FIRE AT MIDNIGHT

"I warned you," Kit murmured, "that if ever you gave me the slightest encouragement, I'd kiss you again."

Norah had known. She had known from the very instant he ushered her into the darkness that he meant to kiss her. The truth washed over her in a warm wave, drowning any protest she might have uttered.

He caught her against his chest. For one breathless moment he held her, his fingers smoothing the fine hairs at the nape of her neck.

His arms tightened; his fingers plunged into her hair, dislodging a few pins. Norah strained upward on tiptoe and reached for the shining world of passion he offered.

The kiss went on and on, an eternity of heaven.

FIRE AT MIDNIGHT

BARBARA DAWSON SMITH

An Avon Romantic Treasure

AVON BOOKS ◆ NEW YORK

FIRE AT MIDNIGHT is an original publication of Avon Books. This
work has never before appeared in book form. This work is a novel.
Any similarity to actual persons or events is purely coincidental.

AVON BOOKS
A division of
The Hearst Corporation
1350 Avenue of the Americas
New York, New York 10019

Copyright © 1992 by Barbara Dawson Smith
Excerpt from *Only With Your Love* copyright © 1992 by Lisa Kleypas
Published by arrangement with the author
Library of Congress Catalog Card Number: 92-90134
ISBN: 0-380-76275-7

First Avon Books Printing: September 1992

AVON TRADEMARK REG. U.S. PAT. OFF. AND IN OTHER COUNTRIES, MARCA
REGISTRADA, HECHO EN U.S.A.

Printed in the U.S.A.

RA 10 9 8 7 6 5 4 3 2 1

Dedicated to
the greatest critique group in the world
and my best writing buddies:
Joyce Bell, Arnette Lamb, and Susan Wiggs

Chapter 1

London, December 31, 1886

A muffled scream cut through the laughter and chatter of the party.

Lord Christopher Coleridge, marquis of Blackthorne, halted his glass of champagne halfway to his mouth. His keen dark eyes scanned the assemblage at his Mayfair mansion. None of his guests seemed to have noticed the cry. Yet his own skin prickled.

New Year's Eve revelers thronged the grand staircase hall, men in elegant black suits and women in vivid gowns of risque cut. Gaslight glowed on bared shoulders and lavish displays of bosom, a feast of feminine flesh that would scandalize any proper lady. But the women here hardly commanded respect; their purpose lay in the art of gratifying men.

Kit shook off his uneasiness and sipped his champagne. No doubt the cry had emanated from one of the pleasure seekers in the upstairs bedrooms.

". . . perhaps you might agree, Lord Kit?"

A striking brunette trifled with the jet beads adorning her aqua silk bodice, drawing his gaze to her magnificent breasts. In a purely reflexive response, his groin tightened. For the life of him, Kit couldn't recall her name. "I'm sorry," he said. "What did you say?"

"Only that you appear quite . . . alone. And I should be happy to accommodate your desire for adventure." She cocked her head and smiled. "A woman can learn much from a man of your blood."

The stirring of lust vanished. He fixed her with a chilly stare. "A man of my blood?"

She stroked the dusky skin of his hand. "Forgive my boldness, but you are half Hindu, my lord. I'm told the Indians are by nature most skilled in the art of love." Her hand moved lower until her fingertips skimmed across the front of his trousers. "And I hear you're more well-endowed than any milksop Englishman."

Her prejudice raised his hackles and stirred unwelcome memories of another woman whose bigotry had caused a still painful scar on his heart. He caught her wrist. "I *am* an Englishman."

Her eyebrows winged upward. "Please don't be angry. Your allure is so dark, so sensual. All the women want you—"

The shrill cry pealed again, louder this time, piercing his anger. Kit loosed the woman and turned. Guests tilted their heads back. Everyone gazed at the second-floor landing, where marble pillars supported a lofty ceiling painted in the palazzo style. From the shadows of the upstairs hall emerged his mistress, clad in only a cherry-pink corset and black-gartered silk stockings.

Kit frowned at her dishabille. What mischief had Jane Bingham been up to this half an hour past?

Jane stumbled as if inebriated. She clutched at the marble guardrail, dislodging a red bow that anchored a swag of Yuletide greenery. Patches of rouge shone stark against her chalk-white cheeks. Her breasts heaving, she leaned down toward the crowd.

The flow of voices and the clink of glasses quieted. The lilt of piano music ceased. A moment of suspended breathing stretched out.

Into the unnatural silence she sobbed, "He's dead! God love me, he's dead!"

Feminine gasps broke the stillness. Masculine

mutters rippled like waves across the sea of uptilted faces. The whispers and murmurs swelled to a storm tide.

"Dead?" Shuddering, the courtesan looked at him in disgust. "Someone's died *here*, in your house, Lord Kit? How horrid, that you can't even keep your own guests safe."

Kit paid her petty comment no heed. He dropped his glass onto the silver tray of a nearby footman, then shouldered his way through the crush. People stepped back to let him pass. Faces turned to him, some shocked, others curious, and a few amused, as if the disturbance were a carnival act staged for their entertainment.

He ignored them all. If this was another one of her pranks, the Honorable Jane Bingham would have bloody hell to pay.

The crowd thinned near the staircase. He took the marble steps two at a time. Several people now hovered around Jane. Lord Adrian Marlow supported the weeping woman, his usual droll expression sobered.

"What the devil's going on?" Kit asked.

Jane flew into his arms and bawled all the louder. Her sweet perfume of lilacs enveloped him. Her tears drenched his collar.

Adrian shrugged, raking a hand through the sandy-brown Byronic curls that made him irresistible to women. "Sorry, old chum. Dash me if I can wring anything but an ocean of tears out of her."

Jane clung to Kit as tightly as an East End whore to a gold sovereign. Against his black lapel she moaned, "Oh darling, it was dreadful. Dreadful! I've never endured such a fright in all my life."

He tipped her chin up. Perhaps she wasn't jesting after all. Genuine alarm rounded her watery blue eyes, and her pouty lips quivered. Her sunshine hair cascaded in loose waves around her corset. Even with tears wetting her lashes and cheeks, she exuded sensuality.

"Calm yourself," he ordered. "Take a deep breath, then start at the beginning."

Her breasts lifted as Jane obeyed. "I . . . I saw a dead man. I touched him and . . . and he didn't move. His skin felt cold and rubbery, like a three-penny doll." A quiver convulsed her voluptuous body. "Oh, Kit. It was so horrid . . ."

"Sshh." Conscious of the rapt audience thronging the staircase and the hall below, he took off his dinner jacket and draped the finely tailored garment around her shoulders. "Show me where he is."

"He's in your bedroom." Jane pointed unnecessarily down the hall, her voice lifting toward the high pitch of hysteria. "In your very own bed!" A gasp came from the onlookers as she went on, "Oh, I can't bear it. Truly I can't!" Crumpling against his chest, she again lapsed into weeping.

Kit quelled the urge to shake her. He knew Jane. Now that she'd weathered the initial fright, she was playing center stage for all its drama. He pressed his folded handkerchief into her palm. "Here, dry your eyes."

As she sniffled daintily into the square of linen, he propelled her down the dim corridor, their footsteps muffled on the long Turkish runner. A few people peeked curiously out of the bedrooms, amorous couples in various stages of undress.

His own bedroom door stood wide open. The masculine domain held furniture of simple mahogany and draperies of pleated green silk fastened by gold cords. A coal fire snapped on the hearth, and a large framed photograph of the Great Palace in Beijing decorated the mantelpiece. A single gas jet hissed in its cut-glass sconce.

On the four-poster bed lay the corpse.

Kit walked slowly forward. The man rested supine, his hands folded at his trim waist and his eyes closed, as if he were sleeping. A diamond ring winked on one of his fingers and matching sleeve links glinted at his wrists. A pearl-studded watch chain formed a perfect half loop against his black waistcoat. Silver threaded his brown hair, and his face held a distinguished elegance enhanced by middle age. Kit couldn't put a name to the suave features.

The broad chest lay unmoving. He parted the starched cravat and pressed his thumb to the man's throat. Cool flesh. No pulse beat.

Jesus God. How had a stranger ended up dead here?

Mutters and exclamations buzzed through the room.

"Eek! Gives a lady the shivers."

"Quite the handsome gent, don't you say?"

"Imagine, a man in Lord Kit's bed—now that's a first."

"I should have known. Parties like these attract the worst elements."

"Shush. Have a little respect for the dead."

Kit turned. Jane sagged against Adrian and dabbed at the corners of her eyes. Behind her, onlookers crammed the room, vultures scenting the carrion of scandal. Most were mere acquaintances, men he knew from his schooldays at Harrow or from polo matches at the Hurlingham Club, and women whose shapely bodies he remembered better than their names.

"Does anyone know this man?" Kit asked.

The gawkers exchanged glances and shook their heads. Despite their inquisitive expressions, no one ventured any closer.

Adrian thrust Jane into the arms of the nearest man. Then he walked to the foot of the bed. "Rutherford, if memory serves me."

The name rang a familiar note. "The jeweler?" Kit asked.

Adrian nodded. "I purchased a brooch from his shop to give to my grandmama for Christmas. Lovely design, it was." With a thoughtful frown, he gazed at the body. "Heard Rutherford was angling for a royal commission. But he hardly moved in your circle. I didn't know he was your guest."

"He wasn't."

Adrian cocked a sandy eyebrow. "Picked a peculiar place to pass on, then. Heart seizure, would you guess?"

"Perhaps."

Or perhaps not.

It was damned peculiar how tidy Rutherford looked, his watch fob neat, his hands clasped, his cuffs and collar pristine. Even the creases of his trouser legs were knife-straight, right down to the polished black shoes.

As if a loved one had laid him out for view.

Seeking an identification paper, Kit gingerly reached inside the corpse's breast pocket. Even as he touched the cold edge of a calling card case, his hand met dampness. He lifted the lapel slightly. And saw blood.

His stomach lurched. Half hidden inside the man's coat, the red stain darkened the black waistcoat. On the left breast lay an emerald. It looked like the top of a woman's hatpin. Plunged to the hilt into the heart.

Horror jolted Kit. He settled the coat back into place. The onlookers stood too far back to have noticed the dark blemish. Hands icy, he plucked a pasteboard card from the thin gold case; the black print confirmed the victim's name. Maurice Rutherford, Rutherford Jewelers, Bond Street.

Rutherford hadn't settled himself on the bed and then expired in perfect taste. Someone had killed him, then arranged his body here. Deliberately.

Who? And why?

On the bedside table sat a glass identical to the ones downstairs. Kit picked it up and sniffed the dregs. A faint, familiar scent mingled with a sweetish odor. Sherry . . . and opium?

"I'm ringing the police," he said.

Silence spread, as thick as plum pudding. Then the florid-faced Sir Edmond Maybrick harrumphed. "Puts a bit of a damper on things, eh?" He edged toward the door. "Think I'll just toddle along home now."

"Jolly fine notion," echoed Lord Augustus Quimper, his Adam's apple bobbing as he trailed after Maybrick. "No sense in risking a scandal. Don't want the wife to know I've been attending one of *your* parties."

A mass exodus began, men and women alike slinking out of the bedroom. Only Adrian made no move to depart. He leaned against the green silk-draped bedpost, his grin satirical. "Rats from a sinking ship."

"Not from my ship." To the others Kit snapped, "Halt where you stand. No one is going anywhere."

Movement stopped. As one, the congregation peered guiltily back. "Here now," blustered Sir Edmond. "There's no need to involve the lot of us in your unpleasantness."

Distaste flavored Kit's mouth. His most intimate allies were suddenly behaving like hypocrites who would take their pleasure with one of the whores at his party, then deny their presence here, to protect their precious reputations. How could he have ever seen them as his friends? "A pity," he said, "because you're already involved. Wait downstairs, all of you. And reflect on this: the law will consider anyone who leaves the premises a prime suspect."

"Suspect?" said Sir Edmond. "Why, bosh. The fellow obviously suffered some sort of attack."

"He was murdered," Kit said.

Gasps and exclamations burst from the spectators.

A choked cry yanked his gaze to Jane. She stood by the door, her white hands frozen on a blue gown that lay on a Chippendale chair. Now here was another pretty puzzle, Kit thought. Why the devil was her dress in the same room with the dead man?

His overlarge coat slipped from one of Jane's shoulders. Her gaze flitted to the corpse and back to Kit. "Jesus save me," she breathed, and pressed her palms together as if in realization. "If he was murdered, I know who did it!"

"Poison, your lordsh—"

The police surgeon sneezed into a huge handkerchief. The resulting blast echoed through the grand staircase hall.

The guests shrank back. For over an hour, they had milled about, talking in hushed tones and awaiting the outcome of the investigation. The merry atmosphere had given way to the somberness of mourners at a wake. Midnight had come and gone, the start of the Queen's Jubilee Year all but forgotten.

"Poison?" Kit repeated. "You're sure?"

The surgeon adjusted the rimless spectacles perched on his reddened nose. "Quite, your lordship," he said in a nasal tone. "The pupils were contracted, a sign of morphine poisoning. Likely the dose caused respiratory failure even before the hatpin pierced the heart."

The news gripped Kit in a fist as frigid as the draft seeping through the tall window behind him. Jabbing in the hatpin when the victim was already dead seemed an act of unnecessary savagery, of merciless hatred. Who could be so inhuman?

Detective-Inspector Harvey Wadding stepped forward. His long, horsey face reflected no annoyance that he'd been rousted out of bed on a cold winter night, only awe at his elegant surroundings. "If I might speak, your lordship."

"Yes?"

"The glass you gave me contains an opium derivative in the form of morphine. A lethal dose can work in under an hour."

"And I was dressing in my bedroom only three hours before the body was discovered," Kit said.

Wadding made a note. "Excellent. That should help establish the time of death."

"I trust you'll verify your conjecture with a postmortem."

"Straightaway, your lordship." Wadding turned to the surgeon. "Get on it immediately, Partridge."

"My men are loading the body on the mortuary cart right now." Partridge sketched a bow, sneezed again, and scurried off, honking into his handkerchief.

Wadding focused reverent brown eyes on Kit. "You mentioned an eyewitness, m'lord?"

"Yes. Follow me."

Kit led the way into the library. Cigar smoke and spirits almost masked the leather scent of book bindings. He wished to God he could be alone in his sanctum, kick off his shoes, and study the racing forms.

But Jane Bingham occupied his favorite wing chair. Like a queen on a throne, she perched on the cushion before a half circle of admirers. She had donned her gown of cerulean satin. A tiara with a centerpiece of doves in diamonds and sapphires glittered in her upswept blond hair.

"I hear you've been poisoning your guests, Blackie." The familiar voice spoke from behind Kit; a familiar resentment pricked him into turning.

A slim man lounged just inside the double doors, his arm propped on a glass-fronted bookcase. Wearing a dandified gray suit with a red rosebud in his lapel, his fair sidewhiskers and mustache perfectly barbered, he might have been a tailor's dummy.

"I don't recall inviting you, Carlyle," Kit said.

Lord Bruce Abernathy, Viscount Carlyle, picked up a framed photograph of a racehorse and grimaced at it. "I saw the mortuary wagon from my town house across the square. I was most concerned about the reception you give your guests."

"I am most concerned that you would dare invade my home," Kit said. "I should toss you out with the rubbish."

"Tut, tut. Still the same savage beast you were at Harrow." Setting down the picture, Bruce curled his lips into an aristocratic cross between a sneer and a smile. "I understand, Inspector, that the victim was given an overdose. It's common knowledge that Indians have a fondness for opium."

Wadding turned to Kit. "Do you keep morphine in the house, m'lord?"

Kit seethed at Bruce's implication. With effort, he kept his voice even. "No, but one of my servants may. Please feel free to ask them any questions you like."

The policeman ducked his head apologetically. "Yes, m'lord."

"Just remember," Bruce murmured, "as the saying goes, blood will tell."

The insult festered like a long-buried thorn. Kit cared little for Bruce's bigoted opinions and taunting insults, yet he was conscious of the others in the library who avoided his eyes and took sudden interest in the book-lined walls.

"It seems we established long ago that your blood is no bluer than mine." Kit gazed pointedly at the scar that lifted one of Bruce's eyebrows in perpetual question, the only imperfection in his aristocratic face.

Bruce's expression darkened as he fingered the indentation. His mouth settled into a sulk. "Crass as ever," he muttered.

Impatient with the bickering, Kit waved the group toward the hall. "Everyone out. Except you, Jane. Oh, and Carlyle, if you would be so kind as to shut the doors as you depart."

Following the others, Bruce stalked out, his posture so stiff and straight he might have had a poker stuffed up his bottom. The tall doors closed with an ungentle bang.

Kit settled himself on the edge of his polished oak desk. "Jane, this is Detective-Inspector Wadding of Scotland Yard. Inspector Wadding, may I present the Honorable Jane Bingham."

"A great pleasure, Miss Bingham."

Pad and pencil gripped in his rawboned hands, Wadding almost tiptoed toward Jane, as if she were a goddess on an altar and he the humble supplicant.

Though faced with a gangly commoner in thread-
bare tweeds, Jane reacted as she did to anyone in
trousers; her lips curved into a come-hither smile
and her fingers stroked the blue feather boa draped
over her cleavage. Wadding's eyes glazed over.

In spite of his black mood, Kit suppressed a grin.
"You may proceed, Inspector."

Wadding blinked and refocused. "Er, yes. Did you
know the unfortunate, Miss Bingham?"

"Only through tidbits of gossip. Rumor says he
kept a mistress."

The inspector's brows perked. "Would you know
the woman's name?"

"I'm afraid not." Jane batted her lashes. "He's a
commoner. We hardly shared the same social circle."

"If you could tell me precisely what you saw,
then."

"It was the most horrid experience," she said,
shuddering. "I was walking along the passage upstairs, after a visit to the necessary room. That's
when I saw *her*." Jane leaned forward on the chair,
her breasts pillowing above her bodice, and added
in a stage whisper, "She must have just murdered
Rutherford."

"A woman, you say?" Wadding asked in confusion.

"Yes. She was stealing out of his lordship's bedchamber. Naturally I wondered what mischief she'd
been at. One never knows who might have slipped
into the house, what with the riffraff roaming the
streets of London. Thank God for the bravery of our
police. Why, one time the neighbor's nasty cat
sneaked into my house and went after my doves,
and I summoned a constable—"

"The facts, please," Kit broke in.

She moistened her lips. "Of course, my lord. I
called out to the woman. But she didn't stop. She
disappeared down the servants' stairway at the end
of the hall." Gasping, she raised her hand to her

mouth. "Oh, dear God. Do you suppose his *mistress* murdered him?"

"We shall strive to find out." Wadding jotted something in his notebook. "Can you describe the woman?"

"It was quite shadowy and her face was veiled. But she wore a scarlet cloak with jet fringe."

Kit shifted against the hard surface of the desk. The vague description failed to pinpoint any woman at the party. "Was she short or tall?" he prodded. "Fat or thin? Did you note the color of her hair?"

Jane lifted her dazzling white shoulders in a shrug. "She was a bit on the tall side, I suppose. Oh . . . and her hat had one of those high turban brims that are all the rage, and a splendid tuft of white ostrich feathers." She glanced at Kit from beneath her lashes and wriggled in a way that suggested an image of her naked and restless. "I've been simply pining for one like it."

Her coquettish manner rang a discordant note into the dirge of tragedy. "And that's all you recall?" he asked.

"I'm afraid so. But she must be the murderess. She was running from the scene of the crime."

"So after she'd gone," Wadding said, "you went into the—ahem—bedroom."

"Of course. Someone had to check and see that none of his lordship's valuables had been stolen."

The inspector scratched his protruding ear with his pencil. Kit knew he burned to ask how well-acquainted she was with the contents of the master's chambers. "Er, yes," said Wadding. "Did you notice anything amiss?"

Lips curled, Jane looked him up and down. "Why, I found the dead man, what else?"

"Beg pardon, Miss Bingham. Didn't mean to offend. But any detail you can remember might aid in the investigation."

"I'll contact you if I think of anything more." With a royal wave of dismissal, she glided up from the chair. "If you'll excuse me, I'm near to swooning from shock and fatigue. Would you mind escorting me upstairs, Kit?''

''Yes, I would mind.''

''You would?''

''It seems there's a piece missing from your story. An essential piece.''

''I can't imagine what you mean.''

''Sit down and I'll tell you.''

Wariness chased across her sensual features. ''I really am so very tired. Why don't we go upstairs and talk alone?''

''Sit.''

As always, she obeyed his command, though she thrust out her lower lip.

Hands on his hips, Kit walked toward her. He knew Jane—and himself—too well to go upstairs with her at the moment. She'd try to entice him into bed rather than answer his questions. He was in no mood to ward off her tenacious eroticism.

The daughter of a baron, Jane had grown up motherless and half forgotten by her bookish father, an amateur archeologist who traveled abroad for months at a time, leaving her in the care of servants. At the tender age of fourteen, she had learned about sex by seducing the footman. At sixteen, she had abandoned any pretense at propriety and embraced a succession of noble lovers. At twenty, she had met Kit and acceded to his demand that she remain faithful to him.

Now, only a few months into their torrid affair, he wondered how far he could trust her. God help her if she'd played him for a fool.

Firelight sparkled off the sapphires in her hair, the gems a glittering echo of her eyes. ''When you came running to the second-floor balcony,'' he said, ''you were wearing only your undergarments. I should like to know how your gown came to be draped over a chair in my bedroom.''

''Aha,'' muttered Wadding, scribbling madly in his notebook.

A carmine flush deepened the rouge on her

cheeks. Gritting her teeth, she glanced at the inspector. "Kit, for the love of God!" she said in a scandalized undertone. "I hardly think a lady's lingerie should enter into a conversation with a stranger. And with a common public servant at that."

"The police are investigating a murder. I want the truth."

The tip of her tongue darted over her lips. "Are you sure you wouldn't rather go upstairs?" she purred.

Wadding made a strangled sound and shifted his big feet.

Kit cocked a black eyebrow. The mantelpiece clock ticked into the silence and the coal fire hissed in the grate. He kept his hard gaze aimed at Jane.

She lowered her eyes and huffed out a sigh. "Oh, have it your way, then. When I first went into the bedroom, I didn't realize Rutherford was dead. I thought he was only asleep."

"I see. You planned to give him a nice surprise when he awoke."

"It isn't what you think," she said, straightening her rounded shoulders. "For pity's sake, I only meant to play a harmless little joke on the man."

"Explain yourself."

She lifted her chin in mulish defiance. "I was going to tell him we'd been seen together and I would tell his wife."

His wife. Kit hadn't considered a bereaved widow. "Rutherford was married? How did you know?"

Jane shrugged. "He's one of the contenders the Princess of Wales is considering to make her Jubilee tiara. His wife was mentioned in one of the gossip columns. Besides, a handsome fellow like him would have a proper little wife tucked away, a homely gray-haired matron who probably thought of Britannia while they engaged in intercourse."

A choked cough came from Wadding. "Ahem—there is indeed a widow, your lordship. One of my constables found the address. Mrs. Rutherford lives in"—the inspector consulted his notebook—"Pendleman Square."

"There, you see?" said Jane. "A woman knows these things."

Irked by her smugness and suspecting she was still hiding something, Kit snapped, "So you intended to blackmail Rutherford."

"It was an innocent prank. I would have led him on, then told him the truth."

"And how do you know he was the sort of man to appreciate your pranks?"

"A bit of fun never hurt anyone. It isn't as if I'd nicked the crown jewels."

"But a man was murdered. Your little 'prank' could land you behind bars."

Her cheeks blanched. "I didn't commit a crime. You see that, don't you, Inspector?" Leaping up, she seized Wadding's hand and clasped it to her bosom.

Redness shot up his long neck and colored his equine face. "M-Miss Bingham . . ."

"You shan't arrest me, shall you? Oh, please say you shan't."

"N-no. Of course not . . . a lovely lady like you . . ."

"Thank you." She released him and went to Kit, rubbing against his sleeve like a kitten soliciting affection. "There, you see, darling? I've done nothing wrong. Please don't be angry." She murmured for his ear alone, "It's certainly no worse an escapade than the time I had myself served naked to you on a covered platter."

The memory tickled his ill humor. Jane may well have lied about the blackmail scheme; he suspected her true intent had been to seduce Rutherford. At least Kit felt confident that her vices leaned toward hot-blooded sex rather than cold-blooded murder.

And she preferred sapphires. She didn't own an emerald hatpin.

"We'll talk more later," he said. "Run along now."

"But Kit, darling—"

"Tell Herriot I'd like him to escort you home."

"Oh, but can't I stay—"

"Not tonight." He honed his voice to sharp command.

She clamped her mouth shut and tossed the blue boa around her shoulders. Apparently seeing the value of retreat, she minced out of the library, her shapely hips swaying. Wadding stared after her, his neck craned and his eyes bugged.

"Inspector," Kit said.

The lanky man swerved back, almost dropping pencil and pad. "Er, yes, m'lord?"

"You'll want to interview all the women present, account for their whereabouts during the evening, see if any of them knew Rutherford."

"That is the procedure in such a tragedy, m'lord." Wadding pulled a glum face. "But I rather doubt we'll be so lucky as to find a lady wearing a scarlet cloak trimmed in jet."

"One of my servants may have seen her on the back stair. And Rutherford wasn't on the guest list. He very likely came in the back way as well."

"With your permission, I'll send a constable to the kitchen. Then I fear I must be on my way to convey the sad news to the widow." Wadding bowed and went out.

The widow again. Stark reality struck Kit in the face. Doubtless she slumbered in peaceful unawareness of her husband's grisly fate. Kit pictured her abrupt awakening by a maid, her plump fingers trembling as she dressed in the predawn chill, her anxiety as she hastened downstairs to face the police, the sagging of her matronly face as she heard the news . . .

The image melted into the lovely features of his own stepmother. He could well imagine her grief should she ever receive a tragic announcement; he could feel the sorrow of his brother and sisters. He breathed a prayer of thanksgiving that his parents were alive and hale, safe at their estate in Kent.

Did Rutherford leave children, too? God forbid they should suffer because Kit Coleridge had provided the perfect setting for a murder.

Come morning, Kit resolved, he would pay Mrs. Rutherford a visit and offer his condolences. It was the least he could do.

He returned to the grand staircase hall. A burly constable moved among the crowd, laboriously recording each guest's name on a dog-eared notepad. One by one, the noblemen and their *demi-mondaines* were allowed to gather top hats and mantles and overcoats, and to slip out into the dead of the winter night. At last even the policemen departed. Kit dismissed the squad of bleary-eyed maids and footmen. The tidying-up could wait until the morning.

He stood in the dark, the cavernous hall illuminated by a meager bar of light from the library. Usually he welcomed the solitary sensation in the aftermath of a ball. Tonight he felt too drained and uneasy, too disenchanted with the unprincipled side he saw in himself. Was this what his decadent lifestyle had turned him into, a man who would host the sort of gathering where a murder would occur? The incident struck Kit as a graphic illustration of how low he had sunk.

His friends had been anxious to flee, to divorce themselves from him. No, not friends. Acquaintances without a shred of faithfulness. Kit faced the hard truth: they had been using him, taking advantage of his frequent parties and the whores he hired as entertainment.

He pressed his hands to his burning eyes. Damn, he was tired. Tired of living on the edge of society. Tired of having hypocrites as companions. He felt the sudden need to make himself into a better man, but he scarcely knew where to begin. How could he erase the reputation blackened by years of dissipation?

Though the linens had been changed, the notion of sleeping in the bed so recently occupied by a corpse repulsed Kit. He walked into the library, closed the doors, and removed his coat and shoes. With a sigh, he loosened his stiff collar. Then he eased into the wing chair by the hearth and stretched his stockinged feet toward the low blaze.

Unable to find a solution to his own inner dilemma, he turned his mind to wrestling with the mystery. Why would a jeweler steal into a private party, only to end up dead in the master suite? Was the woman in the scarlet cloak his mistress? Why would she want to kill him . . . and why here, of all places? To confuse the police?

Or to implicate Kit? Troubled, he shifted position. Could someone hate him enough to commit murder? Carlyle? He was too much the coward. Then someone else who thought a half-caste had no place in high society? Kit grimaced. Were he to list the bigots who had turned a cold shoulder to him over the years, he would fill a yard of paper.

He tried to imagine himself in Rutherford's shoes. Had he comprehended that he had been poisoned? Had he panicked and fought his assailant? No, he showed no sign of a struggle. Perhaps he had realized nothing at all, just gone to sleep, never to awaken . . .

Questions danced inside Kit's head like the flames sputtering in the grate. Fatigue gritted his eyes. He closed them for a moment and rolled his head against the back of the chair. Lassitude sucked him into a vat of warm treacle.

He succumbed to the irresistible darkness.

He was cold, bitterly cold.

A speck in the vast landscape of the Himalayas, he stood alone on a snowy slope. The wind lashed his naked body. Ice crystals sheathed his brown flesh and transformed him into the likeness of a white man. But he was still a savage underneath the outer trappings. He wanted to cry out for help, but his throat was frozen, his limbs frigid. The frosty shield locked him forever in isolation from a world that judged a man by the color of his skin.

A sound pierced the ice. A distant knocking. Then voices, coming closer. Footsteps.

Relax, Kit thought. Help is on the way.

He opened his bleary eyes. Reality struck. He was slouched in the wing chair, his legs extended toward the dead ashes in the grate. Watery sunlight poured through the slit in the draperies.

Damn, but he was chilled to the bone. He lifted his head and felt a beastly crick in his neck. The mantelpiece clock drew his gaze. Jesus God. Who would call at six-forty in the morning?

Before he could rise, the library doors opened. A footman marched in, a black cloak over his arm. Half hidden behind him glided a woman.

"M'lord!" exclaimed Herriot, his cheeks reddening, his brown eyes as round as the gold crested buttons on his livery. "I'm sorry, most awfully sorry. Didn't know you was in here. The lady, she was most insistent on seein' you. I . . . I'll show her elsewhere until your lordship be ready." He started to back out, almost colliding with the caller.

As if she hadn't heard, the veiled woman came into the library, her slender figure clad in unrelieved black.

Standing up, Kit plowed his hand through his hair and stepped into his shoes. He felt cold and rumpled and churlish. "If you'll excuse me," he said to her as he started toward the door. "I'll join you in a few moments."

"No. I will speak to you immediately."

The ragged edge to her voice caught his attention. He stopped. To Herriot, he said, "Send Betsy to light the fire. It's freezing in here."

"Aye, m'lord." The servant bowed and dashed out.

The woman hovered in the middle of the room. She wore black suede gloves and fingered her only adornment, the brooch pinned at her throat, an exquisite knot of seed pearls set in onyx. The high-collared gown fell to a straight skirt with a modest bustle, and seemed designed to disguise the womanly curves of her hips and waist.

She lifted the veil and drew it back. His chest clenched and his weariness slid away.

The filtered dawn light gave her skin the translucence of a cameo. Her fine cheekbones bore a natural winter-kissed flush more lovely than any color out of a pot. Beneath a black ribboned fedora, her curly red hair was scraped into a topknot, as if she were determined to tame its sensual beauty into ladylike neatness.

Kit gaped like a schoolboy at a sweetshop window. Heat banished the chill from him. He wanted to undress her. He wanted to see her titian waves cascading around her slim white body.

He formed the most charming smile he could manage, given his unshaven state. "I don't believe we've met. I'm Christopher Coleridge. My friends call me Kit."

She raised one auburn eyebrow. Fingers fisted at her sides, she came closer and stopped a few feet from him. Her long-lashed green eyes perused him with relentless intensity. She viewed him with the cool distaste one might afford a poisonous snake.

"My name is Norah Rutherford," she said. "I came to see where my husband was murdered."

Chapter 2

Clinging to the frayed threads of her composure, Norah tasted the bitter satisfaction of catching the marquis off guard. His smile faded, though the set of his mouth retained its naturally wicked slant. Hands at his hips, he regarded her with a boldness that confirmed his notorious reputation.

She had expected a libertine. He hadn't disappointed her. The image of a self-indulgent aristocrat after a long night of debauchery, he stood coatless, his collar hanging open. Black hairs curled at the unbuttoned top of his shirt. Fine lines of weariness bracketed his mouth and eyes. An unshaven shadow hugged the teak-hard contours of his jaw and cheeks.

Yet even in his unkempt condition, Lord Christopher Coleridge commanded attention. His rugged muscularity and tousled onyx hair oddly reminded her of the promise of perfection in an uncut gem. He had tiger's eyes, dark and direct and dangerous.

She had heard rumors of his wild parties, whispers of his gambling and womanizing. No true lady considered him proper company, especially unchaperoned. But today, shock and disbelief had overpowered her scruples.

"Please sit down, Mrs. Rutherford." Coming closer, he extended a bronzed hand.

Panic constricted her chest. She stepped out of his

reach. By custom she should curtsy, but her pride rebelled at paying homage to a man who preyed upon weak women. "Thank you, but I prefer to stand. This is hardly a social call."

"Of course. I sincerely regret the unfortunate circumstance that brings you here."

His sympathy, the very gentleness of his tone fired the icy void in her heart. She disliked platitudes, especially from this philanderer. "My husband's death was more than mere misfortune. According to Inspector Wadding, it was murder."

He paused in the act of donning his formal coat. "Yes. I had intended to call on you today and offer my condolences."

"Never mind that. I would rather you tell me exactly what happened."

"I doubt I can add anything to what the inspector already said to you." His voice lowered. "But please know, Mrs. Rutherford, that I hold myself accountable. If I can atone by helping you and your children in any way . . ."

Untimely tears prickled at the back of her throat. Norah swallowed her secret sorrow and looked at the soiled glassware littering a side table. She felt as used and empty as those vessels. "Maurice and I were never blessed with children."

"I'd be happy to help you make any arrangements," the marquis went on softly. "I'll notify your acquaintances, or do whatever else I can to make this tragedy more bearable for you."

His persistent kindness nearly undid her. She held tightly to her control and reminded herself that his sympathy rang false. He only wanted to unburden himself of guilt. "If you truly wish to be of service, your lordship, you may start by showing me where my husband died."

Frowning, he cocked his head. "There's nothing to see. My servants have tidied up."

"Nevertheless, you'll show me upstairs now." She pivoted toward the hall. "Or I shall find the way myself."

Lord Blackthorne stood still, a predator garbed in the finely tailored suit of a gentleman. In a flash of black humor, she guessed this was the most unorthodox reason a woman had ever used to get herself into his bedroom.

Shrugging, he motioned to the door. "Since you insist."

They went out into the lofty hall and up a staircase so grand ten people abreast could ascend its marble glory. A team of servants bustled to and fro, clearing away the glassware from the New Year's Eve party, sweeping cigar butts and other debris from the beautiful palazzo floor, polishing the smudges on the newel post. A footman balanced himself on a tall ladder and unfastened the Yuletide greenery looped along the balcony.

A fog of unreality swathed Norah. The tap of her footsteps mingled with the heavier echo of Kit Coleridge's shoes on the marble steps. She glanced sideways at him. Thoughtful absorption firmed his exotic dark features. He exuded an aura of banked energy, his vitality and strength evident in his springing steps. Her own limbs felt as dead and stiff as coral, and so brittle they might shatter with the slightest handling.

He opened the door at the end of the upstairs passage and ushered her inside. Fabrics in the rich hue of Siberian jade lent the bedroom a surprisingly cheery comfort. Silver-framed photographs decorated the tabletops. Her numbed senses registered the warmth of the fire and the faint masculine aromas of shaving soap and earthy musk.

She paused, aware of Lord Blackthorne standing silently behind her. She had expected something murky and foreign and cavelike, the lair of a tiger. From nowhere came the image of him luring a woman here, charming her with the mesmeric music of his voice, enticing her with the hypnotic luster of his eyes, and then pouncing, stroking, overpowering her . . .

Norah forced down a shudder and walked to the

foot of the bed. Pale sunbeams trickled through the windows, slid past the silk hangings, and pooled on the plush bower within. The pillows were plumped, the ivory linens smooth with the sheen of satin, the goosedown coverlet thick and inviting. A place to sit and read. A place to cuddle on a cold night.

A place to die.

She groped within herself for grief, but found only a dreamlike void, as if her soul had separated from her body. As if she hovered above the well-appointed room and looked down at the woman standing by the empty bed, her face bleached of color against the jet-black of her gown, her fingers twined together. She fancied herself a painting on display at the Royal Academy: *Young Widow Faces Tragedy*.

Beside a vase of hothouse calla lilies on the nightstand, metal glinted. Her heart took a tumble and brought her crashing back to earth. On stiff legs, she went to examine the object. The fluted gold match case was topped by a lustrous pearl set in a bed of rose diamonds.

"What's the matter?" asked Kit Coleridge, from behind her.

"It's Maurice's matchbox," she whispered. "The one I gave him for Christmas."

Kit picked up the small piece and examined it, the gold bright in his topaz-brown hands. "It must have fallen from his pocket. The maid probably found it when she was tidying up." His gaze lifted to Norah. "May I take it? The police may consider it a clue."

"Of course."

As he went to put it on a side table, she stood immobile by the bed. Against her anesthetized skin came the sensation of warmth on her cheeks, a wetness which seeped from her eyes and slid down, spattering like raindrops on her hands. She gazed at the splotches of moisture on her gloves. The suede would be ruined. Winnifred would scold. And Maurice wouldn't be present to temper his cousin's crossness.

He was dead.

The desperate disbelief that had propelled Norah here in the wintry dawn abruptly fled. Oh, Blessed Virgin. He had been consorting with another woman. And Norah hadn't even guessed.

The cruel blow deprived her of breath. She felt as naive as she had been as a young bride who had escaped the confinement of a Belgian convent only to have her romantic dreams strangled by the bonds of marriage. Long ago she had accepted that Maurice kept a part of himself closed to her. Didn't every man? Didn't she hide a part of herself, too?

A virtuous wife refrained from plaguing her husband with questions; she performed her duties with grace and modesty. By force of willpower, Norah had disciplined her baseborn tendency toward disobedience and outspokenness, even when Maurice refused to publicly acknowledge her artistic talents. Even on the infrequent nights when he exercised his conjugal rights. Even when he was detained evening after evening at his club.

His absences had grown more numerous in the past half year. How foolish she had been not to realize. All those evenings he must have been meeting a scarlet woman in a scarlet cloak.

The faithless blackguard. With the filthy coin of deceit, he had repaid her efforts to be a worthy wife. From a corner of her mind crept a shameful sense of relief and liberation . . .

Her rigid control crumbled. A floodgate of feelings spewed forth. She trembled under the onrush of fury and frustration. Her body ached and burned and hurt. Her heart pounded a terrible, suffocating rhythm.

The bed loomed before her, the site of sinful luxury where Maurice had betrayed his vows and ripped apart the fabric of her life. All for his own manly selfishness. The clamor inside her surged to a storm tide. Rage misted her vision.

She reached blindly for a pillow and hurled it aside. Glass crashed. The sound barely penetrated the roaring in her ears. She threw herself on the bed and tore at the counterpane. Her fingernails raked the sheets. Sobbing breaths burdened her chest.

She hammered the mattress. "How could you do this to me?" she gasped. "How could you do this?" She knew no curse black enough to express the humiliation heaped upon her by a cheating husband.

Arms like steel bars locked around her, caged her frenzy. "Mrs. Rutherford . . . Norah . . . stop. Please stop."

She bucked within the restraint. "Let me go!"

"Calm yourself." The voice slid over her, as low pitched and soothing as the purr of a cat. "Don't fight me. I only want to help you."

Warm breath blew against her cheek. She lay trapped, wriggling uselessly against the coverlet, pinned by the heat and hardness pressed along the length of her.

"Go ahead and weep. I'm here for you. For as long as you wish."

Weakness saturated her limbs. She melted into the satin sheets. Her crying shuddered to a halt. A blessed blanket of deliverance sheltered her from the malestrom of emotion. Like water running from a sieve, the madness swirled away and left her shaken and vulnerable.

Hands turned her, guided her head onto the solid pillow of a shoulder. Her cheek met the smooth linen of a shirt. She kept her mind tightly shut to all but the comfort radiating from the embrace. With each slowing breath, she drew in the fragrance of a man, alien yet agreeable. She felt the pleasing pressure of lips moving against her brow, and the lulling stroke of fingers over her wet cheeks. A whimper of need rippled in her throat. From where the sound arose she could not fathom. She knew only that she needed the strength of his arms, needed the closeness of this man . . .

"There now," he murmured in her ear. "You'll be fine, Norah. I'll take care of you."

Kit Coleridge. It was Lord Christopher Coleridge holding her, kissing her forehead.

Awareness burned a path of color up Norah's cheeks. She thrust her head back. His flagrantly handsome features loomed so near she could discern each individual black lash that shaded his tiger's eyes. The fullness of his lower lip, the soft slant of his mouth suggested wicked intimacies, profane pleasures.

She was lying beside the most notorious rake in England. In the bed where her husband had died mere hours ago.

She scrambled into a sitting position. The tumbled state of the bedding horrified her. The shards of a crystal vase were strewn on the floor. A water spot anointed the fine carpet. The crushed lilies emitted a sickly funereal odor.

Sweet heaven, she had lost control and behaved like a virago. Even worse, she had clung to Kit Coleridge with the shamelessness of a trollop.

He rolled to his feet and reached out to her.

Fear of his touch sent Norah flying backward. Her spine met the mahogany headboard. "Stay away! Stay away, you blackhearted scoundrel."

Her slur wounded Kit like a dagger plunged into his chest. From the prison of his memory escaped another jeering, female voice: *You're Blackie . . . a heathen from India.* As if it were yesterday instead of fifteen years ago, he saw Emma Woodferne recoiling from him, her fair face twisted by disgust.

Gall choked his throat. He stepped back, his movements rigid. "You needn't be alarmed, Mrs. Rutherford. I meant only to straighten your hat."

"I can manage." She yanked at the crooked fedora, then stood and smoothed her black skirt.

Her somber aloofness, the tear tracks marring her pale cheeks, somehow sparked defensiveness in him. "I'm hardly a savage, to force a woman to my will. Or perhaps you came here expecting me to be dressed in a turban and loincloth, as if I'd just stepped off my elephant. Perhaps you expected my house to be filled with statues of pagan gods, like some godawful Hindu shrine.''

She blinked. ''No, I didn't.''

At her blank expression his anger eased, leaving him at a loss. He had overreacted to her insult. Norah Rutherford had just suffered the terrible shock of learning she was a widow; of course she would flinch from him.

God, she must have loved her husband, to weep so violently. Kit felt more guilty than ever for hosting the party where her husband had been murdered, and he honed his determination to help her. Hunger throbbed inside him. If only he could inspire a love so powerful in a woman, a love so compelling in its intensity.

She stepped back, glass crunching beneath her shoes. ''Pardon my lapse in manners,'' she said stiffly. ''If you'll send me a bill, I'll pay for the vase.''

''Never mind the bloody vase. Are you sure you're all right?''

''Of course. I wouldn't dream of inconveniencing you.''

''Your husband died in my bed. I understand why you're distraught.''

Norah mastered her runaway emotions. Lord Kit Coleridge watched her with the intent eyes of a friend. For an instant she felt drawn to him; then his pretense of concern affronted her. ''Do you, my lord? Pardon me if I mistrust compassion in a man who recreated Sodom and Gomorrah in his own home.''

His lips compressed. So, she thought, his high and mighty lordship had hoped to keep his bawdy revels a secret.

''You're overwrought,'' he said. ''Please come back downstairs. Betsy will have made up the fire by now. I'll ring for a cup of tea—''

''Bother your wretched tea. I came here for answers, not refreshments.''

He settled his hand against the bedpost. ''Ask away, then. I'll gladly share what little I know.''

"You can start by confessing the truth about this woman in the scarlet cloak. You must know her name since you asked her into your home."

"Didn't Wadding tell you? The police surmise that she and your husband slipped in through the servants' entrance at the rear of the house."

"Oh?" Norah let the word convey her disbelief. "Maurice was a respected jeweler, a proper gentleman. He was no thief to creep in back doors. He would never have entered your house without an invitation." Or would he? she wondered in anguished chagrin. How well had she really known him?

"Nevertheless he did." With bland dark eyes, the marquis regarded her. "He wasn't on my guest list."

"Then one of your visitors must have taken the liberty of asking him along."

"So why didn't he come in the front door? No one recalled seeing him. Not even the footman stationed at the door could identify him. That brings us to the most logical conclusion."

"Or the most convenient one," she flung back.

Kit Coleridge stood still, yet the slight rise and fall of his broad chest drew her attention to the muscular power outlined by his white shirt and black coat. With his mouth tightened and his eyes narrowed, he made a formidable opponent. "Kindly explain yourself."

Norah pressed her fingers into her skirt. She mustn't let him frighten her. "I mean you may be protecting the woman who murdered my husband."

"I?" His brow creased. "Why would I protect a murderess?"

"Perhaps she's one of your conquests."

He snorted in disbelief. "Surely you can't believe I'd protect a woman who'd cuckolded me."

With your husband. The unspoken words galled Norah. She forced herself to face the ugly truth. For whatever unknown purpose, Maurice had stolen into this bedroom. With a woman who was not his wife.

She tried to ignore her anger and put herself in his place, tried to imagine what he had been thinking and feeling. But the man whose habits she had known over the nine years of their marriage suddenly had died a stranger. The raw wound of his unfaithfulness smarted more than even sorrow at his death. Yet in her most secret depths, she admitted to a feeling of release from the odious bondage of physical union.

Fingering the brooch at her throat, she walked to the window. A lacework of frost etched the glass panes. She rubbed a clear spot with the heel of her gloved hand. Across the street stretched Berkeley Square, a long quadrilateral composed of brown grass with leaf-bare plane trees and deserted pathways. Few people braved the blustery New Year's morning, only servants about their early errands and a bundled-up driver perched atop his hansom cab. The faint clatter and banging from downstairs underscored the silence in the bedroom.

Her chest ached. She had planned to spend a peaceful day sketching at her desk. Instead she stood in a stranger's bedroom and contemplated an uncertain future.

"Forgive me for intruding on your grief." The deep-pitched timbre of Kit Coleridge's voice sounded closer. "Yet have you considered that you might know the culprit yourself?"

She swung around, gripping the cold windowsill behind her. "How could I? I had no idea Maurice even consorted with *your* kind of female."

Again, he fixed her with his feral stare. "My personal preferences are not at issue. I would rather take a close look at everyone you and your husband knew."

"Why should you bother yourself?"

"The incident happened in my home. That carries a certain responsibility."

"Or perhaps you're afraid of gossip, of newspapers spreading the word that the exalted marquis of Blackthorne hosts the sort of parties where decent folk end up murdered."

His face might have been a bronze sculpture, etched lines of cold arrogance. "Think whatever you like, Mrs. Rutherford. But if you sincerely wish to see justice served, you'll cooperate."

Shame slithered past her anger. He suggested the sensible path, a start toward finding the truth. Norah forced herself to think. "I'm sorry, but I can't imagine any woman of my acquaintance who would commit murder."

"And the men? It's possible that a man paid this woman to do the deed."

She shook her head. "This is madness. Maurice and I don't . . . didn't befriend murderers."

"Perhaps it's someone you don't know well." Hands clasped behind his back, Kit Coleridge paced the leaf design of the carpet. "Did your husband have any enemies?"

"Of course not. Maurice might have been as opinionated as any man, but he got on well with people. After all, he needed finesse to deal with the most demanding of our highborn customers."

A slight quirk of his dark brows gave the only sign that the marquis had noticed her irony. "Perhaps he had a professional rival. I understand he was contemplating a royal commission. To make a tiara for the Princess of Wales to wear at the Queen's Jubilee in June."

"Yes. We . . . he had competitors, other jewelers who plan to submit their own designs." Worry over the commission seized Norah; she forced her mind back to the murder. "But to kill him? I can't imagine who would have done so."

"Yet someone did. Had he quarreled with anyone recently?"

One argument echoed an unwelcome refrain in her memory. But she had no intention of spilling out her private life to a stranger. "Maurice had occasional disagreements with people. Don't we all?"

"Yes, and in the heat of the moment, we can speak unduly harsh words. We can stir passions that might otherwise remain dormant."

"What are you saying?"

He hesitated, one black eyebrow arched in keen absorption, as if he were assessing a flawed jewel. "I'm afraid the police will consider you a prime suspect, Mrs. Rutherford."

Her lungs froze in breathless surprise. "That is utterly preposterous."

"But unavoidable. Who would have more motive to kill her philandering husband than the injured wife?"

The allusion to Maurice's infidelity cut into Norah. "I can prove my whereabouts last night."

"So where were you?"

He stood with his hands on his hips, the coat pushed back to reveal his trim waist and the powerful breadth of his chest. Resentment pricked her. She needn't justify herself to this stranger. "That is between me and the police. Besides, you're ignoring one salient point."

"What's that?"

"Why kill him here?" She pointed her index finger at the marquis. "Why did the murderess involve you, your lordship?"

Moodiness descended over his face. He rubbed the back of his neck as if it pained him. "I wish I knew."

Clutching the black velvet of her skirt, Norah took a step toward him. By heaven, she must unravel the mystery. "Maybe *you* killed him."

He glared down at her, his mouth taut and pale. "I beg your pardon? What, pray, was my motive for doing in your husband?"

His sarcasm angered her. She lifted her chin. "Inspector Wadding confirmed that Maurice may have been robbed. You see, when my husband left home, he was carrying an expensive diamond he meant to deliver to a client. That diamond is now missing."

His gaze sharpened. "Who is the client?"

"I don't know." She extricated herself from the bitter swamp of memory. "Maurice didn't tell me."

"I see. So you think I robbed your husband, stuck him with a hatpin, and arranged him in my own bed. All in the midst of a party in which scores of eyewitnesses can vouch for me."

Put in bald terms, the scenerio seemed absurd. Whirling, she retreated to the drafty windowsill. "Inspector Wadding said there was only one witness—a woman who was your guest."

"Yes, that's true."

"I should like to speak to her."

He shook his head decisively. "It would serve no purpose, Mrs. Rutherford. She's already told her story to the police."

"Unless she lied at your urging."

"Oh? Where is your proof of my lie?"

His affronted glare daunted Norah. His hands were balled at his sides, his mouth tight, his dark eyes glittering. She wondered how far Lord Christopher Coleridge would go to protect his sterling name. What if he *were* more involved than he admitted?

She must tread carefully. She mustn't forget he was a tiger, dangerous and unpredictable. And probably above the law.

"Perhaps *lie* is too strong a word," she amended. "I merely thought you or the police might have intimidated the witness into saying what you wanted to hear."

His lips quirked unexpectedly into a half smile so impudent and appealing that she glimpsed his allure to a certain type of female. Not herself, of course. "So," he said, "you think I bullied the poor woman?"

"It's possible. I wish to meet the witness. To hear her account for myself."

"I'm sorry, but she isn't available. She left last night—"

"No, I didn't."

The husky sound of Jane's voice made Kit spin around. His heart jerked. "What the devil—"

His mistress stood in the shadowed doorway of the dressing room. Her blond hair cascaded in an immodest mass down to her waist. She wore his maroon silk smoking jacket . . . and nothing else, judging by her naked calves.

Trust Jane to make a dramatic entrance.

He flashed a look at Mrs. Rutherford. Across the bridge of her nose, a charming cluster of freckles sprinkled her pearly skin. High color tinted her cheeks. She held herself stiff and straight, one auburn eyebrow arched, her eyes jewel-green in the morning light.

Bloody hell. He could imagine the condemning thoughts racing inside Norah Rutherford's head. She had accused him of murder; now she had proof to denounce him as a philanderer, too. Shame washed over him. Damn, he was weary of being judged a lecher, a walking phallus with no more to offer a woman than an illicit romp in bed. He needed more than meaningless sexual encounters. He knew a desperate wish to see Norah Rutherford's lovely features kindle with esteem and admiration instead of suspicion and censure.

Like the lady of the household, Jane stepped into the bedroom. "I don't mind answering your questions, Mrs. Rutherford," she said in her best upper-crust tone. "But first, allow me to extend my deepest—"

"Please refrain from extending anything." Kit strode grimly to intercept her. "Why are you still here?" he said in a harsh whisper. "It's quite obvious you're been eavesdropping."

"I fell asleep on the cot." Jane waved a hand at the dressing room. "Your voices awakened me. I could hardly avoid overhearing you, darling." She spoke as if he were the one at fault.

"Then I'm sure you'll hear this clearly enough: get back in there and attire yourself properly."

"I've nothing to hide—"

"Go."

"But Kit, darling—"

"Now."

Her kittenish features settled into a fine sulk. She yanked at the tasseled tie of the robe and minced away in a huff.

"Stop," said Norah Rutherford. "I insist on having a word with you."

Jane swirled back around, the image of injured womanhood. "Yes?"

Jesus God. Things were going from bad to worse.

Kit stepped to Norah's side. "Come with me, Mrs. Rutherford. We'll wait downstairs."

Ignoring him, she focused on Jane. "Pardon me, but are you the witness?"

"The one and only." She smoothed her palms over the dressing gown. "I'm the Honorable Jane Bingham. What was it you wished to ask me?"

Norah Rutherford's gaze traveled up and down his mistress. "I've changed my mind. I believe my questions have been answered adequately already." She turned to Kit, and her withering look revealed her doubts of his witness and her condemnation of him. "Thank you for your hospitality, my lord. I can see myself out."

Tongue-tied with a woman for the first time in his adult life, he watched Norah Rutherford walk out the bedroom door.

He saw himself through her eyes, a self-indulgent profligate whose most notable achievement was his sexual conquests. A man whose word she mistrusted. A man she denounced as a blackhearted scoundrel. The insult still pained him. He prayed her opinion didn't stem from his half-caste heritage.

He massaged the crick in his neck. Damn, he felt old and jaded. Hell of a condition to develop before he'd even reached his thirtieth birthday.

His charm had always won him favor with women. He fulfilled their erotic fantasies and gratified his own physical urges. Yet no woman had ever brought lasting joy to his life. The future loomed before him, an endless string of aimless affairs and fair-weather friends. Suddenly Kit yearned to find the great love his father and stepmother shared.

The powerful love that had driven Norah Rutherford to tear at the bed in mindless grief.

Misgivings assaulted him. He wasn't sure he knew how to love a woman completely, to offer her spiritual and emotional support. But if learning by example could work, his parents were fine teachers. He had grown up protected in a close-knit family, and not until he went off to boarding school had he been forced to fight prejudice against his damnable Indian blood.

"Well!" said Jane. "I never expected Rutherford's widow to be so young. Thank heavens I wasn't cursed with hair in that bold red hue."

In grim humor, Kit watched Jane primp her sleek tresses. "Thank heavens indeed. You're bold enough just as you are."

She draped herself against his chest. "Oh, darling. You're not still angry with me for intruding, are you? I waited ever so long for you to come to bed last night."

"What torment you must have suffered. Since you'd failed to scratch your itch with Rutherford."

A tiny frown disturbed her sultry expression. "I told you last night, I never meant to seduce him—"

"Spare me the lie." Shaking her off, Kit walked away and worked at his sleeve link. "I know your proclivities too well. And they don't lean toward fidelity."

"Fidelity! That's as antiquated an idea as those dusty relics my father is forever digging up."

Kit unbuttoned his shirt. "Nevertheless, faithfulness was our agreement."

"Come now, nothing really happened." From behind him, she glided her fingertips over his ear. The heat of her body left him cold. "And speaking of proclivities, mine are telling me a certain stallion needs to ride his mare."

He pulled away. "For once you're wrong."

"Then why are you undressing?"

"I'm going to wash up. And you're going home." Impelled by weariness and discontent, he made a snap decision. "For good."

Her provocative mouth opened and closed. She planted her hands on her hips. "Just like that, you're pitching me out?"

"Just like that." Seeing the baffled shock in her blue eyes, he gentled his tone. "It's inevitable, Jane. You always move on to another man every few months."

"On my own terms, yes."

"I'm sorry, but this time it'll be on my terms."

Her lower lip thrust out. Her eyes narrowed to slits. She glanced at the rumpled bed, then poked her spike-nailed finger at him. "It's that woman."

"What woman?" he scoffed, going into the dressing room to deposit his sleeve links on the clothespress.

"That Rutherford woman." Jane followed him. "You're taken with that prissy, sharp-tongued widow."

"That isn't true." But even as he spoke, Kit felt the truth burning like a fire inside his chest.

"Hah! Now who's lying? I saw how you looked at her." With an ill-humored curse, Jane snatched up the untidy heap of her clothing. "But the joke's on you, my lord. You'll never get your prodigious cock under *her* skirts. I know her kind—she's the sort who keeps herself locked in a chastity belt. And her husband probably swallowed the key before he died." Jane tossed one final glare as she headed for the door, trailing a silk stocking. "You'll regret spurning Jane Bingham. I'll make bloody certain of that!"

Kit only half heard her diatribe. Memory enthralled him with the feel of Norah Rutherford's body beneath his, the passionate spirit hidden behind her ladylike facade, the ethereal beauty enhanced by her keen mind. He ached to think that the ice of grief encased her in sadness.

If only he could help her.

Yet in his heart he feared she would never accept help from a reprobate. God, maybe he was a fool for hoping she wasn't prejudiced. Hadn't he learned his lesson about snide Englishwomen at the tender age of fourteen? As much as he tried to dam them, the painful images came flooding back.

Images of Emma Woodferne.

The first time he had seen Emma, she had been sitting on a wrought-iron bench outside the headmaster's office. Kit had been studying in the cavernous silence of the refectory, his private retreat whenever his classmates shunned or taunted him.

Peering idly out the leaded window, he spied her in the garden. The unusual sight of a girl at a boys' school riveted him; she must have been there to fetch her brother home for the weekend. The fresh green of early spring foliage made a backdrop for her radiant features. She was a wood nymph with petal-white skin, an aura as pure as newly fallen snow, and an abundance of cinnamon hair draping her shoulders. Her slender form was bent over the primer in her lap.

Kit fell instantly in love. He was racking his brain for an excuse to go out and meet her when her parents emerged from the dormitory with a boy in tow, James Woodferne. Even now, Kit felt his muscles tense with anger. James was a thickset, stupid lad devoted to two sports: cricket and the game of ridiculing Kit about his heritage. How James with his ugly bulldog features and cruel manner had gotten a nymph for a sister, Kit couldn't say.

But he dared not introduce himself to her now. Torn by frustration, he watched her depart with her family. Only by shamelessly rifling through James's trunk was Kit able to discover her name, in a letter she'd written to her brother, full of poignantly girlish complaints about her studies with a governess.

Emma. Emma Woodferne. Even the name held an unearthly quality, sweet and mysterious.

The following weekend, he left a sprig of violets

on the wrought-iron bench, with her name written on a card. Then he kept watch out the refectory window. He had almost given up when at sunset she strolled into the garden, a wand-slim fairy gliding with grace and beauty through the shadows of early evening. She found the violets and lifted them to her nose, then tucked them into her white lace collar.

Her expressive blue eyes and delighted smile encouraged Kit. She looked around, as if to search the bushes and trees for her secret admirer. He stayed hidden inside the darkened refectory. She would come to love him; slowly he would win her affections. Only then would he reveal himself.

The next week he left her a belated Valentine with a poem he'd laboriously composed when he ought to have been studying his algebra. He scored woefully low on his exam, but earned the prize of Emma's pleasure when she read the love verse.

Each week, he left her another small treasure: a lace handkerchief embroidered with her initials, a cluster of fragile forget-me-nots, a sketch of her refined profile. After a time, he began to pen her letters, too, extolling her virtues and lauding her loveliness. He could tell by the spring in her step as she hastened to the bench, and by the brilliance of her smile, that she cherished each new gift.

His own parents asked in bewilderment why Kit never wanted to come home on the weekends anymore. He wove a tale of needing to study, of enjoying the quiet atmosphere when many of the other boys were gone. Lying shamed him, yet he couldn't disclose to anyone his love for Emma Woodferne.

Until the summer holidays fast approached, and he faced the prospect of not seeing her again until autumn. That Friday, he scraped up his courage and changed into his best suit. He even took a razor to the black fuzz that was beginning to sprout on his cheeks and jaw. Then he slipped into the refectory to wait.

She came through the garden gate and hurried to

the bench. Today he had left the most expensive gift of all, a crystal bottle of perfume, which had required him to save his allowance for a month. Smiling, she sat down and sniffed daintily at the bottle, then applied a dab from the stopper to each wrist.

Now. He must go to her now.

His palms sweating and his heart thumping, he opened the heavy oak door and went outside, into the balmy twilight. Emma would love him, he told himself. She wasn't like her nasty brother. She was a nymph, shining with goodness and purity.

Reckless hope spurred Kit down the stone path. She looked up, the smile fading on her flawless complexion. The delicate scent of gardenias wafted through the air. Before he could turn coward, he sank to one knee and reverently kissed the back of her pearl-smooth hand. "Miss Woodferne. Emma." Her name tasted as sweet as forbidden wine on his lips.

"Who are you?"

The harsh demand daunted him for a moment; then he realized she hadn't yet connected him with the gifts. "I'm Christopher Coleridge. I left you the perfume and all the other things. I've waited so long to tell you—"

"*You!*" She recoiled, yanking her hand free and shrinking against the back of the bench. Horror lit her blue eyes. "But you're . . . Blackie! My brother says you're a heathen, from the wilds of India."

Then she had hurled the perfume bottle onto the flagstone path, where his costly present smashed into a thousand shards. Numb with disbelief, he had watched her run out of the garden, leaving only the reek of gardenias and the terrible wound of rejection throbbing inside him.

Kit came back to the present to find himself slumped against the dressing room wall. Emma's prejudice still burned inside his chest like a white-hot fist. That pain scorched him worse than what had followed. On learning of the episode, James Woodferne and five of his cohorts, Bruce Abernathy included, had ganged up on Kit, blackening both his eyes and bloodying his nose. With a parting punch, Bruce had warned him never to touch a white woman again. The stern headmaster had been quick to blame Kit for instigating a fight. Only the close of the term had kept him from being expelled.

And only the scars on his soul remained. Those scars hid a resentment toward the mother he had never known, the woman who had passed on the legacy of Hindu heritage that had festered like a thorn in his side.

He moved into the bedroom and paced to the window, where an icy draft seeped. He had decided back then to pretend that the slurs didn't matter, to hold himself aloof from women. In time he had discovered an advantage to his sensual nature: he became adept at flattery and at enticing the physical passion of cool English beauties. He had used their bodies while guarding his own emotions behind a shield of indifference. There was an infinite number of ladies who willingly set aside their scruples for the chance to bed a wealthy, titled lord.

But now the years of pointless pleasure left him ashamed, in need of warmth and light to fill the void within him. In need of a woman like Norah Rutherford.

You blackhearted scoundrel.

He winced at her acid words. Surely Norah Rutherford had been referring to his reputation as a philanderer, and not to the color of his skin. His soul cried out for the love and grief that had driven her to tear at his sheets in agony. He wanted to feel emotions as deeply as she did, to know the loyalty and adoration of a good woman.

But first he must end the affairs and the worthless parties. He must find the sense of honor that lurked beneath the trappings of a rogue. He must prove to Norah Rutherford that he was a changed man, a man of integrity.

The fierce desire to clear his name goaded Kit. By

God, he'd unravel the mystery of her husband's death. He'd prove himself worthy of her. He'd win her respect.

And in the process he'd thaw her heart.

Chapter 3

If they didn't stop discussing it, she would lose her temper.

She wanted to scream. She wanted to curse. She wanted to add her own acid commentary.

Instead Norah sat quietly on the medallion-backed sofa in her parlor. As the conversation swirled around her, she used pencil and sketch pad as an outlet for her frustration. In quick bold strokes she captured the profile of the man sitting beside her.

Jerome St. Claire wore his double-breasted coat with the easy elegance of an aristocrat. A monogrammed handkerchief peeked from his pocket. His wavy silver hair held the faint sheen of macassar oil. Norah sketched his high brow, the patrician straightness of his nose, the neatly trimmed mustache over lips that usually perked upward in the aspect of a man who viewed life as a whimsical adventure.

But today Jerome wasn't smiling.

His face bore a look of sober tolerance as Maurice's cousin Winnifred told her own embellished version of the past week's events.

"It was the most dignified funeral I have ever seen." A sturdy, handsome woman of forty-two, she held her chin high and her shoulders virtuously squared beneath her gown of black bombazine. She touched a crape-edged handkerchief to her tearless brown eyes. "The hearse was pulled by no less than four black horses decorated with twenty-three plumes of ostrich feathers. We engaged only the best for dear Maurice, of course."

"Of course," Jerome murmured.

"He was so well-loved. Near two hundred mourners attended the service at St. George's. The Reverend Mr. Newberry gave a stirring eulogy about Maurice's faithful attendance at church and his admirable character." She dabbed her eyes again. "Oh, Mr. St. Claire, can you imagine how everyone grieved for my dear departed cousin? There he lay in the fine oak coffin that was draped by a magnificent black velvet pall. He looked so distinguished, so venerable, so eminently respectable—"

"We're entranced by your excellent description," Norah broke in. She restrained the urge to remind Winnifred that she and Maurice had clashed more often than not. "But perhaps Jerome doesn't care to hear every particular."

Winnifred aimed her disapproving gaze at Norah. "Can you in good conscience take so little interest in your own husband's demise? These past seven days you've left me to receive most of our sympathy callers."

"Only because you entertain them so well."

"Thank you." Winnifred, clearly missing the irony, released a long-suffering sigh. A martyred tautness pinched her lips. "A lady must perform her duties, however distressing or unpleasant."

Jerome grasped Norah's hand. The firmness of his grip matched the intensity of his blue eyes. "I'm so very sorry I was away during your ordeal. If only I'd given you the name of my hotel in Naples, you might have wired me the unhappy news."

Affection softened her ill humor. Their friendship extended back to the early days of her marriage, when as a close acquaintance of the Rutherford family, he had been the only one to notice her lonely confusion, the only one to coax laughter from a disillusioned young bride. "You're here now," she said, "and that's all that matters."

"I'll be in London for at least a fortnight. Then I'm to meet with a client in Hamburg at the end of the month. I may be able to change the appointment—"

"Please don't on my account," Norah said. "It's kind of you, but you mustn't alter your life to accommodate me."

"Would that I could have spared you this misfortune," he burst out, his hand squeezing hers. The fervency in his expression was extinguished; only a somber shadow remained. He sat back. "If it won't distress you, I would like to ask a few more questions."

"I don't mind. I want answers myself."

"I'm unclear about the circumstances of Maurice's death. How was he acquainted with the marquis of Blackthorne?"

Norah clenched the pencil. Over and over, she had relived the memory of their meeting. She felt a strange, unsettling throb every time she thought of his tigerish eyes, every time she recalled the heat of his body pressed to hers. "Maurice wasn't invited to the party," she said, doodling on the pad again. "His lordship claims no knowledge of how my husband came to be there."

"Praise heavens we've quelled the rumors of Maurice being associated with that half-caste," Winnifred said. "Can you imagine the scandal if word gets out? I let everyone believe that Maurice died of a seizure here at home."

"You told a falsehood," quavered a voice from a corner of the room. "That was wrong."

Ivy sat in a biscuit-tufted chair by the window. Haloed by the hazy afternoon light that filtered through the fine lace curtain, Maurice's maiden sister was hunched over her tatting like a crone at her spell casting. Although only six years her brother's senior, Ivy seemed ancient. A dainty cap shrouded her thin gray hair. She wore unrelieved black, as she

had since the death of her parents some thirty years
past. Rimless spectacles magnified her aquamarine
eyes. Her orange-striped cat, Marmalade, slumbered
at her feet.

"Bosh!" said Winnifred, angling herself toward
Ivy. "Is it a sin to spare our family's reputation?
Even you should see the necessity of protecting the
respected name of Rutherford."

"A lie is a lie." Ivy dropped her lacework and
leaned earnestly forward, her spidery hands gripping the arms of the chair. "God will surely punish
you. He will punish all of us."

"Nonsense. Mr. Teodecki says the good Lord will
forgive our need to stifle the evil breath of gossip."

"Oh, dear. Then Mr. Teodecki must be careful lest
he also endanger his eternal soul."

Norah stopped drawing. "I'm afraid Winnifred is
right, Ivy. The scandal would drive customers away
from the jewelry shop."

Winnifred arched her bristly brown eyebrows.
"And we would no longer be able to afford this
house. You wouldn't wish to move away, would
you? Of course not."

Ivy's face went as white as the lace in her lap.
"This is my brother's home. You can't sell it."

"Norah owns the house now," said Winnifred.
"Or have you already forgotten that Maurice left
everything to her? You and I live here on her suffer-
ance."

Ivy blinked, her eyes like opaque blue-green jewels behind the thick glasses. Her fingers trembled on
the brocade of the chair. "Norah will take care of
me. She wouldn't sell my home."

Norah cast a furious look at Winnifred. "That's
absolutely right, Ivy. You've nothing to fret about."

A sigh wisped from the older woman. She rum-
maged first in the voluminous pocket of her apron,
then in her sewing basket on the floor. "Where is
my shuttle? Winnie, did you hide it again?"

"Really!" huffed Winnifred. "You're the one who

forever hides things, then can't remember where you put them. The shuttle is right there in your lap."

"Oh. Oh, my. So it is."

"Maurice was right about your forgetfulness. What if one night you neglect to snuff your candle and burn the house down? It might be safer for all of us if you lived somewhere else, under the proper care of doctors—"

"Stop it," Norah snapped. "You'll frighten her."

"Don't put me away!" Ivy leaped up, shuttle and thread tumbling to the carpet. Marmalade awoke and streaked away. "Please, Norah, don't let her lock me up in that dreadful place. I'd be all alone. I couldn't bear it. I couldn't."

Laying aside her pencil and pad, Norah crossed the parlor. She took her sister-in-law's hand. Papery skin covered remarkably strong bones. "No one is sending you anywhere." She spoke with quiet firmness. "Now do sit down. I'll fetch your things."

Ivy wilted into the chair. Marmalade crept back and curled into sleep. Norah collected the lacework and placed it in Ivy's shaking hands.

"Oh, thank you. You've always been so very kind to me. Now I simply must finish this tablecloth for the morning room." As if her work were a talisman against the outside world, Ivy crouched over her tatting, her fingers flying over shuttle and thread.

Poor dear, Norah thought. The house dripped with the fruit of her labor—the tall window panels, the antimacassars on every chair, the bedspreads and napkins and lampshades. Norah tolerated the frilly decorations because their creation kept Ivy content.

"If you've no objections," Jerome said, "I'll ring for tea."

"Thank you."

As he tugged the bell rope by the fireplace, Norah lowered herself to the settee. After giving the parlor maid instructions, he took his seat beside Norah. Quietly he said, "We need assurance that the police won't let the story slip to a newspaper reporter."

"Inspector Wadding seemed a discreet man," Norah said.

"What about the guests? I understand his lordship's parties attract large crowds."

"None of the gentlemen would dare to speak out for fear of ruining his own good name."

"There were also a number of ladies present."

Winnifred snorted. "Ladies! How loosely you use the word, Mr. St. Claire. Only one class of female would attend a soiree hosted by the marquis of Blackthorne."

Norah saw a vivid picture of the Honorable Jane Bingham garbed in his lordship's oversized maroon robe . . . and nothing else. Their intimate relationship had been as obvious as an inclusion trapped within a piece of amber. Norah had felt the inexplicable urge to slap his lordship's too-handsome face.

The only witness to the murder was his mistress.

Oddly, Norah felt no enmity toward Jane Bingham. Jane was a woman who openly embraced the darker side of human nature. A woman who lured men to her bed without the blessing of holy matrimony. The alien idea both repulsed and intrigued Norah. She wished she'd had the chance to find out why a woman of Jane's genteel birth had strayed so far from the path of grace. She wondered why any woman would seek the painful physical union only men craved. For money?

Toying with her pencil, she realized with a jolt that she'd sketched a picture of Lord Kit Coleridge . . . the high cheekbones and brow, the pitch-black hair, the devilish eyes. She slapped the pad shut. She had always prided herself on being open-minded. One person ought not impose his prejudices on another.

Nevertheless, she resented him for the way he lived, spending his lust on one woman after another. He possessed an allure that enslaved a certain type of female. No person deserved so much power over another. Jane might even have lied at his bidding.

Norah pondered the possibility. He and Maurice hadn't known each other. So why would his lordship ask Jane to concoct a tale of seeing a woman in scarlet? Had they conspired to rob Maurice?

"Norah?" Concern etched Jerome's distinguished features. "Are you quite well?"

"Pardon me. I was distracted." She fumbled to pick up the thread of conversation. "Inspector Wadding assured me the female guests likely won't spread any rumors. Drawing the attention of society would threaten . . . their way of life."

Jerome nodded. "Of course. No gentleman would ally himself with a woman who was known to be indiscreet."

"Wadding should never have come here in the first place," Winnifred snapped. "Only a common sort like him would plague the bereaved family with impertinent questions so soon after our loss." She waved her black-edged handkerchief like a flag of honor. "Can you imagine, him thinking one of *us* the guilty party? I sent him packing, you can be certain of that."

"When did he visit?" Jerome asked.

"A few days ago, after the reading of the will," Norah said.

"This sordid investigation appalls me," Winnifred went on. "A Rutherford would never willingly involve himself with a vulgar class of female. Clearly, Maurice was lured there by an unsavory trick. His murderess must have stolen the jewel."

Frowning, Jerome sat straighter. "What jewel?"

"Maurice told me he was delivering a twelve-carat South African diamond to a client that night," Norah explained. "I don't know who, or even if he handed over the gem. But it wasn't found on his body."

Eyes narrowed, Jerome stroked his mustache. "Is the buyer logged in the ledger?"

Norah shook her head. "I couldn't find the reference. Perhaps Maurice meant to record the sale when he went to the shop the next day."

Winnifred leaned forward in a conspiratorial manner. "I say they should start their search with Lord Blackthorne. Now there's a devil who would stoop to any wickedness. Who knows, he might have hired this woman to rob Maurice and do him in."

"He's heir to the duke of Lamborough," Jerome pointed out. "The Coleridges are one of the wealthiest families in the land. Why would he stoop to stealing?"

"Because he's also half Hindu," Winnifred stated, with a sage nod. "And the Hindu race is amoral by nature. God alone knows what compelled the present duke to marry a woman of dark skin."

"The duchess of Lamborough is from India?" Norah asked.

"No. That one was murdered in the Sepoy Mutiny, some thirty years ago. The present duchess is the marquis of Blackthorne's stepmother." Winnifred shook her handkerchief again. "You mark my words, he's our culprit. You know what they say about bad blood."

Unexpected anger flared in Norah, like heat rising from the smoldering ashes of memory. Long ago she had overheard the nuns at the convent whisper, *Pauvre petite. She is the product of sin. She can never wash away the taint of her bad blood.*

"His lordship's lineage is hardly responsible for his character, Winnifred. People choose whether to be good or evil."

"I agree with Norah," Jerome murmured. His lips quirked into a sly smile. "If people were judged by their pedigree, none of us here would belong in this elegant setting. Not even you."

Winnifred turned beet-red. "Fiddle. Mr. Teodecki says his lordship openly consorts with wicked women. Why, he even had the gall to bring one of his *demi-mondaines* into the jewelry shop."

Norah tensed, her fingers digging into the settee cushion. Jane? Or another of his conquests?

Her mind vaulted to another startling thought.

Perhaps this was the connection between Maurice and Lord Kit Coleridge.

"Did he?" she asked, feigning casualness. "When?"

"A few months ago, or so I gathered."

"Who was she?"

"I don't know." Winnifred peered suspiciously. "Why should you care to acquaint yourself with the identity of such a woman?"

"I like to know our clientele. I hadn't realized his lordship had ever purchased anything from us."

"He hasn't. Mr. Teodecki said they looked at diamond brooches. And what do you suppose happened next? The ill-bred hussy made a scene, of course. She begged for an expensive ring. His lordship refused to purchase it and half dragged her out the door."

"I see. And he never returned?"

"No, thank goodness. Vulgar displays only drive away the more respectable customers."

"Maurice never mentioned the incident to me." Even as she spoke, Norah tasted the bitter reason why. Seldom had he shared the particulars of his workday because he had believed a woman should take no interest in commerce. Only rarely had Norah been allowed to visit the jewelry shop.

Winnifred rose to give the bell rope an imperious tug. "Where is that Lizzie with our tea? Likely flirting with the footman again. One of these days I shall be forced to dismiss her—"

The doors clicked open. The butler, Culpepper, loomed against the dimness of the hall. A silver tray in his white-gloved hands, he walked at a stately pace toward Norah.

"A visitor, Mrs. Rutherford."

Stifling a sigh at the thought of enduring platitudes from yet another sympathizer, she plucked the calling card from the salver. The unglazed square held simple black print which lacked the usual flourishes and curlicues.

She read the name. Her corset squeezed her ribs. Her heart galloped and her palms dampened.

She reined in her emotions. "Please show his lordship in."

Culpepper retreated. Winnifred sank back onto her chair, smoothing her black gown and tidying her plainly styled brown hair. "His lordship? Good gracious, it isn't every day we can boast a titled visitor. Quickly now, tell me who . . ."

Footsteps sounded from the entry hall. Norah couldn't have spoken anyway. As the visitor strode into view, a strange pressure tautened her throat. She might have termed the feeling anticipation if the notion weren't preposterous.

On the threshold stood Lord Kit Coleridge.

He looked the perfect gentleman today. The white cravat formed a dazzling contrast to his bronzed features. His suit matched the onyx shade of his hair. He wore his clothing with faultless refinement, yet at the same time something in his manner suggested a wilder spirit caged within the civilized exterior.

Norah's every nerve blazed to life. It was the first time she had seen him since that terrible morning a week ago. He hadn't bestirred himself to attend the funeral. Nor had he bothered to send her a sympathy note. So much for his avowed intent to make the tragedy easier for her, she thought. So much for his desire to help her see justice served. His compassion was as fraudulent as paste diamonds.

So why had he bothered to come here?

His gaze swept the parlor and stopped on her. With difficulty, she met his dark regard. Ungovernable heat crept up her neck and scorched her cheeks. In the past she had excelled in commanding her emotions.

But Lord Kit Coleridge had witnessed her one loss of control. He had seen her rip at his bed. He had held her close while she wept and thrashed. He had stroked her wet face and kissed her forehead.

The memory washed her entire body in warmth.

She had the uncomfortable feeling that her thoughts lay naked to him.

Rising from the settee, she dipped into the smooth curtsy required by etiquette. "Good afternoon, your lordship. What a surprise to see you."

"The pleasure is mine, Mrs. Rutherford."

He walked to her. His hand swallowed hers and he drew her upright, as if impatient with her homage. His grip was firm, his skin cold from the outdoors. His long fingers brushed her sensitive inner wrist. He stood too tall, too close. His touch frightened her and she pulled away.

Lizzie entered with the silver tea service. Norah willed strength into her wobbly knees. "We were about to have our tea," she said. "Will you join us?"

"If I'm not imposing," said the marquis.

"Of course not." She dispatched the servant after another cup. Jerome greeted him with a jerky nod colder than his usual warmth. Winnifred sank into the obligatory obeisance, though the rigidity of her pose conveyed disapproval.

Lord Kit Coleridge crossed the parlor and approached Ivy, who sat alone, a delicate spider spinning her web of lace. "You must be Miss Rutherford. May I escort you to tea? I should be most disappointed if you remain so far from us."

Her face bloomed with girlish prettiness. She set down her tatting and accepted his arm. "Oh, my. What a kind gentleman."

How had he known Ivy's identity? Norah couldn't answer the question, but his generosity in including the old woman softened her heart. She poured the tea while Winnifred passed around the hazlenut biscuits and apple sponge cake. Kit Coleridge declined to sit and stood by the fireplace, the bone china cup absurdly dainty in his large swarthy hand.

"Miss Ivy," he said, "you manage your loss with the grace of a true lady."

Ivy blinked behind her round glasses. "How sweet of you to say so. Maurice took the very best care of us. We all miss him."

"Humph." Winnifred made a sound that could be interpreted as agreement or otherwise. She perched like a stiff crow on the wing chair and regarded his lordship. "I'm sure I speak for everyone when I say we are pleased that you would do us the honor of visiting our home, my lord."

He focused his intense eyes on her. "On the contrary, all of you do me the greater honor by tolerating my presence. I'm aware how little you must think of my character."

The case clock ticked into the silence. Norah sank onto the settee. Jerome cocked his head in thoughtful surprise. Ivy sipped her tea in bright-eyed innocence.

Winnifred looked dumbstruck. "Oh?" she said on a nervous laugh. "I'm sure I don't know what you mean."

"Thank you for trying to spare my feelings. But in light of your recent tragedy, may we dispense with banalities and speak honestly with each other?"

"Honestly?" she squeaked, the word foreign on her lips.

"Yes." He drank, then swirled the dregs in his cup. "Over the years I've earned the reputation of being a rake. Now your cousin has died under my roof, at the sort of party I must refrain from describing in the company of gentle folk." His gaze traveled from Winnifred to Jerome to Ivy, and tarried on Norah just long enough to make her heart tumble. "I came here today because I wish to make amends. I want all of you to know that Maurice Rutherford did not die entirely in vain."

Flabbergasted, Norah said, "Kindly explain yourself."

"My unwitting role in your misfortune forced me to face my own failings. I took a close look at the way I live." He grimaced. "The dissolute man I saw appalled me. Henceforth, I intend to mend my immoral ways and behave like a true gentleman."

His eloquence roused Norah's suspicions. His

humble tone was too suave, too facile to be genuine. He must be ingratiating himself.

But for what purpose?

"Oh, my," said Ivy, her eyes flooding with tears. "That is most noble of you."

"It's far too soon to praise me." Lord Blackthorne passed her his starched handkerchief. "As the first step toward my goal, I accept any burden of blame you place upon my shoulders. And I welcome any penance you might wish to visit upon me."

Winnifred's jaw flapped. "I hardly know what to say."

Ivy removed her spectacles to blot her eyes. "You, my lord, are a saint among men."

"Saints are a rare commodity," Jerome observed, one silver eyebrow winged in droll disbelief as he helped himself to a biscuit. "Some of us achieve that stature in name only."

Kit Coleridge set his cup on the tea table. He straightened, one hand pushing back his coat to reveal his tapered waist. "What about you, Mrs. Rutherford?" he said softly. "Have you any desire to punish me?"

Flecks of gold glinted in his dark eyes, like tantalizing secrets awaiting discovery. Norah inhaled the smoky heat of her tea and caught a whiff of his masculine musk. His purpose still eluded her. Was he sincere? Or was he a smooth-tongued charlatan who wished to absolve himself of guilt?

"Vengeance is for those who cannot let go of bitterness," she murmured. "I would never presume to pass judgment on you."

"Indeed. I'm relieved to hear so."

By his half smile, Norah suspected that he knew her true feelings about him, that she had indeed found him wanting. The impulse to challenge him provoked her. "However, if you truly wish to prove yourself . . ."

"I do."

"As a token of your sincerity, then, perhaps you wold make a small donation."

He swept her a courtly bow. "Name your charity. I'll have my accountant issue a check in the morning."

Typical aristocrat, she thought, using his wealth as a panacea. "I don't mean money. I mean a contribution of your time and expertise."

An inky lock of hair slipped to his forehead, marring his perfect image and giving him the aspect of a rogue. "I'm delighted that you see desirable skills in me."

Was he teasing her or not? Frustrated, she said, "You need only the ability to read and an abundance of patience. I presume you have both?"

"I attended Trinity College. And my stepmother says I showed patience even as an infant, when I survived a trek across wartorn India. Will that do?"

He hadn't been very patient with Jane. Anticipating his reaction, Norah smiled. "Your task is to help me two mornings a week at the Sweeny Academy for Orphans. Beginning tomorrow."

One of his eyebrows cocked upward. "Help in what capacity?"

"As a teacher. I instruct the children to read and write."

Rather than retract his offer in disgust, he merely said, "How admirable of you. I'm pleased to assist you however I can."

His compliance surprised her. Regretting her impulsive invitation, she shifted on the cushion. The way he watched her was most unsettling . . . as if she were a magnificent diamond and he a prince among thieves.

"This is outrageous." Winnifred half choked on a bite of cake. "Norah, how can you ask a man of his lordship's stature to consort with filthy urchins from Seven Dials and the like?"

"The children are washed and properly dressed," Norah said. "If other people were freer with their time, I would not be forced to impose on him." She

clamped her lips. The marquis had so jangled her
nerves that she resorted to bickering.

"Well! Would you criticize me when I manage this
household?" Winnifred lifted her teacup in an all-
encompassing gesture. "No one ever offers to
lighten *my* burdens."

"Because you excel at your tasks," Jerome put in
smoothly. "Maurice often told me how much he val-
ued your sense of duty."

"Bosh. He acted as if I were no more important
than a dusty relic in a curiosity shop." But the
grumpy line of her mouth eased.

"Did you and Maurice often argue?" Kit Coleridge asked.

"Why, er, no . . ."

He watched Winnifred closely. Like a lightning
bolt, his purpose hit Norah. He considered Winnifred a murder suspect. He had come here to
question all of them.

Disbelief warred with anger. "I hardly think Winnifred's domestic merits could interest you, Lord
Blackthorne."

His lordship's scrutiny entrapped her. "On the
contrary, you . . . and your family fascinate me."

"Norah has important things to do, too," piped
Ivy. "She designs lovely pieces of jewelry."

Norah's stomach plunged. Only a handful of people knew her secret. If word slipped out about her
unladylike profession, she risked becoming *persona
non grata* in society, when she had struggled so long
to erase the taint of her bastardy.

Winnifred wiped her mouth with a lace napkin.
"Don't heed Ivy's prattling, my lord. She sometimes gets confused." To Ivy, she muttered, "Perhaps you should return to your tatting, cousin."

Ivy firmed her chin in an earnestly stubborn
expression. "I shan't let you bully me this time,
Winnie. His lordship can be entrusted with our secret. Can't you, Lord Blackthorne?"

He placed his hand over his heart in a faintly the-
atrical gesture. "You have my word of honor."

"On your new status as a gentleman?" Norah asked, her tone ironic.

"A man has to start somewhere." Grinning, he nodded to Ivy. "Go on, Miss Rutherford."

"For years Maurice struggled for success. No one seemed taken with *his* jewelry. Then he married Norah and started to use her pretty designs. Rutherford Jewelers became a smashing success." Ivy nimbly jumped up and looked through Norah's sketch pad until she found a drawing of earrings and a pendant with a lotus blossom motif. "See? The duchess of Kent paid thousands for this set."

Kit Coleridge took the pad. "Lovely." He riffled through the pages, stopped and studied a sheet, then slanted Norah a concentrated look from beneath the black slash of his eyebrows. "You continue to amaze me, Mrs. Rutherford."

"Men do find it difficult to accept talent or intelligence in a woman." She rose and retrieved the sketch pad. Clutching it like a shield to her breast, she moved near Jerome. Standing made her feel less at a disadvantage to Kit Coleridge.

"Norah may be a gifted artist, your lordship, but she is also a lady," Jerome said in a hard-edged tone. "I trust you shan't forget that."

The two men exchanged a long glance, intense and cryptic. "I have the utmost respect for her," the marquis murmured, and turned to address Norah. "So now you'll head Rutherford Jewelers?"

Her stomach contracted with a yearning so acute it left her shaken. She fiddled with the pasteboard cover of the sketch pad. Maurice had left no instructions, but she knew his wishes in her heart. He would have ordered her to remain behind the scenes. He would have forbidden her to take an active role. He would have wanted her to appoint a man to oversee the business.

But Maurice no longer dictated her actions.

The realization struck away the cobwebs of indecision, the uncertainty that had lingered since his death. The future loomed before her, radiant with hope.

A heady waft of freedom lifted her. "Yes," she said firmly. "Yes, I *will* take over the shop. I'll start tomorrow afternoon."

Winnifred's fork clattered onto her plate. "But Mr. Teodecki is to be the new manager."

"Who is Mr. Teodecki?" asked the marquis.

"The head craftsman," Jerome said. "He's a superior artisan, but . . ." His tone softened. "Forgive me, Winnifred, but he's not a leader of men."

"Why, you upstart," she sputtered. "He has plans for expanding the store, for drawing in new customers . . ."

Kit Coleridge watched her closely. "Indeed?" he murmured.

Norah's heart beat faster. So now he was adding Thaddeus to his list of suspects. A niggling fear kept her silent. What if the marquis were right? What if someone close to her *had* orchestrated the murder? No, she simply couldn't believe that.

"Mr. Thaddeus Teodecki is Winnie's beau," said Ivy, peering up at Lord Blackthorne over the rim of her teacup. "It's so romantic, so tragic. He is the grandson of a Polish count—"

"Prince," snapped Winnifred. "His grandfather was Prince Leopold of Krakow until the rabble government deposed him. So you see, Mr. Teodecki is far more suited to governing the staff than a mere woman."

Pity tempered Norah's resentment. Winnifred had been crushed to discover that Maurice had left her no dowry. Now even her hope for elevating Thaddeus's salary had been dashed. Norah resolved to rectify the injustice somehow. "The responsibility is mine," she said. "From now on, I shall be spending my days at the shop."

"You won't win the commission from the Princess of Wales. You mark my words."

"Thank you for the warning." Norah pressed her

damp palms together. "But I shall manage just fine."

"Had you borne an heir to carry on the Rutherford name," Winnifred grumbled, "you would have no time to meddle in manly affairs."

The criticism sliced open the scar on Norah's emotions and released the sting of pain. She felt as empty as a mollusk shell in which no pearl had grown. Her life had taken a different course, she comforted herself. One that graced her with newfound opportunity and independence.

"That is quite enough," she murmured. "Remember our guest."

Winnifred closed her mouth. Her robust features drew into a scowl. Then she lowered her gaze to the cake crumbs on her plate.

Kit Coleridge's face was as smooth and sleekly handsome as a bronze mask. Yet a perceptive light glowed in his keen dark eyes. Despite the sketch pad flattening her breasts, Norah again had the eerie sensation that her feelings lay open to his scrutiny.

She went to the window and feigned an interest in the dreary January scene. Dusk settled like gray fog over the cobbled street and barren trees. A hansom cab clattered past, the horse releasing its breath in misty plumes.

The others were making small talk about Jerome's business trip to Italy. Norah bent to stroke Marmalade. The cat stretched and yawned. Its purr vibrated against her cold hand.

The future unrolled in an endless series of evenings, she and Winnifred and Ivy seated near the hearth, the tall clock in the corner ticking away their lives. Two old maids and a widow. Each year a little grayer, a little lonelier, a little more eccentric.

She banished the maudlin image and moved restlessly around the parlor, smoothing a lace doily, straightening a framed print of *The Last Supper*. Her

new plan for her life left nothing to spare for sentiment. Tomorrow she would begin work.

But first she would go to the school. With Lord
Kit Coleridge.

His gaze stalked her. She could feel it burning into
her back, following the shape of her torso, sliding
down over her modest bustle and black skirt. Irritation bit at her stomach. Wait until he faced a roomful of boisterous orphans; his fine and fancy lordship
would retract his spurious vow to change his wicked
ways. He would turn tail and run. Smiling at the
ridiculous image, she swung around to find him
standing directly behind her.

"May I speak to you in private for a moment, Mrs.
Rutherford?"

He had crept up on the silent paws of a tiger. She
tamed the wild beating of her heart. Her alarm was
irrational. She had nothing to fear from him.

"As you like." Ignoring Winnifred's sulk, Norah
told Jerome, "His lordship and I will be in the morning room."

Jerome tightened his lips. He surged up and put
his arm around her. "I'll go with you."

So Jerome distrusted the marquis, too. His protectiveness warmed her. "Thank you, but finish your
tea. We'll only be gone a moment."

Leaving the parlor, she felt Kit Coleridge's hand
brush her back. It was the impersonal touch of a
gentleman, yet awareness prickled her skin. His
imposing presence struck the air from her lungs.
Petticoats swishing, she swept quickly down the
dim hall. The chill in the air made her long for her
shawl.

He seemed not to notice her discomposure. As
they entered the morning room, he examined the
frilly decor of Wedgwood blue and white lace, the
round table and cozy chairs, the fringed lamps. A
gas sconce hissed, shedding pale golden light over
the furnishings.

He fingered the lace shrouding a sideboard, the
snowy cloth stark against his dusky skin. "How kind

of you to use so much of your sister-in-law's handi-work in your house."

"This is Ivy's home, too. She has every right to display her tatting." Uneasy with his praise, Norah minimized her compassion. "Why did you wish to see me?"

"Because we have a few things to discuss alone." He planted his palms on the table and lowered his voice to a velvet murmur. "First of which, Mrs. Rutherford, I want to know why you drew a picture of me."

Heat suffused her cheeks. "Pardon?"

"I saw the likeness in your sketch pad, a flattering one, I might add. May I venture to guess you've been thinking of me?"

She cast about for a retort to cover her confusion. "You interest me in the same sense as any creature, including our cat. If you'd snooped further, you'd have seen sketches of Marmalade, too."

"A pity. *Your* welfare has been uppermost in *my* mind."

His eyes glowed like midnight fire in his sinfully attractive face. Her breathlessness came back with a vengeance. "Oh?" she said. "If you're so deeply concerned, you might have attended the funeral."

He straightened. "Surely you know I couldn't have."

"Why not?"

"For one, I didn't know you needed me."

"I don't need you."

He lowered his eyes a moment, and she could almost swear her words had cut him deeply. "I also wanted to spare you the embarrassment. No one is supposed to know your husband died at my house. The gossips would have worn out their tongues wondering what respects the no-torious marquis of Blackthorne owed to Maurice Rutherford."

His logic and thoughtfulness took her aback. "I see your point," she conceded. "I shouldn't have leaped to the wrong conclusion. Please forgive me."

"Of course." He touched a cluster of hothouse camellias left from a funereal tribute, the petals forlornly edged in brown. "I also wanted you to know that I haven't been idle this past week."

"That concern never crossed my mind," she lied.

"I did my best to track down your husband's mistress."

The starch left her legs. Norah wilted into a chair by the table. Why would he bother? "I thought ferreting into people's private affairs was the task of the police."

"They lack my connections in society. The gentry will reveal their secrets to one of their own before they tell a commoner."

Half afraid to voice the questions clamoring in her mind, she nodded slowly. "Tell me what you found."

Kit Coleridge went to gaze out the window. "I scoured every club, questioned acquaintances and strangers alike, even bribed a few butlers and housemaids."

"And?"

"And I couldn't find even a trace of her." He swung around. "Though many have heard the rumors, not a single person knows her identity."

Norah's breath emerged in a painful whoosh. "Someone must know her! Perhaps Jerome. He and Maurice have been friends for years." She started to rise. "Why didn't I think to ask him?"

"Don't trouble yourself," said Kit Coleridge. "I've already spoken to him."

"You have?"

"Yes. I caught him as he returned home from Italy this morning, before he came to see you."

She sat in stunned silence. Jerome hadn't breathed a word. Of course, he wouldn't, she realized. He was too protective of her. "That's why you seemed to know everyone in my family."

"Yes." Lord Blackthorne knelt before Norah

and gathered her hands in his. The shock of his familiarity, coupled with his unforeseen news, paralyzed her. "Mr. St. Claire knew nothing of a paramour, either," he said gravely. "I'm beginning to wonder if your husband's mistress even exists."

A slow pounding assailed her insides. "Don't be absurd. A ghost didn't thrust a hatpin into his heart."

"I know. But perhaps we all snatched at a false assumption."

"Then who was the woman dressed in scarlet? A thief who panicked?"

"Perhaps. I suspect she was someone your husband knew, someone close to him." Kit Coleridge bared his white teeth in a look both fierce and gentle. "Possibly even someone from this household."

All heat fled her body. Jerking her hands free, she sprang from the chair and pushed past him. "How dare you come in here and accuse my family." Her voice vibrated with anger. "Ivy couldn't have murdered her own brother—she was too devoted to him. And Winnifred might bluster, but she's hardly a killer."

He leaped to his feet and towered over her like a dark archangel. "She said she wanted to marry Thaddeus Teodecki. Perhaps she had counted on a legacy in your husband's will."

Norah swallowed the prickle of tears at the back of her throat. "Regardless, the police will prove it was someone else."

"They may indeed. God, I hope they do." He pressed his hand to her shoulder in the soothing gesture of a friend. "Trust me, Norah. I would never willingly cause you pain—"

"Madam?" Culpepper's voice rang from the doorway. Contrary to his unflappable nature, he wrung his gloved hands. "Pardon me, but that policeman is back. I put him in the kitchen."

Norah gathered her scattered thoughts. "Inspector Wadding?"

"Yes, madam. I asked him to return at a more convenient time, but he was most insistent on speaking to you and the other ladies."

"Please show him into the parlor, then."

"As you wish, madam." The butler bowed and departed.

"Let's see what he wants," the marquis murmured. "We can finish our talk later."

They reached the parlor at the same time as the inspector. Clad in worn tweeds, he gripped a tattered pad and the stub of a pencil, which he used to scratch his long ear. "Ahem—beg pardon for intruding, ma'am."

"It's quite all right." Norah had no patience for small talk. "Have you learned something?"

"Not yet." Wadding shifted his big feet. "Er, if it won't be too distressing, I must show you something."

"Do you mean to say you haven't caught the murderess yet?" demanded Winnifred, surging up from her chair. "It's been a week already. How long will that hussy roam free? She's a menace to decent folk—"

"Please let the man speak," Norah said. "Inspector, feel free to ask anything that will bring my husband's killer to justice."

Wadding fumbled with pad and pencil, then groped in his pocket. "I'd like to see if any of you might know the owner of this. I've showed it to most everyone at the scene of the crime, but nobody knows who it belongs to."

The others gathered around as he unfolded a frayed bit of gray felt. In his palm, a large Siberian emerald glinted in a gold collet setting. From the gem stretched a thin, wickedly long shaft.

"My gracious," Ivy said, her hand on her faded cheek. "It's so very pretty."

Wadding glanced grimly around the group. "It's the hatpin that was stuck in Mr. Rutherford's heart."

Winnifred gasped. Lord Blackthorne frowned. Jerome released a hissing breath as Ivy sagged against him.

Dizziness swamped Norah. She swallowed hard against a rising nausea. It couldn't be true; it was too horrid. The admission pushed past the dryness in her throat.

"The hatpin is mine."

Chapter 4

"**I** understand Mrs. Rutherford had dinner with both of you on New Year's Eve," Kit said.

His voice echoed within the plastered walls of the refectory. Two long tables lined with benches comprised the sole furnishings. Beside him, he could see Norah's lustrous hair and slim body, but he kept his gaze trained on the couple before him.

The Reverend and Mrs. Sweeny made an unlikely couple, Kit thought. Elias was a taciturn man with sparse sandy whiskers and a consumptive cough. His high boiled collar propped up his bald head like an egg perched in an eggcup. In contrast, Verna Sweeny had an abundance of brown corkscrew curls, a pudding face with black currant eyes, and a smiling mouth. She cradled a sleeping baby in her pudgy arms.

Mrs. Sweeny smiled at Norah. "Indeed we did have the poor darling to dinner. How dare the police try to accuse her of doing in her own husband! I told Inspector Wadding that Reverend Sweeny and I will vouch for her in any court of law. Isn't that so, Reverend?"

He coughed and nodded. "Yes, dearest."

"Thank you both," Norah said. "I appreciate your kindness." She hesitated, then added, "May I hold the baby?"

"Of course," Mrs. Sweeny said. "John is the

newest addition to our orphanage. A constable found the wee lad abandoned in an alley yesterday, howling for his dinner.''

"In such cold weather.'' Her brow furrowed, Norah gathered the slumbering infant close to her breast. Tenderness eased her lovely features and brought a wistful smile to her lips. She smoothed her hand over his tiny, blanket-swathed form, then caressed his downy hair and rosy cheeks. ''Oh, isn't he sweet? His mother must have been in dire straits to leave him.''

Kit wished Norah would regard him so warmly. He wished she would look at him at all. In the few minutes since he'd met her here at the school, she had granted him only a perfunctory greeting.

"John'll have a safe place with us.'' Taking the baby back, Verna Sweeny shivered, her doughy chin jiggling. "But I'm more concerned about you, Norah. To think Mr. Rutherford might be alive today if only he'd come along like you asked him.''

Kit's attention perked up. "He was invited here?''

" 'Course he was. But Norah said he had another engagement. I know he disapproved of our school, but it isn't seemly for a husband and wife to go their separate ways on a holiday. Isn't that so, Reverend?''

Elias Sweeny coughed an assent. Kit wondered how the preacher managed to speak long enough to deliver a sermon. On the other hand, his congregation must cherish his brevity.

"If you'll excuse us, we must be getting to the children now,'' Norah said, with a last lingering look at the infant. "Your lordship, I'll show you to your classroom.''

As he accompanied her to the door, Mrs. Sweeny called out after them, "We're quite overwhelmed by your generosity, my lord. An angel surely must have sent you to relieve our burdens.''

Kit stared at Norah. "An angel indeed.''

"Amen!'' the Reverend added, clasping a black-bound Bible to his sunken chest. In a rare burst of fervency, he added, "May God reward you in the afterlife!"

Bother the afterlife, Kit thought, indulging in an irreverent study of Norah Rutherford's slender back as she led him down a musty passage. Now there was one reward he hoped to collect in the temporal world.

A black snood imprisoned her curly red hair at the nape of her neck. A black lacy scarf draped her shoulders. The bustle on her black woolen gown swayed enticingly as she walked.

Black, black, black.

The dismal reminder of her grief daunted Kit. Only a degenerate like him would lust after a widow whose beloved husband was barely cold in the grave. She deserved at least a year or more to mourn. Even then, she might never want a rogue who had known more women than Lothario. In a way Kit couldn't blame her for thinking the worst of him. He himself had woven the soiled cloth of his reputation. He ought to turn around right now and walk out the door. Leaving her to her grief would be an act of courtesy, the act of a true gentleman.

But he was a lovesick fool.

Kit tried to fathom his powerful longing for a woman who clearly disliked him, a typical, priggish English lady who judged him by the color of his skin. A lady like Emma Woodferne.

The old hurt clamored for release. He fought down the appalling sickness of rejection and concentrated on Norah Rutherford, marching along the passage like a crusader on her way to save the world.

The image endeared her to him. Norah wasn't a typical English lady, not by any stretch of the imagination. He thought about the tender emotions she kept hidden, the artistic talent that created jewelry of exquisite beauty, the generous nature that caused her to drape her house in lace and devote her mornings to teaching orphans. She adored children, judging by the way she had cuddled the abandoned infant. He envisioned her nursing his baby at her full breast, and imagined himself someday sharing with her the boisterous, loving family of his youth.

And he knew why Norah Rutherford was the one woman who could put an end to his bachelorhood.

Kit rallied his determination. He would prove himself a commendable man. She believed him incapable of change, so he must use this opportunity to establish his reformed nature.

At the end of the passage, they reached a steep staircase. An uncurtained window overlooked a deserted courtyard. The chanting of girlish voices floated from somewhere in the distance. Norah glanced over her shoulder at him. Morning sunshine gilded the freckles dusted on the dainty bridge of her nose.

"The boys' classroom is upstairs." She clutched her skirt in preparation to ascending.

"Wait."

She paused, one foot poised on the bottom step. Her heady scent of roses swirled around him. Her very nearness fired his loins even as her cool expression smote his heart. "What is it?" she asked. "Don't tell me you've changed your mind already."

Her supercilious expectancy irked him. "No. But we never had the chance to finish our talk."

"You were there when I answered Inspector Wadding's questions. I see no point in repeating my explanation about the hatpin."

Kit tried a different approach. "Where did your husband tell you he was going on the night he died?"

Her clear green gaze skittered away. "He didn't say."

"Didn't he ask you to accompany him?"

"No. Not that it's any of your concern."

He could see only her profile, as pure and precious as one of her designs. Pride and pain etched her expression. He burned to know how she had fallen in love with a man twice her age, what they had in common besides a passion for jewelry. On a hunch, Kit said, "Did you and he often socialize apart?"

Her back stiffened. She whirled on him, her fingers enmeshed in the folds of her skirt. "I don't care for your prying. My private life is my own."

Her frosty tone hurt, yet he kept his expression meek. If it took a year, two years, even a lifetime, he would win her over with gentlemanly charm and shatter her negative image of him. "Kindly accept my apology, Mrs. Rutherford. I'm merely trying to get a picture of your late husband's habits. In the interest of finding out who wished him dead."

She gazed at Kit as if weighing his sincerity. He remembered how good she had felt clasped in his arms. Despite the chill in the school, his insides felt like a furnace. From far away came a girl's high voice lisping the alphabet: *Q, R, Eth, T* . . .

Norah sighed, and the rigidity of her features eased. "Please excuse my discourteous manner, your lordship. I realize you're only trying to help."

The lavender shadows beneath her eyes indicated a sleepless night. He ached to hold her, not just as a lover, but as a friend. "Then tell me what happened when you asked your husband to dine with the Sweenys."

She clutched her shawl and turned toward the small courtyard outside. "They issued the invitation when I came to visit the children that morning. Maurice and I hadn't made plans for the evening, so I'd hoped . . . Well, the Sweenys were so kind that I couldn't bear to refuse them again."

"Again?"

"Yes. They encouraged me to be honest with Maurice." She bent her head and studied her clasped hands. Her hair glowed like fire against her alabaster skin. "You see, I hadn't quite told him of my work here."

He took a step closer. "Why not?"

"I was afraid he'd forbid me to associate with a lower class of people."

The haughty bastard. How could she have loved

a man like him? Kit kept his expression neutral. "And did he forbid you?"

"Actually, no." Forehead pleated, she had the hazy aspect of a person puzzling over the past. She absently turned the wide gold wedding band on her finger. "When Maurice came home that afternoon, I conveyed the invitation. He was displeased, but distracted somehow."

"What did he do? Scold you?"

"He . . . barely spoke to me. He only said something had come up, and he had to go out. He didn't even try to stop me from accepting the Sweenys' invitation myself."

The swine had left his loving wife and gone to meet the woman who murdered him. Damn, who was the red-caped female? "Where did he usually go when he went out in the evenings?"

"To his club." Norah bit her lip. "Or so he said."

Her tormented uncertainty made Kit long to touch her. Afraid she'd spurn him, he propped his hand against the wall. A flake of plaster drifted onto his coat sleeve. Absently brushing it off, he said, "You told Wadding that on Boxing Day, when you discovered the setting was loose, you gave the hatpin to Maurice."

"Yes. He took it into the shop for repair. He must have done so, because it was fixed."

"Did Mr. Teodecki mend it?"

"Why, no." Her auburn brows arched in surprise. "Thaddeus is a master craftsman. Simple repairs are done by an assistant."

"I see. So we don't even know if it disappeared at the shop or when Maurice brought it back home."

She sighed again. "No."

"But one fact is certain." Kit hardened his jaw against an upsurge of rage and fear. "Whoever stole the hatpin wanted *you* to be accused of the murder."

She shook her head in vigorous denial. Feathery curls haloed her face. "I don't believe that. The hatpin could have been in Maurice's pocket. The murderess probably found it by chance."

Norah's distress coiled deep inside Kit, so much that he couldn't keep from touching her. Grasping her shoulders, he knew a keen awareness of both her softness and her strength. "But neither Ivy nor Winnifred could offer a solid alibi for her whereabouts that night."

She jerked back. "That doesn't make one of them a murderess. There must be another explanation."

"We have to start somewhere," he said, daunted by her vehemence yet determined to help her. "How about Winnifred? She's a woman of forceful opinions. Did she and Maurice have a falling out?"

Norah clamped her lips into an obstinate line.

"For God's sake," Kit snapped in frustration, "do you really want to live in the same house with the woman who murdered your husband? At least think about the possibility that she might be your cousin!"

Norah's composure crumpled. A terrible shudder of anguish racked her body. Tears rolled down her cheeks. "I've done nothing but think!" she burst out. "How else do you suppose I've occupied myself since yesterday?"

She sank onto a step and pressed her hands to her eyes. Her misery sparked an answering agony in Kit and, again, the overpowering urge to offer comfort in the best way he knew how. Lowering himself to the wooden stair, he caught her against his chest and fancied she wanted him not merely for human solace, but for himself, for the man who had only just glimpsed his heart's desire.

"Norah," he entreated. "I want to help. Please let me."

She melted into his arms—but only for a second. Then her body tensed. Like a panicked filly, she shied away, the cramped stairwell permitting only a few inches between them. She dashed fiercely at her tears and gulped hard.

"Stop it," she cried. "Stop touching me. I am not one of your hussies."

Her disgust hit him like a physical blow. He breathed deeply to dispel the hot rush of pain. "I know," he murmured. "I'm only trying to assist you."

"Why? Out of boredom? Is your life so empty that you have to seek amusement by stalking a murderess?"

"No!" Kit's voice strangled to a stop. He saw the kernel of truth in her accusation, for his days and nights had been a meaningless round of parties, an empty game of carnal pleasures.

But how could he explain that he had a sense of purpose at last? He couldn't. Norah would trust actions, not mere words.

"I regret the necessity of questioning your loved ones," he said. "But we can't risk letting your husband's killer go free."

"Let the police handle the case."

"Unfortunately, the police are getting nowhere."

The cold breath of dread tickled his spine. If someone had meant for Norah to be accused of murder, the attempt had failed. Had the murderess wanted only to draw attention away from herself?

Or had her true purpose been to see Norah executed for the crime? What if she tried again?

No, he couldn't believe danger stalked her. The notion seemed inconceivable in this bright, clean place. Hoots of boyish laughter wafted down the stairs. The summery fragrance of roses eddied from Norah. Winter sunlight drenched her in radiance.

She drew herself up in perfect posture. Twin spots of pink colored her cheeks. "Pardon my lapse in manners," she said in a formal voice. "I'm ready to cooperate now."

He was beginning to think she used politeness as a shield. "For God's sake, I'm not so callous as to criticize your manners when you're overwrought. There's nothing wrong with expressing your feelings."

She lifted an eyebrow. Without preamble, she said, "Winnifred has no independent means of support and Maurice denied her a dowry. He opposed her marriage to Thaddeus."

"Why?"

"He called Thaddeus a common workman, despite his royal blood. Maurice claimed he was doing his duty simply by providing Winnifred a home."

The revelation made Kit see the ill-tempered woman in a kinder light. "So she's been an unpaid servant."

"Yes, since long before I married into the family. Maurice once hinted at a bequest for her in his will, but . . . he must not have gotten around to adding it." As if suffering a sudden chill, Norah pulled her shawl tighter. "Do you suppose her desire for money and marriage could make her hate him so much?"

"It's a possibility," Kit said gently. "What about Thaddeus Teodecki? Could he have abetted her in a murder plot?"

Norah frowned. "He's a quiet man. I'm not sure I know him well enough even to hazard a guess."

"They had dinner together at his boardinghouse early in the evening, or so Winnifred claimed. Then she returned home and went straight to her room."

"Without seeing anyone," Norah murmured. "Or anyone seeing her."

She sat lost in thought. Kit wanted to stroke away the worry lines on her forehead, but knew with a pang that his touch offended her. After a moment, he asked, "How about Ivy? She said she had a headache and went to bed early."

"Yes."

"Do you know of any reason why she might hate her brother?"

Norah gnawed her lower lip and turned her gaze to her lap.

"You do know something, don't you? Something you didn't tell the police." When she remained silent, he urged, "Talk to me, Norah. Please."

She flung up her chin, her glare fierce. "I never gave you leave to address me so intimately."

Damn, she must be proud of her married name. He swallowed and said, "Pardon me. What happened that gave Ivy a headache? Did she and Maurice disagree?''

Norah surged to her feet, petticoats rustling. Her expression troubled, she pressed back against the window frame. ''Yes! Yes, they did.''

''What about?''

She took a deep breath and paced before the staircase. ''When he came home, he hung his coat on the hall rack. He left a small jeweler's case in the inside pocket. Later, Culpepper saw Ivy examining the coat. But Ivy claimed she never touched the case.''

''And what happened?''

''Maurice was frantic when he couldn't find the case. He said it contained a twelve-carat diamond he wanted to deliver to a client that evening.''

''To whom?''

''He didn't say.'' She threw up her hands in despair. ''But Maurice found the case in Ivy's sewing basket. He said the diamond was safe inside.''

''Wasn't the stone insured?''

Her brow wrinkled. ''I don't know. Maurice was furious. He . . . he threatened to put Ivy away in a sanitarium.'' Her voice fell to an anguished whisper. ''A madhouse.''

Fragile Ivy, who expressed herself in lacy designs, would wither away in the cold, inhuman atmosphere of an institution. Kit's opinion of Maurice Rutherford sank even lower. ''A beastly threat to give a charming old soul.''

''I know. I told Maurice so.'' Norah rubbed her arms. ''Ivy is forgetful at times, but who isn't? A poor memory is hardly evidence of insanity.''

But murder might be. The unspoken words hovered like an evil specter in Kit's mind. ''Did your husband play cards?''

She blinked. ''Most parlor games bored him. Why?''

''I thought perhaps he might have incurred gambling debts—obligations he couldn't pay.''

She regarded him coldly. ''My husband was not

a wastrel to squander his hard-earned money on hedonistic pursuits.''

Ouch, Kit thought. Her jab pushed him over the
edge of frustration. ''No, he was only a skinflint who
refused to dower his cousin and wanted to lock his
own sister in a madhouse.''

She reared back as if slapped. ''Lest you forget,
Maurice died in *your* bed. Perhaps one of your for-
mer mistresses was seeking revenge on you for
spurning her.''

Sitting on the stair, he felt like a schoolboy facing
the governess. He focused on the onyx and pearl
mourning pin fastened at her throat. ''I've considered that. I plan to interview each of them as soon
as I can.''

''*That* should keep you busy for the next ten years
at least,'' she said tartly. ''In the meantime, I should
like to know why you lied to me.''

His gaze bolted to hers. ''Lied? About what?''

''You claimed you didn't know my husband. But
I understand you came into Rutherford Jewelers
once. With one of your females.''

To his mortification, Kit felt a flush travel up his
neck to his cheeks. He hoped his dark skin hid the
color. ''Who told you?''

''Winnifred heard about the incident from Thaddeus. So you don't deny it?''

''No. But I never spoke to your husband. A salesman showed me some brooches, that's all.''

''How do I know you're telling the truth?'' She
looked him up and down. ''I want you to know that
even as you examine the people in my life, your
lordship, *I* intend to be examining *you.*''

She held herself so prim, so priggish, he felt furious and amused all at once. Obeying an irresistible
impulse, he said in his most silken voice, ''I'm always happy to oblige a pretty woman. If it pleases
you, we can go to my house straightaway and you
can begin your examination.''

Her face blanched. She gripped the shawl so tight
over her breasts that her knuckles went white against

the black lacework. "In case you've forgotten, you have work to do. And you've made me late enough already."

She went past him and scurried up the stairway. Glimpsing her slim ankles and plain black stockings, Kit followed at a slower pace. Hadn't she recognized his teasing tone? Any other woman of his acquaintance would have giggled and flirted. Of course, he wasn't used to decent women.

Yet Norah's manner seemed to reflect a high emotion beyond ladylike coyness or the offended sensibilities of a recent widow. Fear? Absurd. Unless she felt repulsed. He went cold inside. Perhaps his half-caste blood really did repel her.

He stared down at his feet, the polished leather shoes ridiculously elegant against the plain wooden steps. God, *was* he a stupid fool? Or dare he dream that once he proved his dedication to changing his knavish nature, she would soften toward him?

The noise of boyish voices grew louder. At the top of the stairs, Kit found Norah waiting in a narrow passage much like the one below. The plastered walls bore embroidered beatitudes in simple wooden frames. She swept open a door. Like steam gushing from a valve, laughter and shouts poured out.

She ushered him inside. "Your classroom, my lord."

Her face wore a bland expression. Yet he could have sworn her green eyes twinkled. Then the roomful of boys captured his attention. Roomful of devils, he amended.

In a cleared space at the back, two youths fought a sword battle with long wooden pointers. The other boys were gathered around, cheering. A few at the rear stood on benches and peered over the crowd. The dull crack of sticks rang with the clamor of voices.

Bloody hell. He was supposed to teach these rapscallions?

Kit swung around to ask Norah for assistance. The door was shut. She had gone.

The truth slapped him in the face. What a damned fool he was. Of course she had never meant to help him. She expected him to fail. Hell, she *wanted* him to fail. So she could prove him incapable of achieving any ideal higher than a romp in bed.

Panic gripped him in an iron fist. Now what? Somehow he had expected younger orphans, five or six years old. He had pictured neat rows of tractable children, their shiny faces uptilted to drink in his every word.

Not these almost-grown savages.

The lads didn't notice his presence. One of the swordsmen was a big brute of a boy with spiky black hair and wolflike cunning in his eyes. His scrawny opponent, a towhead with fair freckled skin and crooked teeth, fought gamely back, parrying every thrust and sidestepping the low blows.

The combat sparked a painful memory of Kit's own schooldays. Because of his stepmother's excellent tutelage, he had entered boarding school one form higher than other boys his age. Consequently he had been among the smallest in his class. That, along with his dusky Hindu skin, had made him a prime target for fagging. The bigger boys, James Woodferne included, had forced Kit to tote their books and fill their coal scuttles, to endure kicks and curses and vile nicknames like Blackie. Until he'd grown large and crafty enough to avenge himself on their ringleader, Lord Bruce Abernathy.

Yet even that satisfying encounter, which had left a permanent scar on Bruce's eyebrow, failed to erase the scars on Kit's heart. The memory of his helplessness still stung like an unhealed wound.

He rallied himself to his present dilemma. Boys were like sheep. They would follow wherever led. Discipline the leader, and the rest of the group would fall into line.

Hell, he just might have a chance to prove Norah wrong. And to win her admiration.

Kit put his fingers to his lips and whistled. The shrill sound sliced through the din.

Heads swung around. The lads poked each other in the ribs. A few mutters and comments broke the sudden silence.

"Ye're in trouble now, Lark," one gleeful voice called.

The spike-haired bully named Lark lowered his makeshift sword. "Shut yer trap, Gaff. Where's Billy? Bleedin' barstard was the lookout."

A stout youth wearing a bright red kerchief cowered against the wall. "I got a penny ridin' on you," Billy whined. "Can't expect me to keep me eyes peeled to the door—"

"Quit yer snivelin'. That goes for the lot o' you." Lark swung the stick and the other boys shrank back. He aimed a scowl at Kit. " 'Oo're you?"

"An' where's the Rev?" demanded another boy.

Hostile echoes of the question swept the group.

Good God, Kit thought. No wonder the Reverend Elias Sweeny had been so eager to hand over the job.

"The 'Rev' won't be teaching you today." With more brashness than confidence, Kit strode forward. The boys opened a path for him. He stopped before Lark, whose belligerent eyes were on level with Kit's chin. "I'm your new master, Mr. Coleridge," he said, deeming it judicious to conceal his nobility.

Lark studied the tailored cut of Kit's suit. "You ain't no teacher. Ye're a bleedin' toff."

"Toff or not, I'm in charge here." Kit wrested the pointer from Lark. The younger lad, who crouched a yard away, gave up his weapon more willingly. Kit slapped the pair of long sticks against the palm of his hand. The wood made a satisfying whack. "I wonder," he mused, "whose ears shall I box?"

"Screeve," Lark said quickly. " 'E started it. 'E tried to kick me in me better parts."

"Well, Screeve?" asked Kit, looking down at the youth. "What have you to say for yourself?"

Screeve clamped his lips tight. Though his chest still heaved from exertion, his narrow shoulders were squared and his steady blue eyes flashed stubbornness. The boy wouldn't tattle, not even to implicate a brute and save himself.

From the guilty looks that passed among the other classmates, Kit guessed more had touched off the conflict than Lark would confess. Kit sympathized with their tribal solidarity. What else did these street boys have but pride? Just staying alive was a daunting task.

"See?" Lark bragged. " 'E can't deny it. Go on, cane 'im, if ye're really the master."

"I'll give the orders here," Kit said. And maybe he could teach the youngsters a survival skill in the process.

On impulse he tossed the stick back to Lark. The lad caught it in mid-air. " 'Ey! What're you doin'?"

"We're going to have a quick lesson in swordplay. You were a sloppy fighter."

Lark stared as if Kit had sprouted fangs. "If ye're thinkin' t' trick me—"

Kit smacked his pointer against his opponent's. *"En garde!"*

Before Lark could do more than blink, Kit dealt him a series of swift blows. Forced into retreat, the boy lashed out with his makeshift sword. His grip was clumsy, his thrusts wild. The air resounded with the whack of wood on wood.

Lark's spine met the corner. His tongue stuck in the corner of his mouth, he gamely deflected the attack. Kit feinted to the right. Lark swung in that direction. With the ease of practice, Kit pinned the tip of his pointer against the boy's stocky chest.

"Give up or die."

Lark's jaw dropped. His stick clattered to the floor. His panting rasped into the silence.

His classmates gathered around. "Blimey!" said Billy. " 'Ow'd you do that so quick, sir?"

"I put him on the defensive. Then I tricked him." Kit looked around at the sea of interested faces. "Brawn might be an asset in a fight, but cleverness can conquer even the biggest bully."

"Will you teach us, sir?" Screeve asked, his tow-head upturned.

"If you like."

The enthusiastic clamor almost deafened Kit. With Screeve as a partner, Kit demonstrated several techniques, showing the lads how to hold their weapon, how to fight on the offensive. "Don't strike out blindly. Discipline your thrusts. Watch for a weak spot. Think about what your opponent will do next."

The boys eagerly imitated him, using imaginary swords to engage each other in mock combat. Twenty minutes of exercise had vented their excess energy, Kit finally decided. Despite the groans and protests, he put the sticks away and turned to Lark. Subdued but not beaten, the lad glowered back.

"Something tells me you were collecting penny bets for thrashing a smaller boy," Kit said. "I needn't check with the Reverend to know that gambling breaks the house rules. Not to mention fighting."

Lark's gaze wavered. "But Screeve's always lordin' 'is learnin' over the lot o' us."

The bully glowered toward the corner, where a tattered book lay on the floor. Kit scooped up the slim volume. The pasteboard cover depicted a sinister man in black clothing and slouch hat, a length of rope in his dirty hands as he crept around the corner of a stone mansion toward an unsuspecting lady. The six-penny novel was entitled *The Madman of Mayfair*.

Aha, Kit thought. "This is your book?" he asked Screeve.

"Yes," the towhead admitted defiantly. "I didn't steal it, though. I found it lying in the rubbish at Farringdon Market."

Kit wondered at the boy's cultured accent. "I didn't say you'd stolen it. I merely meant to ask if you would share the story with the other boys."

"Lark wouldn't know a book from privy paper. He'd probably use the pages to wipe his arse."

Lark snarled like a wolf and lunged. Kit grabbed the boy's rough-spun shirt. "That's enough."

The boy brandished his fists at Screeve. "Think ye're so 'igh an' mighty 'cause yer dad were a screever 'oo could write fancy letters."

Screeve squared his scrawny shoulders. "He was a gentleman down on his luck."

" 'E were a thief just like me own dad were. You ain't no better'n me."

"I said, that's quite enough," Kit bellowed. "There's a time to fight and a time to talk."

Lark thrust out his lower lip. Screeve took sudden interest in his scuffed boots.

Kit released Lark. "I want you two to shake hands."

"Ain't gonna—"

"I shall never—"

"No more arguing," Kit said in a steely tone. "Make your choice between a handshake and a caning."

The boys eyed each other with identical sullen expressions. Then their hands flashed out in a brief touch. The fastest handclasp in history, Kit thought, the cold sweat on his skin warming with relief. But who was he to argue with success?

"Now," he said, "you're all going to take a turn at the book."

Twenty pairs of eyes stared uncomprehendingly.

"I want to know how well each of you can read," he explained.

Billy waggled his pudgy hand in the air. "But the Rev made us recite from the 'Oly Scripture."

"My method is different." Stifling a twinge of conscience, and deeming it wise not to humiliate Lark, Kit handed the book to Billy. "You go first."

The youth went as red as his kerchief. "Me, guvnor?"

"Yes, you."

Misgivings written over his mottled face, Billy slowly opened the volume. He planted his thickset finger at the first sentence. " 'It was a . . . a . . .' "

Kit peered over his shoulder. " 'Quiet.' "

" ' . . . quiet day in Du . . . Duberry Place . . .' "

Pitiful, Kit thought with a wrench of compassion. Inside half an hour, he unmasked the deplorable truth. Other than Screeve, who could recite with the eloquence of a Shakespearean soliloquist, Billy was one of the best readers in the class. A few like Lark could decipher only a simple word or two.

Yet they all wanted to hear the story and sat entranced on their benches as the tale unfolded of the madman stalking the mews behind fancy mansions and strangling lone servant women, of the brave constable who slowly tracked a trail of clues leading to the murderer. Just as the hero's sweetheart, a sweet-tempered lady's maid, faced the evil killer in terror, Kit clapped the book shut. "We'll read the next chapter tomorrow."

Lark sat with his brown eyes wide. "Mrs. R's 'usband were murdered in cold blood, weren't 'e? By a tart in a red cape."

"Where did you hear about that?" Kit asked sharply.

"The Rev's missus were grievin' an' carryin' on," Billy said. " 'Er and the Rev went t' the funeral, y'know."

"The murderess is still at large, isn't she?" Screeve said.

"Aye," added Lark in a stage whisper. "An' she could strike again, stick 'er 'atpin into some other unsuspectin' bloke—"

"That's quite enough," Kit broke in. Good God, maybe he shouldn't have read them the lurid novel. "You're not to bother Mrs. Rutherford with your questions. Now let's get to your lessons."

The boys grumbled but set to work, some writing their alphabet on the chalkboard, the more advanced students taking turns reciting from the Bible on the lectern. Kit regarded them with unqualified pride and weak-kneed relief. Lord, who would have imagined these rascally imps would settle down to penmanship and recitation? And with a master whose greatest educational accomplishment to date had been initiating bored ladies into the art of love-making.

He liked the glow of success he felt now, the un-adorned pleasure of helping others. It filled the empty feeling inside him, yet infused him with the keen hunger for more in his life than parties and mistresses.

But doubtless Norah would condemn both his method of bribery and his choice of reading matter. He hid *The Madman of Mayfair* inside his breast pocket. She need never know his teaching techniques.

He moved from boy to boy, checking on their work. Lark sheepishly displayed his crude rendering of the alphabet. The *S*'s and *J*'s were backward, but Kit praised him nonetheless. The youth shrugged and attempted to look nonchalant, though his shoulders were squared with self-importance.

Now if Norah would only hurry up and witness this spirit of industriousness, Kit thought, he might even believe in miracles.

Chapter 5

S he prayed for a miracle.

When no lightning bolt of wisdom streaked down from the heavens, Norah huffed in disgust. She flung her pencil onto the ledger, propped her elbows on the desk, and massaged her weary eyes. The squiggly numbers danced like dervishes in her brain. Each time she tried to add them, the long columns of digits yielded a different sum.

She slapped the leather-bound volume shut. Arithmetic had never been her forte. Even simple household accounts mystified her. But there was no need to rush, she reminded herself. The vault held adequate cash to meet the payroll. She could go over the ledger another day.

Allowing herself a moment's rest, Norah lounged against the cushioned chair. It was the only comfortable seat in the office, the spacious room Maurice had occupied until three weeks ago. The gray afternoon light oozed over the white-and-gilt Louis XIV furnishings. The decor was too extravagant, too pretentious for her tastes. The spindly guest chair looked as if it couldn't support an elf. The pearly paint on the desk hid the rich patina of oak. From above the ornately carved mantel, the portrait of a cavalier in a long feathered hat glared balefully at her.

But with a fierce feeling of reverence, Norah cherished every stick of furniture right down to the gold-leafed rubbish bin. Rutherford Jewelers belonged to her now, from the pens and inkpot on the desk to the diamonds and rubies in the walk-in vault.

She picked up a presentation box from the desk. Designed to hold a parure, or matching set of jewelry, the green nephrite box had rose diamond chips set in a silver trellis pattern. Her fingertip brushed the *MR* stamped into the base. Sudden jealousy consumed her. *She* had designed the piece. *Her* initials ought to be emblazoned across the bottom.

Norah swallowed the unladylike swell of resentment and set down the box. Henceforth, she could take credit for her own work. She would supervise every piece from design to polishing and see her own trademark imprinted on each one. The daring thought inspired the dream that once had been only a sparkling jewellike secret to be drawn out and revered in privacy.

Yet frustration dimmed her spirits. If Maurice had included her in the daily routine, she might be able to decipher the ledgers. She knew more about serving tea than managing a business. Assuming leadership a fortnight ago had been an act of courage . . . or the act of a fool.

She still wasn't sure which.

Norah plucked the pencil from inside the ledger. Mistrustful of accountants, Maurice had tallied the records himself. Which meant she lacked even a bookkeeper to consult. Whom could she rely on for advice?

Lord Christopher Coleridge.

She tried to banish his image from her mind, but his wicked eyes and pirate smile lingered. He was as trustworthy as sunshine on a winter's day in London. An idle rich man like him would disdain a topic as crass as finances. Doubtless his knowledge of money matters extended to how much coin he should spend on French perfume and Worth gowns to pamper his mistress, the Honorable Jane Bingham.

Yet he had kept his pledge to help out at the Sweeny Academy for Orphans, and amazingly he was succeeding at the task. He stood at the front of the classroom as if he were born to the role of teacher. How had he inspired such awe and interest in the boys?

Nibbling the wooden end of her pencil, Norah pondered the enigma. He certainly hadn't caned the lads. They had acted eager, not subdued. Somehow he had bred loyalty into them, for they kept mum about his methods. The conspiracy of silence intrigued her. She must sleuth out the truth.

Teaching must be another game to him, she decided. He had seized her suggestion as a personal challenge, a dare of sorts, another gamble to win. Like any profligate nobleman, he would tire of the sport soon enough and go in search of new amusement. Just as he would weary of pursuing the puzzle of Maurice's death.

Yet she acknowledged a softening inside her. For all his shortcomings, Kit Coleridge had worked wonders with the boys, Lark in particular. He had yanked the youth from the pit of delinquency and dragged him by the scruff of the neck into a world of possibilities. The Sweenys had almost given up on saving the orphan from a wretched life of crime. But after only a few sessions of the marquis's tutelage, Lark could read whole sentences. Hope lifted her heart; someday he might obtain a suitable post as a merchant or a teacher.

A shaft of memory pierced her with pain. She worked at the orphanage to fulfill her longing for a houseful of children. As a lonely girl surrounded by nuns too involved in their prayers to notice her, she had once imagined having a large, loving family. Over the years her bright hope had dimmed to a flicker and now had died with Maurice. Some flaw in her body had kept her from conceiving. She could find only one spark of solace in the matter. Never again need she fetter herself to a husband, never again endure a man's hands groping her in the dark . . .

Peter Bagley, one of the craftsmen, poked his ruddy face into her office. His leather work apron stretched across his portly middle. "A man to see you, Mrs. Rutherford. He raised a ruckus when he found out the master had passed on."

Norah stood, and the ring of keys at her waist jingled faintly. "Who is he?"

Bagley shrugged. "Wouldn't give his name. Dressed fine enough, but vulgar. Says Mr. Rutherford owed him money. I bade him wait by the back door, lest he offend the customers in the showroom."

"Thank you. Show him in here, please."

Bagley's lip curled beneath his sweeping mustache. "Mr. Rutherford wouldn't have wanted you to meet alone with that sort."

"Thank you. But Mr. Rutherford can hardly object now."

"Suit yourself, then."

As he sauntered out, Norah caught herself clenching her fists so hard that her nails left little half-moon shapes on the tender skin of her palms. Would she ever overcome the disapproval of the men here? Already two workers had resigned rather than take orders from a woman. The attitude of the others ranged from quiet distrust to outright enmity.

Everyone expected her to fail, from the gem cutters to the metalsmiths, from the assistants to the salesmen. Even though they now knew that many of the pieces they had been making and marketing came from her designs, her talent.

Footsteps drew her attention to the door. A great hulk of a man strode inside, his gait lopsided from a slight limp. He wore a black cloth coat and trousers, and a shiny silk hat which he swept off. When he bowed, Norah saw that his oiled brown hair had been combed carefully over a bald spot. Despite his dapper dress, he exuded a coarseness that repelled her. Thick sidewhiskers half concealed his sallow complexion. His squat features brought to mind a toad.

Maurice had owed money to this man?

The stranger sent his hat sailing onto the desk. With an impropriety that made her skin crawl, he looked up and down her black-gowned figure. "My, my. Ye're as tempting as a fancy tea cake. Ol' Maurice never mentioned that he kept a pretty piece like you 'idden away."

"I beg your pardon?" she said, icing her voice with politeness. "How may I help you?"

"Me name's Albert Goswell. Me friends call me Bertie—like the Prince o' Wales, you know." He paused, his vested chest puffed out like a bullfrog seeking notice by a female.

Deliberately Norah remained standing. She must learn to hold her ground with men. "Kindly state your business, Mr. Goswell."

Without asking, he flung himself into a gilt chair; it creaked ominously under his weight. He peered up at her. "So," he said, sneering, "yer husband didn't mention ol' Bertie, eh?"

"Indeed, he did not."

"Fancy that. An' me an' 'im almost like partners."

"Do explain yourself. Or I shall be forced to show you to the door."

" 'Ere now, don't bust yer corset." Goswell grinned, displaying a set of gold-capped teeth. "I only come by for me first monthly payment."

Cold fingers of apprehension tingled her spine. "Payment?"

"Aye. 'Tis two days overdue and I ain't a patient bloke." He propped his booted feet on the white desk and shook his stubby finger at her. "Yer man might've passed on, but ye're still bound ter meet 'is obligations. Owed me a pretty pile o' coin, 'e did."

"How much?"

"Twelve thousand gold sovereigns."

Norah's legs threatened to give way. Willpower held

her upright. She had drawers full of precious gems in the vault. Even so, the huge sum staggered her.

"Why would my husband borrow so much from you?"

"I ain't a nosy man. I don't ask no questions."

Hiding her dismay and disbelief, she gazed into his crafty eyes and grasped at a strengthening thread of anger. She'd heard of scoundrels who victimized the bereaved. "What proof have you?" she demanded. "How do I know you didn't hear about my husband's death and seize this chance to bilk me?"

"Me? Swindle an 'elpless widow? Why, you wound me, you do. Bertie Goswell's an honest man, 'e is. The proof's right 'ere."

Goswell swung his boots down, leaving black smudges on the white painted desk. He reached inside his coat, drew out a paper, and spread it across the ledger book. His nearness gave her a cloying whiff of his oily hair tonic.

Willing her hand not to shake, she picked up the document and scanned it. Dated the previous November, it stated that Maurice Rutherford of Rutherford Jewelers, Bond Street, London, had agreed to repay the loan at the rate of one thousand pounds per month, at a ten percent interest rate, compounded monthly, whatever that meant. Across the bottom of the page unrolled Maurice's tidy, familiar signature.

She itched to fling the paper into the fire.

Goswell intercepted her glance at the hearth and smiled. "I got me another copy tucked away safe, I do. Both signed and lawful."

"I should like my solicitor to examine this."

"Please yerself. Just don't be gettin' any notions about cheatin' ol' Bertie."

Swallowing, Norah kept her expression neutral. "I fully intend to repay you, Mr. Goswell. Once I confirm the legality of the document."

"Oh, no," said Goswell. His mouth hardened into a cruel line. He stabbed his finger toward her face.

"You ain't gonna weasel out o' this one, missus. You owe me a payment today."

"I don't keep large amounts of coin lying about," she said. "You'll simply have to wait until the will has been probated. That's the best I can offer you."

"Is it now?" Goswell snatched up the presentation box and turned it over in his hairy hands. " 'Andsome piece. Real silver and diamonds. Must be worth a pretty penny. Aye, an' it might even be the price o' givin' you a fortnight's extension." He tossed the box into the air and deftly caught it, tucking it under his arm.

"Put that down—"

"Now mind your manners, missus. Me favors ain't cheap, you know. You owe me—lemme see, 'ow do you fine folk call it? A token o' good faith, eh?" He clapped on his top hat. "Cheerio, Mrs. Maurice. Bertie Goswell'll be back afore you know it."

Whistling a gay ditty, he limped out the door.

For long moments Norah stood petrified, her breath searing her chest with icy fire. In jerky movements, she made the sign of the cross. Then she thrust the document into the desk drawer. Feeling soiled, she scrubbed her hands together. A fortnight. She had a fortnight. Surely if need be, she could sell some gems and scrape together the cash.

Never before had she met a lout of Goswell's ilk. As thick as the sickening scent of his hair oil, the stench of his corruption tainted the room. The need to escape pricked her.

Rushing from the office, she passed through the high-ceilinged workroom, where gas lamps augmented the watery daylight seeping through the wall of windows. She scarcely noticed the artisans at work, or the clink of hammers and the metallic aromas that usually gratified her.

The mystery of why Maurice had gone to the vile moneylender poisoned her spirits. If the shop was short of funds, why had he not borrowed from a bank? Surely his credit was beyond reproach.

And to where had the twelve thousand gold sovereigns vanished? The ledger had held no such immense entry. Had Maurice bought a supply of stones? Or perhaps the South African diamond that had vanished on the night of his death?

No, a twelve-carat diamond would account for only a fraction of the sum. Suddenly Norah recalled the design for the Jubilee tiara. Its centerpiece was to be a spectacular lavender diamond known as Fire at Midnight. Had Maurice been forced to borrow to buy that legendary diamond for the royal tiara? Again she resented him for sharing so little information about the business.

She emerged into the showroom. Plush carpeting in a subtle rose pattern cushioned her feet. A pair of Waterford chandeliers sparkled against a scalloped recess in the ceiling. Glass display cases lined in black velvet discreetly exhibited the jewelry, necklaces and chokers, scarf pins and opera glasses, rings and bracelets. On this dreary January afternoon, only a few customers roamed the premises, each attended by an elegantly dressed salesman.

Norah leaned against a tall mahogany cabinet. A great weight of fear crushed her chest. Dear Blessèd Virgin. What if she couldn't pay back the money? What if Bertie seized the store? What if she had to relinquish the wonderful dream that had only just become a reality? What if Ivy and Winnifred were thrown into the gutter of poverty?

"Mrs. Rutherford?"

She blinked at the tall woman clad in a minivertrimmed cloak. Fine age lines enhanced her lovely features, and a lavender velvet hat with a white egret feather crowned her graying hair.

"Lady Carlyle," Norah murmured, plucking the name from the fog inside her head. She had met the noblewoman months earlier, on a rare visit to the shop. "How are you?"

"Never mind me." Her ladyship touched a gloved hand to Norah's arm. "You look altogether too pale, my dear. Please, let me help you to a chair."

"No, thank you. That's won't be necessary. It was overly warm in my office, that's all."

Lady Carlyle still looked worried. "May I offer my sincerest sympathy on your recent loss? I know what a difficult time this must be for you, the first few weeks of adjustment, if I may speak so frankly."

Her kindly manner put Norah at ease. "Of course you may."

"I'm pleased to see you here at the shop," Lady Carlyle said. "Society might deem it proper for a widow to mourn in the privacy of her home, but when my own Hubert passed on a year ago, I found it comforting to occupy my days with worthwhile pursuits, to help me escape all the memories." She pressed Norah's hand. "You do the same, dear, no matter what any small-minded person says to the contrary."

Norah smiled shakily. After Winnifred's harping, she welcomed a noncritical person. "Your words are a comfort. I've had my doubts over whether I was doing the right thing."

"You're to be commended for carrying on your husband's legacy. You have so many lovely pieces here." Her ladyship indicated a necklace sparkling against the black velvet interior of a display case. "May I see this one?"

"Certainly." Norah opened the cabinet with a key from the ring hanging from her waist. Reverently she drew out the necklace; diamond brilliants formed five stars which dangled from a sapphire-studded band. The beauty of the stones, the delicacy of their weight, brought a fierce rush of pleasure to her heart.

"How exquisite. The band represents the sky." Lady Carlyle stroked her gloved fingertip over the midnight-blue stones lying in Norah's palm.

"A head frame comes with the necklace. If you like, you can convert it into a tiara."

"Indeed? How versatile." The noblewoman studied the jewelry another moment, then tilted her elegant head at Norah. "Speaking of tiaras, will you still compete for the Jubilee commission?"

Norah's stomach curled. "I hope so."

"I'm glad. I understand from the Princess Alexandra that your husband had located a diamond nearly as fabulous as the Koh-i-noor in the crown jewels."

"Yes, the gem is called Fire at Midnight. It's the only lavender diamond known to exist."

A thought continued to trouble Norah. In response to her repeated questions, Maurice had admitted in November that his agent, a Mr. Upchurch, had already departed for India to purchase the fabled gem. But whether or not Upchurch had taken the loan money with him, she didn't know.

Impatient and frustrated, she resolved to send a telegram to India and find out. She needed Fire at Midnight. Winning the royal commission would secure her professional reputation.

"I'm waiting to hear from my agent," she added. "He's negotiating with the maharaja of Rampur."

"How proud you must have been of your husband." Lady Carlyle touched the star necklace again. "He was a brilliant designer."

Conscious of the fine gemstones in her hand, Norah braced herself against disapproval. "Thank you," she murmured. "But I designed this necklace. And most of the other pieces here."

"Did you? Why, how very clever." Lady Carlyle's gray-green eyes lit with a glow of awed surprise. "I never dreamed you were so talented, Mrs. Rutherford. Or that you shared my own love for art."

Her unexpected praise warmed Norah. Yet a strange sadness seemed hidden within her ladyship, a melancholy that Norah ached to banish. "If you like this necklace, I would be happy to wrap it for you—"

"I think not." A man stepped up behind Lady Carlyle. Fair-haired and slim, he wore a buttoned topcoat with a red silk handkerchief peeking from the breast pocket. A gold-knobbed walking stick was tucked under his arm, and white kid gloves concealed his hands. His scarred eyebrow lifted as he looked at the necklace Norah held, and his mouth formed a thin line beneath a perfectly trimmed mustache. "Gaudy piece," he commented. "And inappropriate for your mourning period, Mother. Come along now. I've little patience for standing about and chatting with shopkeepers."

His frosty blue eyes swept over Norah. The distaste there chilled her as much as his rudeness angered her.

The animation fled Lady Carlyle's countenance. She lowered her gaze like a scolded dog. "Certainly, Bruce," she murmured. "Good day, Mrs. Rutherford."

"Please come back soon, my lady," Norah said, pointedly ignoring her son. "You're always welcome."

She watched them walk toward the door. She had the unpalatable sense of being dismissed like a nameless servant. The brief intimacy between her and Lady Carlyle might never have existed. Odd, how such a free-minded woman had overlooked her son's discourtesy and acceded to his wishes. The ambiguity uncovered an emptyness in Norah, a vague feeling of loss.

Pauvre petite. She is the product of sin. She can never wash away the taint of her bad blood.

Nonsense, she told herself. Lord Carlyle didn't know of her bastardy. He was only another haughty aristocrat who believed himself superior to anyone beneath his own exalted stature.

A tall, dark man approached the shop. He paused to greet the Carlyles, then strode inside. The din of street noise rushed in before the beveled glass door quietly closed.

Oh, no. Not him again.

Norah's spirits took a giddy jump. At the same time, the impulse to flee clamored within her.

Indecision held her immobile. Lord Kit Coleridge

had already seen her, anyway. He moved through the exclusive shop like a bee homing in on a rose.

Hatless, his coat collar turned up against the icy weather, he walked with assurance and strength. Ah, he is handsome, she thought. As perfect and pleasing to the eye as the Black Prince's ruby. That must be why his image stole into her mind so often. Because she appreciated beauty in any form.

At present he looked irked, embroiled in inner thought. The crease marring his brow smoothed when he came up to her. "I see you've met Lord Carlyle," he whispered for her ears alone. "Prissy swine, isn't he?"

Norah swallowed a startled laugh. "I've seen his sort a number of times here at the shop," she said in a low-pitched voice. "His uncharitable attitude seems to be representative of the nobility."

"You wound me. Not all of us are so uncharitable. Here, I brought you a gift." Lord Kit held out a small parcel.

She gazed at him in surprise. "For what occasion?"

"Need there be one?"

With a single step, he closed the gap between them and pressed the package into her free hand. He smelled of crisp, cold weather and his own faint, exotic musk. Surreptitiously she glanced around the shop; the breadth of his body half shielded her from the prying eyes of customers and salesmen.

Her heart thumping, Norah set down the parcel while she carefully replaced the star necklace on its velvet bed inside the display case. Maurice had given her presents on her birthday, on their wedding anniversary, and on Christmas. But never so unexpectedly. She felt awkward, unsure of what to do. "I shouldn't accept this," she murmured.

"Open it," Kit urged.

Curiosity prodded her into untying the string. Beneath her fumbling fingers, the brown paper crackled. Inside lay a dog-eared novel with a garishly illustrated cover.

She eyed Lord Kit in puzzlement. *"The Madman of Mayfair?"*

"Yes." He ducked his head in an oddly boyish gesture, then cleared his throat. "I have a confession to make."

"Confessions seem to be becoming a habit with you," she couldn't resist saying.

"Yes, well. This is something that's been weighing on my conscience. Something I've kept from you."

She couldn't imagine what his guilty expression had to do with the six-penny book in her hand. Half jokingly she said, "Don't tell me you're the author of this rubbish?"

His black eyebrows shot up. His white teeth flashed in a meltingly attractive smile. "Sorry, I can't claim that honor."

"Then kindly get to the point."

"The point is the boys."

"The boys?"

"At the school. You see, I know you've been wondering how I got them interested in reading. Well . . ."

The Madman of Mayfair suddenly stung her fingers. The book thunked onto the glass-topped counter. She glanced around to make sure no one else in the shop had noticed. *"That?"* she whispered. *"That* is what you've been using to educate impressionable young minds?"

He shrugged self-consciously. "The lads liked it."

"Of course—they don't know any better. But the children need to learn how to survive in polite society." She jabbed her finger at the book. "This is melodramatic drivel, without a lesson or a moral to speak of."

"It does have a moral. Justice and honor prevail in the end." Lord Kit planted his hands on the display cabinet and put his face closer to hers. "Have you ever read one?"

Wary at his nearness, she retreated a step. "Of course not."

"Then please withhold judgment." He pushed the book toward her. "I hadn't read one either before last week, and I was pleasantly surprised. That's why I decided to confess my secret and pass the novel on to you. I thought you might consider using popular literature in your class, too."

He looked so hopeful and appealing that Norah caught herself from melting toward him. She folded her arms. "My girls are studying *The Illustrated Manners Book*. It's a classic of well-bred accomplishments and good behavior, to enable them to find work someday in millinery shops or as lady's maids."

Lord Kit grinned. "Commendable, but I can imagine how well rascals like Lark and Billy and Screeve would like *your* book. They need to learn more useful skills."

"Reverend Sweeny is under the impression they're reading the Holy Bible."

"And so they are—for part of their lesson. But I had to find a more creative way to hold their attention."

"With this?" Using thumb and forefinger, she gingerly picked up the lurid novel by the spine. "Where in heaven's name did you unearth it?"

"Never mind that. The object is to teach the boys to read. Unless you'd rather see them back on the streets again."

The marquis had a point, Norah admitted. A vital, indisputable point. *Was* she being too closed-minded? She, who prided herself on avoiding prejudice? Somehow Kit Coleridge seemed to bring out the worst in her. He made her search inside herself and see her own faults.

She rewrapped the book in brown paper. "Very well, I'll look this over."

"I knew you'd listen to reason." Smiling, he rounded the counter, his hands thrust in the pockets of his coat.

His nearness rattled her. Only, she thought, because he alone had witnessed her most private emotional outburst. She would gladly pay the cost of the

Koh-i-noor diamond to erase that embarrassing episode. She still quivered to recall the pressure of his mouth against her brow, the feel of his hard body entrapping her.

"Now," he said, "I should like to meet Mr. Thaddeus Teodecki."

Her lips parted at the abrupt reminder of the mystery. "I thought you'd lost interest in investigating the murder."

"Then you're wrong. I have a few questions to put to Mr. Teodecki. Is he here?"

"He's working in the back."

She led Lord Kit through the passageway, past the door to the vault, and to the workshop. Rows of craftsmen sat at their benches, each workstation consisting of a desk with a half-circular indentation from which hung a leather skin to catch the lemel, or scraps of precious metal. Each man had his own set of tools—handsaws and tweezers, tongs and pliers.

At a round table sat a group of assistants shaping gold wire. Norah sorted through the low level of noise, the rasp of a file, the ping-ping of hammering, the thump of a hand drill. The thrill of ownership seized her heart. Despite the guarded glances from the men, she felt proud and confident as she escorted Lord Kit through her domain.

In front of the bank of windows, she found Thaddeus standing at his workbench. Tall and stoop-shouldered, he had a crowning glory of wavy brown hair, its neatness identifying it as his one vanity. He bent over the desk to position a wooden jig, which held a single pearl in preparation for drilling.

"Mr. Teodecki?" she said. "Excuse me."

He pivoted and bowed. His pointed goatee gave him a faintly sinister air. "Good afternoon, Mrs. Rutherford," he said, the trace of a Polish accent in his voice.

In deference to her, he rolled down his shirt sleeves. He always acted too respectful, too humble.

She wondered what thoughts lay behind his composed expression.

"Lord Blackthorne, I should like you to meet Mr. Teodecki, one of our master craftsmen. Mr. Teodecki, his lordship has some questions for you."

Lord Kit held out his hand and Thaddeus gravely shook it. "Miss Winnifred mentioned you," he said.

"Ah. And she praised your artistry to me. May I see what you're working on?"

Thaddeus moved aside. "As you wish, my lord."

On the table lay the almost finished piece, a foliage design sprigged with collet-set diamonds from which hung three tiers of flawless, milky pearls. Lord Kit leaned closer to study the sketch tacked to the backboard of the desk.

"It's a stomacher brooch," Norah murmured. "A commission for Lady Churchill."

He straightened. "It's unusual and stunning . . . lovely. I'm beginning to recognize your unique style."

His admiring smile curled her insides. "Thank you." Of course his compliment pleased her, she thought. The act of publicly acknowledging her work was still new and exciting, a hunger to be satisfied, like consuming a forbidden fruit.

Lord Kit turned to Thaddeus. "What do you think of Mrs. Rutherford's talent?"

"I am happy to render her handsome creations."

"How long have you known that she designed the jewelry and not her husband?"

Thaddeus stroked his goatee. He glanced hesitantly at Norah. "Several years ago, Miss Winnifred told me the truth. Of course, I would never have betrayed her confidence."

"Of course." Lord Kit paused. "She wanted you to manage the shop. You must have been disappointed to remain in your present position."

A tiny compression of Thaddeus's lips gave his only indication of emotion, though whether of annoyance or anger, Norah couldn't discern. "I am an artisan, no more and no less," he said. "And I shall remain so, despite Miss Winnifred's grandiose dreams."

The marquis peered closely at Thaddeus. "Did you see the hatpin Mr. Rutherford brought here for repair after Christmas?"

"If you refer to the one which caused his death, then I did not." Thaddeus made a disdainful gesture. "Assistants perform the minor repairs."

"I understand you once took morphine, did you not?"

The query took Norah unawares. Her fingers tensed around the paper-wrapped book. Dear God, was it true? Could drugs tie Thaddeus to the murder?

But he merely nodded. "Last year I suffered from a bout of headaches, and my physician prescribed the capsules. I used up the medicine months ago. Since you consider me a suspect, I will give the name of my doctor so you may verify this." He scribbled the name on a slip of paper.

"Thank you for your cooperation, Mr. Teodecki."

Thaddeus clicked his heels and bowed. "I only pray you find Mr. Rutherford's slayer, your lordship."

They left him at his worktable, a modest and grave man already reabsorbed in his labor.

Burning with questions, Norah conducted Lord Kit into her office. The sight of the ledger on her desk jarred her. Dear Blessed Virgin. She had almost forgotten about the repulsive Bertie Goswell and her financial problems.

More and more she could see that Lord Kit Coleridge possessed the power of commanding her attention; he also had an instinct for handling people. Both traits lay at the root of his charm . . . and explained why he fascinated her even as the force of his masculine nature discomposed her.

He shrugged out of his topcoat and slung it onto the gilded rack by the door. Hands on his hips, he stood watching her. "Why did you let your husband take credit for your work?"

His implied criticism roused Norah's ire. "What else was I to do?"

"Claim your just due, of course."

"How simple you make it sound. But women must live within the restrictions imposed by society. At least Maurice was kind enough to allow me the chance to see my designs grace the people who can afford them."

"Kind?" The marquis strolled closer, his eyes dark and alive. "Selfish and cowardly is more to the point. I suspect it would have hurt his pride to admit that his wife had far more talent than he did."

Norah had long thought so herself, but the private person inside her refused to admit it aloud. Especially not to Kit Coleridge. "Men are always so quick to imprison women with the rules of society. Then they have the temerity to blame us for conforming to their rigid guidelines."

"Not all men think alike. I, for one, appreciate cleverness in a woman."

The smoldering fervency on his face sparked an uneasy fire in Norah. She retreated to the desk and dropped *The Madman of Mayfair* onto the loan document, venting the steam inside her by slamming the drawer. "Enough philosophizing. I want to know how you found out about the morphine."

Raising an eyebrow at the spindly chairs, Lord Kit settled onto the edge of the desk. "From Ivy. I had tea with her yesterday."

Norah sank into the chair behind the desk. The ease with which he invaded her private life rankled her. She folded her hands atop the ledger. "She didn't tell me you'd been by."

"Because I asked her not to. I wanted the chance to speak to Thaddeus first. To see what I could glean from his response, which, as it turns out, revealed little enough."

"You didn't trust me to judge my own employee?"

"Please. Let's call a truce." He feathered his fingertips over her hand, prickling her skin in a strangely pleasant way. ''I was only thinking of you. After all, you have to work with him every day. Better he should resent me for considering him a suspect.''

She jerked her hands into her lap and twisted her wedding band. His smile sobered, as if she'd hurt him by pulling away. Playing on her sympathies, she thought, was the trick of a seducer, a manipulator. Yet somehow his steady gaze melted the stiffness in her muscles. He had a way of disarming her, diluting her resentment.

''How did Ivy find out?'' Norah asked.

''Months ago, she overheard Thaddeus asking Winnifred to fetch his prescription from the chemist. I suspect Ivy hears a lot that people don't realize.''

Fear and worry tangled Norah's insides. She'd spent many a sleepless night turning over the problem in her mind. ''Do you really suppose Thaddeus or Winnifred murdered Maurice?''

Lord Kit blew a sigh. ''Someone laced his sherry with morphine.''

''But morphine is as common as diamonds in South Africa. Anyone could have gotten some. People take the drug for ailments ranging from rheumatism to nervousness.''

''Norah, your husband was impeccably dressed and there was no sign of a struggle. He must have been killed by someone he knew and trusted.''

Feeling ill, Norah sat back. She pictured Maurice climbing the darkened back stairs of Lord Blackthorne's mansion, the convivial sounds of the party drifting from the distance, the mysterious woman in scarlet clinging to his arm. Stealing into a stranger's bedroom, Maurice had drunk the glass of poisoned sherry. What had he been thinking? Feeling? Had he been lured there? Had he spent his last moments believing himself safe in the company of a friend . . . a cousin . . . even a sister?

Or had he been kissing and caressing his mistress even as he slipped into a drug-induced coma? Another horrid but plausible thought choked Norah.

Had the woman found his touch so painful, so repulsive that she'd murdered him on impulse?

"Did you love him so much, then?"

The softly spoken question tiptoed into her awareness. Norah blinked. Sitting on the desk, Kit Coleridge leaned toward her, his elbows propped on his thigh and his hands clasped beneath his chin. His bronzed features wore a look of mesmerizing intensity, a concentration that entranced her. It took a second for her to recall his question.

She got up and went to the window. "I was very fond of Maurice. He was my husband."

"That wasn't what I asked. I wondered how *much* you loved him."

An ache opened inside her. If only Kit knew the truth. But he never would. "Are you seeing me as a suspect again?" she asked icily. "Wasn't the word of the Sweenys good enough for you?"

"I didn't mean to imply that you'd killed him."

"Then why are you questioning me?"

He raked his fingers through his hair, mussing the straight midnight strands into the look of a libertine. "I was curious, that's all. Forgive me for prying."

How a man of his reputation could appear so innocent, could even make her feel guilty for her coldness, Norah didn't know. Frost rimed the windowpane and she rubbed her fingertip over the ice. There wasn't much to see outside; the office overlooked the alley and the brick wall of the adjacent tobacconist's shop.

"If you're quite through," she said over her shoulder, "I have work to do."

"There is one other reason I came here. I want to commission a set of matching jewelry . . . necklace, bracelet, brooch, and earrings."

She turned in surprise. "A parure? For whom?"

One corner of his mouth tilted into a secretive smile. "A lady."

Distaste struck Norah with lightning force. He must intend to give the magnificent gift to Jane Bingham.

She squelched her displeasure. If he wanted to squander his wealth, that was his choice. Considering the amount she owed to Bertie Goswell, she should appreciate the commission. "Well," she said. "What exactly did you have in mind? South African diamonds? Burmese rubies? Kashmirian sapphires?"

"I don't know. I leave everything to your creative judgment. Cost is no object."

"What is this . . . lady's taste?"

"She's attracted to me." His smile deepened with boundless conceit.

"You'll have to tell me more than that," Norah said. "Is she bold? Shy? Feminine?"

His idle gaze roamed her up and down, as if seeing the image of another woman. "She's a bit unconventional."

"Any woman who engages in your sort of relationship is unconventional," Norah snapped without thinking.

"Perhaps." Oddly, a flush darkened his cheeks. He rose from the desk and strolled around the office, touching a swan dish here and a jade table clock there. "Let me think. She's witty. Intelligent. Warmhearted." He angled an inscrutable glance over his shoulder. "And of course very beautiful."

"A paragon." Norah struggled to keep the sharpness from her tone. How could he speak so highly of a hussy? "How lucky you are."

"I think so." Lord Kit came closer and fingered the brocade drapery beside her. "Design something unusual. Something *you* would like, Norah. I trust your taste."

"Thank you." His scent and nearness, the intimate use of her name, threatened to scatter her thoughts. She had never before met a man who exuded seduction, a man who focused his natural charisma on any and every woman he met. She moved away on the pretext of picking up her sketch pad. "Perhaps a celestial motif with diamonds and moonstones. Very delicate and pretty."

On the wings of inspiration, she penciled a stylized moon against a bed of diamond chips. "I could even do some haircombs if you like. Or a diadem."

He peered over her shoulder and his warmth brushed her back. "Ah," he said, his breath tickling her ear. "Lovely. I knew I could depend on you to come up with something original, even ingenious."

His praise glowed within her. She kept her tone crisp and businesslike. "You'll want to see a complete set of sketches before we begin the actual work."

"Of course. When can you have them ready?"

"If you'll give me until next week . . . ?"

He nodded and walked away to don his topcoat. "Excellent. I confess I'm most anxious to present the jewels to my lady."

That strange twisting sensation assailed Norah's stomach again. Before she could stop the words, she blurted, "Miss Bingham strikes me as the type who might prefer something more flamboyant. Are you sure she'll like my design?"

Lord Kit paused with his hand on the doorknob. His dark eyes gleamed with an obscure amusement. "You must have misunderstood me," he murmured. "I never said the gems were for Miss Bingham. You see, she and I have parted ways."

Chapter 6

"Women."

The incisive voice jabbed into Kit's concentration. He turned from his contemplation of the fire and looked at the man slouched in the wing chair in his parlor. "Pardon?"

"Women," repeated Adrian, his brown Byronic curls framing a droll expression. "I was beginning to fear not even *that* topic would engage your attention. For the last ten minutes, you haven't heard a word I've said."

"Sorry." Going to the sideboard, Kit splashed more brandy into his glass. He downed half in one stinging gulp, then lowered himself into a chair opposite Adrian and propped his feet on a stool. "Go on now. You have my complete attention."

"No one's seen you with any women. You haven't attended a single party in weeks. You haven't even been out to Hurlingham. The fellows at the club have been wondering why you haven't been exercising your horses."

"That's what stable lads are for."

"You haven't been racing any of the horses, either."

"It's been too bloody cold."

Adrian cocked an eyebrow and grinned. "Ah, so you've been chasing warmer prey. Do tell me about her."

Norah's likeness burned into Kit's soul, the hair as red and shining as a ruby, the skin as smooth and lustrous as a pearl, the eyes as cool and mysterious as jade. For once he felt disinclined to trade tales of conquest. He wanted to keep her all for himself. Besides, he hadn't even come close to conquering her. "Never mind."

"Rumor has it you're after the widow of that jeweler chap, the fellow found murdered in your bed. The story in this morning's news sheet will only fertilize the gossip."

Kit cast a grim glance at the blackened remains of yellow newspaper in the grate. The shock and surprise of reading the report of the murder still reverberated inside him. "Only the bored read that drivel."

Adrian curled his lip. "I beg your pardon?"

"Sorry. Just do me a favor and don't remind me that everyone in London is reading the true account of Maurice Rutherford's death."

"Come now, no secrets between friends," Adrian cajoled. "She must be a hot filly to lift her tail when her husband's not a month in his grave."

"For God's sake, leave off!" Kit slammed his drink on the side table and surged up. "I won't hear you talk about Norah that way. She's a lady."

Unfazed, Adrian idly leafed through a copy of *The Kama Sutra*, then paused to examine one of the erotic illustrations. "Touchy, aren't you? Most intriguing. I never knew a little scandal to transform you into Sir Lancelot."

"Jesus God," Kit muttered. Half embarrassed and half angry, he prowled his library. This lovesick obsession with a woman had never happened to him before. He had always been able to withhold his emotions, to enjoy women without laying himself open to hurt. Until now. "Can't we discuss something else?"

"I'm only trying to spur you back into your old self. I say, will you look at this?" Adrian turned the book to display a painting of an entwined, naked couple. "I wouldn't have thought these acrobatics humanly possible, hmm?"

"Amazing," Kit said dryly. "To think there's something you haven't tried."

Adrian tsked. "I could say the same for you, old boy. In all the years I've known you, you've been faithful only to unfaithfulness."

"Then it's time for me to change." The power of conviction strengthened Kit. He couldn't continue skimming along the surface of relationships, never delving fathoms deep into the pain and joy of commitment. "Maybe I'm ready to settle on one woman."

"More pressure from your father, eh?"

"No. I haven't been home since Christmas."

Adrian's mouth slanted downward even as he shot upright. The book slid from his lap and thunked onto the Persian carpet. "Ye gods! Don't say you of all men have been struck by Cupid's arrow."

Humor glinted into Kit's dark mood. Like him, Lord Adrian Marlow spurned polite society in favor of more sinful pastimes. But unlike Kit, who had confined himself to romantic liaisons, Adrian was a dedicated thrill-seeker forever in search of new amusement, from smoking opium in the dens of the Devil's Acre to sailing over Paris in a hot-air balloon. His current challenge, one he'd been pursuing for the past year, was to seduce the wife of every member of Parliament under the age of forty.

Kit winced inwardly. That was precisely the sort of libertine Norah thought *him*. She still mistrusted his ability to reform, even though he'd dedicated himself to investigating the murder and teaching her orphan boys. Even though he'd tried to show his honesty five days ago by confessing about the sixpenny novel.

Out of desperation, he'd been forced to resort to subterfuge. Surely she couldn't despise a man who ordered a complete set of her jewelry. Once she found out the recipient of the parure, surely she would relent. In the meantime, a spot of jealousy gave him hope that at least she cared for him.

He drummed his fingers on the mantelpiece. *If* she were truly jealous. Being in love was so new to him. God Almighty, what if his plan fizzled? What if only his monstrous pride made him believe that beneath her chilly manner Norah truly needed him? What if she reacted to his proposal with shock and disgust—

"You're doing it again," said Adrian.

"Doing what?"

"Not listening. You can't explode a bomb and then leave me to sort through the debris."

"What exactly do you want to know?"

Adrian sat with his hands tucked beneath his chin, like a lost boy deprived of a playmate. "Tell me you're jesting. That you only mean to make the widow Rutherford your mistress."

Pity touched Kit. How could he explain to a nonbeliever the exquisite agony of falling in love? "Marriage is hardly a death sentence," he said inadequately. "I only hope I can convince Norah to accept my suit."

"By God, you *are* serious." Then Adrian brightened. "But you haven't asked her yet?"

"No."

"And she's in mourning. Can't hobble yourself to her for at least two years. Anything can happen in that time."

Precisely, Kit thought. The idea of Norah giving her heart to another man gored him like a sword. In particular, he couldn't forget the possessive way Jerome St. Claire regarded her, as if she were his personal property.

"To hell with convention." Kit slapped his palm on the mantel, the framed photographs rattling. "If I thought I could convince her, I'd elope with her tomorrow."

Adrian grimaced, his shoulders again drooping with gloom. "You're truly set on this course to hell, then."

"I prefer to call it a course to heaven." In sudden

curiosity Kit looked at his friend. "Surely even you've given a thought to begetting an heir someday."

"Ye gods, you sound like my father. The old curmudgeon keeps nagging me to sire the twelfth earl, and I'm not even number eleven yet. He wants me to have a whole litter of brats besides." Adrian shuddered. "One whelp tucked away in the country is the most I could ever tolerate. Even so I refuse to give up my freedom until I pass forty at the very least."

Kit chuckled. "What if you fall in love before then?"

"It'll never happen." Adrian shook a finger. "I'll make you this vow. I'll marry if and when I meet a woman—a respectable lady—who's bold enough to sneak into Buckingham Palace and make love to me in Queen Victoria's own bed." Satisfied with the impossibility of his requirement, he eased back into his chair.

"I wonder what your father would think of your criterion for a bride?"

"I rather suppose he'd chain me to a mustachioed nag as long as her blood was blue." Combing his fingers through his curls, Adrian assumed a thoughtful frown. "Speaking of bloodlines, old chap, word has it Norah Rutherford is baseborn."

"Jesus God," Kit said in mock fear. "This half-caste could never bear the disgrace."

"Now don't get sarcastic with me. Even though you've faced down plenty of bigots over the years, we're speaking of marriage here. I'm wondering what the duke will say."

"The small-minded people of society can go to the devil. As for my father, he's tolerant enough."

"Ah yes. How could I forget what he gave you on your eighteenth birthday?" Adrian picked up *The Kama Sutra* and flipped the pages again. "This book and a box of condoms. I remember envying you his indulgence."

The memory wrested a smile from Kit. Then he

looked down at the grate, and his grin crumpled like the ashes of newspaper he scattered with the toe of his shoe. His father had also advised him to treat women with respect. "Unfortunately, my father won't be so indulgent when he sees today's newspaper story about a murder under my roof. If I know him, he's scribbling off a telegram this very moment, demanding my presence at once. I might as well resign myself to spending the next few days in Kent."

"Who do you suppose leaked the story to the scandal sheets?" Adrian asked.

An iron band of hatred clenched Kit's chest. Over the years he'd learned to turn the other cheek. But not this time.

This time Norah would be hurt by the scandal.

Softly he said, "I've a notion who the culprit is. Bruce Abernathy."

"Mmm. The sly goat never gives up, does he?"

"He will this time." Kit smiled harshly. "Once I come back to London, I mean to pay him a call."

"I'm so glad you came to call." Norah drew her visitor over to the parlor sofa and seated herself beside him. "How I've missed you this past week."

"I bought a copy of the *Times* at a stall in Hamburg. But the newspaper was two days outdated. The moment I read the story, I caught the first train back to Le Havre."

"Thank you. But you needn't have hurried so."

"Norah, I had to be with you now that people know Maurice was murdered." Frowning, Jerome St. Claire clasped her hands tight. His skin retained a trace of cold from the outdoors and his silver hair was untypically mussed. "I couldn't bear to think of you enduring the gossip alone."

Reluctant to worry him any further, she fabricated a smile. He needn't know about the snubs on the street, the whispers at the shop, the snooping reporters who had been hounding her for more dirt until she had run them out of the store. "Nothing earthshaking has happened. Besides, I have Ivy and Winnifred.''

"Those two." Uttering a snort, he loosed her hands. "Ivy, bless her soul, wouldn't comprehend cruelty until it slapped her in the face. And Winifred? I wouldn't trust that shrew not to join the rest of society in vilifying you." He glanced around. "By the way, where are the grand dames?"

"Winnifred is mending the linens, I think." Norah touched a lace doily on the side table. "And Ivy is tatting in bed. She's having one of her bad days."

"Hmm. The poor dear. I hate to think of any nasty gossip reaching her maidenly ears."

"I've done my best to protect her."

Jerome narrowed his blue eyes. "And meanwhile, who'll protect you?"

"Let the old biddies cluck all they like," Norah said with an airy wave of her hand. "You should know by now that I'm not one to crave socializing— it was Maurice who enjoyed those endless soirees and dinner parties."

Jerome looked unconvinced. "Nobody had better shun you in front of me, by God. Or I'll give the wretch a lecture about rudeness and manners."

Warmed by his loyalty, she smiled. "Thank you, but I'm sure that won't be necessary."

"What about the shop? Has the gossip affected your clientele?"

The strong voice of temptation bade her to tell him about the vile usurer, Bertie Goswell, and the missing twelve thousand sovereigns. A month ago, she would have spilled her troubles to Jerome. But with dawning independence, she wanted to solve her own problems. To that end, she had scheduled a meeting with the bank director on Monday; he would answer her financial questions.

"Business is off a bit, yes," she admitted. "But that's likely due to the postholiday season." Her heart lurched as she thought of Kit. "And I *have* won a choice commission. Things will pick up even more when the weather grows warmer."

Concern continued to crease Jerome's brow. "Speaking of commissions, have you finished your entry in the competition for the royal tiara?"

"Not yet." Norah thought of the unanswered telegram to Upchurch; the agent must not have reached India and purchased Fire at Midnight yet. With effort, she controlled her impatience. "But you needn't worry. I have the diamonds in the vault." Most of them, anyway, she added silently. If she told Jerome the truth, he'd try to interfere.

He nodded, though his head remained cocked at a worried angle. "Norah, not everyone will accept that a woman can be a fine designer. People believe the success of Rutherford Jewelers depended on Maurice's artistic talents, not yours."

"Then I shall have to prove otherwise to them."

"The scandal surrounding his death is bound to drive away even the most loyal of customers."

"I'll manage somehow."

"But you're alone now." He touched her black sleeve. "Let me at least act as your business adviser. I know I'm often gone for weeks at a time—"

"Six months last summer and autumn."

"Er, yes. But nevertheless, you need a man to watch out for you. God knows, you never had a father around as a child."

The sadness on his face threatened the firm ground of her determination. "Stop trying to coddle me," she said, more sharply than usual. "I'm an adult woman, and I don't need a parent. I can take care of myself."

Lizzie walked in to deliver the tea tray and then left. Brisk and businesslike, Norah set herself to pouring. When she passed Jerome his cup, she noticed a strange pensiveness shuttering his fine-lined features.

"Forgive me for presuming to manage your life," he murmured. "Sometimes I forget you're no longer the innocent sixteen-year-old girl who crossed the North Sea to marry a virtual stranger."

"And I'm sorry I snapped at you." Contrite, she

hugged him. His scent of tobacco and peppermint wrapped her in the comfort of an old friend. So many times over the years, when Norah had been left alone while Maurice spent the evenings at his club, Jerome had been there, to escort her to the theater or to simply enliven her solitary dinner. "Oh, Jerome. You are a dear."

The tautness on his face eased into a whimsical grin. "A cup of hot tea on a cold day and a beautiful woman for company. Now how could a man ask for more?"

Norah offered a plate of pastries. "You could ask for an apricot tart."

"Ah," he said, helping himself. "Monsieur Fontaine does bake the best tarts this side of Paris." He ate in silence a moment, then asked, "Have the police uncovered any new evidence?"

"Very little, I'm afraid." Disquiet stirred to life inside Norah. "Did you know that Mr. Teodecki once took morphine?"

"No. Now that's a twist . . ." Jerome fingered his lace napkin. "Well, at least it sounds as if Inspector Wadding is doing his job."

"It wasn't the inspector who found out. It was Lord Blackthorne." Norah's stomach fluttered. His name tasted as hot on her lips as the tea in her cup. She'd thought long and hard about their last encounter over a week ago, when he'd left her with the news of his break from Jane Bingham. According to Reverend Sweeny, Kit had gone out of town on business.

Business indeed, she thought. More likely he had shirked his classroom duties at the orphanage so he could run off on an illicit assignation with a new lover.

The notion scalded Norah. His lack of morality had irked her from their very first meeting, when he'd caught her on his bed and kissed her brow. With reckless disregard for respect and fidelity, he flitted from one conquest to the next. To Kit Coleridge, women were playthings to be bought with diamonds and moonstones.

Jerome threw down his napkin. "I must say, I don't care for his lordship's interference. It would be far better for your reputation if he divorced himself from the case."

"Whether I approve or not, he's been involved from the start."

"And now people are wondering why Maurice attended a party hosted by that profligate." Jerome leaped up and began to pace, his hands thrust in the pockets of his impeccable gray suit. Anger radiated from his jerky steps. "Blast it all, I wish I knew the answer."

Norah nibbled at a tart. The apricot pastry melted on her tongue, but she was too distracted to enjoy its sweetness. "I understand it was quite the hedonistic gathering. Perhaps Maurice went there at the urging of his mistress."

Jerome came closer and tilted her chin up. "Norah, I swear before God that if Maurice kept a paramour, I never knew about her."

"Maybe he simply didn't tell you."

"Men talk about . . . these things. But he never breathed a word. And believe me, if I'd ever thought Maurice had hurt you, I'd have killed him myself."

The bloodthirsty tightness on his face startled her. "Truly?"

His savagery faded. "For heaven's sake, Norah, I'm only speaking figuratively." Smiling, he tapped the tip of her nose. "Besides, infidelity makes no sense. Why would any husband stray from a lovely wife like you?"

Because the sexual act repulsed me . . .

She dragged herself from the mire of memory. Jerome was teasing to make her feel better. Yet she could still see fury shadowing his eyes, along with something almost furtive. Was he trying to distract her? From what?

Before she could sort through the puzzling impression, Culpepper knocked and entered the parlor. His white-gloved hands held a salver on which lay a small parcel. "A delivery for you, madam."

"From whom?"

"I'm afraid I don't know. Someone knocked and left it on the front step." He gave her the parcel and departed.

Her name was written across the top in a feminine hand, with scrolls and curlicues. The aroma of lilacs clung to the floral paper. The tissue rustling, she unwrapped the box and lifted the lid.

Inside lay a heap of rubbery objects. Mystified, she picked one up. It dangled limply from her fingers. "What in the world is this?"

Jerome snatched it from her. His cheeks blanched; then red color suffused his face. "What in the hell . . . !"

She had never before heard him curse. "Tell me what's wrong, Jerome. What is that?"

His mouth opened and closed. He stuck the floppy article in his pocket. "It isn't important. I'll take care of this."

He reached for the box, but she hugged it to her chest. "For heaven's sake. I deserve to know what was delivered to me."

He tilted his head to the ceiling, a muscle in his jaw working. Then he exhaled loudly and muttered, "It's a condom."

"A condom?"

"A sheath." Obviously discomposed, he hesitated. "Sometimes a man uses one when he's . . . with a woman."

A thunderbolt of awareness exploded in Norah. She forced herself to hold his gaze. "But . . . for what purpose?"

"To protect against disease. Or to prevent conception."

Her gaze fell to the contents of the box. Unwillingly her mind conjured a picture of how the condom fit a man. Even as she suppressed a shudder of revulsion, another thought made her giddy.

Was this why she hadn't conceived? Had Maurice used these?

No, she thought, the brief hope flickering out. He had sometimes forced her hand on him. Even in the dark she would have known this rubbery sensation.

"I'd like to know who the devil played such a trick on you," Jerome snapped. "Is there a note?"

"I'll look." Pushing aside the clammy sheaths, Norah found a card tucked in the side. Aloud she read, " 'If I may offer a piece of advice from one woman to another, use these. After all, a moment of prevention is better than being burdened with an illegitimate brat. J.B.

" 'P.S. His lordship will expect you to order his condoms with extra length.' "

Norah's pulse drummed in her ears. She gripped the box so tightly her nails dug into the pasteboard. His lordship. She might have guessed that even being acquainted with Kit Coleridge would soil her with his filth. If he had left her alone, Jane wouldn't have gotten the wrong idea.

"Who is J.B.?" Jerome asked in angry bewilderment.

"Jane Bingham." Hands shaking, Norah dropped the card back into the box and replaced the lid. "One of Lord Blackthorne's lovers."

"How dare she slander you like this! Why would she imply that you and he were carrying on?"

"I don't know. But I intend to find out."

The hot lava of rage propelled Norah to her feet. She would find out for herself if Kit Coleridge had returned from his tryst. Brushing past Jerome, she sped into the foyer. "Culpepper!" Her voice echoed, shrill and loud.

The butler opened the green baize door at the end of the passageway, a silver polishing rag in his hand and an apron around his thick middle. "Madam?" he said in surprise.

"Fetch my mantle and gloves immediately. And order the carriage brought round."

"Yes, madam." He vanished.

Jerome appeared. "Where are you going?"

Marching from the newel post to the parlor entry and back again, she shook the box at him. "To give these to the person who needs them most."

"I don't understand."

"You don't need to. This is my problem and I'll manage it."

Concern creased his brow. "This isn't like you, Norah, to go flying off the handle."

He was right. Then again, what had restraint ever gained her? For too many years, she'd held her emotions in check. Now the volcano of independence inside her seethed for release. "Pardon my abruptness. I'll explain everything to you later—"

A staccato rapping interrupted her. Annoyed, she flung open the front door. On the front step stood Lord Kit Coleridge.

Like a blast of wintry wind, his unexpected presence froze her. Eight days' absence had only magnified his handsomeness. A lock of black hair dipped rakishly over his brow. Healthy color glowed on his bronzed cheeks. His taupe ulster made him seem taller, more princely than ever. He carried a large sack at his side.

"How delightful to see you again, Mrs. Rutherford."

His wolfish smile fed the fury bubbling inside her. "Well!" she snapped. "You've saved me a trip."

"Pardon?"

"I was just on my way to visit you."

His keen eyes devoured her form. "Then do ask me in. It's cold out here."

Without awaiting her permission, he brushed past her. She took meager pleasure in slamming the door just as Culpepper hastened in with her mantle.

"My plans have changed," she told the butler. "I'll be staying in after all."

"Er, yes, madam." Bristly brows arched, he waited while the marquis put down his parcel, peeled off his gloves, and removed his coat.

Lord Kit narrowed his eyes. "Good afternoon, Mr. St. Claire."

Jerome nodded curtly. "Your lordship."

The marquis looked from Jerome to Norah. "I have the distinct impression I've interrupted something."

"Heavens, no." Norah clutched at both the box and her temper. "More to the point, you've *started* something."

His face sobered. He strode forward and took her hand. "Have you learned the identity of the murderess?"

"No."

"Then is it that news story? Has someone insulted you? Tell me who."

His show of protectiveness and the gentle pressure of his fingers rattled her. She stepped away. "It's nothing like that. If you'll come into the privacy of the parlor—"

"Whatever is the ruckus down here?" Like a sharp-eyed Hera poking her head from the clouds, Winnifred materialized at the head of the stairs. "Oh, we have visitors." Her tone lowered to genteel politeness. "Good afternoon, Mr. St. Claire. And your lordship."

"Ah, Miss Rutherford," he said as she descended the steps. "How good to see you again."

She curtsied. "If I may echo the sentiment, my lord."

He peered closely at her. "You might be interested to know that last week, I had the pleasure of meeting your fiance, Mr. Teodecki."

"Yes, he told me." The pinched lines bracketing her mouth deepened, as if she were debating whether to revile Lord Kit for considering Thaddeus a murder suspect. Her posture rigid, she swung to Norah and said in an undertone, "Your voice carried all the way into the sewing room. You disturbed my mending."

On the verge of exploding, Norah said tightly,

"Then do return to your work. After all, you can eavesdrop from there as well as from here."

Winnifred's jaw dropped. "How dare you speak to me so uncivilly?"

Norah bit back another retort. Better she should expend her ire on the man who had sparked it. "Pardon me. It's just that I'm anxious to have a word with Lord Blackthorne. Alone."

"Far be it from me to intrude where I'm not wanted. If you gentlemen will excuse me." With an injured sniff, Winnifred flounced up the stairs.

Jerome took Norah's arm. "I think we had better move into the parlor," he murmured.

"Yes." Automatically, she let him escort her.

Lord Kit followed and deposited his sack on a chair. "Perhaps you would be so kind as to leave us now, Mr. St. Claire."

Jerome kept his protective stance at her side. His eyes as hard as agates, he said, "With all due respect, my lord, I wouldn't leave a withered spinster alone with you."

"Since Norah doesn't fall into that category, you're excused."

Norah fingered the sharp edges of the box. The haughty way Lord Kit assumed control fanned the flames of her anger. "Your lordship, it isn't your place to order my guests out of my house."

"I was merely trying to expedite matters—"

"When I require your help, I'll ask for it." His jaw went rigid, but she swung around, her petticoats rustling. "Jerome, I must ask you to wait in the morning room."

"I hardly think—"

"I'm a widow, remember? Not a girl fresh out of the convent."

His fists clenched and unclenched. His lips compressed beneath his silver mustache. Then he made a jerky bow. "As you wish, then. I'll be nearby if you need me." He strode out and closed the doors.

"He spends a good deal of time on the continent, doesn't he?" Kit asked. Like a tiger on the prowl, he paced the parlor, pausing only to pet Marmalade, who snoozed on the hearth. "What sort of business is he involved in?"

"He buys and sells jewelry for the nobility. Those who lack the ready cash to keep up their huge estates."

"Ah. A pawnbroker to the elite."

"No!" Her temper flared dangerously hot. "He's engaged in a legitimate business. He acts as an intermediary for those aristocrats who have squandered their inheritance. Those who disdain to go into a shop and sell the gems themselves."

"You're quick to defend him. Why?"

"I won't have you criticize Jerome. He's a dear friend, my guardian angel."

An odd tension hovered about the marquis. He stopped pacing and focused his dark eyes on her. "I see. Perhaps he hopes to become more to you than a protector."

Norah stared blankly. Then his ugly meaning struck. The restraint on her fury burst.

"How dare you?" she said, swooping toward him. "How dare you reduce a cherished friendship to your own misbegotten standards?"

She tore open the box and hurled the contents at him. He ducked, but a shower of condoms rained over him.

"Jesus God!"

Transfixed, she stood, her chest heaving. She had meant to give him the vulgar objects, not sling them like a fishwife from Billingsgate Market.

The fire crackled a merry note into the charged silence. Kit Coleridge swiped at the sheaths clinging to his broad shoulders. Condoms draped his black hair like a cap. Another dangled from his ear. The sight awakened her dormant sense of humor. Assailed by a weakening rush of mirth, Norah sank onto the settee and hugged the empty box in an effort to contain her laughter.

"You look bloody proud of yourself," he snapped,

plucking off his makeshift hat and tousling his hair in the process.

A giggle broke from her. "And you look absurd."

He grimaced. "What the devil are you doing with these things, anyway?"

"They were delivered to me. A gift from the Honorable Jane Bingham."

He froze for a moment, then dropped a condom onto the carpet. A crimson flush heightened his teak-hued skin. "That sounds like one of her tricks," he muttered. "I should have anticipated she'd make you her next victim."

"Oh?" Norah scoffed. "It's utterly ridiculous of Miss Bingham to imagine that you and I could ever become involved."

As if sharing the loathsome thought, Lord Kit scowled. Going down on one knee, he scraped the condoms into a pile. Then he got up and came toward her, his hands overflowing with the floppy objects. He seemed to have trouble meeting her eyes.

"The box," he mumbled.

His awkward manner amazed Norah. The suave Kit Coleridge, embarrassed? This was a moment to savor. Yet somehow her triumph dissolved into tenderness, into the shocking desire to straighten the onyx strands of his hair, to smooth the furrow on his brow.

Numbly she held up the container, and he dumped the condoms inside. Then he strode away to shove the box into his sack.

He returned with a bouquet of pale pink roses. "Perhaps you'll find this gift more to your liking."

Flabbergasted, Norah looked from his handsome face to the blooms. Her fingers curled around the ribbon-wrapped stems. Why had he brought her roses?

The question faded before the irresistible aroma, and she buried her face in the velvety flowers. The exquisite perfume drenched her senses and transported her back to the convent where she had grown up. Once again she could feel the warmth of the sun on her back, and beneath her the cool stone bench where she sat swinging her bare feet. Bees hummed in the arbor. The statue of the Virgin Mary smiled from its mossy niche, and an archway of roses flowed downward to neatly tended beds. She reveled in the guilty delight of stealing out of chapel, heard the distant murmur of the nuns reciting the litany . . .

"Tell me what you're thinking."

Lord Kit's deep voice ended with wistful memory. She found him seated beside her, his hands clasped, his elbows resting on his knees. His solemn expression somehow crept into her heart. "The roses reminded me of the convent where I once lived in Belgium."

"So that's why you teach the orphans, because you grew up without parents, too."

Feeling the sting of old bitterness, she nodded. "My mother gave birth to me there, then left me to be raised by the nuns."

"Who was she?"

"I don't know. I'll never know. The Mother Superior would only say I was conceived in sin, and that my mother was a lady who had made a wicked mistake."

"Hypocritical Christians." He gave a snort of disgust. "You could hardly be held responsible for the circumstances of your own conception. A precious little girl is a blessing from God."

His defense peeled away her reserve. "When I was young, I used to imagine her coming to fetch me. She would embrace me, tell me how dearly she regretted giving me up. Together we would find my father and live as a real family . . ." Norah blinked to clear the film of moisture from her eyes. Confused that she would reveal her most cherished dream, she bent her head and rubbed her fingertip over the baby-soft petals of one pink bloom. "How silly of me. I don't know why I'm telling you this."

"You need to let your feelings out." Kit touched

her chin and brought her face toward him. "We're kindred spirits, you know."

"Pardon?"

"You and I have both felt the barbs of prejudice. We've both suffered from our parentage. You because of your illegitimacy, and me because of my dark skin—the legacy of my Indian mother."

She ached to ask him about his past, but the warm pressure of his fingers suddenly felt intolerably familiar. His closeness threatened her equilibrium. She could see the faint shading of black stubble that delineated his jaw, and the hint of softness to his lower lip that brought to mind hedonistic pleasures. His masculine scent, his alluring eyes, snared her in the chains of panic.

On shaky legs, she got up and moved away. "It's not the same at all. You were born to the aristocracy. I've had to earn my place in society."

Kit gripped his fists as if to face an unseen opponent. "I've had to fight, too. Bullies like Lord Carlyle when I was a schoolboy and then bigots like Winnifred."

Norah didn't want to feel the affinity of a common bond. She didn't want to accept the unveiled confession that made him human and vulnerable. She busied herself with putting the bouquet into a vase on the bookcase. "Don't blame it all on the color of your skin. You've helped alienate yourself by flaunting your mistresses."

"Agreed. I've wasted much of my life going from woman to woman, trying to prove that I don't need anyone." His voice lowered to a silken murmur. "But lately I've come to the conclusion that I was wrong."

His frankness startled her into turning. With the indolence of a maharaja, he lounged with his arms draped across the back of the settee. "What do you mean?" she asked.

"I'd like to find a special woman and marry her, to settle down and start a family of my own."

"Oh." The notion of him wedding a society debutante set off a disagreeable churning inside Norah. Now she knew for whom he'd ordered the parure. He had probably already chosen his future bride, an English rose who would tame the rogue, a fertile woman who would bear him a nursery full of children. Denying an intolerable ache, she cast about for a neutral topic. "Where did you find roses in the middle of winter?"

"At my parents' house in Kent. They have a conservatory."

"So that's where you've been. I wondered." The words slipped out before she could stop them. How preposterous to want to know anything more about him and his relations.

"You're changing the subject," he said, rising to his feet. "But so much the better. Did you miss me?"

He was toying with her, as he did with all women. She knew by the cocky tilt of his eyebrow, the wicked slant of his smile. "It isn't a question of missing," she said stiffly. "I only wondered why you didn't come to the orphanage this week."

"I told Reverend Sweeny I'd be out of town."

So he had. And she had spent the week imagining him engaged in unspeakable acts with his most current paramour. "I also wondered when you'd stop by and approve the sketches of the parure."

He glanced around. "Are they here?"

"No, I left them at my office."

"I'll be there tomorrow morning."

"Tomorrow is Sunday." She recalled her appointment with the bank director on Monday afternoon. "Come by on Tuesday."

"All right. Promptly after class." He strolled around the parlor, then hunkered down to pet Marmalade again. Norah watched, mesmerized, as the stroking motion of his big hand made the cat stretch and purr. Did he stroke his women with the same gentleness? "By the way," he added, "have you read the book?"

"What book?"

Crouched, Kit looked up and grinned. *"The Madman of Mayfair."*

He so flustered her, she'd almost forgotten the novel. She smoothed the antimacassar over a chair. "Yes, I have."

"And?"

"It's an entertaining story," she said honestly. "A trifle heavy on the melodrama, but I can appreciate that boys would enjoy the tale of a madman stalking the houses of the rich."

He stood up, his hands on his hips and his jaw held high, like the majestic statue of a hero. "And do you also appreciate the fact that I've redeemed myself? Certainly if I can teach a classroom of orphans, you can't denounce me as a worthless profligate."

"Your work is to be commended."

"Thank you."

His charming smile could have melted the frost from the windows. But his magic was an illusion, she reminded herself, a trick with no real substance. "On the other hand . . ."

He sauntered toward her. "Yes?"

Uneasy with his proximity, she went to the tea table and made a show of gathering up the dishes. "I'm sorry. I should have rung for more tea."

"Bother the tea." He gently pried a cup from her fingers, but kept hold of her hand. "Norah, tell me what you're thinking."

Awareness of his male body, the powerful muscles beneath the garb of a gentleman, set her heart to hammering. Wresting free, she retreated. "I'm thinking you've done a fine job with Lark and the other boys. But you can't let them down by vanishing for days at a time. Respect is more than a game to be won."

Displeasure darkening his face, he stalked her. "Then you don't believe I've truly changed?"

"Exactly. You might intend to marry, but you won't remain faithful to one woman. Your disappearance this week proves you're incapable of loyalty."

Her spine met the hard surface of the wall. His hands shot out to bracket her. Too late, she knew the quivering panic of a cornered rabbit. Though he didn't touch her, his sensual allure radiated like hot rays of sunshine.

"I intend to prove you wrong," he said in a velvet undertone.

She felt breathless, scorched by desperation. Yet spurred by the devil of defiance inside her, she threw back her head and met his gaze squarely. "You won't. A tiger can't change its stripes. You're even depraved enough to kiss a bereaved widow the morning after her husband died."

He frowned. "Kiss? What are you talking about?"

She regretted bringing up so volatile a memory. "Never mind."

Norah tried to duck past him, but he lowered his arms, keeping her in a gentle but firm cage. "No, you don't," he said. "If you make an accusation, you must at least do me the honor of explaining yourself."

She drew a lungful of air and indignation. "You had the gall to trap me on your bed—"

"You flung yourself on the bed."

"But you lay down right on top of me—"

"I was trying to help you, to calm you."

"But you didn't have to press your lips to my forehead."

His dark gaze pierced hers. Then he arched his neck and chuckled. "You call *that* a kiss?"

Her cheeks burned. "I certainly don't call it a handshake."

Amusement gleamed in his eyes, along with a heavy-lidded fire. Before she could move, he lightly traced his fingertip over her lips. "My dearest Norah. Whenever you're ready to learn *my* definition of a kiss, I'll be happy to oblige you."

As abruptly as he'd snared her, he stepped away.

Without another word, he picked up his sack and left the parlor.

Norah stood caught in the prison of her own thoughts. Her mouth still tingled from his caress. Her body retained the heat of his closeness. She told herself she was wrong, that she had misunderstood him. But suddenly everything made sense—his gift of the roses, his dedication to solving the mystery, his subtle persistence in touching her. Certainty burned hot and cold through her veins, pooling like icy ardor in her belly.

Kit Coleridge meant for *her* to be his next conquest.

Chapter 7

Someone was following him.

Kit swung on his heel toward the barren expanse of Berkeley Square. Yellow light pooled beneath the gas lamps on the residential side of the street, but the park lay in shadow. He reknotted his scarf and plunged his hands into the pockets of his ulster. It was a bitter evening in early February, the stars glittering in the black sky. A hansom clattered down the street, then a brougham drawn by a fine pair of grays. The few passersby hurried along the walkway, their heads bent against the cold and their breath forming tiny clouds of smoke.

No one seemed to take notice of him. He must have imagined the sensation of being followed.

Kit resumed his walk around the perimeter of Berkeley Square. His heated encounter with Norah on Saturday had left a prickly sensitivity on his skin. Christ, he had wanted so desperately to kiss her that his loins still ached. He would see her tomorrow, when he went to her shop to approve the parure. And he would hold his carnal desires in check. He didn't want to scare her off.

For a widow, she possessed a naive quality that both intrigued and frustrated him. Maurice Rutherford must have been an inept lover, the typical stodgy Englishman who believed only a male could enjoy the sexual act.

Damn, what qualities had Norah loved in a man so small-minded? A man twice her age? Her strict convent upbringing must have blinded her to his faults.

And to her own sensuality.

Kit blew out a frosty breath. If ever a woman needed erotic awakening, she was Norah Rutherford. Fiery anger had caused her to hurl the condoms at him. Unbridled joy had lit her face as she inhaled the scent of his roses. Dormant desire had quickened her breath when he'd trapped her against the wall.

She wanted him. But she wasn't ready to admit the truth. Not even to herself.

It's utterly ridiculous to imagine that you and I could ever become involved.

He hunched his shoulders against the memory of her wintry words, so like Emma Woodferne's cruel denunciation. From the mists of memory came the disgusted look on Emma's fair face, her shock and revulsion at learning that Kit was the secret admirer who had left her posies and poems.

He shook his head with desperate, concentrated effort. Norah was unique, a sensitive woman still reeling from the blow of her husband's murder. Kit couldn't let himself fear that she disdained him for his mixed blood. His reputation appalled her, not his heritage. She herself had said that more than the color of his skin made him an outcast; he had alienated himself by flaunting his mistresses.

Her insightful comment was a bitter pill for Kit to swallow. He truly *had* used women, out of the urgent need to insulate himself from hurt. But in the process he had cut himself off from love and honor.

No more. Now he had a purpose, to win Norah's respect and to earn her affections. By God, he would break down the wall of her mistrust. He'd rip it apart brick by brick if necessary. And he must be patient, for she needed time to overcome the loss of her adored husband.

Kit reached his destination, a town house opposite the square from his own mansion. The three-story edifice loomed above, the windows glowing like malevolent eyes. The damp chill spurred him up the steps. He seized the ram's head knocker and rapped hard.

Once more, the notion of being watched raised the hairs on the back of his neck. He peered around, but saw nothing out of the ordinary, only a crossing sweeper plying his broom and a maidservant trudging along the curbstone.

A prissy-faced footman opened the door. "Yes?"

"I should like to see his lordship," Kit stated.

"I'm sorry, sir. He isn't receiving callers."

"He'll see me." Kit brushed past the servant. "Tell your master that Lord Blackthorne would like a word with him. Immediately."

The footman's outraged expression smoothed into boot-licking respect. "Yes, m'lord. Forgive me, but I'm new here, didn't recognize a neighbor. Please permit me to take your coat."

"No. I'll only be a moment. Now get on with you."

"Of course, m'lord."

The man minced up the curving staircase. Kit strolled into the drawing room. Warmth roared from the hearth, though the decor of ornate plasterwork and mirrored walls left him cold. He toasted his hands over the fire, then walked around the room and eyed a marble statue of a nude Apollo, a crystal bottle topped by a ruby-studded stopper, a strut clock in enameled burgundy. A wry smile nudged at his lips. Lately he preferred a homelike decor, with dozens of lace antimacassars draped over the furniture and a marmalade cat snoozing on the hearth.

The only appealing item was a small watercolor half hidden behind a gilt lamp. The painting depicted a quaint country garden overgrown with purple larkspurs and pink roses. The tiny signature in the lower corner identified the artist as Eleanor Abernathy. A pity Bruce possessed so little of his mother's sensitivity.

Going to the grand piano in the corner, Kit idly depressed a series of ivory keys. Tinkling notes rained into the air.

"What a surprise," came a voice from behind him. "I wouldn't have thought you civilized enough to play."

Lord Bruce Abernathy stood in the doorway, a red carnation tucked into the lapel of his charcoal-gray tailored suit. One fair eyebrow tilted upward in an unnatural, diabolical look. The curl of his lip, so familiar and so superior, stirred a nauseating fury in Kit.

Determined to hold on to his temper, he shoved his fists into his coat pockets. "I don't play," he said bluntly. "Not the piano, nor cat and mouse games with you."

"I'm afraid I don't know what you mean."

"You bloody well do. No one but you would have leaked the story to the press about Rutherford's murder."

"Tut, tut, Blackie," Bruce said on a laugh. "Don't come crying to me with your troubles. If you choose to embroil yourself in scandal, you must face the consequences like a man. Now if you'll excuse me, I was dressing for a dinner party."

Kit sprang forward and spun the viscount back around by his arm. "If you're a man, you'll admit to my face that you went tattling to the press."

"I didn't! Better you should look to your own whore as the culprit."

"Jane Bingham?"

"That's right."

Startled but still suspicious, Kit released Bruce. "How do you know what she did?"

"Because she came to me and asked me to corroborate her story. In case the press wouldn't believe a woman. But I refused to soil myself with your filth."

"If you're lying to me, Carlyle, you'll be mopping up your own blood in a minute."

Bruce brushed off his pristine coat sleeve. "Keep your hands to yourself, you beast."

"You've had only a taste of my brutishness." The thought of Norah enduring slander enraged Kit, but he restrained himself by remembering his pledge to make her love him. He couldn't afford a brawl. "If you dare spread any gossip about the Rutherford murder, I'll do more than scar you. I'll scrape off your other eyebrow with a very dull razor."

He plucked the red carnation from Bruce's lapel and ground it to shreds beneath his heel. The crushed petals reeked a clove scent.

Bruce shrank back. His gaze faltered. "Get out of my house."

"Gladly."

Once outside, Kit paused on the sidewalk to let the cold air cool the heat of his anger. More than worry over Norah caused his roiling emotions; the old feelings of inadequacy and helplessness still lurked like a dark cancerous growth deep within him. Impatient with the weakness, he buried it and started toward home.

Jane, damn her. First the condoms, now the gossip to the newspapers. He'd had enough of her pranks. He resolved to give her a short but strict lecture on appropriate behavior.

Across the road, something moved in the gloom of the park. He spied the pale flash of a face. Someone lurked behind the thick trunk of a plane tree.

He had been right about one thing tonight. He *was* being followed. Kit strode swiftly down the walkway. By God, he would find out once and for all who dared spy on him. And why.

He stayed on the residential side, where the street lamps cast a hazy golden glow. Few pedestrians braved the chilly night. Even the crossing sweeper had gone home.

From the corner of his eye, he could discern the shadowy shape slinking from tree to tree, pursuing him. Witless scum. If the man were a footpad, then he'd better start praying to St. George.

Upon reaching the intersection, Kit headed down the side street. The corner mansion lay in darkness; the earl of Hawkesford and his American countess must be away at their country manor with their brood of young children.

The ache for a devoted family of his own washed over Kit in an untimely wave. He steeled his will to the task at hand.

Luck met him. Near the entry to the mews, the gas lamp had gone out. When he reached the shadowed area, he ducked into the alley and flattened himself to the stone wall. The cold gritty stone met his cheek. A gust of icy wind buffeted him.

He waited.

The ripe scents of manure and rubbish assailed his nose. Within moments came the light patter of someone running. Then a pause. The stalker must be searching for his prey.

The steps resumed, slower, more cautious. As they neared his hiding place, Kit tensed himself for battle.

Her hands full of diamonds, Norah sat alone at the small table in the vault. The gems sparkled in the light of the oil lamp. The hush of nighttime allowed her to hear the quiet rhythm of her own breathing and the far-off sound of the wind rattling the eaves.

She had fallen into the habit of working late every night. Since her duties as owner of the shop ranged from settling disputes between the workmen to supervising the delicate assembling of each piece of jewelry, she had little time left to herself. Norah cherished the silence of evening when she could work in private.

Now, her entire awareness focused on the gems. She lifted them to her mouth and reveled in the cold feel of genuine diamonds. Paste gems, made of cheap glass, felt warm to the lips. It was one trick used to determine the authenticity of a stone.

Cradled in her palms, the diamonds looked like

chips of ice. Pear-drop brilliants in graduated sizes, they had been shaped by the finest gem cutter in Amsterdam. She intended to use these stones to create the tiara for the Princess of Wales.

Norah could see the design in her mind. It was a simple yet elegant scroll, curving around the head with the cobweb texture of fine lace. Lightweight platinum would render the settings almost invisible, so the sparkling stones appeared like dewdrops floating on air.

But the tiara required a spectacular gem at its apex. Since Princess Alexandra favored purple stones, Norah intended to use the only lavender diamond known to exist. Fire at Midnight.

Her stomach plunged. She hadn't yet heard from Upchurch that the maharaja of Rampur was willing to sell the fabled gem, or if the agent needed her to send the purchase money for the ninety-eight carat stone. Today, her meeting with the bank director had unearthed a dismaying discovery. Back in November, Maurice had nearly defaulted on a loan. The bank had demanded full repayment and threatened court action.

He must have turned to Bertie Goswell in desperation.

The shop account held only a handful of guineas. The message had been implicit in the snobbish tilt of the banker's chin, in the distaste with which he regarded her. If the trustees had encountered difficulty in dealing with a jeweler who embroiled himself in scandal, they most certainly would refuse to extend credit to his widow.

How had Maurice squandered their wealth? Was the answer the key to his murder? And where would she find the ready cash to pay back the oily Mr. Goswell?

Her limbs went weak, uncorking the stress she had kept bottled up all day. She bent and touched her forehead to the diamonds in her hands. Black Monday, she termed the day. It had been doomed from the moment she had set foot in the shop, for

her solicitor had been waiting in her office to pro-
claim Goswell's loan document legal and binding.

In a scant few days her fortnight's grace period
would end. The usurer would strut back into her
office, demanding his due.

Norah raised her chin and studied the rows of
steel drawers lining the walls. She faced the appalling prospect of reimbursing Goswell from her cache
of gems here. Even given her limited business
knowledge, she saw the danger in surrendering the
raw materials required to produce additional pieces
of jewelry. She lacked the resources to replace the
precious stones.

On the other hand, because of the scandal of
Maurice's murder reported in the newspapers, the
shop's clientele had dwindled to a trickle of curiosity
seekers, along with an occasional pesky reporter.
Even though she had the one commission from Kit,
soon she might cease needing new stock to replen-
ish the showroom.

Her spirits funneled downward in a long, dizzying spiral. Dear Blessed Virgin. If only she could be
as carefree, as confident of unlimited riches as Kit
Coleridge.

The thought of him stopped her plunge into the
fathomless shaft of despair. Her heart cavorted
against her rib cage. Closing her fingers over the
hard gemstones, Norah tried to deny the pleasant
disturbance inside her.

But the feeling persisted, sparkling like a diamond
in the brick wall around her emotions. As wicked as
the truth might be, deep down she felt flattered that
Lord Kit found her so appealing he would choose
her as his next conquest.

Yet she hadn't seen him in two days, not since
Saturday. If he were truly intent on ensnaring her,
wouldn't he come around more often? Or was the
tiger playing with his prey?

*Whenever you're ready to learn my definition of a kiss,
I'll be happy to oblige you.*

The memory of his silken voice tingled over her

skin. Not that she ever intended to take him up on his offer, of course. She must represent a challenge to him, the one woman immune to his considerable charm. He had a method of mesmerizing a woman, of edging too close and stealing her will to resist. He would demand her full attention and her undivided loyalty. That was the way of men; they wanted to be coddled but they also wanted to control.

Norah curbed a violent shiver. She must stop thinking about Kit Coleridge.

Leaving the table, she went to the single opened drawer and let the diamonds trickle gently into the black velvet interior. The feel of the cold stones rolling from her fingers gave her an almost sinful jolt of pleasure.

A passionate sense of ownership clasped her chest. Giving these precious stones to a man like Goswell was a sacrilege, a violation of their beauty.

Yet she saw no other way of her financial dilemma.

The scrape of footsteps came from the passage outside. Into the vault stepped a burly man in braided uniform. Lines of age burrowed into his frowning, bulldog features. He brandished a cavalry sword. "You all right, ma'am?"

"Of course, Captain Ackerman. Shouldn't I be?"

Steel grated as the guard slid his weapon back into its sheath. "Thought I heard a noise," he said, sounding almost disappointed. "But it must've been you."

"Why aren't you carrying your lantern?"

"Can't collar a thief if he sees you coming." Ackerman jabbed his thumb at the medals adorning his chest. "I got eyes like a cat, I do. I was chief scout in the Abyssinian War, sneaked right up to the fortress of Magdala at midnight, and spotted a way over the walls. We won that war for the Queen, we did."

Norah smiled. The pensioned-off military man never lost a chance to relate his exploits. His loyalty was a comfort after the hostility she endured from some of her other male employees. "How good to know I'm safe, that I can depend on you."

Clapping his hand on the sword hilt, he came to attention. "No robber will sneak past Captain Archibald J. Ackerman, late of the Queen's Dragoon Guards."

He started to pivot on his heel, then returned. "Forgot something." He pulled a jeweler's case from his pocket and slapped it on the table. "I found this on the floor out front and didn't know where it belonged. Cheerio, ma'am." Ackerman marched off to patrol the premises.

Norah picked up the box and idly opened it. The empty, white velvet interior felt as soft as baby's down to her fingertips. Each single piece of jewelry purchased at the shop was nested in a case of the finest Russian black leather lined with white velvet. The containers came in varying sizes and shapes; this square one reminded her of the case Maurice had brought home on the night of his murder.

A thought tiptoed from the recesses of her memory and pounced on her with staggering force. But there *had* been a difference.

She frowned, thinking hard. When that jeweler's case had disappeared, then turned up in Ivy's sewing basket, Maurice had opened it to check the contents. And Norah had glimpsed a flash of red fabric.

Until now she had forgotten the detail. Their row over his threat to put Ivy in a sanitarium had distracted her.

She snapped the lid shut, and sat for a few moments, pondering the riddle. Either Maurice had given the South African diamond to his murderess, or she had stolen it. With mounting excitement, Norah realized that if by some slim chance she could find the red-lined case, it could provide incriminating evidence.

Resolutely she snatched up the oil lamp. She left the vault and followed the narrow passageway to the workroom. There, the faint glow of night filtered through the lofty wall of windows. Gloom lurked in the corners, beneath desks and workbenches. The air seemed unnaturally quiet without the tap of hammers, the murmur of voices, the clink of metal. Only the scrape of a tree branch on a windowpane disturbed the silence.

Captain Ackerman's presence on the premises reassured her. She found Thaddeus's workbench and slid onto the stool. Higher than a conventional table, the wooden surface was pristine, though scarred. Mallets and drills and saws hung in tidy rows. The tray beneath the semicircular cutout had been swept clean of precious gold particles. The spotlessness was exactly what she would expect from a meticulous man like Thaddeus Teodecki.

She wrestled with a moment's guilt at invading his private domain. The domain of Winnifred's prince. No money could be spared for a dowry now.

Norah cleared her mind of emotion. Even if she possessed all the wealth in the world, she must first determine if Thaddeus and Winnifred had conspired together to commit the murder.

She opened the top drawer and found loops of delicate gold and silver wire. The next held files in various lengths. She moved methodically down the stack of drawers, which revealed every manner of supply from calipers to buffing cloths. At the back of a drawer, her fingers met the smooth square of a calling card. She pulled it out, tilting it to the light. Frederick Gage, Gage and Brookman Goldsmiths, Ltd., Regent Street.

Why would Thaddeus have a card from another jeweler? Did he intend to seek another post? Another, more disturbing possibility occurred to her. Surely he wouldn't steal gems and resell them. Or would he?

Dismayed, Norah tucked the card back into its hiding place. She mustn't jump to conclusions. Tomorrow she would ask Thaddeus for an explanation.

In the meantime, she must think. Another employee could have hated Maurice. Peter Bagley? Or one of the other craftsmen?

A gust of wind thumped the tree limb against the window glass. The eerie sound, along with the chilly air, made her shiver. Drawing her shawl more securely around her shoulders, she hurried through the task of inspecting each desk. By the time an hour passed, she had found no red-lined jeweler's case.

Discouraged, she headed slowly away. Her footsteps echoed in the cavernous workroom, then grew muffled on the Turkish runner outside her office. Darkness shrouded the short passageway. Why had Ackerman turned off the gas jet?

Crossing her threshold, she half-stumbled across a large object. The light of her lamp illuminated the brawny shape of Captain Ackerman. The guard lay sprawled on his back, arms and legs splayed, his weathered face in repose.

With a gasp, Norah shrank against the door frame. Her heart galloped. She sank to her knees beside him.

Willing herself not to shake, she put her ear to his chest. She detected the weak rhythmic rise and fall of breathing, the faint beat of his heart.

Praise God, he was alive. She gingerly turned his head and saw a bloodied lump matting his gray hair. Had he taken a misstep and fallen?

Or had an intruder attacked him? His drawn sword rested on the carpet near his slack hand. He had reported hearing a noise . . .

Silence suffocated Norah like a thick glove. She heard the tiny tick-tick of a clock and the thump of her own pulse. Her palm slick, she reached for the lamp. She must bridle the fear rampaging inside her.

She must run for help.

Even as she started to stand, Norah sensed the swoosh of movement in the passageway behind her. A scream gathered in her throat. She whirled. A black shape surged from the shadows, and a heavy object knocked her off balance.

She staggered against the door frame. Pain burst

on the side of her skull. The lamp slipped from her fingers. Through a fog of dizziness she heard the tinkle of glass breaking, smelled the reek of spilled oil.

Flames as brilliant as diamonds blinded her.

In the icy gloom of the mews, Kit stood taut, ready for action. The fever of anticipation heated his veins. Damn, he was spoiling for a fight.

The footsteps came closer. The rasp of breathing sounded inches away. Kit leaped out.

He caught the brigand around the chest and yanked him backward. A solid body thumped against him. The man loosed a squeal of alarm, choked off when Kit hooked an arm around the skinny throat. The stalker squirmed and bucked.

Kit wrenched back one arm. A cry broke from the would-be thief. He went limp, sobbing like a child.

"Ow! Ow!" Fright radiated from his quivering muscles, his compact body. " 'Elp! Somebody 'elp me!"

"Quit your sniveling."

Disgusted, Kit marched his captive into the light of the nearest lamp. Keeping the wiry arm in a lock, he prepared to search for a weapon.

His violent mood dissipated like steam into the frosty night. He had seized not a man, but a lad. A lad with familiar wolfish eyes and spiky black hair. Lark.

Kit let go. The boy staggered against the iron post of the lamp. "Oooh." His breath whooshed out like smoke from a fired pistol. "Jesus! You scared me, sir."

"I bloody well meant to." Annoyed and exasperated, Kit planted his fists at his hips. "I ought to tan your hide too. Would you care to explain why you've been following me?"

Lark rubbed his arm, his expression sheepish. "You weren't suppose t' see me."

"Well, I did. So answer me."

"Uh . . . we been guardin' you."

"Guarding me?"

"Aye." Lark sniffed, then scrubbed his nose on his coat sleeve. "Me an' the boys been takin' turns, sir. We couldn't let you come t' no 'arm."

"Harm from what?"

"From that 'orrible murderess, o' course."

Frowning, Kit cocked his head. "Are you referring to the woman who killed Mrs. Rutherford's husband?"

"Aye. We 'eard the Rev say you was searchin' fer clues, on account o' the fact that she did in Mr. R at yer 'ouse. Me and the boys was afraid you might be 'er next victim."

Warmed by their concern, Kit tempered his sharp tone. "You needn't worry about me. I'm not in the slightest danger."

"Mrs. R's husband might've thought that, too." Lark glanced furtively to and fro. "But the murderess could be lurkin' anywheres. Round any corner. Waitin' t' leap out an' jab you with 'er 'atpin." Lowering his voice to a stage whisper, he added, "The madwoman o' Mayfair."

Torn between amusement and chagrin, Kit bit back a smile. Good Christ, if Norah knew how that six-penny novel was coming back to haunt him, she'd give him a blistering I-told-you-so. "And what did you intend to do if the murderess attacked me?"

"Why, whistle fer a constable, o' course." Lark reached into the pocket of his coat and pulled out a butcher knife. The blade glinted in the gaslight as he jabbed it into the night air. "An' then I'd poke 'er in the gullet."

Kit snatched away the weapon. "Where did you get this?"

Lark scowled. "I borrowed it from the Sweenys' kitchen. I ain't no thief."

"I never said you were." Kit forced himself to speak calmly. "Lark, this is a deadly weapon. What if you'd cut yourself? Or stabbed the wrong person by mistake?"

"I been careful," Lark said, drawing himself up

so he stood on eye level with Kit's cravat. "I'm almost a man, I am."

"I know you are." Kit racked his brain for a way to protect the boy without injuring his pride. "I'm flattered by your effort to keep me safe. But this is a matter warranting extreme caution. If the 'madwoman' should happen to see you lurking about, you might frighten her off before I could nab her."

Lark scratched his untidy hair. "Didn't think o' that."

"That's why I need your cooperation. Your promise that you'll stop trailing me."

"I dunno . . ."

Kit clapped his hand onto the boy's shoulder. In a tone of man-to-man confidence, he said, "Perhaps it would satisfy you and the other lads if I carried a pistol from now on. I hadn't considered my own danger, and I must thank you for bringing the oversight to my attention."

Lark locked his thumbs in his lapels. "Any bloke what knew the way o' the streets would've done the same, sir."

Kit held out the knife. "I trust you'll return this to the Sweenys, then?"

"Aye, sir." Lark put the weapon in his pocket. "If you carry yer gun, me an' the lads'll leave you be."

"We've a bargain then. Shall we shake like gentlemen?" Lark hesitated, then thrust out his stubby paw. Grasping it, Kit hid a smile of relief. "Now you must have missed your supper. Come along and my cook will fix you a plate of bangers and mash."

The boy's eyes rounded with awe. "Me, eat in yer fancy 'ouse?"

"Why not?" Kit said. "All of my friends are welcome there."

As they started across the cobbled street and toward the square, Lark strutted like a cock. "Wait'll the lads 'ear about this."

"Let's keep mum about our little discussion though, shall we? We don't want word reaching

Mrs. Rutherford's ears. She might be frightened by this talk of a madwoman running rampant.''

"Aye." Lark ducked his head in an oddly guilty air. "Er, there be somethin' else I didn't tell you, sir . . .''

But Kit's attention was distracted by the pudgy boy standing before the wrought-iron fence. "Isn't that Billy in front of my house?''

"Cor! The barstard was supposed t' be guardin' Mrs. R!''

"Guarding—?'' The news caught Kit unawares. He ought to have guessed the boys' zeal for detection would extend to Norah as well. Another thought jolted him. Why had Billy deserted his post?

Apprehension froze Kit's lungs. He quickened his steps, Lark running beside him. As they neared the mansion, Kit could see Billy tossing pebbles at the windows, though most of the missiles fell short.

"Here now,'' Kit called. "What's going on?''

Billy spun around in a crouch, fists raised. Then he straightened. "Oh, sir. Sir! Praise Jesus, ye're 'ere!''

" 'Course 'e's 'ere,'' Lark snapped. "What're you doin' throwin' rocks at the master's 'ouse?''

"Bleedin' doorman wouldn't let me in.'' Billy blubbered loudly and honked into a crumpled red kerchief. "I didn't know 'ow else t' signal you, m'lord.''

"Signal me for what?'' Kit demanded.

" 'Tis Mrs. R.'' The boy fell to his knees and latched on to the hem of Kit's ulster. "Sumfink turrible's 'appened. Turrible!''

Kit yanked Billy upright. "Then for God's sake, tell me!''

"She was at her jewel shop. I was scoutin' the place from the alley.'' Billy gulped noisily. "There were a fire! I seen it through the window!''

"When?''

" 'Alf an hour ago. When I spied the flames I come runnin' straight 'ere fer 'elp. 'Tis the madwoman o' Mayfair fer sure!''

"Blinkin' coward!" Lark cuffed the boy on the ear. "Why didn't you stay and 'elp Mrs. R—"

"Fetch the fire brigade," Kit snapped. "And for God's sake keep yourselves out of trouble!"

Wheeling around, he sprinted down the sidewalk, the ulster flapping around his thighs.

Dear God, let Norah be safe.

A lone hansom came down the street. He whistled. When the cab kept going, he leaped out into the road. The horse snorted and stopped, so close its plumes of warm breath enveloped Kit.

The high-seated driver waved his long whip. " 'Ere now. You'll git yerself killed that way."

"I need a ride."

"Goin' 'ome fer the night—"

"There's half a crown if you can get me to Bond Street in under five minutes."

"Why didn't you say so? 'Op in."

Spurred by dread, Kit jumped inside. He couldn't bear to think he might be too late already. Wheels clattering and hooves ringing, the hansom took off like a shot.

Chapter 8

*D**ear God, let Norah be safe.*
   The breakneck speed of the cab jostled Kit from one side of the small seat to the other. Frantic with worry, he kept the front window open and gripped the edge of the door. He shivered as much from fear as from the arctic wind slapping his face.

The stench of cinders tainted the air. He tried to assure himself the smell meant nothing. On this frigid February night, smoke puffed from a hundred thousand chimneys across London.

His heart thundered as fast as the hooves striking the cobbled pavement. The rough ride jarred his bones. His mind conjured the horrifying image of Norah's charred body lying amid the smoldering ruins.

Dear God, let her be safe.

The stores and office buildings of Bond Street loomed ahead. As the cab careened around the corner, he saw a crowd gathered before the jewelry shop. Darkness shrouded the bow-front windows of the showroom.

He tamped a spark of relief. Norah's office lay at the rear, where Billy had spied the fire.

Before the cab came to a complete halt, Kit sprang out and flipped a coin to the driver. Straining to see toward the back of the building, he glimpsed a faint glow and a sluggish cloud of black smoke.

148

His heart surged with renewed alarm. God, what if he was too late? Watching for Norah, he shouldered a path through the swarm of gentlemen and whores and urchins.

"I say, you trod on my foot!"

"Git t' the back. We was 'ere first."

Kit ignored the gibes and protests. He focused on the noise emanating from behind the shop, the shouts of men, the clamor of the fire brigade. He broke out of the throng and ran.

The constable who held back the curiosity seekers shook his truncheon. " 'Ere now! You can't go back there!"

"Out of my way."

Kit plunged down the narrow side alley. He vaulted over piles of rubbish and half slipped in the gutter. Flying ash stung his eyes. Blinking to clear his vision, he came upon an orderly scene unlike the Hades he expected.

A pair of horse-drawn fire engines waited a short distance down the alley. Along the back wall of the shop, broken windowpanes stared like blackened eyes. Soot darkened the bricks. The door sagged open. Sparks danced in the air. Down at the far corner of the building occupied by Norah's office, several firemen aimed their long hose at the small blaze while another man pumped. Water spurted; the flames steadily diminished.

Peering frantically around, Kit saw no sign of Norah.

He caught the arm of the stocky man directing the firemen. "Did you get everyone out?"

"The constable found the guard laying 'alf dead on the floor. Ambulance took the poor devil away." Rubbing his begrimed face, the fire chief added, "Got lucky on this one. Somebody called the alarm on one of them newfangled telephones. We was 'ere lickety split."

"What about Mrs. Rutherford? Did you see her?"

"Mrs. 'Oo?" The fire chief frowned. "Oh, you

mean that 'andsome, red-haired lady who says she owns the place?''

"That's her."

He snorted. "Tried to run back inside—after sumfink—jewels, I think she said. Feather-witted female. I sent 'er up to the street to wait with the constable." The chief shook a filthy finger. "You oughta get up there, too, sir."

"Thank you. I will."

Half overjoyed and half uneasy, Kit stepped back. Norah hadn't been out front. Christ, she wouldn't really be foolish enough to venture back inside, would she?

Bilious fear lurched in him. Whenever she spoke of the shop, fervor lit her eyes. Yes, she might indeed put herself in peril.

He glanced back. At the end of the building, the firemen were engrossed in battling the remnants of the fire. When the chief turned away, Kit darted to the door and slipped inside.

The hellish glow flickered through the smoky interior of the workroom. From what little he could see, the fire was confined to the office area. Embers sizzled and popped under the hissing stream of water. Fleetingly he wondered how the blaze had begun. A dropped lamp or a spark from the hearth could ignite an inferno. Or perhaps a flammable substance used in jewelry making.

Acrid cinders darkened the air. Coughing, Kit pulled his scarf over his nose and ducked low to avoid the worst of the smoke. Even so, his throat burned and his mouth tasted of ashes.

Jewels, the chief had said. Norah must have gone to the showroom. Damn her, Kit thought in sudden savagery. As soon as he found her, he'd shake sense into her pretty head.

Unless she lay somewhere in the gloom here. Unconscious . . . or dead.

Eyes slitted, he hastened across the workroom. He stubbed his leg on the sharp corner of a table and cursed. His groping hands located a doorknob, cool to his touch. The gloomy passage led to the front of the shop.

He shut the door behind him. The smoke thinned. The distant shouts of the firemen masked his footsteps. Using the wall as a guide, he felt his way forward. A glimmer penetrated the haze.

Before he reached the showroom, he came upon a walk-in vault lined with steel drawers. On the center table a candle guttered, its yellow light penetrating the fine mist of ash in the air.

And near the wall knelt Norah.

Exultation halted him. Her ebony gown pooled around her, she was concentrating on wrestling free a jammed drawer. Soot smudged her alabaster complexion. A scowl pleated her smooth brow. Uttering a sigh, she paused to massage the side of her head, further mussing the untidy mass of red curls that tumbled down her slender back.

She had never looked lovelier.

Norah shoved at the drawer again. It slammed shut. Then she plucked a key from the ring dangling chatelaine-style from her waist. Metal grated as she opened the next drawer down.

Bits of green scattered the black-lined interior. Quickly she began scooping the emeralds into a sack.

Like a match flaring, fury scorched Kit. While the place burned around her ears, she coolly collected her plunder.

He strode into the vault. "What the devil do you think you're doing?"

She spun on her haunches. She clutched the bag in one grimy hand and the emeralds in the other. Her eyes, as jewel-bright as the stones, rounded in surprise.

"Kit!"

Her familiar use of his name, the husky rasp of her voice, barely penetrated his anger. He snatched the sack from her. "Have you gone mad? Get out of here."

She shot to her feet. "This is my shop. You've no

right to order me around. What are you doing here, anyway?"

"I'm trying to keep you safe. You've no right to risk your life to save a pile of damned stones."

"The fire's under control. So I'm perfectly safe."

"Then why couldn't you have waited?" With each sentence, he jabbed his finger toward her face. "The flames could flare up again. You could be trapped in here. You could die from inhaling the smoke."

Norah knocked his hand away. "It's a risk I have to take. The back door is broken and I haven't a guard. Didn't you see all the people out there?" She waved toward the front of the building. "As soon as the firemen leave, they'll loot my shop."

"For God's sake, there's a constable."

"And what about when *he* leaves?" She clasped her hand to her breast, emeralds glinting between her sooty fingers, the gold wedding band smudged. "As God is my witness, I won't let anyone steal what belongs to me."

An impassioned glow lit her features, a glow Kit ached to inspire. Frustration sizzled through him. Jesus God! He wished she would hug him as tightly as those stones.

"Damn your jewels to hell."

He pried open her fingers. Gems went flying, clattering over the carpeted floor, winking green in the candlelight.

"How dare you!" Firing a deadly look at him, Norah dropped to her hands and knees and began gathering up the emeralds. "Do you have any idea what these stones are worth? But, of course, you wouldn't care. You have money to burn. Well, I don't."

Riveted by her provocative posture, Kit barely heard. Her hiked-up hem revealed the shapeliness of her ankles. Enhanced by the bustle, her derriere wiggled invitingly. Her hair bobbed around her in long corkscrews of fire.

Fury and desire seared a path to his groin. He wanted to undo the row of jet buttons down her back, to unlace her tight corset, to slide his hands around her unbound breasts. He wanted her to crawl naked over his hot body instead of chasing after cold rocks.

To hell with gentlemanly restraint.

He dropped the sack and pulled Norah up, catching her between himself and the wall of steel drawers. She dropped the gems and thrust her palms against his chest.

Eyes widening, she began, "What do you think you're—"

He slid his fingers into her hair, tilted her head back, and let his kiss answer her. The breath left her in a warm gust of shock that filled him with her scent of cinders and roses. Taking advantage of her parted lips, he ran the tip of his tongue along the inside of her mouth, exploring her moistness, coaxing her toward arousal. He refused to think about any blaze beyond the one inside his body. He refused to consider that Norah might despise him when she came to her senses. He cared only about the lustful urges driving him and the brilliant splendor of kissing her at last.

She stood as stiff as a china doll within his embrace. Her fingers convulsed around his shoulders, but she didn't push him away. The heat of his anger funneled into the fierce desire to feel her soften and respond. He deepened his assault, using skills developed over a decade of wooing ladies whose scruples demanded a token resistance. His tongue commenced a slow dance, withdrawing from her mouth, then dipping inside again, the rhythm an erotic echo of lovemaking.

She turned her head away, though her fingers continued to hold tight to him. "Don't," she whispered. "Please don't."

Despite her husky protest, the swiftness of her breathing encouraged him. He sensed the indecision in her, the voluptuous desires rising against rigid morals. Her body exuded a torrid sensuality that excited him to a fever pitch. Cradling her neck with one hand, he nuzzled his lips along her soot-streaked jaw to her ear, where he brushed aside a curled lock of hair and let his breath tickle her. His lips nibbled the tenderness of her skin, his tongue finding the delicate whorls of her ear.

A shiver rippled through her. "Kit," she moaned on a warm exhalation. "Oh, please . . ."

"Please go on?" he said silkily. "My pleasure."

He moved his mouth to hers again, kissing her with all the fire in his blood, with all the mastery of a rogue. All the women he had kissed before were mere appetizers before the feast of Norah. Against his chest, he could feel the rapid rise and fall of her breasts. His hands slid down her arms, followed the corset-defined shape of her bosom and waist, then reached with practiced ease beneath her bustle to discover the pliant curve of her buttocks. Despite the impediment of their clothing, he lifted her to him, rubbing his hardness against the nest of her femininity. The exquisite friction wrested a groan from him.

Norah jerked her face away. The back of her head banged against the metal drawers. Her fists battered his jaw and jolted him back to reality. "Stop it. *Stop!*"

More surprised than hurt, Kit stepped back. She scrambled away, stumbling on the hem of her gown and catching herself with a hand on the table. She brought herself up straight. Her eyes were wild, her cheeks flushed, her bosom heaving.

"Don't you understand the meaning of the word *no*?" she cried out. "I asked you to stop and I meant it."

The vehemence of real pain in her voice shocked Kit. He reached his hand to her. "Norah, what's wrong?"

"Stay away." She retreated until her spine met the back wall of the vault. Then she crossed her arms over her breasts as if to ward off attack. "Stay away, you blackguard. Or I'll scream."

Awareness chilled his ardor. He had misinterpreted her response. Her shiver had been one of disgust, not passion. His kiss had revolted her.

The bitter taste of ash in his mouth came from more than the smoky haze. Christ, she must think him a callous heathen. Like so many others, she must loathe his mixed blood.

Yet the tense quality about her reached past his torment. Genuine fright lurked beneath her bravado. She watched him with the vigilance of a rabbit facing a tiger.

Perhaps more than prejudicial disgust sparked her violent reaction. She was a grieving widow. Damn, he had forsaken his vow to slowly reveal his love and her need.

Or did another reason lie behind her panic? Had she never known the pleasures of the sexual act?

Kit doused his burning curiosity. "You needn't be afraid of me," he said gently. "I'm not the madman of Mayfair."

She held her head high. "I know that. But I still didn't want you to kiss me."

"I respect your choice—"

"You didn't a minute ago."

"Despite your low opinion of me, I've yet to force a woman."

"Then don't touch me ever again."

Her sharp tone speared him. Breathing deeply against the pain, he gambled on the truth. "I can't make you a promise like that. Norah, I find you very attractive—"

"Save your glib compliments for your next paramour."

"I'm not spouting empty words, I'm being frank. I've never met a woman like you before. I admire more than your physical beauty. I admire your talent and your strength and your tender heart."

Her lips parted. Her eyes softened in confusion. Taking a step closer, he lowered his voice. "I've no desire to hurt you or frighten you. But if you ever give me the slightest encouragement, I *will* kiss you again."

The rigidity eased from her posture and she lowered her arms. She met his gaze squarely. Curls shimmering around her shoulders, she shook her head in quick, decisive denial. "I shan't ever offer you encouragement. So that's that."

"I think I made that too easy for you," Kit muttered, half regretting his spurt of honesty. "You certainly know how to stroke a man's self-assurance."

"That's all you really want, someone to boost your male conceit. A woman who will pamper you, a woman who exists only to please you." Norah plucked an emerald from the floor and rolled it between her fingers. "Well, I have a life beyond being a man's possession. I won't be your next conquest."

Irritated, he paced the small vault. The knowledge that he'd blackened his own reputation dogged his heels. "I never said I wanted to conquer you. Can't we meet as equals?"

"Hah. Your definition of *equal* is a woman willing to shed her clothes as quickly as you."

"For God's sake, I only kissed you," he shot back. "You're acting like a damned outraged virgin. Didn't you enjoy kissing your husband?"

The wary look returned to her eyes. Her hand convulsed around the green stone. "I'll thank you not to curse."

"You're evading my question."

She shrank back, but kept her chin lifted. A pink flush underlay the smudges on her cheeks. "And you're prying where you're not welcome."

"How the devil else am I to understand you? You certainly don't volunteer any information."

"There's nothing I want to tell you."

Kit blew a sound of disgust. "Fine. So let's get the hell out of here, then." Striding to the door, he peered out. A thin haze of smoke obscured the corridor. He could still hear the muted calls of the firemen, the crackle of distant flames.

"I shan't budge until I have all my jewels," Norah said.

"God, you're obstinate. I'll send over a few of my footmen to watch the shop tonight. Perhaps that will convince you to save your own life."

Her fists met her hips. "Thank you, but I can take care of myself."

"Oh?" He let his voice convey disbelief. "You'll empty the rest of the drawers, gather up the jewelry from the showroom, then carry it home all by yourself?"

"Yes."

"I see. You'll have quite a few sacks to lift. Suppose a footpad decides to relieve you of your burden?"

"That isn't your concern."

Norah made no move to collect her treasure trove. She fingered the key ring at her waist. A familiar stubborn line firmed her lips.

Lips he ached to kiss again, despite her infuriating independence. One taste of her luscious warmth had whetted his appetite. But he might as well wish for a piece of the moon.

Resentment broke the thread of his restraint. "Do you know what your problem is, Norah?"

"I hardly think—"

"Your problem is that you have too much damned fool pride. More pride than the nobility you profess to scorn."

"That isn't true—"

"Jesus God! Then why can't you accept help from anyone?" Kit whacked his fist on the wall. The metal drawers rattled. The pain that shot up his arm underscored the agony in his chest. He couldn't stop the hurt that seeped into his voice. "Or is it just me you despise?"

She stood quietly, a cinder-smudged goddess cloaked in copper hair. Her direct gaze wavered; her luxurious lashes lowered. She bent to pick up the sack of gems.

"All right," she murmured, "I accept your offer."

* * *

Her heart thrumming, Norah peered out the window of the carriage. Her breath misted the cold glass, and she rubbed it with the heel of her gloved hand. Through the swirl of snow flurries, she glimpsed the opulent town homes of Mayfair. She must be nearing Berkeley Square.

Nervousness tickled like a thousand beating wings in her stomach. She smoothed her crape-trimmed mantle and her best black velvet gown beneath. She had taken special care with her appearance. This morning she had lingered in the bath for a full hour, scrubbing the ashy stench from her skin and hair. She had drawn up her unruly tresses into a looser, softer style.

A style that would please a connoisseur of women. Kit Coleridge appreciated femininity. Today, she desperately needed to charm him.

I admire more than your physical beauty. I admire your talent and your strength and your tender heart.

He mouthed empty flattery, honeyed phrases meant to lure her into his trap. Or was he sincere?

Dear Blessed Virgin. She no longer knew what to think of him. His earthy nature both intrigued and alarmed her. His honesty and vulnerability rattled all her preconceptions of him. She itched for pencil and paper with which to capture his fascinating facets.

Norah absently massaged the soreness at the right side of her head. After a sleepless night she knew the futility of trying to dam the flood of memory. His kiss had shaken her, the bold caress of his hands, the shocking invasion of his tongue. The profound experience sent hot-cold tingles over her skin.

Whenever you're ready to learn my definition of a kiss, I'll be happy to oblige you.

She closed her eyes. Now she understood Kit's meaning, and knew why he'd been amused by her offended reaction to his lips on her brow. Maurice had never kissed her intimately. Her husband had never kissed her at all, other than an occasional dry peck on the cheek. On the rare occasions when he exercised his conjugal rights, he had turned out the lights and removed his robe in the darkness . . .

The shadows in her mind shifted. She lay waiting in bed, but the rustle of clothing came from Kit. He slid naked beneath the covers and reached for her. He immersed her mouth in another drowning kiss. His fingers glided sure and strong up her bare legs. Then he positioned her to receive his burning invasion . . .

Shuddering, Norah opened her eyes. The sensation was not entirely born of revulsion. The hint of trembly excitement baffled her. Praise God, she was free. She would never, ever submit to physical intimacy again.

Her breath formed a cloud in the chilly air. Besides, Kit Coleridge used women. She discounted his protestations to the contrary. A man couldn't change. The heart-wrenching early years of her marriage had taught her the fruitlessness of attempting to reshape a man's basic nature.

Therefore, his kiss should have insulted her. She should have been outraged. Why hadn't she instantly drawn away? Why had she felt the dark pull of curiosity? Why had she longed to melt in his arms and let him have his wicked way?

And why was she thinking about his kiss when she had more vital problems at stake?

Kit had caught her at a vulnerable moment. A moment when her hopes and dreams, her newfound liberty, teetered on the brink of catastrophe. Dear God. She might yet tumble into the chasm of poverty. And drag Winnifred and Ivy into ruin with her.

No. Her plan would succeed. It *must* succeed.

She rubbed her aching head again. *Count your blessings*, old Sister Simone used to scold. Things could be worse. At least the thief hadn't broken into the vault or looted the showroom. She must have surprised him right after he'd knocked out poor Captain Ackerman. Thankfully the fire had fright-

ened the man away. She repressed a swell of panic
and fear. Lord, she had had a run of bad luck . . .
her husband murdered and now a fire at the shop,
all in a little over a month. But she mustn't dwell
upon the hideous episodes. Better she should focus
on the task at hand.

*Why can't you accept help from anyone? Or is it just
me you despise?*

The raw pain in Kit's voice still shamed her. Norah
shifted on the cold leather seat. She also recalled the
hurt on his face when she had called him a blackguard. Despite his unsavory reputation, he possessed his own brand of honor. She, who prided
herself on ladylike virtues, had behaved like an un-
grateful wretch.

But perhaps he would give her a second chance.
It was her only hope.

Fingers trembling, she caressed her costly amethyst necklace. One of her favorites, the design of
deep purple stones formed a garland scattered across
a silver trellis framework. She wore the gems for the
last time. Beginning tomorrow, she would exercise
every economy. Her precious collection of jewelry
would be returned to the shop. The French chef
would be let go. The carriage would be sold. She
could make do with a hired hansom or the public
omnibus. Winnifred would complain about the fru-
gality, but so be it.

The carriage rocked to a halt before Kit's towering gray stone mansion. The butterflies in her
stomach took flight again. Taking a deep breath,
she reminded herself that she was safe. Kit had
promised never to force her into a physical relationship. She believed him. So she had nothing to
fear.

Norah silently reviewed her tactics. She would be
cool, businesslike. She would state her case in persuasive words. She would reveal no hint of the chaos
his kiss had stirred in her.

Determination sustained her as she went up the

steps. A poker-faced butler took her wrap, ushered her into the library, and shut the double doors.

Kit's domain. She had been here once before, the morning after the murder. That day she had been too distraught to form more than a fleeting impression of a masculine den. In the air she detected the faint aroma of leather and musk, the scents she associated with Kit. Restless, she wandered to one of the tall bookshelves and scanned the eclectic titles, from a well-thumbed volume of *Geological Evidences of the Antiquity of Man* by Charles Lyell to a rare edition of Milton's *Paradise Lost*. For a man who followed the superficial pursuits of a lothario, he took interest in profound topics.

The indistinct scratchings of handwriting indented the leather pad on the desk. A haphazard collection of fountain pens stood in a cup of Chinese porcelain; splotches of black ink marred the blue-on-white design.

She picked up a silver-framed photograph of a family. Unlike the typical stiff studio pose, these people exuded a lively joy that caught at her heart. The blond woman rested her head on her husband's broad shoulder. Both smiled down at the six children gathered around the garden bench. The tallest boy, as dark-haired as his father, tweaked one of his sister's fair ringlets.

Kit. Even as a youth, he'd been uncommonly handsome and an incorrigible tease. How disconcerting to think of him as part of a large, loving family. Perhaps he did possess a hidden capacity for faithfulness.

I'd like to find a special woman and marry her, start a family of my own.

Yearning puddled within Norah as she remembered his casual announcement. She had focused her girlish dreams on a similar goal. But fate had rendered her body barren.

Regretfully she set down the photograph. She would find contentment in her jewelry designing. She would become the greatest jeweler in the empire. Her plan depended upon making this interview a success.

Another flurry of misgivings unsettled her. What was keeping Kit?

She opened the doors and peered out. The sound of footsteps drew her attention to the opulent staircase. Surprise jabbed her. Down the marble steps glided the Honorable Jane Bingham.

A pair of doves made of ostrich tips wagged in her fair hair. An evening gown of blue tulle dotted by white velvet bows adorned her voluptuous body. Her decolletage displayed a generous portion of her bosom. The frock was unsuitable for the afternoon . . . or perhaps Jane had worn the dress the night before and was just now going home. Norah felt instantly dowdy, like a black crow eyeing a fine bluebird.

Behind Jane, Kit descended the stairs. Irritation firmed his high cheekbones and thinned his mouth. The gaslight burnished his bronzed skin. The pearl-gray suit and white cravat magnified his swarthy handsomeness. He and Jane made a beautiful couple, she so pale and he so dark.

They must have come from his bedroom. So much for his avowal that he'd ended their liaison. Perhaps Jane was the woman he'd chosen to marry.

Norah wondered why the truth hurt. His personal affairs didn't involve her. After all, she had secrets of her own.

Jane sailed across the foyer. "Ah, Mrs. Rutherford. What a delight to see you again."

"Good afternoon," Norah managed stiffly.

"Poor darling, you look devastated. The marquis told me all the pitiful details of last night's tragic fire." Jane tossed a sultry smile over her bare shoulder at Kit, then looked back at Norah. "Kit and I do like to share."

A hint of color washed his cheeks. "You were on your way out."

His teak-dark fingers curled possessively around Jane's white arm. Violent resentment attacked Norah.

She clenched the velvet folds of her gown to keep from clawing both their faces. Blast him for discussing her personal life with his hussy.

Her veins iced. Had he also told Jane about the kiss?

As they started toward the door, Norah called out, "Don't go so quickly, Miss Bingham. I haven't yet thanked you for your charming gift."

Jane loosed a trill of laughter. "Ah yes, the unmentionables. I do hope I didn't shock you."

"Not at all. You'll be pleased to know I've already put them to very good use." By throwing the condoms at Kit, Norah thought.

Jane's mouth pinched into a tart line. "You and I should have tea in a few months. We'll have so much more in common. After all, Kit will be sniffing after a new bitch by then—"

"That's enough," he snapped.

"She deserves to know—"

"Get out."

"But you haven't ordered my carriage brought round—"

"Now."

The butler appeared and handed Jane her wrap. She marched out into a blast of snow flurries. The slam of the door echoed in the cavernous hall.

A muscle worked in Kit's jaw as he strode to Norah. Large and masculine, he loomed over her. His nearness made her quake. His tiger's eyes moved keenly over her fancy gown and her amethysts, then bored into her face.

"What's wrong?" he said. "Did you have a problem with the new guards you hired?"

He made no move to touch her. After the shattering kiss of the night before, Norah had trouble meeting his dark gaze. "No. They came highly recommended by the agency you suggested. And the carpenter repaired the door already."

"What about the broken windows?"

"The glazier started work this morning, too. The building should be secure by evening. Of course, the fire and smoke damage still remain to be assessed . . ." The thought of her mission dried her throat. "May we speak in private? I have a matter of importance to discuss with you."

"Of course." His hand warm at her waist, he guided her into the library. "I have something to tell you, too."

His words jolted her. Would he announce that he had patched up his rift with Jane?

The instant they entered the room, he left Norah's side, as if he detested the need for gentlemanly courtesy. He acted so formal, unlike the ardent man who had trapped her against the wall last night and caressed her as if she were his own precious jewel.

Her heart throbbed in the hollow of her chest. Too agitated to sit, she went to the hearth. "Please pardon me for arriving without notice. I didn't mean to interrupt your . . . meeting."

Kit settled himself onto the edge of the desk. "You didn't. As I said, Jane was on her way out."

"Oh." Unable to stop herself, Norah blurted, "I thought you weren't seeing her anymore."

He raised an eyebrow. "I thought you weren't interested in my private affairs."

"Miss Bingham's presence took me by surprise, that's all."

"Indeed? No doubt you expected a whole parade of women to come trooping out of my bedroom."

Her cheeks heated. "I had no expectations whatsoever."

"Then perhaps you'd be interested to know why I sent for Jane—"

"You needn't recount all the details," Norah said quickly. "Unlike Miss Bingham, I don't thrive on gossip."

He grimaced. "Believe me, I know. However, there *is* one item of interest to you." Resting his elbows on his powerful thighs, he leaned forward, his gaze intent. "If you've been wondering how the newspapers found out about the murder, Jane leaked the story."

Norah wilted into a chair. "Are you sure?"

"She admitted as much. I warned her that if she plays any more tricks on either of us, I'll make damned certain that not even a cabbage farmer will take her into his bed."

"But why would she want to hurt me? Surely she knows that you and I aren't . . . involved."

"Contrary to what she claims, I've told her nothing about us, beyond mentioning the fire. Nevertheless, she was shrewd enough to guess that I broke off with her because of you, Norah."

His hard-chiseled features showed only aloofness. The frostiness of her rejection must have killed his attraction to her. She ought to rejoice. Instead, a peculiar sensation of loss settled like a rock in her stomach.

Unable to look at him, she lowered her eyes. At their first meeting, Kit had been standing by the very chair in which she sat. He'd been unshaven and tousled, his smile boyishly charming. She feathered her fingertips over the fine lace draping the leather arm. Odd, she didn't remember these doilies positioned here.

She sat up straight. "This is Ivy's handiwork."

"Yes."

Tenderness as soft as cat's paws padded into her heart. "How kind of you to display it."

He toyed with the pens on the desk. "God forbid you should mistake me for a compassionate man. She gave me a few pieces the last time I took tea with her, that's all."

He spoke curtly as if to minimize his softness. Because he was embarrassed to show sensitivity? She wished she knew him well enough to guess. "Ivy didn't mention you'd come by. When did you see her last?"

"Yesterday, while you were working late." He let the fountain pen clatter back into the porcelain cup. "Norah, why don't you get to the point?"

"What point?"

"Tell me why you're here, all dressed up in jewels and velvet." His hard gaze slid up and down her, like a gem cutter examining an imperfect stone. "Did you want something from me?"

The blunt question flustered her. She touched her necklace for courage. Matching six-carat drops dangled from her earlobes. For the first year of mourning, a widow was allowed to wear only simple pieces made of jet or onyx. But Norah wanted to look her best today. She wanted to appear prosperous, as if she didn't need him. The masquerade formed part of her stratagem.

Kit leaned against the desk. A forbidding expression shadowed his masculine features. His arms were folded across his wide chest. Blessed Virgin, he appeared in no mood to grant favors. Especially to the woman who'd rebuffed him.

But she couldn't retreat now. She had nowhere else to turn.

Moistening her parched lips, she groped for her memorized speech. "I did come here to ask you something," she admitted. "But first, I must apologize for my rude behavior last night. You were gracious enough to offer your help, and I should have accepted immediately."

"Yes."

"I can only plead that I was shaken by the traumatic events."

"Are you referring to the fire? Or my kiss?"

"Both. I mean, the fire," she amended quickly. "You see, if the stones had been stolen, I would have been left in dire financial straits."

"Surely you're insured."

She shook her head. "Maurice didn't believe in insurance. Just as he didn't believe in accountants. Apparently he preferred to retain complete control of the business."

"That's utter nonsense. Insurance is a sensible practice."

"I agree." Scouring the bitterness from her

voice, she twisted her gold wedding band. "Over the past few weeks I've been finding out all sorts of oddities about my husband's methods of business."

"Such as?"

She hesitated. Voicing the facts gave her a vague feeling of disloyalty, as if she were betraying Maurice's memory. "For one, the bank had refused to lend him any more money. And for another, he'd gone to a usurer in order to pay off his . . . our debts."

Kit narrowed his eyes. "Debts? I was under the impression that the shop was doing well—at least up until his death."

"I thought so, too. But there's very little cash left. And since word got out about Maurice's murder, only curiosity seekers have come in. The stones are my only assets."

"Surely there's an enormous profit on jewelry. Where has the money been going?"

She lifted her shoulders in despair. "I don't know. The ledgers are a mystery to me. I took them to an accountant, but he couldn't decipher some of the symbols and notations. There were curious debits to initials I don't recognize."

Kit thrust his hands in his pockets and began to pace the room. "And you think all this—his liabilities—may be related to Maurice's murder?"

The keen observation caught her off guard. "No. I mean, I hadn't considered the possibility." She wrung her fingers. "That's not why I'm telling you this."

"Then why *are* you telling me this, Norah?"

She wrestled with a final attack of guilt. Nonsense. He'd offered his aid; she might have already burned her bridges with him, but she'd never know without asking. Besides, she was speaking of business, not pleasure.

His darkly handsome form loomed only a few feet away. His unflinching regard made her unaccountably warm in a way that both fascinated and frightened her. She took a deep breath, then released it slowly.

"I need an investor," she said huskily. "Please, Kit, will you help me?"

Chapter 9

Kit's face might have been chiseled from agate. He looked her over, as if assessing her sincerity. Norah held herself straight. Clearly, he no longer had any romantic interest in her. The success of the shop depended upon her artistic ability and business acumen. He had every right to ascertain the integrity of her offer.

Now that she'd taken the plunge, she felt more confident, ready to present her list of persuasive arguments. "I think you'll find the shop an excellent investment," she began. "It's in a choice location near Mayfair. As soon as the scandal dies down business will pick up. Granted I've suffered a few setbacks recently, but the tiara will win me royal patronage—"

Kit held up his broad palm. "There's no need to convince me. I'll help you."

She closed her mouth, then opened it. "Just like that, you'll agree?"

"My money and your talent." Beneath his finely tailored suit, his shoulders lifted in a shrug. "I'm always willing to gamble on a winning combination."

The specter of failure lifted from her soul, like a door opening to a world of bright possibilities. She hadn't discerned until this moment the depth of her fear. Finding her voice, she managed to say, "I'm pleased you think so."

"I have only one stipulation."

"Yes?"

"I want to be more than a silent investor."

Suspicion dimmed her sparkle. Gripping the chair arms, she watched him pace toward her, a sleek predator moving in for the kill. A slow, warm pounding started deep inside her. "I thought we'd settled that issue last night," she said.

He stopped abruptly. "For God's sake, Norah. I'm not referring to the bedroom. Surely you don't believe I'd stoop to buying your favors—or imagine you would sell them."

The lowering of his brow, the tightening of his lips, cracked his stony facade. He looked annoyed, but wounded too. Yesterday she had convinced herself that she had injured only his male pride. Now she wondered if his feelings for her ran deeper, if she had truly caused him emotional pain.

The thought rattled her. "I'm sorry," she murmured. "I misunderstood. I'm also sorry for calling you a blackguard yesterday. I meant no slur against your heritage."

Her apology eased the tension bedeviling Kit. Not her words as much as the utter sincerity in her unblinking green eyes, the candor softening her lower lip. God save him, he'd hand over his entire fortune if it made her happy. Who would have thought she would march in here today and present him with this golden opportunity to win her over?

He wanted to kick up his heels in exultation. Instead, he sat down in the chair opposite her and loosely laced his hands. "If I'm to invest in your shop, I intend to keep a close watch on where my money is going."

"That's fair enough."

"I want a fifty-fifty venture."

"Of course you're entitled to an equal share of the profits. And I'll pay back all the money you lend me plus interest."

"I'm speaking of more than the revenues. We'll split everything down the middle, including the work. You do the designing and oversee the production, and I'll take care of the business end. If I'm to straighten out the finances, I'll need access to the ledgers and the inventory list. Starting tomorrow."

His meaning crashed into Norah like a slab of granite. "You're coming to the shop every day?"

"Yes."

"But you can't."

"Why not?"

"Because . . ." She picked up a lace doily and drew it through her fingers, over and over. The prospect of working so closely with Kit disturbed her. She had counted on him to supply the capital, accept his portion of the profits, and go on his merry way. "Because you have other things to do."

"Such as?"

"Well . . . whatever you've always done."

He leaned indolently against the chair, the burgundy leather a choice backdrop for his exotic features. "I raced horses. Attended parties. And, of course, romanced women." Again, he subjected her to a potent scrutiny that made her toes curl. "All pursuits I'd give up for the chance to work at a real job."

She searched for an excuse to dissuade him. "You'll grow bored."

"I doubt that."

"You won't have time to teach the boys."

"You manage. So will I."

"What about the murder investigation?"

"What about it?"

"You said you wanted to find the killer."

"Then let's look upon this as a golden opportunity," he said. "I'll have a chance to observe Thaddeus Teodecki. Besides, maybe there's a clue in the ledgers."

She dropped the doily and snapped her fingers. "Thaddeus. The fire made me almost forget."

Quickly she told Kit about the business card she had found.

"Good work," he said, approval glinting in his brown eyes. "Perhaps he was stealing gems. I'll look into the matter."

"We'll both look into it."

One corner of his mouth curled upward. "Does that mean we're partners, then?"

His silky tone immersed her in a choppy sea of uncertainty. Never had she expected to meet a man who could make her quake inside with one bold look, a man who could make her melt with one warm compliment, a man who could make her shiver with one casual touch. This couldn't be happening, not to her. She groped for the life raft of anger. "I suppose you think you can't trust me with your money. Because I'm a woman."

To her surprise he smiled warmly, displaying even white teeth and dazzling her senses. "I think you can accomplish anything you set your mind to doing, Norah. However, you're an artist, a designer. I doubt you enjoy plodding through a mire of numbers."

"You're a marquis and heir to a dukedom," she countered. "I doubt you want to dirty your hands with a commoner's work."

The smile vanished. He sat forward, his face sober. "I want to work for the same reasons you design jewelry, Norah. To challenge myself. To gain a sense of accomplishment. To find worth in my life."

The parallels between them shook the foundations of his image. In a startling flash, she saw beyond the suave nobleman to the man within, a man with needs equal to her own, a man with doubts and dreams, a man who could admit to human longings. Unaccountably, she recalled the smooth slide of his lips against hers and the heat of his hard body pressed to hers.

Feeling warm, Norah rose and went to the window. A cold draft restored her senses. He might be lying. Why would he abandon his plush life in favor of work? "You may still change your mind. I haven't told you everything."

"Skeletons in your closet?" He quirked a diabolical eyebrow. "This sounds interesting."

"It's about the moneylender. His name is Bertie Goswell." She rubbed her arms at the chilling memory. "Back in November, Maurice borrowed twelve thousand sovereigns from him. A week and a half ago, Goswell came to me and demanded the first payment. He gave me a fortnight to come up with the cash. He is . . . not a pleasant man."

Fists clenched, Kit surged to his feet. "Did he threaten you?"

"Not in so many words. But I have to pay him a thousand pounds by the end of this week. And I simply don't have the money without selling some of the jewels from the vault."

"Why did your husband need the money?"

She lifted her hands, palms out. "I'm not certain. Perhaps to purchase Fire at Midnight, the center stone for the royal tiara."

"I see. Well, forget about Goswell. I'll take care of him."

His defense weakened her knees. She clutched the icy windowsill behind her. "Thank you."

Kit prowled toward her, then stopped a few feet away. "You could have told me about your financial problems before today."

She found herself watching his sensual mouth, remembering his kiss. She wrenched her gaze away. "You're a stranger. I'm an independent woman. This is only a minor setback."

"I can't blame you for wanting to succeed on your own. Maurice kept you under his tight thumb for nine years."

His criticism annoyed her. Yet she couldn't deny the truth in his statement. "My husband owned the shop, not me. He had every right to do business the way he saw fit."

"Even if it meant claiming your designs as his own? Even if it meant leaving you in debt? Even if it meant leaving you to deal with a backstreet moneylender?" Kit leaned forward and skimmed his fingers down her sleeve in the idle gesture of a friend. "Norah, I admire your loyalty. But you deserve far better than the muddle he left you."

She thought so, too, but to voice her doubts seemed an act of betrayal. Absently she moved the heavy gold wedding band up and down her finger. "I do have to meet the payroll, buy supplies, and manage a hundred other expenses. It's more than I can handle on my own. Finances simply aren't my strong suit."

"You can't expect to be a genius at everything. My stepmother says I'm hopeless at appreciating the classics of literature."

She glanced toward the desk. "You have *Paradise Lost* on your shelf there."

Humor brightened his eyes to topaz. "That's Mother's old copy. She gave it to me for my eighteenth birthday. I read it to please her, but to be honest, I much prefer the racing forms. Until recently, that is.'

"Oh." Hearing the fondness in his voice when he spoke of his stepmother, Norah felt a queer tightening inside her. "Well. The fire made me realize that I was taking too much on myself. I needed to ask someone for help."

His eyes caressed her. "I'm glad you came to me. What made you change your mind?"

"I should think that's obvious," she said lightly. "You have money."

"Doesn't Jerome St. Claire?"

The keen edge to Kit's voice intrigued her. His skin drawn taut over his high cheekbones, he stood with his hand braced on the back of the wing chair. He waited, watching her as if his very life depended upon her reply.

"Jerome was Maurice's friend," she said. "I hoped to avoid telling him about the predicament Maurice left me in. Besides, Jerome is too . . . paternal, too gallant. He'd feel obliged to take on all of my problems in addition to his own work."

"I'd call him possessive," Kit stated. "He'd like to own you like those jewels he pawns for the rich."

Anger flared in her. "He cares for me—I've told you so before. I resent you putting a sordid connotation on our friendship."

Kit thrust up his hands in a parody of alarm. "I'm sorry. Please don't start throwing things at me again."

Norah realized she was gripping her wedding band like a rock about to be hurled. His reference to the condoms caused an absurd bubbling of mirth in her. Unbidden, a smile rose to her lips. "Relax, my lord. I promise not to get violent."

Lowering his arms, he smiled back. "Thank God for that. I wouldn't wish to regret our partnership."

He could look so utterly appealing, his eyes warm and dark, his handsome features as alluring as those of a foreign prince. She slipped the circlet back down her finger, the weight familiar and constricting, ending the brief closeness of humor. "You're misjudging Jerome," she said.

"Trust me to recognize obsession in a man. He covets you, Norah."

"The way Jane covets you?"

"No. That's different."

"How?"

"She'll go after anything in trousers. But Jerome wants only you."

Was Kit right? She shook her head. "Well, I don't believe you. He's an honorable, upstanding gentleman."

"So am I. At least I'm trying to be." His voice mellowed to a velvet murmur and he reached for her hand. "You need a younger man. A man who can be your equal partner in more than mere business."

His thumb stroked over her knuckles and smoothed the fine hairs on the back of her hand. Lassitude purled over her, a sweetly sharp feeling that made her feel light-headed. A single, stunning thought blazed like a comet across the firmament of her soul. Kit still desired her. She could see the fire illuminating the gold flecks in his eyes. His body heat tingled up her arm and warmed her breasts. He stood so close, she might touch the faintly stubbled strength of his jaw; she might unbutton his shirt and learn the hair-roughened contours of his chest . . .

Curiosity and panic churned in her stomach. She pulled her hand free. "I don't need anyone," she said. "Not that way. Not ever again."

"Why? What happened between you and Maurice that made you dislike physical intimacy?"

"Nothing!"

"Something about it bothers you. I can't even touch your hand without you flinching."

"You're invading my privacy."

"You're evading the issue."

She pressed her palms to her aching head and shrank against the frosty windowpane. "Stop it. Stop!" Hearing the high edge to her words, she lowered her voice. "Your questions are rude and insufferable. We're business partners, no more and no less."

"Norah, forgive me." His gentle hands drew her arms down, then slowly let go. "I hope you'll answer me someday. In the meantime, please don't ever be afraid of me."

Sincerity haunted his eyes. He seemed disappointed, yet somehow he also looked as swept away as she by the powerful currents between them. The storm tide of alarm ebbed, leaving a peculiar glow on the shores of her heart, like the sensuous softness of warm sand against her skin. Their kiss illuminated her memory, the taste of his mouth and the tenderness of his caresses. Again, she swayed with the inexplicable urge to touch him, to be touched by him . . .

A knock sounded. Kit scowled at the library door. "Come in."

A boyishly attractive footman entered. "Beg your

pardon, m'lord. Inspector Wadding is here. You did leave orders never to keep him waiting."

"Send him in, Herriot."

As the retainer departed, Norah said, "Do you suppose the police have found the murderess?"

Kit shrugged, then cocked his head at her. "How would that make you feel?"

"Relieved. Free, somehow." The honesty of her words shamed her. "Is that beastly of me? To consider the mystery of his death a burden?"

"God, no. You can't dwell on the past forever. You need to get on with your life."

He stroked her arm with the intimacy of a companion, and this time she felt an acute sense of privation when he drew back and turned to the doorway.

Detective-Inspector Harvey Wadding stepped into the library. His shoulders hunched like those of a schoolboy summoned to the master's office, he gazed reverently at the ornate ceiling and rich furnishings. His gaze stopped on Norah. He bent into a rusty bow and stammered a greeting.

Kit suppressed a wry grin of kinship. So the gangly inspector was staggered by Norah's unconventional beauty, too. The softer hairstyle barely restrained the riot of coppery curls. The low-cut gown and amethyst necklace complemented her pearly skin. Kit wanted to slide his hand inside her bodice and . . . He clamped a lid over the untimely fantasy. "Please proceed, Inspector."

"Er, yes. So glad I've caught up to you, Mrs. Rutherford. I went to your home, and Miss Ivy Rutherford directed me here."

Norah hastened forward. "What is it? What did you wish to tell me?"

Wadding blinked. "I was hoping *you* would tell *me* something. I've some questions about the fire last night."

So they hadn't identified the killer, Kit thought on a stab of disappointment. He was beginning to think the woman would never be found. Norah would never again be free to love.

"Certainly I'll cooperate," she said. "But . . . are you working on this case, too?"

"Yes."

"Why would a fire involve the police?" Kit broke in, fixing the inspector with a frown. "Do you suspect arson?"

"Oh, heavens no, the blaze started when I dropped my lamp," Norah explained. "I told that to the constable last night."

"Indeed so," Wadding said. "Today I went to St. Mary's Hospital and interviewed the guard." He consulted his dog-eared notepad. "A Captain Archibald J. Ackerman."

"How *is* Captain Ackerman?" Norah asked. "I sent Winnifred with a basket of pastries and jam to visit him, but she hadn't returned when I left."

"Yes, I saw Miss Rutherford on my way out of the ward. Quite the opinionated female on the role of the police." A crimson blush stained Wadding's horsey face. "Ahem—I mean no criticism toward your kin, ma'am."

"I understand."

"The captain is suffering from a concussion, but he's otherwise well. Unfortunately, he could add little to your story. He didn't see the intruder, either."

"Intruder?" The news struck Kit with the stinging force of an ice storm. He wheeled toward Norah. "You never said anything about an intruder."

Her lips parted. Her gaze shifted, then returned to his face. She lifted her hands, palms up. "I'm sorry, Kit. In all the excitement, I must have forgotten."

"Forgotten." The word tasted bitter in his mouth. She didn't trust him any more now than she had the day they met.

"She's a lucky woman," Wadding stated. "Luckier than many a poor soul at the hands of a heinous criminal. The intruder was frightened off by the fire.

Mrs. Rutherford suffered only a glancing blow to the head.''

Kit felt like an actor thrust into a play in which he didn't know the lines. "Blow? What blow?''

"The intruder struck her on the right side of the head.'' The inspector peered at his notepad again. "According to her testimony to the constable, she ducked when the man swung at her. When she dropped the lamp and the fire started, the suspect ran off before she could see his face.''

Kit rushed to her. In the silky nest of hair behind her ear, his shaking fingers met a nasty lump. "Are you all right?'' he said hoarsely.

"I'm fine, just a slight headache. The blow only stunned me, so I ran outside and summoned a constable. He helped me pull out Captain Ackerman, then telephoned the fire brigade.'' She lowered her chin in a sheepish expression. "I suppose I should have told you earlier.''

"Yes, by God. You might have been killed.''

"But I wasn't.'' Her fingers brushed his wrist like the tentative sweep of a butterfly's wings. It was the first time she had ever touched him of her own volition, and despite his wrath he felt the sting of desire. His distraction vanished when she added, "Please don't be angry. It was only an oversight.''

More likely it was her damned independence. His heart beat a furious tattoo against his ribs. He wanted to blister her ears with curses, but the presence of the inspector deterred him. "You get coshed over the head, forget to mention it, and call it an oversight?''

"I . . . had other things on my mind.''

"Ah yes,'' he said coldly. "Your precious jewels.''

Her emerald gaze skimmed over his face, then darted to the inspector, who stood gaping at the interplay.

Kit focused a glare at the policeman. "Proceed with your questions,'' he commanded.

"Ahem—yes, m'lord, of course.'' Wadding

scratched his long ear. "Was anything stolen, Mrs. Rutherford?"

"I don't believe so. I kept a copy of the inventory secured in the vault. When I went into the shop this morning, I spent several hours checking the catalogue."

"Did you itemize the jewels in the showroom as well?"

"Yes. Several of the craftsmen helped me. I intend to do a more thorough check tomorrow."

"Hmm. The office was gutted, though. Could you make a list of what was burned?"

She nodded. "I'll be happy to, but it was mostly furniture. Thank goodness the ledgers were at my accountant's office." She pensively rubbed the amethysts at her throat. "The only item of value destroyed was a sketchbook of my designs."

Wadding blinked, apparently uncomprehending of the loss. "Could anything have been stolen from the files? Important papers, perhaps? Loan documents?"

The color washed from Norah's face. "I'm not sure. Why do you ask?"

Wadding hesitated, shifting his large feet.

Kit braced his hand at her slender waist. She must be stricken by the frightening memory of the moneylender. "Get to the point, Inspector," he snapped. "Do you see a connection between the intruder and the murder of Mrs. Rutherford's husband?"

"As a matter of fact, I do have another conjecture about the unfortunate's death. Perhaps I may speak to you alone, m'lord—"

"No," Norah said. "Whatever you have to say concerning my late husband, I would like to hear."

Wadding shot Kit an appealing look. "Your lordship?"

Kit feathered his fingertips over Norah's rigid back. He ached to spare her any suffering. But she had the right to listen. "State your theory."

"Yes, m'lord." Lowering his gaze, Wadding moved his pad from one rawboned hand to the other. "Mrs. Rutherford, I regret to say I've uncovered evidence that your husband was deeply in debt."

She stood very still. "I'd found that out myself, just recently."

The embarrassed red faded from his complexion. "Er, yes. He had dealings with a usurer from the Seven Dials area. Man by the name of Albert Goswell."

"Who told you that?" Kit asked sharply.

"Sorry, but I daren't name my informant—"

"Peter Bagley, no doubt," Norah murmured. She glanced up at Kit, her eyes like moist green jewels against the paleness of her features. "He's one of my craftsmen. He showed Goswell into my office."

The pain of betrayal on her face tightened Kit's throat. "I'll show the bastard into the gutter, then."

"Please. I have nothing to hide." Her voice composed, she frowned at the inspector. "Do you think Mr. Goswell had something to do with what happened?"

"It's one possibility. Could be he was aiming to steal back his money. I've been trying to pin something on that slippery eel for years. His kind don't care what laws they break."

"But you're forgetting one thing," Kit said. "Even if the intruder and the murder *are* connected somehow, Goswell had no motive to kill Maurice Rutherford. The loan hadn't even come due yet."

"Aye, that brings us to a more likely possibility." Wadding paused, glumness pulling at his long face. "Goswell mightn't be involved in either crime. Forgive me for saying so, ma'am, but your husband may have owed a debt to someone else, too."

Norah sank onto a leather chair. "You're referring to the woman who killed him."

"Then there may have been another loan document in Maurice's desk," Kit said, pacing slowly before the shelves crowded with books. "One that could have linked the woman to the murder."

The inspector nodded. "She may have hired an

accomplice to steal back the paper. Do you recall seeing any notes or papers like that, Mrs. Rutherford?"

"I'm afraid not. With so much other work, I hadn't gone through all the old files yet."

"Ma'am, I hesitate to ask this again, but have you recalled anything at all that could lead us to your husband's mistress?"

Closing her eyes a moment, Norah pressed her fingers to her brow. "No. No, nothing."

"A pity. With your permission, ma'am, my constables will search the ruined office for evidence."

"Of course."

Wadding bent his lanky frame into a bow and scurried out the door, leaving them alone in the library.

Norah sat with her hands tucked beneath her chin as she gazed into the coal blaze on the hearth. Her mournful expression washed Kit in tenderness and tainted him with despair. He swore under his breath. Maurice Rutherford had left her mired in debt and scandal. He hadn't deserved her adoration, her loyalty.

Then again, maybe the cad had done Kit a service. Her coming here today had been like manna from heaven.

She was using him. He knew that and accepted it as a minor nuisance. Because, of all men, she had chosen *him*. Surely he could break down the barrier of her mistrust.

Yet even their partnership couldn't expunge the jealousy eating at his heart.

He hunkered down before her chair. "For God's sake, Norah. You ought to give your love to an honorable man who will care for you, not the memory of a self-centered hypocrite."

Her forehead wrinkled. "Pardon?"

"Weren't you thinking about Maurice?"

"Why, no. It was my sketch pad. All my drawings from the last six months were burned to cinders."

"Oh." His frustration winked out like fire plunged

into water. "I'm sorry. I suppose you lost your sketch for the royal commission?"

"Yes, but I can redraw it from memory." She paused. "My design for your parure was in the notebook, too."

He gently circled her wrists with both his thumbs and forefingers, when he really wanted to kiss her until she welcomed him into her heart. The tiny shush of her breathing sounded over the snap of the fire. At least she didn't pull away. He reveled in the small victory.

"Hmm," he said. "I'll have to wait a little longer to present the gift."

"You're not in a hurry, then?"

"I am, but I can restrain myself."

She slanted him a look from beneath the copper-tipped fringe of her lashes. "I don't mean to pry, but it would help to know the name of the recipient. I much prefer to tailor a commission to a specific person."

The stiffness to her voice pleased him. He repressed a smile. If she were jealous, there might yet be hope that she would open herself to him. "That's my secret. Partners needn't tell each other everything."

Norah extracted her hands and lowered them to her lap. In a formal tone, she began, "Your lordship . . ."

"Kit."

"Yes, well. I really *should* have told you about the intruder. I'm truly sorry."

The reminder cast a shadow over his lightened spirits. A fearsome suspicion lurked in the gloom of his mind. What if the criminal had been seeking not jewels or a loan document, but Norah herself? After all, the murderess had used Norah's hatpin. Perhaps in an effort to see Norah executed for the crime . . .

He absorbed her soft beauty, the halo of crimson curls enhancing the pure skin of her face, the dusting of freckles across the bridge of her nose, the noble tilt of her chin.

Damn, why would anyone want to see her dead?

He leaned back on his heels, Indian fashion, in the way he'd sometimes seen his father sit. "I'm glad you mentioned the intruder. We're going to set down some rules."

"Rules?"

"Yes," he stated. "For one, there'll be no more working after hours." He ticked off the items on his fingers. "I'll come by for you in my carriage each morning. I'll escort you home each evening. You're not to leave the building alone, either."

"Oh, for heaven's sake," she grumbled. "I need a partner, not a bodyguard."

She sat so proud and so alone . . . no husband, no parents, no relations to turn to. Ivy and Winnifred he discounted. One was too sweet and the other too sour. As for Jerome . . . Kit resolved to fill her need for a male companion.

He ached to lock Norah safely away, his own priceless jewel hidden in the plush confines of his Devon estate. But even velvet bonds would chafe her. "I shan't get in your way," he promised. "Neither will I stand by and let you be hurt again."

"The break-in was likely an isolated incident, done by a random thief."

"Then the jewels might lure another robber, especially if he knows you're alone at the shop." He hated to alarm her with vague suspicions, yet he burned with the need to warn her. "Someone killed your husband, Norah. Until we know why, it's best to take precautions."

She studied him, her hand stealing up to touch the lump behind her ear. At last she nodded. "If you're taking on your share of the work, I suppose I won't need to stay late anyway."

"Excellent."

But even her concession failed to quiet his troubled thoughts. Why *would* someone want her dead?

The unresolved question dug like talons into his peace of mind. Damn, he lacked too many facts.

Slowly Kit rose to his feet. A half-formed idea took shape.

Perhaps there *was* something else he could do.

Chapter 10

"**M**um?"
The boyish voice drew Norah's attention from the milky sheen of a moonstone. She placed her loupe and the stone on her desk. Around the high wooden screen that formed the wall of her temporary office peered a lad with wolfish eyes and scruffy black hair that poked out in disarray.

"Lark," she said in surprise. "What are you doing here?"

"Come t' see you, mum."

The noise of sawing and hammering echoed in the shop and obscured the quieter sounds of the craftsmen at work beyond her corner cubicle. She waved the boy closer. "Please, come in. I can hardly hear you over the din."

Lark jerked a glance backward. Cap in hand, he strutted the few feet to her desk. His cheeks were red from the cold outside. "Buildin' you a new office, is they? I knew 'is lordship would take care o' you."

His implication bothered Norah. Even as a fledgling, the male of the species assumed the dominant role. The female had to work harder to gain any ground. "A woman doesn't need a man to watch over her, Lark. We're perfectly capable of managing our own affairs. Don't forget, the British Empire is ruled by a queen."

Lark scratched his untidy hair. "Beggin' yer pardon, mum, but are you sayin' girls is as clever as boys?"

"Yes." She surprised herself with the force of her conviction. It was true, she reflected, despite the nuns teaching her to be humble and subservient, despite Maurice expecting her to act the modest and feminine wife.

"But . . . don't some man got t' be the master?"

"No. Men and women can work together as equals."

"Equals?" Lark tasted the word as if it were a worm. "You mean I gotta be equal mates with 'Enrietta Banks?"

"Even her." Smiling, Norah pushed away from the desk. "Why aren't you in school today?"

"Snuck out o' teatime. The Rev and his missus pairs us lads off with the girls." He crinkled his pug nose. "Teachin' us manners, y'know."

"Let me guess. Henrietta Banks is your partner."

"Aye, an' she waggles 'er baby finger when she 'olds 'er cup." He made a comedy of slurping tea, his stubby finger extended. "Like she were a royal princess instead of dollymop's brat."

"Henrietta can't help that her mother was a maid-servant fallen on hard times." Norah went to the spirit lamp in the corner. Her cubicle abutted the brick side wall of the shop. "I was just about to make tea myself. Perhaps you'd join me."

"No, ma'am. I mean, thanks, but I come 'ere t' work."

She swung around, tea canister in hand. "To work?"

"Aye, mum. I was 'opin' you'd gimme a job." He bent his head and scuffed the toe of his boot over the carpet. "I'd like t' earn me own way in the world."

"But what about your schooling? You're learning to read so well."

"I know, mum. I want t' come after class an' work a few hours, till closin' up time."

"I see." She set down the canister. "What sort of job did you have in mind?"

He craned his neck to see past the screen. "I can sweep floors an' wash windows an' empty the rubbish bins an' such. Ain't no job too 'umble for me." Lark got down on one knee and clapped his palms together in prayerful supplication. "Please, mum, say yes. I know I ain't worth much. Just a few coppers is all."

His zealous appeal touched her heart. Perhaps she'd been wrong to think a bully like Lark lacked ambition; then again, perhaps Kit had inspired a sense of responsibility in the boys. The thought nestled warmly inside her.

She put the water pot on to boil. "You underestimate yourself, Lark. You're worth ten shillings a week at the very least."

"Then I got the post?"

"Yes. You may start immediately with the window washing. But if you fall behind in your studies, you're fired."

He wiggled forward on his knees, seized the hem of her gown, and kissed it. "Oh, thank you, mum. You won't regret it. On me dad's own gravestone, I vow you won't."

Half embarrassed, she reached down to grasp his stocky arms. "Come now, stand up and I'll introduce you around the shop—"

"What's going on here?"

Hands planted on his hips, Kit towered in the opening beside the screen. He had discarded his coat and cravat and rolled back his cuffs halfway up his muscled forearms. The white linen shirt made a brilliant contrast to his topaz skin. Irritation scored his forehead, and his black eyebrows clashed into a frown.

"Blimey." Lark bounded to his feet, hunched his shoulders, and turned his cap to his hands. "Didn't know you was 'ere, m'lord."

"I'm supervising the workmen in Mrs. Rutherford's new office. Why *you're* here is more the question."

"I been chattin' with Mrs. R. I'll be off now."

As he edged toward the door, he gave Norah a small, furtive shake of his spiky hair.

Puzzled, she said, "I thought you wanted to begin work today, Lark. Have you changed your mind about the job?"

"Uh . . ."

"Job? Why aren't you in school practicing the verbs I assigned yesterday?" Kit took a step to the side to block the opening and folded his arms across his broad chest. "Ah. I'm beginning to see what mischief you're about."

The disapproval in his tone surprised Norah. "It's enterprising of Lark to seek employment for a few hours after school. He deserves praise for his resourcefulness."

Lark puffed out his chest. "I do at that. I—"

Kit glared him into silence. "He's resourceful, all right. I'll grant him that."

"For heaven's sake, you should be proud of him." She brushed her hand over the desk and blew the sawdust off her fingers. "With all this dust from the construction, we could use help with the custodial duties."

"You might have consulted me, Norah. May I remind you, we haven't enough work to keep our craftsmen busy."

His dictatorial manner honed her anger. She drew herself up. "You can't expect the craftsmen to empty the rubbish. Besides, it isn't often we have the opportunity to hire a worker as clever and enthusiastic as Lark."

"I'm worth ten shillin's a week, I am." Lark jabbed his thumbs at his lapels. "Me and Mrs. R, we got us a bargain. Men and women can work together like equals, y'know."

A lone hammer punctuated the thickness of tension. Kit's taut mouth eased into its naturally sensual slant. "Interesting philosophy," he said dryly, aiming a look at Norah. "I wonder where you heard it."

She pressed her lips together to discipline a smile. "Never mind that. The point is that Lark needs this job. And he is precisely the sort of dedicated employee this shop needs."

A crash sounded from the direction of the office, followed by a muffled curse. The pounding ceased for a moment, then resumed its rat-a-tat beat.

Raking his fingers through his hair, Kit angled a distracted glance over his shoulder. "All right," he told Lark. "Your first task is to go to the Silver Swan Restaurant and fetch the crew sandwiches for their tea. But when you get back I'll want a word with you."

He flipped Lark a coin; the boy snatched it in midair. "Aye, sir." He motioned Kit down and whispered in his ear.

Kit glowered, but nodded. "Out with you."

The boy bolted into the workroom. A moment later, the back door slammed.

Kit lounged against the tall wooden screen, arms crossed, his sinews and muscles rigidly defined. Norah rotated the wedding band on her finger. She wished he had the decency to button up his collar. She wished *she* had the decency to tear her gaze from the glimpse of his teak-hued chest. Even after more than two weeks, she could recall the vivid experience of his kiss, the demanding pressure of his mouth, the invasive caress of his hands. The memory made her oddly light-headed, as if she had been sipping champagne.

Determined to hide her disconcerting reaction, she said, "Would you care for a cup of tea?"

"I was hoping you'd offer."

The white flash of his smile melted her legs. Norah retreated to dip a spoon into the canister of tea. His nearness heightened her senses. The small pot of water bubbled on the spirit lamp. The dryness of sawdust tickled her nose, along with a metallic aroma from the enameling kiln and the rich scent of the tea. In between the construction noise, she could detect the muted sounds of industry beyond the screen—the rasp of files, the hum of conversation, the solid tap of a hammer on gold.

"Well," she murmured over her shoulder, "what was so secret between you and Lark that I couldn't hear?"

"It's no secret. He asked if I was carrying my pistol."

She spun around. Tea leaves scattered over the hot water and onto the tiny oak table. "Pistol! Why would you carry a weapon?"

"Lark and I made a pact the night of the fire." Kit lowered his voice to a murmur. "He agreed to stop following me if I'd keep a gun on me at all times."

"I don't understand. Why was he following you?"

"He had a misguided desire to protect me." A slight quirk of Kit's mouth indicated both humor and chagrin. "From the madwoman of Mayfair."

"The mad*man* from the book?" Realization shuddered through her. "Oh . . . you mean the woman who murdered Maurice."

"Precisely. The boys were following you, too. That's why I got here so quickly that night—Billy spotted the fire from the alley behind the shop."

"Why didn't you tell me this before?"

"We've both been caught up in restoring the shop."

"I see." Slowly Norah set out two china mugs. She had taken Kit's presence that night for granted; he had an uncanny way of appearing whenever she needed him. Another thought quickened her pulse beat. "Did Billy see the intruder? Could he give the police a description?"

"Unfortunately not. The poor lad was in a fine panic when he ran off to fetch me."

She watched the black leaves settle to the bottom of the teapot, swirling like the dark longings inside her. "So Lark and the boys are afraid the murderess might come after me . . . or you."

"Exactly."

"I do hope you corrected them."

Kit prowled the tiny space around her desk. He picked up her loupe, peered through it, then set it back down. "There's a chance they may be right, Norah. It worries me that someone may have intended to hurt you."

In her memory the dark shape leaped from the gloom. She stifled another shiver. "Don't be absurd. It's hardly extraordinary for a jewelry shop to be a target for robbery. I got in the way, that's all."

"He hit Ackerman, too. So the guard couldn't come to your aid."

"Captain Ackerman is back on the job now, so all's well that ends well. I think we should put the incident behind us."

Kit flattened his palms on the desk and leaned toward her. "And what about Wadding's theory? The burglar could have been hired by the murderess to steal an incriminating paper that Maurice left behind."

"All the files were burned, so there's no evidence left. And no further cause to worry. Or to carry a weapon."

"I pray to God you're right. She's already killed at least once. The next time may be easier."

His ominous tone tiptoed like a spider over Norah's skin. The idea of herself in danger seemed absurd, like the melodrama in a six-penny novel. She heated her cold hands on the pot while she poured the tea. "Do you think Lark wanted a job here so he can play constable and track down the murderess?"

Kit sat on the edge of the desk and steepled his long fingers beneath his jaw. "Precisely. He knew I'd try to stop him from interfering. So he appealed to you."

"Well, I think it's sweet of him. We should encourage his desire to help other people, Kit."

A look of smoldering sensuality lit his face. He skimmed his fingertips over the back of her wrist, the sensation so startling and delightful that she nearly dropped her mug. "I'm pleased you've finally decided to end the formality and call me by my first name."

A different sort of chill invaded her, settled in the depths of her belly, and grew as smoky-warm as the tea on her tongue. She banished the feeling. He'd find a noble wife soon, a woman who would bear his children. "We've been working together for weeks," she said crisply. "We needn't stand on ceremony."

"You called me Kit the night of the fire, too."

"Did I? I don't remember," she lied.

"You did."

His confident tone implied an intimacy that made her restless and uncomfortable. She inched toward the brick wall, as far away as she could given the minuscule dimensions of her office. "We were speaking of Lark. I do hope we keep him on."

Kit drained the contents of his mug, making her aware of his strong brown throat and unbuttoned collar. "I suppose there's no harm in his presence. So long as you leave at a reasonable hour, he won't be tempted to linger and get himself into trouble. I'll take you both home."

"Agreed." The arrangement would ease the awkwardness of riding alone with Kit, when the interior of his brougham enclosed them in a shadowed bower. Her nerves were rubbed raw from having spent over a fortnight enduring the occasional brush of his hand against hers, inhaling his male scent, listening to the caress of his deep voice. And trying to fathom why he affected her so.

She curled her hands around the cup and said, "*Do* you have a pistol?"

He reached into his pocket and drew out a pearl-handled gun the size of his broad hand. "Small, but effective in quelling any intruders."

Norah grimaced. "Surely you won't need it."

"It's a precaution, that's all." He tucked the weapon back into his trouser pocket and picked up the moonstone from her desk. Cut *en cabochon*, the jewel shone with a faintly bluish tinge in the gathering dusk. "If nothing else," he added, "maybe I'll stop another thief from trying to steal your gems."

He had every right to say *our gems*. Already he had ferreted out Bertie Goswell and repaid the entire twelve thousand sovereigns plus interest. He had taken charge of reconstructing the damaged portion of the shop. He had gone over the ledgers with his own accountant. Best of all, he had freed her to create and design.

Of late, she had found herself rethinking her opinion of him. Maybe he really *had* changed.

"Moonstone," he said, peering through her loupe at the semiprecious gem. "A form of feldspar?" He looked to her for confirmation.

"Correct. Can you guess where it's from?"

"Testing me again?"

"You seem to enjoy it. So, answer my question."

He thought a minute. "Siam?"

"Close. Ceylon." A sense of loss tainted her artistic pride. "It's to be one of the center stones in the necklace for your parure."

"Perfect. You couldn't have chosen better." Smiling, he rubbed the pad of his thumb over the smooth rounded surface, the motion hypnotizing her. "When will the set be ready?"

She dragged her gaze to his. "In about a week. Thaddeus is working on the bracelet right now."

"May I watch later?"

"If you like."

"We'll look together."

His financial investment granted him the right to pry in the shop wherever he liked. Yet Kit asked permission and included her. Not once had he lorded his superior position over her. More and more she glimpsed the gentleman inside the trappings of a rogue. Rather than reassuring her, the distinction somehow made her feel gawky, overly conscious of her own common background.

Pauvre petite. She is the product of sin. She can never wash away the taint of her bad blood.

"What are you thinking about?" Kit asked. "You look so serious."

"Nothing important." Pierced by his stare, Norah put her teacup down with a thunk. "Shall we go?"

She started out, her skirts brushing him in the small space despite her effort to maintain a distance. He grasped her arm and drew her back into the cubicle, where the screen hid them from the workmen.

"Not until I tell you why I came in here." He lowered his voice. "Norah, you should know—"

A burst of hammering muffled his words. Automatically she leaned closer. "Pardon?"

Kit put his mouth close to her ear. "I found proof in an old ledger that Maurice was deeply in debt when he married you. Fifteen years ago, when he first opened the shop, he made a huge investment. That liability isn't entirely paid off yet."

His breath blew rhythmically against her neck. The warm sensation stole inside her high collar, crept down into her corset, and tingled over her breasts. "I . . ." With difficulty, she absorbed his words. He was saying that nine years of marriage had been founded on the lie of prosperity. "I didn't know that."

Kit snorted in disgust. "I'm not surprised. Doubtless he wanted to impress you with his wealth. I suspect he had too much pride to let his wife think he couldn't provide for her."

The rasp of sawing joined the pounding. The cacophony disturbed her far less than Kit's nearness. She forced herself to think back. "Maurice was a lavish spender, too. He had the finest Saville Row suits, kept a fancy carriage, belonged to the best clubs, entertained his society friends."

His friends. In the tumultuous weeks since the funeral, none had paid more than a duty call. After sizing them up and discarding them as suspects, she had let their names and faces fade from her mind like poorly cut stones.

"Then five years ago," Kit went on, "Maurice

borrowed heavily again when he moved to this location, a more expensive shop.''

''That's about when I began doing much of the design work. He also expanded the stock.''

''That accounts for the disappearance of some of the profits.'' Kit paused, his eyes moody and his expression grim. ''There's something else you should know.''

''More bad news?''

''The one initial investor Maurice hadn't fully repaid is Jerome St. Claire.''

Stunned, Norah sank onto the desk. ''Jerome? He never mentioned Maurice owing him any money.''

''Jerome is the consummate gentleman.''

For once, she ignored his acid tone. ''Dear Blessed Virgin. I'll have to pay him back. How much do I owe him?''

''We owe him six thousand pounds.''

Squeezing her eyes shut, she raised both hands to her mouth. Her sigh wisped between her fingers. ''I feel as if I'm in a pit that gets deeper every time I try to climb out.''

''Norah, don't be despondent. I'll see that Jerome is repaid.''

The independent side of her chafed at the need to ask for more help. Yet when Kit's hand feathered over her cheek, she felt herself drowning in the scandalous desire to turn her head and kiss his palm, to take the pads of his fingers into her mouth and taste his warm flesh.

She snapped her eyes open. How could she yearn for what would only lead to a disgusting experience? Kit wasn't the man for her. No man was.

He stood over her, so close she could see the faint black stubble peppering his cheeks and jaw. His half smile suggested sin and sensuality. Perception gleamed in his brown velvet gaze, a keen understanding that invaded her mind and read her most intimate thoughts.

The impression rattled her. He couldn't possibly have guessed her absurd longing.

Could he?

Breathlessly she admitted, "It seems I'm always depending on you to settle my debts."

"You've already begun to repay me, partner." He tapped her on the nose. "Don't forget the parure."

"Speaking of which, shall we go see Thaddeus now?"

She rose, but Kit caught her arm again. "There's one more thing."

"Yes?" She stared, entranced by the circle of his brown fingers on her tender white wrist.

"Remember the calling card you found in Thaddeus's drawer?"

Between the commotion of rebuilding and the turmoil of working with Kit, she had let the matter slide to the back of her mind. "Yes. From Frederick Gage."

"This morning I paid a call on Mr. Gage." Kit paused, and in the dusky light a shadow seemed to slip over his face. "Thaddeus wasn't looking for another post. Nor was he stealing jewels. He sought Mr. Gage's sponsorship. You see, Thaddeus intends to submit his own design for the Jubilee tiara."

The air slid from her lungs. "Thaddeus, a designer?" The notion jolted her as much as his underhanded action.

"He's a traitor." Kit rubbed the inside of her wrist. "Norah, this gives him another motive for killing your husband. He may have been trying to get rid of a rival, first Maurice and now you. Winnifred could have encouraged him in the matter."

"No, I can't believe that. He's practically my cousin-in-law." She wrested her hand free. "I'll speak to him on the matter."

"Better you should leave him to me. He could be dangerous—"

"No." She turned on her heel before Kit could object. Beyond the screen, long rows of hanging gaslights penetrated the gloom of late afternoon. Sawdust floated on the air. Against the far end of the workroom, the wooden framework for her new

office stretched from floor to ceiling. The crew of four
nailed up the wall planks, steadily enclosing the
space.

As she passed Peter Bagley at his workbench, he
stood up and gestured, his ruddy face disgruntled.
Pointedly ignoring Kit, Bagley said, "Mrs. Rutherford, I need a word with you."

She paused. "Of course."

"I shouldn't be restringing pearls." He waved a
disdainful hand at the lustrous set lying on the
scarred surface of his desk. "I grasp the temporary
need for economy, but we must rehire some of our
employees. This is the work of an apprentice."

Blessed Virgin, what next? She couldn't afford
more trouble. "Lady Muldoon specifically requested
your excellent services. She simply doesn't trust
anyone but you."

His bulbous nose tipped pridefully into the air.
"I'll make an exception this time, then."

As she walked on, Kit whispered in her ear, "Very
diplomatic, Mrs. Rutherford. I would have booted
the old goat out the door."

"And gotten stuck with restringing the pearls
yourself," she murmured dryly.

To her surprise, when they arrived at Thaddeus's
desk, they found Winnifred and Ivy there talking to
him. Light through the wall of windows outlined his
rounded shoulders and his magnificent pelt of wavy
hair. The similarities between him and Winnifred
struck Norah. Of uniform physique, both had brown
hair and hazel eyes. Yet Winnifred looked like a
dowdy crow beside a sovereign eagle.

Ivy waved her lace handkerchief. Behind the
round spectacles, her eyes glowed like aquamarines,
the color youthful against her ancient features.
"Hullo!" she called over the hammering. "Winnie
and I rode here on the omnibus. I sat beside the
most fascinating man, an actor from the Savoy Theatre—"

"Humph." Winnifred brushed her black gloves as
if they were soiled. "Rubbing elbows with the com-

mon folk. All because we can't afford to keep a carriage.''

"Oh, don't be a prune on such a splendid occasion, Winnie. We've come to take tea at the Silver Swan. Won't you join us, Norah?'' Like a bright-eyed wren, Ivy dipped her head. "You too, Lord Blackthorne.''

"Thank you,'' Norah said, "but his lordship and I have already had our tea in my office.''

"Alone?'' Winnifred elevated a bristly eyebrow. "I hardly think that's proper. Especially with a man of dubious reputation.''

"Come now, Miss Rutherford,'' Kit said, his voice low so that no one beyond their small group could hear. "Even *I* would stop short of ravishing your cousin-in-law where anyone could walk in on us.''

Winnifred went beet-red. "Can you blame me for worrying? Her reputation reflects upon myself and dear Ivy. Time was when Norah stayed home, where she belongs. People are whispering about your unseemly partnership.''

The warmth of Kit's hand at her waist gave Norah the courage to ask, "Who is whispering? I should like to know their names.''

"A lady never repeats gossip.'' Winnifred thinned her lips in a virtuous line.

"Then the people you overheard must not have been ladies,'' Kit said dryly. "Ergo, we can ignore their small-minded comments.''

"Gossip is a lamentable pastime of society,'' Thaddeus murmured. "If one ventures into a hornet's nest, one must expect to get stung.''

His bland gaze wandered over Norah. At one time she would have thought his words an innocuous comment on rumormongers; now she wondered if he also jeered at her effort to perform a man's job.

"There'll be no more innuendos in this shop.'' The hard edge of Kit's voice sliced through the construction noise. "Should I hear anyone sully Mrs.

Rutherford's name, I shall teach him the error of his ways.''

He glanced around the group. Thaddeus stood aloof, Winnifred grumpy, Ivy round-eyed.

Kit's gallantry glowed inside Norah. How would she carry on once he left, as he surely would someday? To cover her confusion, she stepped toward the workbench. ''Mr. Teodecki, Lord Blackthorne would like to view the bracelet.''

The craftsman clicked his heels. ''As you wish, my lord.''

On the scarred surface of the desk lay a spool of silver wire, along with needle-fine pliers and a file. The loose-weave bracelet was stretched out and nearly finished. Pebble-sized moonstones studded the filigree work, like luminescent orbs scattering the heavens. Between the moonstones, diamond chips formed tiny stars.

''Oh my,'' Ivy said, a white handkerchief clutched to her crape bodice. ''How very pretty. It reminds me of teardrops on lace.''

Winnifred curled her lip. ''Silver? How common. And the diamonds are rather modest.''

''You've a keen eye, dearest.'' Thaddeus stroked his pointed goatee. ''It's no inconvenience to replace the chips with larger diamonds, my lord.''

Norah detected a hint of superciliousness in his tone, as if he would have designed a more elaborate parure. Misgivings assaulted her. Had she ventured too far in the unconventional design? *She* liked the airy feel of the jewelry, but would a noble-bred debutante prefer heavy gold and thumb-sized diamonds? Of course, maybe she wouldn't care as long as the gift came from Lord Kit Coleridge.

Kit stroked his brown finger over the delicate bracelet. ''This is perfect. I wouldn't alter a single stone. Your workmanship is superior, Mr. Teodecki.''

He bowed. ''Thank you.''

''My lord, you must have a special lady in mind for so . . . interesting a piece,'' Winnifred observed.

Kit merely smiled, a wolfish quirk of his mouth that roused a spasm of unwanted curiosity in Norah. Why was he so secretive? Because the parure was destined to grace his chosen wife, she thought. He must be waiting to disclose her name until the announcement of their betrothal.

Disliking her contrary emotions, Norah focused on business. "If it's no inconvenience, Mr. Teodecki, I would like a word with you alone."

He arched an eyebrow. "Of course, Mrs. Rutherford."

"But our tea—" began Winnifred.

"We promise to keep your fiancé only a few moments," Kit said. "If you ladies will excuse us."

"I don't mind waiting," Ivy said. "Norah, may I walk around and look at all the lovely jewels?"

"Yes. Please, make yourselves at home."

Ivy gaily waved goodbye. Winnifred clutched her black reticule and glowered.

"We'll go to the vault," Norah said. "At the moment it's the only place where we can speak privately."

She led the two men out of the workroom and down the gaslit passageway. The carpeting muffled their footsteps. As she unlocked the vault, she glimpsed several customers browsing the elegant showroom beyond the passage. At least the storm of scandal seemed to be abating. Over the past few weeks, more and more clients had come trickling back.

She entered the vault. Kit closed the door, and blessed silence reigned. After lighting the brass lamp on the table, he crossed his arms and leaned against the drawer-lined wall.

At least they wouldn't have another quarrel over who would direct the interview, Norah thought. She didn't know whether to be relieved or nervous. Clasping her damp hands, she looked at Thaddeus, who was waiting by the door. The yellow light cast shadows over his thin features crowned by a sweep of brown hair.

"Mr. Teodecki, I understand you've had dealings with Frederick Gage."

His face blanched. He lifted his hand halfway, then dropped it to his side. In a hollow tone he said, "How did you find out?"

"Never mind that. I know you're planning to submit a tiara of your own design for the royal commission. And you needed the sponsorship of a respected jeweler."

"Yes. I have little money of my own and no means to purchase the necessary stones." His voice was stiff, his shoulders squared.

"Why did you not ask me or Maurice to help you?"

His lips compressed. His eyes flashed with anger. "I did so, just before Christmas. But Mr. Rutherford insisted that I devote myself to making the jewelry. He said that developing my own style would distract me from my work, perhaps so much that I would be tempted to make alterations in your designs."

Norah understood his resentment. From the distance of time, she could see that Maurice had cared for only his own interests. How dare he stifle the need to create rather than craft? She kept her expression neutral. "How long have you been designing?"

"For years, a little bit here, a little bit there." He made a dismissing motion. "Small pieces I sold to insignificant shops."

"Until you approached Mr. Gage four weeks ago," Kit added.

"Yes." Thaddeus held himself with the hauteur of a king. "He offered to hire me, but I felt . . . I could not leave Mrs. Rutherford, considering her recent tragedies."

"How noble of you," Kit drawled.

Thaddeus ignored the sarcasm. "Even Miss Winnifred did not know of my plans until recently. I had hoped we might at last . . ." He lowered his eyes.

He had hoped to earn enough money to marry Winnifred. The unspoken words softened the pain of his betrayal.

Yet Kit's frown reflected the suspicions clawing at Norah's mind. In his quest to win the commission, had Thaddeus stolen the South African diamond? Had he murdered Maurice in a fit of fury? Beyond Winnifred's word, Thaddeus had no alibi for his whereabouts on New Year's Eve.

He bowed to Norah. "If you will excuse me, I will pack my belongings now and leave." His back straight and his face composed, he reached for the doorknob.

"Wait," Norah said on impulse.

He eyed her warily. "I have committed no criminal act, I swear so on the holy bones of St. Stanislaus. If you mean to call in the police—"

"No, I don't." She looked to Kit for guidance, but his stony expression offered no clue to his thoughts. If Thaddeus left now, she knew, the ill feelings would linger. When he and Winnifred married, she might never see them again. Winnifred might even influence Ivy to move out. Exasperating as they sometimes might be, they were Norah's only family. "I would like you to stay on at Rutherford Jewelers."

Thaddeus gaped at her. "But . . . how can I? I have made myself your rival."

"I expected competitors. The Princess of Wales will make her own choice."

A moment of silence ticked away. He bowed his head. "You are not like your husband, Mrs. Rutherford. I am ashamed to have deceived you."

Norah took a step toward him. "You've been a diligent employee and a superb craftsman. If you prefer to work for Mr. Gage, then go with my blessings. But I should like to give you the freedom to design, too. So long as you vow never to lie to me again."

Thaddeus stood unmoving. Then with surprising suddenness, he crossed to her, bent on one knee, and pressed his lips to the back of her hand. The bristly brush of his goatee tickled her skin. In a choked voice, he said, "May God reward you for your kindness. Of course you have my word of honor."

His courtly gesture was oddly reminiscent of Lark kissing her hem. For the second time that day, she found herself embarrassed and deeply touched. "I would be delighted to see some of your designs later," she said, drawing her hand free. "For now, though, please escort Winnifred and Ivy to their tea."

He rose. Moisture glinted in his eyes. "You will not regret your decision to trust me." He strode out of the vault, closing the door behind him.

Her throat felt thick, her eyes hot. She took a calming breath and turned to Kit. His moody frown and stiff pose invaded the sensitivity inside her, brought an unwelcome start of dismay.

"You don't approve," she stated.

His expression eased into a heavy, heated smile; his black lashes lowered into a lazy perusal of her. "On the contrary," he said, "I'm glad you have a tender heart."

Every time she tried to summon dislike for him, he caught her off guard. "Then why were you scowling?"

"I'm wondering why you can soften toward other men and not toward me."

The wistful curve of his mouth suggested vulnerability. Lamplight gleamed off his black hair and midnight eyes, making him impossibly attractive. The memory of the last time they'd been alone in the vault came flashing back, the aggressiveness of his kiss, the hardness of his body, the warmth of his embrace. A peculiar weakness spread through her, the sensation akin to the breathless wonder she felt on viewing the crown jewels. With effort, she reminded herself that he wanted to conquer her, to chalk her name off his list of challenges.

"If I've acted unduly harsh toward you," she said, "please forgive me. Personal feelings have no place in our business arrangement." Her words sounded stilted, even to her own ears.

His solemn expression held a bleak quality that made her chest ache. Abruptly he said, "You were sixteen when you married Maurice, were you not?"

She nodded. "But what has that to do with our partnership?"

"From what I've gathered, the marriage was arranged."

"Yes, by the Mother Superior." Lest he misunderstand, Norah added, "I did have a choice. I could have refused the offer."

"So why didn't you?" Kit pushed away from the wall and strolled toward her. "Why did you marry a man twice your age, a man you hardly knew?"

She forced herself to hold her ground against his advance, even though panic nipped at her composure. "I wanted to escape the convent. I wanted . . ."

Kit stopped mere inches from her and pressed one palm on the table. "Wanted what?"

His faint aroma of musk unfurled like tendrils of fire around her senses. She blurted, "I wanted something I never had: a family of my own, lots of children to love."

"You and Maurice never had any children."

He breathed the comment on a soft note of sympathy. Untimely tears blurred her eyes. Blinking hard, she looked down at her wedding band. "No. And a gentleman wouldn't say so."

"Come now, we're friends." The gentle nudge of his fingers brought her chin up. "You could marry again, Norah. You could have a second chance."

The brilliant rays of unfulfilled dreams illuminated her mind; firmly she slammed the door on impossible hopes. She stepped back and shook her head emphatically. "Never."

"Never?"

"You heard me. I've no wish to surrender my independence to an autocratic man."

His fingers drummed the table. "Marriage needn't be a prison. Not if you choose the right man. Tell me what qualities you'd require in the ideal husband."

She hugged her arms to her bosom. If only he knew that for her, marriage had been worse than a prison. Never again would she endure the degradation of physical coupling. "This conversation is absurd."

"Perhaps, but humor me." His mouth easing into a dazzling smile, he added, "Please?"

He looked so appealing, so exotically handsome, her heart seemed to melt downward, to puddle in a slow, warm pulse beat in her loins. The strange sensation disconcerted her. How could she feel drawn to him when she knew the ultimate intimacy he would demand of his mistress?

Yet she focused on the shiny wall of drawers beyond him and found herself saying, "I would want a man who shared my interests in jewelry and art, a man who would treat me with the respect of a friend. He would be my knight in shining armor, a man of untarnished honor and faithfulness. He would commit his heart and soul to me, and never hurt me . . ."

Her voice soft and unguarded, she faltered to a stop. Her gaze strayed irresistibly to Kit and she found him watching her, one arm propped on the other, his fingers framing his perfect cheekbone. A paragon. The description jolted her. If she didn't know better, she might have thought *him* a masterpiece, the ideal of masculinity.

"Suppose you find that man?" Kit asked. "Would you change your mind about remarrying?"

A miserable emptiness opened inside her. The raw and painful feeling startled her; she thought she had adjusted to the course of her life, by letting her career as a jewelry designer fulfill her need for happiness and worth. But suddenly her soul cried out for more. She ached to share her lonely life with a caring husband and a houseful of children. The futility of her longing clenched in her breast like a fiery knot. On the ragged edge of emotion, she almost blurted, *What's the use? I can't conceive. No man wants a barren woman.*

Her near-slip mortified her. She sidled away from Kit, away from his tempting warmth and the fantasy that could never come true. "Excuse me. I have work to do."

Blindly she stormed out of the vault. How foolish to voice her broken dreams to a rake of the caliber of Kit Coleridge.

She headed for the sanctuary of her makeshift office. Thaddeus and the Misses Rutherford were nowhere to be seen. The hammering had stopped; the laborers sat on sawhorses, drinking their tea and munching sandwiches. Lark perched in their midst, gesturing and talking, no doubt earning indulgent grins for his imaginative tale.

Restless and aching, Norah plunged into her cubicle. The sight of a parcel on her desk penetrated her distress. Frowning, she picked up the package. Printed in black letters was the address: Mrs. N. Rutherford, Rutherford Jewelers, Bond Street.

The paper crackled as she unwrapped it to find a leather jeweler's case stamped *RJ* in Romanesque type, the shop's trademark. Had someone returned a defective piece?

She opened the case. In a nest of crimson velvet lay an egg-sized brooch that looked vaguely familiar and frankly sentimental. The minute pastoral scene depicted a willow tree with a raven weeping seed pearl tears. A small ivory sarcophagus sat beneath the tree.

Mourning jewelry. Grimacing, she touched the stiffened leaves, made of gray human hair. She had never understood the popularity of keeping morbid relics of the deceased.

Why would someone send the brooch to her?

Norah turned it over in her hands. No inscription embellished the gold back.

Spying the tiny hinges, she found the clasp and flipped it open with her thumb. She recoiled as the contents spilled out.

Chapter 11

A short while later, Norah studied the faces of the people assembled around her desk. Thaddeus frowned in concern, Winnifred pursed her lips in disapproval, and Ivy blinked in perplexity as she twisted her lacy handkerchief around her gnarled fingers. Lark hovered in the entry to the cubicle, his eyes agog as he hopped from one foot to the other in an effort to see past Winnifred's thickset form.

Kit's swarthy palm cupped the dull metallic gleam of gold. But he ignored the brooch and studied the silver and brown strands scattered over the oak desk.

"You're certain that's Maurice's hair?" he asked Norah.

"Yes." Now that the initial shock had passed, she could speak calmly, without the shuddering queasiness in her stomach. "If you've any doubt, the engraving inside the brooch should convince you."

One black eyebrow edged upward as he read the inscription: " 'Whose hair I wear, I love most dear. Maurice Rutherford, 31 December 1886.' "

"Oh my." Ivy reached beneath her spectacles to dab at her eyes. "It was never meant to honor my brother's demise. Maurice made the brooch himself thirty years ago, as a remembrance of our parents' passing. It was the very first piece of jewelry he ever crafted. I wore it to church every Sunday, until it was stolen."

Aha, Norah thought. So that was why the brooch had looked familiar.

Winnifred snorted. ''The brooch wasn't stolen, Ivy. You lost it out on the street somewhere, just as you lost your hat last week. Given half a chance, you'd misplace your own head.''

Ivy's lip quivered. ''That isn't true. Someone filched my precious memento.''

''I see. A footpad walked into our house, ignored the silver and jewels, and went straight up into your chamber to take a near-worthless brooch, did he? How ridiculous can you be—''

''Stop your bickering.'' Norah's patience snapped. ''Clearly the brooch wasn't lost, Winnifred, because someone took it to play this cruel trick on me.''

The air reverberated with tension. Lark poked his head past Winnifred, the whites of his eyes vivid against his street-rough features. In a dramatic whisper he said, ''It ain't just anyone. It's 'er. The madwoman o' Mayfair.''

''Madwoman?'' Thaddeus craned his neck to glare at the boy. ''You surely cannot mean the female who murdered Mr. Rutherford.''

''Aye, I do.''

Hearing her own suspicion voiced aloud jarred Norah. Dear Blessed Virgin. Why would someone go to the trouble of stealing the brooch and delivering it to her? Even worse, who would clip a lock of Maurice's hair, then hold on to it for so many weeks?

A chill slithered over her skin and dampened her palms. Someone who loved him? Or someone who hated him?

''Hush, Lark,'' Kit said, glowering at the boy. ''Miss Ivy, when did you first notice the brooch was gone?''

''Last November seventeenth.'' Setting her chin as if to dare Winnifred to disagree, Ivy added, ''I remember especially, since it was Marmalade's ninth birthday.''

Kit snapped the brooch shut and placed it on the

desk. "And no one here saw the piece again until Lark found the packet on the back step?"

In unison, they all shook their heads.

Lowering his gaze, Lark scuffed the toe of his boot over the carpet. "I should've been quicker fetchin' the tea," he muttered. "I might've nabbed the bloody bitch."

Winnifred harrumphed. "Watch your language, young man."

A red flush augmented the misery on his face. "Beggin' yer pardon, mum."

"Winnifred, I'll chastise my own employees, thank you." In a softer tone, Norah added, "Lark, you had no way of knowing what was inside the parcel."

"But I thought 'twas a odd place t' leave mail." He scrubbed his nose on his sleeve. "I should've gone lookin' down the alley at least." He hung his head lower. "Maybe you'll be wantin' Screeve t' work 'ere instead o' me. If I ain't gonna be no use—"

"Your job is not to chase down criminals," Kit broke in. "You may return to work now. There's sawdust an inch thick in the new office."

"Aye, sir." His gloom visibly lifting, Lark dashed out.

Thaddeus opened the brooch with his thumb. He studied the inside inscription through Norah's loupe. "This lettering was done by an amateur." His slight sneer as he set the brooch down conveyed his opinion of the artisan.

Curious, she leaned forward. "Why do you say so?"

"The engraving tool slipped a fraction on the R, and the loops on the eights and the six aren't uniform."

"May I see?" She picked up the piece. In her initial paralysis, she hadn't thought to scrutinize the jewelry for clues. "Heavens, you're right."

"An excellent observation, Thaddeus," Kit said. "That may help identify the culprit. Miss Ivy, do you mind if I keep the brooch for a few days and show it to the police? I promise to take especial care of it.''

"Of course," she said. "I trust you completely, my lord."

Kit pocketed the brooch. "Mrs. Rutherford and I will look into this matter. You may go now."

Winnifred and Ivy filed out, Thaddeus bringing up the rear. At the door Ivy turned back, a spry figure swathed in mourning, her wrinkled cheeks snow-white against the black crape of her gown. She shook a motherly finger at Norah. "Please don't tarry here too late, dear. It simply isn't safe."

Suppressing a shiver, Norah watched Ivy leave. What if she were the one? Could her guileless features hide a cunning mind? Had she only *said* she misplaced the brooch? If so, she was an actress worthy of the Savoy Theatre.

Then had Winnifred purloined the brooch? When Maurice's body had been laid out in the parlor, had she crept downstairs in the dark of night and snipped a few strands of his hair? The gruesome image left Norah cold and uncertain. Grumpy or not, Winnifred wasn't a furtive woman. She stated her opinions in plain terms.

And what about Thaddeus? He possessed the tools to engrave the brooch. Had he left deliberate flaws in the inscription as a way to point the finger of suspicion away from himself? After all, he'd be the one to notice the defects. Could he desire the Jubilee commission so much he'd kill Maurice, then try to frighten her with a malicious gift?

The gentle pressure of Kit's hand moved over her back. "I'm sorry you have to suspect your own family, Norah."

His massage dissolved her reserve. Yielding to temptation, she turned to rest her head on his shoulder and let herself absorb his strength. Friendship, she thought. Surely there was no danger to her fragile emotions in accepting friendship.

"Oh, Kit. Each of them had the opportunity to

slip the parcel out the back door while we were in the vault.''

''I know, dammit. I know. But anyone could have left the box on the back step. An errand boy, for instance.'' Tension flowed from him, a tension reflected in the tightness of his arms around her. ''Jesus God. I wish I could *do* something. This whole bloody mess infuriates me.''

The steady rise and fall of his chest brushed her breasts in a way that tantalized her nerves. The haven of his arms became a prison. She abandoned his embrace and picked up the black leather jewelry case lying on the desk. ''There's something I almost forgot in all the uproar.'' She snapped open the lid. ''The brooch came in this box. It's lined in crimson velvet.''

''So?''

''So our cases are done in white. Remember the South African diamond that Maurice was supposed to deliver on the night he was murdered? When he checked the box after finding it in Ivy's sewing things, I caught a glimpse of the interior. That case was lined in red, too. And it was the same size and shape. Someone must have altered one of our boxes by switching the lining.''

Kit took the container from her and brushed his finger over the velvet. ''Interesting. If this is the same case, it could prove the murderess also stole the gem. But why would she send you the brooch?''

''Because she resents me.'' Norah looked down at her wedding band, her heart as heavy as the gold on her finger. ''Because she was Maurice's mistress.''

''Perhaps. Then again, perhaps not.''

At the odd note in his tone, Norah tilted her head back. His eyes as black as midnight, he scowled at the screen separating them from the rest of the shop. ''Who else would play such a frightful trick?'' she asked.

''I can think of one other person.''

The thinning of his mouth sparked a hot flash of comprehension. "You don't mean . . . Jane?"

"I do, indeed. Pranks are her specialty."

Norah stared. "Are you saying *she* killed Maurice?"

He slowly shook his head. "Even as avaricious as she is, I can't imagine her killing a man."

"Then how would she get the brooch and the red-lined case? And when did she clip a lock of Maurice's hair?"

Grimacing, Kit pushed the hairs from the desk into the rubbish bin. "Jane is remarkably resourceful. God knows, she had her chance to steal the jewel and cut his hair when she was alone with his body."

And how cleverly she enticed Kit back into her web.

Norah fought down a surge of resentment. She knew the answer before she even asked, "So what will you do?"

"Go see her, of course."

"What the devil is going on here?"

Kit spoke from the doorway of the morning room. His unbuttoned overcoat revealed a tailored suit of charcoal-gray. He shook a familiar necklace, the stones and metal rattling. His expression fierce, he stalked forward like a predator invading the sunny room with its rosewood paneling and sheer lace curtains.

Norah's teacup clattered onto its china saucer. She pushed back her chair by the window and stood. "Why are you here so early? You don't usually call for me until eight o'clock." She glanced beyond him. "Where's Culpepper?"

"Back in the pantry. I told him I'd show myself in." Kit stopped before her and opened his hand, the stones spilling over his large palm. Sunlight struck the delicate silver trelliswork and ignited purple fire in the amethysts. "Answer me, Norah. Why the devil is your necklace displayed for sale in the front window of our shop?"

A sleepless night had chafed her nerves raw. His dictatorial tone rubbed salt into the wound. She poked her index finger at his broad chest. "Stop shouting at me. Better *you* should answer *my* question."

"What question?"

"The one you haven't given me a chance to ask yet. What happened in your meeting with Jane? You said you'd come by yesterday evening, after you'd spoken to her."

His scowl eased a fraction. "I said I'd *try* to come by."

"I waited up until after midnight. How long does it take to ask a simple question? It would have been considerate of you at least to send me a note."

"Please accept my apologies." He dropped the necklace onto the lace tablecloth; it landed between the salt cellar and a sterling toast rack. "Jane was out and didn't return until late. I thought you'd prefer me to wait rather than wake you at three o'clock in the morning."

"You were with Jane Bingham until three? What were you two doing?" Heat rushed over Norah's body. Quickly she amended, "Pardon me. I don't believe I want to know."

A wicked gleam lit his dark expression. He feathered his fingers over her cheek. "Jealous?"

She backed up a step. "You may dally until dawn with whomever you like. I'm only anxious to know if Jane sent the brooch."

He released a weary sigh and passed his hand over his face. "She claims she didn't. I think she's telling the truth."

So he was still susceptible to Jane's wiles. "She's a born liar. How can you be sure of her?"

"If she were lying, she wouldn't have looked me straight in the eyes. She would have tried to distract me."

Norah rubbed her arms beneath her black shawl. She could well imagine the manner of that distraction. Controlling another rise of hot jealousy, she said, "So what do we do next?"

"Let the police handle the matter. Wadding will take the brooch around the city and try to find out who did the engraving."

"That could take days."

"Then you have plenty of time to tell me about the necklace."

Oddly embarrassed, she turned from his stern gaze and crumbled the cold crust of her toast. "I'm selling it."

"That's obvious. The question is, why?"

"I should think you'd know why. I can no longer afford extravagances."

He slapped the table; china rattled. "Good God, Norah. You needn't give up your personal jewels."

"Why do you care if I do or not?"

"Because I know how much you value jewels."

"I shouldn't wear them, anyway. At least not until my first year of mourning is up. By the strictest rules, the amethysts are too ostentatious even for the second year of half mourning."

"Come now, do you truly care so much for convention? I'd hoped you were becoming a more free-thinking woman, Norah." His voice lowered to a caressing murmur. "The amethysts look so lovely against your skin. Remember the day you wore them, when you came to see me after the fire? I neglected to tell you then, but you should always wear black velvet and jewels."

Her heart tumbled, both at the compliment and his implication. She'd worn the amethysts when she'd asked him to invest in her shop. Now his tone suggested a latent immorality in her act, as if her purpose had been to entice him.

"I'm selling the necklace and that's that. I won't be beholden to you for a single penny more than necessary."

He reared back, his face a mask of displeasure. "Ah. So you'll borrow my money, but you want nothing else to do with me."

"I want us to be friends, too."

"Do you?" His eyes bleak and cold, he shoved his hands into his coat pockets. "Then why do you shun me at every turn? Does it degrade you to associate with a half-caste?"

Startled, Norah shook her head. "Your heritage has nothing to do with this discussion."

He slanted an eyebrow. "Then you're not ashamed to be seen with me?"

"Of course not. What a bizarre notion."

"Is it?"

The penetrating quality of his gaze made her wonder what he was thinking and feeling. He reacted so strongly to any slight, real or imagined. What had happened in his past to make him so sensitive? The question perched on the tip of her tongue, but she was afraid to ask it, afraid to open herself to acknowledging his deepest emotions, afraid to strengthen the bond of friendship already linking them.

He leaned toward her, attracting her with his earthy male scent. "Beginning Friday next, there's a special exhibit at the British Museum, featuring gemstones from every corner of the empire, in honor of the Queen's Jubilee Year. You'll go with me to the gala opening."

Her lips parted with an automatic rejection. Recent widows didn't attend public functions in the company of a male nonfamily member. Especially not a man whose illicit romantic affairs had placed him outside the circle of acceptable society.

But if she refused him, he might think his skin color offended her. She couldn't bear to hurt him. In her most private self, she adored his exotic looks. She had to curl her fingers to keep from touching his warm flesh, from stroking the strands of onyx hair that had slipped onto his brow, from tracing his high cheekbones and the strong brown column of his neck.

A wild leap of excitement lodged in her throat. Dear God, she wanted to accept. She wanted to at-

tend the glittering engagement with Lord Kit Coleridge as her escort. The strength of her longing
shocked her. "I'll go," she heard herself say.

He flashed his most beguiling smile. His eyes
glinted with too much triumph for a man who had
looked so heart-meltingly vulnerable only moments
before. "I'll be looking forward to our evening together, Norah."

The gray-haired matron in puce velvet spied Norah
and Kit, stuck her sharp nose in the air, and deliberately veered off into the throng of people at the
British Museum.

Norah had but an instant to wonder at the slight
when Kit steered her straight into the pudgy woman's path. "Why, Lady Romney," he said in a voice
as smooth as pudding. "What a delight. I haven't
seen you in ages."

Unable to avoid them, her ladyship gave a stiff
nod, her multiple chins jiggling. "We hardly frequent the same social circles. I didn't know *you* took
an interest in gemstones."

"I do now, since Mrs. Rutherford and I have become partners." His placid tone didn't fool Norah.
She could feel the rigidity in his muscles where she
held on to his arm. He added, "May I introduce you
to Mrs. Norah Rutherford?"

Mumbling something in between a greeting and a
harrumph, Lady Romney lifted her lorgnette and examined Norah, up and down.

"I'm pleased to meet you, my lady." Determined
to ease the tension, Norah went on, "I see you've
shopped at Rutherford Jewelers. I designed the Ori-
ental pearl collar you're wearing."

Lady Romney clutched her throat as if the jewels
choked her. "I purchased it *before* the scandal." As
if in afterthought, she added, "A pity about your
poor husband."

"Your rudeness is the greater pity," Kit said, his
voice low yet cutting. "One day you'll learn some
manners."

"Well! You always were an impertinent young man." Her fat cheeks flushed, and she shook her lorgnette. "I intend to write to your stepmother about you. I always did feel sorry for her, forced to accept a half-caste as a stepson." Turning, she flounced off in such haste that her bustle bounced on her overstuffed rump.

Norah seethed with resentment. "How dare she insult you."

"The countess of Romney does as she pleases," Kit murmured in Norah's ear, so that none of the other guests could overhear. "The family might count William the Conqueror among their ancestors, but her husband is a drunken lout. Passed out cold last week on the floor of the House of Lords. It proves she's no judge of character."

Despite his attempt to make light of the cut, Norah felt troubled by the chilly reception of icy stares. She clung to the crook of his arm as he led her past haughty duchesses and monocled gentlemen, giggling debutantes and dandified swains. The jeweled hues of ladies' evening gowns wove a spectacular pattern threaded by the black suits of the men. The newfangled electric lighting made the gems on the women sparkle—the ruby-studded necklaces, the floral sapphire earrings, the diamond bowknot brooches.

A few ladies gazed boldly at Kit, and Norah wondered if he had known any of them intimately. Her stomach clenched. Perhaps she shouldn't have come, even with Ivy and Winnifred and Thaddeus trailing somewhere behind as chaperones. People undoubtedly took malicious delight in recounting the scandal of Maurice's death, and the appearance of his widow with the notorious marquis of Blackthorne.

Her cheeks heated. She ducked her head. No doubt everyone assumed she was Kit's mistress.

Mistress to a man with half-Indian blood.

The thought jerked her chin up in a fit of prideful anger. Why let the opinion of these supercilious aristocrats deflate the excitement that had buoyed her all week? Let them trade their mean-spirited rumors. She would enjoy her outing with Kit. More to the point, she would enjoy the exhibition.

Stately columns soared to the high ceiling and led her gaze upward to the classic moldings. Her senses expanded with the echo of voices and the smell of perfume, with the heady delight of viewing the gems. Table cases centered in four spacious rooms displayed the permanent collection of minerals, while the special exposition filled the glass-fronted cabinets around the perimeter of the rooms. The white electric light glinted off a huge chunk of reddish-brown cairngorm from Scotland, and beside it the Eureka diamond, the first diamond found in South Africa.

"A black opal from Australia," Kit said, stopping before a case.

On a bed of white satin, the egg-sized gem sparked mysterious flashes of red and violet inside its midnight depths. "I've never seen one so large," Norah breathed. "A pity we don't sell more opal jewelry. People believe the stone to be unlucky."

"I prefer to think we make our own luck." His voice deepened to rough silk. "Better a man should pursue his heart's desire than wait for the whims of chance."

"And what's a woman to do?"

"Whatever the man tells her."

She would have challenged him, but his tone was teasing. He cocked one eyebrow at a lazy angle. A heavy heat flooded her veins. Flustered, she turned from his mesmerizing gaze. She could feel the tautness of Kit's arm muscles beneath her gloved fingers. Dimly she noted that Winnifred and Ivy and Thaddeus had vanished into the multitude of people.

The throng parted. A rotund man came into view, trailed by a retinue of uniformed men and elegant women. A close-cropped beard and mustache framed his pale features and heavy-lidded eyes. His perfectly tied cravat was anchored by a leek-green peridot of at least ten carats.

Awe left Norah speechless. Queen Victoria's heir. Edward, the Prince of Wales.

"Ah, Blackthorne," he said.

Kit bowed. "How good to see you again, Your Highness."

"I was beginning to think you'd stabled yourself with those racehorses of yours. You even missed Daisy Brooke's reception last week."

"I must beg your pardon, sir. I've been occupied with business matters of late. Jewels, to be precise."

Edward examined Norah with a torpid stare that drifted from her styled red hair to the hem of her black velvet gown. "One jewel in particular, I see. And who might this gem of femininity be?"

Kit covered her hand on his arm. With surprise she realized he was staking his prior claim. She had heard the prince was as ardent a womanizer as he.

"May I present my business partner, Mrs. Rutherford?" Kit said. "She's the brilliant designer who made a success of Rutherford Jewelers."

Glowing with pride, she sank into a deep curtsy. "Your Highness."

The prince waved her up. "An artist? How unusual to make the acquaintance of a lady as talented as she is charming." His gaze strayed to her bosom. "Your necklace quite suits your flawless complexion."

"Thank you," Norah said. "I understand Princess Alexandra favors amethysts."

"Quite so."

"May I suggest," Kit put in smoothly, "that you pay close attention to the tiara Mrs. Rutherford designed for the Jubilee competition? The center gem will be the fabled lavender diamond, Fire at Midnight."

If, Norah thought on a jab of misgiving, Upchurch ever answered her telegrams. She was beginning to worry that the agent had absconded with her money.

The prince perked his graying brows. "Indeed?

By gad, I saw the very stone when I was in India ten years ago. It was owned by a maharaja . . ."

"The maharaja of Rampur," she said.

"Yes. We shall be anxiously awaiting the chance to view your entry, Mrs. Rutherford. If it's half as magnificent as you are, we'll be pleased indeed."

His gaze absorbed her in another blatantly interested sweep. Edward was a married man. His lax moral standards disturbed her, and made her wonder if Kit would also be unfaithful to the woman he wed.

"Blackthorne, do keep in touch. And a pleasure to meet you, Mrs. Rutherford." Edward walked away, followed by his retainers.

Kit focused his moody dark eyes on her. "Well. He admired you. That should stand you in good stead for the competition."

Giddy as much from the meeting as from the terseness of Kit's voice, she couldn't resist teasing, "How enchanting a man he is. Perhaps I'll have the good fortune to renew our acquaintance."

Kit drew her to a deserted corner, between two tall cases. "Norah, be careful where you flirt. Bertie might just take you seriously."

"Jealous?" Reckless caprice spurred her. "Are you afraid I might desert you, my lord, in favor of a prince?"

His handsome face tautened, as if he struggled to master the black storm cloud of his emotions. As quick as a flash of white lightning, he rolled back his head and chuckled. "By God, I can hardly believe it."

"Believe what?"

"You're trying to make me jealous. I'll construe that as a heartening sign."

She gave a delicate snort. Plucking a tartlet from the silver tray of a passing footman, she nibbled at the buttery crust. "Your male conceit overwhelms me. Perhaps I do find His Highness most fascinating."

"Fascinating enough to sleep with him?" Kit said

into her ear, his breath stirring her hair. "If a bed-mate appeals to you, I'll be happy to oblige."

Chills whispered over her skin. Yet somehow the sensation added a sparkle of excitement to the facets of her emotions. Trying to act nonchalant, she took a tiny bite of the tartlet, the damson sweet on her tongue. "Can't a man and a woman simply be friends?"

"Certainly. But it's also natural for them to want more." He grasped her hand, his thumb moving in slow circles over her palm. "Let me tell you what every man thinks when he looks at you, Norah. He wants the chance to undress you, to kiss your smooth white skin, to take you naked into his bed and—"

"What a charming tête-à-tête," spoke a man's voice from behind. "Blackie and the woman in black."

Norah jumped guiltily. For a moment the silken bond of Kit's words held her eyes snared to his. As she watched, the torrid look on his face chilled to arctic hauteur. Curious as to who could elicit the powerful dislike in him, she turned.

A striking, blond-haired couple posed by the ma-hogany wall case. The man wore a slim black suit that accentuated his noble features. A thumb-sized ruby stickpin held his snowy cravat, and a scar lifted one of his eyebrows at a perpetual slant.

Lord Carlyle. With a shiver, she recalled his ar-rogance when he visited her shop. He had been cruel to his own mother.

His companion gave Norah an even more un-pleasant jolt. Clad in peacock-blue satin, the Hon-orable Jane Bingham wore a necklace of sapphire flowers and golden leaves. The feathered aigrette adorning her hair had been mounted *tremblant*, so the sapphire and diamond doves appeared to quiver whenever she moved.

"Bruce." His voice tightly controlled, Kit looked from Lord Carlyle to the woman. "Good evening, Jane. This is a surprise."

"Indeed, my lord?" She held herself as straight and proud as a queen, though her lips pouted. "I'm hardly one to sit home. I have a busy social schedule, you know."

"I meant," he said almost gently, "that I was surprised at your choice of a companion."

"All those beastly tales you told me about dear Bruce were nonsense. In fact, you can be among the first to admire the pretty necklace he gave me." She stroked the piece, then aimed a coy glance at Norah. "It came from Garrard's, the crown jeweler."

"It's lovely. I've seen a number of flower motifs tonight." Pedestrian, Norah thought. *She* would have rearranged the stones into an airy waterfall, a cascade of sapphire teardrops . . .

Lord Carlyle smiled at Jane. "You deserve the best, darling."

Norah studied them with a jaundiced eye. They seemed the consummate couple, as prettily matched as brother and sister. Yet the way Jane fluttered her lashes and cooed at him seemed almost an act. Because she still harbored feelings for Kit?

Had she left the mourning brooch? Maybe Kit was too biased, too ready to believe her. Because he still wanted her.

Tautness defined his mouth and cheekbones. Some unknown problem plagued him. Norah absently finished the tartlet, the damson now tasteless. If he regretted losing Jane . . .

Lord Carlyle's frosty gaze stung Norah. "Where are your manners, Blackthorne? You haven't introduced me."

"Pardon me. Mrs. Rutherford, may I present Lord Carlyle. Carlyle, Mrs. Norah Rutherford."

His lip curled into a faint sneer beneath the blond mustache. "Ah yes, I remember now. The shopkeeper."

Norah suspected he had recognized her from the start. Deep down, his dismissing tone hurt, made her conscious of her common background.

"I see you aren't mourning your poor murdered

husband," Jane said. "Have the police caught the murderess yet?"

The acidity beneath her sweet tone angered Norah. "No, but Kit has been kind enough to help me with the investigation."

Jane laughed. "I know how Kit helps women."

"Odd how no one but you saw the woman in the red cloak. I wonder if you might have been"—Norah deliberately paused—"mistaken."

The superiority vanished from Jane's pretty features. "Do you dare call me a liar?"

"Please, ladies," Kit cut in, with a warning glance at Norah.

Restraining her temper, she vowed to act the lady. She turned to Lord Carlyle. "I haven't seen your mother in the shop lately. I trust she's well?"

For no discernable reason, he scowled. "The viscountess has retired to the country for a time."

"She has a fine eye for jewels. She would have enjoyed the exhibition tonight."

"She's in mourning." His critical gaze raked her black gown. "*She* would have kept to the privacy of her home."

Norah kept her chin high. "Will she return for the Jubilee festivities in June?"

"No." Even as he uttered the curt reply, he swung to Kit. "I say, have you been to the zoology gallery at the other end of this floor? I seem to recall a display that might interest you—stuffed monkeys from India."

Jane tittered behind her gloved hand. "Oh, Bruce. Now don't be naughty."

Kit's arm flexed beneath Norah's fingers. Sympathy wrenched her. For a man of strength and confidence, he was unduly affected by slurs about his skin color.

Just as she herself was sensitive about her bastard birth.

"You never give up, do you, Bruce?" Kit said. "You must be anxious for that matching pair of eyebrows."

"Tut, tut, Blackie. Don't parade your vulgar ancestry in front of a roomful of well-bred people."

On impulse Norah stepped between the two men. Dear God, she had had enough of bigots, this one in particular. "*You* are behaving in a vulgar manner, Lord Carlyle. What a shame a sweet lady like your mother must suffer an insensitive lout for a son."

His mouth opened and closed. His eyes narrowed to blue crystal chips.

Norah whirled and slid her hand into the crook of Kit's arm. "Shall we continue our tour in the next room, my lord? I hear there's a fine collection of lapis lazuli from Afghanistan."

As she marched him toward the archway, she heard Jane's shrill voice chastise Lord Carlyle: "For the love of God, will you allow a commoner to address you so rudely . . . ?"

The crowd noises swallowed the rest of the tirade. Fueled by the remnants of fury, Norah tugged Kit along. People turned and gaped, but she paid them little heed. Her lungs ached from the effort to contain her uncorked emotions. As she started toward the display cases, Kit steered her in the opposite direction.

"What are you doing?" she demanded.

He quailed in mock fear. "God save me," he growled in her ear. "Are you going to snap at me, too?"

She glared, then a gust of humor blew away the steam of her anger. Half of her was mortified at her waspish outburst; the other half reveled in the memory of Bruce's speechlessness.

Her lips tweaked into a smile. Kit strolled out of the mineral exhibit and through the high-vaulted lobby, leading her past the display of a gigantic tortoise shell. A few elegant guests milled about, conversing and studying the artifacts along the walls.

He glanced around, then lifted the crimson velvet rope barring entry to a shadowed room.

"What *are* you doing?" she repeated, half-laughing.

He waggled his eyebrows. "Come along and you'll see."

He waved her under the rope. Too giddy to protest, she ducked into the chamber. Gloom lay thick there, gathered in murky puddles around the skeletons of long-dead reptiles. Ahead, the bones of an enormous fossil gleamed white, luring her deeper into the darkness, until she could reach up and brush her fingertips over its long curved tusks.

Kit loomed behind her, a tall silhouette in the half light. Suddenly conscious of how alone they were, she murmured, "Is this a mastodon?"

"Yes." Glancing at the specimen, he grasped her upper arms. "Norah, I'd like to know why you defended me."

His satin-soft voice floated through the dimness. She could discern the outline of his face, the breadth of his shoulders. Away from the crush of people, the air held a wintry chill, but she felt uncommonly warm.

To avoid his question, she turned the focus on him. "Kit, have people always snubbed you because of your Hindu heritage?"

He stiffened. "Do they? I hadn't noticed."

"Don't prevaricate, please. I'm interested in hearing about your past."

He stood silent for a moment, as if struggling with an inner demon. "I suppose you deserve to know, but where shall I begin?" With a brusque laugh, he went on, "I know. There once was a girl who shunned me, a girl I thought I loved with all my heart."

"What did she do?"

Norah listened in sympathy and dawning anger as he told her about the fourteen-year-old boy who had admired a nymph from afar, and about Emma Woodferne, who had delighted in the gifts left by a secret admirer, only to recoil when she learned his identity. In an emotionless voice, Kit described her disgust and scathing rejection, then the brother and his cronies who had thrashed Kit in retaliation.

Norah heard the rage and pain beneath his nonchalance. She felt her own wrath boil over, scalding her throat, and she reached out impulsively to cup his warm cheeks. "Oh Kit, I'm sorry. I'd like to meet that callous bigot and . . . and slap her face."

Unexpectedly he chuckled, the sound rippling like rich music through the darkness. "There you go again, defending me. Tell me why you keep doing so."

His adept return to their own relationship disconcerted her. "We're friends," she said. "You did the same for me when Winnifred repeated gossip."

"*Are* we only friends?" His thumbs made gentle strokes over her inner arm. "Tonight you showed me the spark beneath your ice. It makes me think you truly care for me."

"Think no more. I dislike bullies, that's all."

He stood unmoving. She could hear the faint buzz of voices from the rooms beyond, could feel the inviting heat of his body and the shivery caress of his hands. "I warned you the night of the fire," he murmured, "that if ever you gave me the slightest encouragement, I'd kiss you again."

She had known. She had known from the very instant he ushered her into the darkness that he meant to kiss her. The truth washed over her in a warm wave, drowning any protest she might have uttered, drowning even her resolve to avoid the loathsome prospect of physical closeness.

He caught her against his chest. The night obscured all but the dusky shape of his features and the tiger-bright burn of his gaze. For one breathless moment he held her, his fingers smoothing the fine hairs at the nape of her neck. He was giving her the chance to retreat, she knew. But the siren call of curiosity drew her, along with the urge to explore the secret longings he roused in her. For too many lonely nights, she had tossed and turned with her inability to explain why he fascinated her so.

Surely one kiss would break the spell. One kiss and no more.

As if wrapped in the misty magic of a dream, she slid her hands over the fine fabric of his coat and up to his strong jaw. "Kit?"

His arms tightened; his fingers plunged into her hair, dislodging a few pins. "My God."

Need wrenched his voice in the instant before his mouth covered hers, slanting downward with sweet, seductive pressure. The warm wooing of his tongue made pleasure flow like molten gold through her veins. She strained upward on tiptoe and reached for the shining world of passion he offered.

The kiss went on and on, an eternity of heaven, yet he felt as solid to her as the earth. Then his mouth left a moist path over her cheek and down to her throat. Threading her fingers through his silky hair, she tilted her head back, the better to feel his fevered kisses. He blew gently against her dampened skin, and prickles danced over every inch of her, even the hidden places under her gown. His large hand reached beneath her necklace and warmed her bosom; then he worked one long finger into the cleft of her corset until he brushed the sensitive peak of her breast.

Awareness exploded inside her body. A moan rose from a place so deep and dark she hadn't known it existed. The wanton sound shocked her half back to reason. "Kit, stop. Please stop."

"Shush." He caught her protest with his mouth. His finger stroked once more over her nipple before he removed his hand. "Don't be frightened, Norah. I only want to show you pleasure."

"Anyone could walk in and see us."

"Is that all you're worried about?" He rubbed his cheek against hers, so she felt the faint brush of stubble. "God, I want you. I don't care who knows it."

Moving his hands beneath her bustle, he cradled her hips against his own. Despite the layers of clothing, she felt the pressure of his maleness, as firm and thick as an oak branch. Her legs quivered with untimely weakness and impossible longing. Even more shamefully confusing was her desire to reach between them and curl her fingers around his hard length.

His lips tenderly tasted the side of her neck. "Let me make love to you, Norah. Let me give you the ultimate joy."

She felt herself sliding into the hot liquid spell of his voice, like a nugget of gold melting into a mold, guided by an expert craftsman. She caught herself on the final plunge.

The ultimate joy? There was no joy in *that*. He wanted to beguile her. He wanted her to forget the burning pain until it was too late to stop his invasion.

The wingbeats of panic fluttered against her rib cage. A sob strangled her throat. "No!"

His hands flexed. "What—?"

She thrust hard at his chest, yanked herself free, and ran.

"Norah!"

She ignored his low-pitched call. Cool air rushed against her hot cheeks. Moisture burned her eyes. She fled past the shadowy shapes of animal skeletons. The swift tap of her feet echoed the hammering of blood in her ears. She must escape the dangerous lassitude that threatened to smother her. She mustn't allow Kit Coleridge to reshape her brilliant future.

Chamber after chamber sped past in a dizzying fog. An occasional skylight spilled a silver stream of moonglow, making the fossils come alive, their eye sockets staring at her, their bony limbs stretching out.

At last a sharp pain in her side forced her to halt. She leaned against a glass case, squeezed her eyes shut, and tipped her head back, until the fire in her lungs subsided.

When she lifted her lashes, a shadow seemed to soar overhead.

Norah gasped, then laughed at her own foolishness. An ancient creature hung from the ceiling, its great skeletal wings spread wide in perpetual flight.

Inside the rows of glass cases, stuffed birds nested in the gloom. She could no longer hear the hum of conversation in the distance. She must have run far from the gallery of minerals.

In a corner of her heart, bitter disappointment lurked. Kit hadn't bothered to follow her. He must have been unaffected by the kiss that had caused a quake in the bedrock of her beliefs.

She had thought herself free at last. But the chains of her newfound desire for him choked with frightful, baffling intensity. How could she yearn for his embrace when she knew—she *knew*—the disgusting finale to their caresses?

In return for her surrender, he would not even offer her the dubious reward of marriage.

Petticoats rustling, she slowly retraced her path. She had been to the museum before, but only to view the Elgin marbles and other antiquities on the ground floor. She had never ventured into the zoology exhibits. Needing time to collect her scattered senses, she wandered past the fossils and attempted to fasten up her disheveled hair. But she had lost too many pins, and her curls flowed in an unruly mass over her shoulders.

An arched doorway led her into a murky chamber with towering white pillars and plastered walls. Here lay specimens of insects, cocoons spun by silk moths, an exotic spider's huge web, clay nests built by African ants.

Something scraped in the next room. Her heart leaped in mingled hope and alarm. A footstep.

"Kit?"

Her voice sounded hollow in the cavernous space. Walking cautiously toward the direction of the noise, she passed a porticoed doorway and found herself in a lofty staircase hall.

A grouping of stuffed black bears reared by the back wall, their giant teeth yellow, their claws washed pale by the moonlight coming through a bank of windows.

Shivering, Norah rubbed her arms against the chill of the night. Her nerves were overwrought. She must have imagined the sound. The museum lay as still as a tomb.

An iron balcony overlooked the gloom of the first floor. She hesitated by the newel post and peered down the broad marble steps. She hadn't passed by here earlier. She was lost.

Should she turn around and grope her way through the labyrinth of rooms? Or should she head downstairs and find another exit?

A vast loneliness enveloped her. Contrary to good sense, she ached to feel the security of Kit's arms enclosing her. What was wrong with her, that she could want him so desperately?

She started to turn back. At the edge of her vision, one of the bears sprang to life. Its feral eyes glittered in a rush of movement.

A scream burst from her throat. The black shape barreled at her, knocked her off balance. She snatched at the iron railing, but her fingers lost the anchor.

"Norah." Her name drifted from afar, like a distant dream.

She felt herself falling down the stairs. The moonlit windows wheeled before her eyes. Pain erupted inside her head. She plunged into darkness.

Chapter 12

D amn, which way had Norah gone?

Kit strode through the north gallery of the museum. His footfalls rang hollow on the wood floor. He passed shadowy cases of toads, lobsters, and crocodiles with maws opened in eternal ferocity. A swordfish hung from the ceiling, in a school of sharks and conger eels and other marine reptiles too large for the display cases.

With every step, Kit flailed himself. He shouldn't have let her rejection of him hurt. He shouldn't have told her that embarrassing episode about Emma Woodferne. He shouldn't have stood there like one of these great stuffed beasts and watched Norah dash into the maze of rooms. He should have followed her instantly.

Damn. He had pressed her too hard with his lust. He had driven her to the brink of tears. Distracted by her allure, he had forgotten his vow to go slowly, to woo her into returning his love.

Yet the memory of her slim body in his arms, the way she had returned his kiss with fire and longing, made his regrets ascend into jubilation. Norah wanted him. No matter how she protested, deep down she felt the same passion as he.

His problem lay in convincing her of his sincerity and overcoming her fears. And in his ability to show her pleasure where she had known heartbreak. A tide of anger crested inside him. Damn her inept husband—

A scream broke the quiet. A female scream.

He pivoted sharply. His elbow struck a giant crab shell mounted on a pedestal. The display teetered, then crashed like cheap pottery to the floor.

Heedless, he yelled, "Norah!"

From the distance came a series of thumps. Then silence.

Kit was already running. His heart thundered as fast as his feet. He shot into another shadowed room.

He cast a frantic look around. The gloom held only cases of nests and webs and insects.

Please God, let the scream have been an illusion. A trick of the eerie surroundings, a prank played by his strung-taut nerves.

"Norah? Norah, where are you?"

Only the harshness of his own breathing answered. On the far side of the chamber loomed a doorway. He pounded through the opening and skidded to a halt. A staircase hall. To his left, arched windows emitted silvery moonlight. To his right, a collection of bears clawed at the gloom.

He hastened to the head of the steps. On the small landing, where the stairway made a ninety-degree turn, lay a puddle of darkness. Paleness gleamed against the inky heap.

A face against a black velvet gown. Framed by a pool of red.

"Norah." Her name emerged from him in an agonized moan.

Kit leaped down the steps, three at a time. He slid onto the marble landing and caught at the hard iron rail to steady himself. One of her arms draped her breast; the other splayed outward on the marble, palm up. The amethyst necklace gleamed against her white bosom.

Dropping to his knees, he gently pressed his finger to the silken skin of her throat. A faint pulse beat rewarded him with a surge of dizzy joy.

He ran his hands down the length of her motion-less form. He could find no visible sign of injury. But she might have fractured a bone, cracked her skull . . . or worse.

He brushed back the curly strands of hair from her face. His hands shook, making his movements clumsy. Her eyes were closed, her lashes like deli-cate fringe against cheeks bleached of color.

Praise God he saw no blood. The dreaded red splash had been her unbound hair.

He lightly rubbed her cheek. "Norah, darling. Wake up. Speak to me."

She lay deathly still. Worry choked the breath from him. Christ, she couldn't die. She couldn't. Not when she shone like a radiant purpose in his aimless existence. Not when his love for her had never had the chance to flower.

He cupped her neck. "Norah, please hear me. Talk to me. Please, please say something." His voice sounded rusty, thickened.

Her chest rose and fell in a sigh. She swayed her head back and forth. Her lashes stirred; then she looked straight up at him. "Kit?"

He restrained the urge to yank her up against him, to guard her close to his heart. He contented himself with stroking her satiny cheek. "I'm here, darling. I'm here."

She lifted her hand to her brow. "My head . . . hurts."

"You've had a nasty fall. Lie still now. I must go fetch a doctor—"

"No!" She caught at his coat sleeve and strained to pull herself up. A shaft of moonlight illuminated her eyes, green as emeralds. "Kit, don't leave me alone!"

Her vehemence wrenched him. "Calm down," he murmured. "You may have fractured a bone. You mustn't move until you've had medical help."

He tried to press her back down, but she squirmed so much he was afraid of hurting her. "I'm fine," she insisted. "There's something I have to tell you—"

"Are you in pain? Show me where your head hurts."

She batted away his hands. "Please stop fussing. I'm bruised, that's all."

"You're not a doctor. You could have suffered a concussion. Or an injury to your spine. Christ, Norah, if you think I'll take any more chances with your life—"

"That's why you mustn't leave me." She braced herself on her elbow. "Kit, someone pushed me."

"What?" he whispered.

She pointed toward the second floor. "I was standing up there, at the top of the stairs. Someone jumped out of the shadows by the bears . . ." A violent shiver shook her.

He tore off his coat and draped it around her shoulders. Fear and fury squeezed his chest. "Are you absolutely sure?"

"Of course I'm sure. I might have banged myself on the head, but I know what I saw."

"Was it a man or a woman?"

"I don't know. Just the dark shape of a person."

He sprang up, drew the pistol from his pocket, and put himself between Norah and the second floor. He scanned the darkness, the cluster of bears beyond the iron balustrade and the corners where the shadows lay as thick as black treacle.

No movement. No gleam of eyes. No hint of someone still lurking there.

"Kit, be careful."

"I am. Did this person look like the intruder who broke into the shop?"

"I don't know," she murmured. "It happened so quickly."

Christ, he'd been careless. Thaddeus and Winnifred and Ivy had attended the exhibit tonight. And a host of people like Bruce Abernathy who resented a man of mixed blood occupying an exalted position in the Upper Ten Thousand.

But why would someone who hated *him* strike out at her?

Jane. Maybe he'd been wrong to believe her protestations of innocence in the mourning brooch incident. And she *was* the only witness to the murderess in the red cloak.

Yet surely she hadn't vanished long enough the night of the New Year's Eve party to kill a man.

One fact settled like a cold rock in Kit's belly. The incident tonight proved his suspicions. Whoever had murdered Maurice Rutherford now meant to kill Norah.

"Do you see anyone?" she asked.

He swung around to find her sitting up. "No. The coward must have run off." Christ, he wouldn't shed this nervous feeling until he got her away from this hall of bones and corpses. "Can you stand?"

"Of course. I'm not an invalid."

Crouching, he slid his arm around her waist and gently helped her to her feet. A cry tore from her, icing his soul. She sagged against him.

"For God's sake! What's wrong?"

"My ankle gave way."

"Does it hurt?"

"A little."

But he could see by the pinched tightness of her mouth that she was minimizing the injury. Anger at the person who'd hurt her swelled inside him like a foul tide. He scooped her into his arms and tightened his muscles around her slender weight.

She clung to his neck. Her scent of roses wafted over him. Her curly hair formed a fiery nimbus in the moonlight, and for one mad moment he saw himself laying her down in a private corner, reaching beneath her velvet skirt and petticoats, and giving her the rapture of life . . .

Ashamed of the untimely fantasy, he closed his mind to all but the need to protect her. He started down the stairs, his footsteps a harsh echo in the mammoth hall.

"Shouldn't we go back upstairs?" she said. "Ivy and Winnifred will be worried."

"I'm sorry, Norah, but we can't afford to trust them. We can't trust anyone until we learn the truth."

He thought she would protest, but she merely rested her head on his shoulder, as if she were too weary to hold it upright. When they reached the shadowed ground floor, she looked at him again. "Where are we going?"

"To the safest place I know."

"But . . . where is that?"

"My house."

Norah awakened to hazy sunlight and a spring garden.

Groggy, she lay beneath the coverlet and studied the four-poster bed with its silk hangings, the fabric abloom with lilacs and roses against a cream background. Draperies of the same floral pattern covered a wall of windows, though light seeped through the cracks to spread a soft radiance throughout the room. In her sleep-drugged mind, the cloth exuded the rich aroma of its flowery print. Until she turned her head and noticed the vase of pink hothouse roses on the nightstand, and beside it, her amethyst necklace.

A coal fire burned in the grate. Near the bed, a uniformed girl sat in an overstuffed chair, her russet head bent over the shirt in her lap, her needle flashing in rhythmic strokes.

The events of the previous night came rushing back to Norah. The dark shape bursting from the shadows. The horror of falling. Kit cradling her in his arms. Kit. Thank God for Kit. He hadn't let go until he had settled her here in his guest bedroom. The doctor had diagnosed a sprained ankle. He had administered a dose of laudanum. That must be why the haze in her mind felt so thick.

The ticking of a clock drew her attention to the marble mantel. She squinted at the gold hands.

Frowning, she squinted again. One o'clock? Surely not.

She cautiously wriggled into a sitting position. Soreness throbbed in her stiff muscles. She winced from the pain that stabbed her ankle.

The rosy-cheeked servant set down her mending and dashed over to prop up the pillows. "Bless me, you slept long and good, m'lady."

"I'm not . . ." Norah paused in confusion. How crass to deny she was a lady. Her head ached dully, making it difficult to think. "I'm Mrs. Rutherford. What is your name?"

"Betsy, mum."

"Is the mantel clock correct, Betsy?"

"Right as rain. Mr. Peacock checks all the clocks, 'isself every morning." Betsy went to the window and drew back the heavy curtains. Sunlight flooded through the sheer lace panels and gilded the elegant furnishings. "Of course, 'e didn't come in this morning. The master gave orders you wasn't to be disturbed."

"I see." Where *was* Kit? Norah swallowed the question.

Betsy approached the bed. "I'll 'elp you to the necessary room."

By leaning on the servant and hopping on her uninjured foot, Norah reached the doorway. Light through a jewel-toned window illuminated a cozy boudoir decorated in purple and ivory.

"Thank you. I can manage from here."

"Are you sure? If I didn't see to your needs, the master'd lop off me 'ead." Her smile denied the gruesome threat. She gestured at the claw-footed tub. "Might I run a bath? A good long soak'd do your soreness good."

Norah wondered what version of the truth Kit had told his staff. Her stomach twisted. Betsy acted so matter-of-fact. Doubtless it was no extraordinary event for the marquis of Blackthorne to have a female guest spend the night.

Oh, dear heaven. Another unpleasant thought

tiptoed into Norah's mind. Her hard-won reputation lay in shreds. People would shake their heads and whisper about her bad blood. No one would believe her stay here had been innocent, despite the impediment of her injury. Yet, oddly, she felt only a twinge of regret. The opinions of society mattered less to her these days. Her heart ached for Kit, for the boy who had suffered the rejection of a cruel girl, and for the man who even now endured the narrow-minded judgments of hypocrites like Lord Carlyle and Lady Romney.

Norah realized Betsy stood waiting. "I'll bathe later," she murmured. "I'd like some tea first."

"Straightaway, mum." Betsy started to go, then turned back. "I near forgot. Two ladies been waitin' downstairs all morning. The one said she wouldn't budge till she saw you."

Winnifred, no doubt. And Ivy. Knowing she would have to parry Winnifred's sharp tongue sooner or later, Norah sighed. "Give me a moment, then send them up, please."

"Yes, mum."

Norah limped into the bathroom. The grape-hued carpet cushioned her bare feet in luxury. Moving gingerly, she availed herself of the convenience, then hobbled to the white sink with its gold faucets and the spigot in the shape of an arched dolphin.

Handsome but decadent, she thought, running her fingertip over the shiny metal. Just like the master of the house.

She washed her hands and face, and dried herself on a thick ivory towel. Then she gripped the cold porcelain sides of the sink and leaned toward the oval mirror. Dear Blessed Virgin. She looked like a hussy after a long night.

One of Kit Coleridge's hussies.

Her hair poured in a riotous red river around her shoulders. Her eyes retained a sultry, sleepy expression. She wore a nightgown of cream-colored silk so fine it revealed the coral shadows of her nipples. Lace hugged the neckline and short sleeves, and

flowed like a bridal train down her back. The exquisite stitchery must have cost a fortune. She tried to
recall who had put it on her, but the effects of the
laudanum fuzzed her mind. Surely Kit hadn't
helped her. Had he?

She blushed over every inch of her body. Then a
disagreeable notion struck away her embarrassment.
This gown must belong to one of Kit's lovers. Jane?

Norah reached in distaste for the buttons at the
back, but stopped. Her own gown had vanished.
Sheer silk won over the prospect of wearing nothing
at all.

A greenish-yellow bruise kissed her jaw. A similar
discoloration graced her left forearm. Her heart
lurched with remembered terror. Against her closed
eyes, she saw the black figure running at her, relived the hard thrust that knocked her off balance,
felt herself falling . . . falling . . .

Then Kit's voice: *I'm here, darling. I'm here.*

She wrenched open her eyes. The dizzy sensation
diminished, though her head still ached and her
stomach felt queasy. Someone wanted her dead. The
realization caught her in a web of horror. She dared
trust no one. No one but Kit. Taking a deep breath,
she pulled herself from the sticky tendrils of fear.

Darling, Kit had called her. She resisted his allure,
yet the endearment curled around her like a soft
blanket.

Limping back into the bedroom, she found a
dressing gown draped over the foot of the bed. She
picked it up, plunged her arms into the sleeves, and
tied the belt tight.

A knock sounded. As Norah swung around, nee-
dles of pain pierced her ankle. She grabbed at the
bedpost. ''Yes?''

The door opened. Kit stuck his head inside. His
jet-black hair and dusky skin formed a striking contrast to his snowy cravat and topaz coat. His doeskin
breeches fit as snugly as a second skin, and outlined
the muscles of his thighs.

Her legs seemed to melt. His perfect grooming

made her even more conscious of her tousled state of undress. "I'm sorry, but I can't see you now—"

"For God's sake, Norah." Silver tea tray balanced on his palm, he strode into the bedroom. "The doctor warned you not to put weight on that ankle."

She clutched the edges of her robe with one hand. "I feel fine," she lied. "Besides, I'm leaning on the post."

He set the tray on the bed. Before she realized his intent, he hoisted her into his arms in a giddy repeat of the night before. "Lean on me instead, partner."

His male aroma made her head reel. She moistened her dry lips. "Kindly put me down."

His stern mouth eased into a decidedly sinful slant. "As you say. I consider it my duty as host to see to your every comfort."

He carried her across the room. Sinking to one knee, he lowered her to a chaise lounge in a sunny spot by the window. With the familiarity of a lover, he arranged the folds of silk around her legs, then checked the wrapping on her ankle.

"The swelling is down."

"I told you I felt better."

"So you did." His midnight gaze traveled from her bare toes back up to her face. "Do you know, this is the first time I've seen you wear anything but black? You look ravishing."

Then ravish me. Norah clamped down on the stupefying thought. Yet she couldn't stop the memory of his kiss from blooming in her mind, the firm pressure of his lips, the sweep of his tongue inside her mouth, the brush of his fingertip over the bare skin of her breast. Despite wisdom and reason, she wanted his hands to explore her body. Her flesh tingled with the temptation to touch him, to be touched by him.

I want you, he'd said last night. *I don't care who knows it.*

Somehow he aroused the same passion in her, Norah reflected in confusion. He stirred cravings no true lady ever felt. Yet his kiss also made her feel clean and good, not filthy and sinful. Somehow he made her want the obscene intimacy of the marriage bed she had just escaped.

"Well!" Winnifred's outraged voice exploded like a pistol shot.

Peering over Kit's shoulder, Norah saw her cousin-in-law sail into the bedroom, followed by Ivy. The women looked like twin crows in their crape-trimmed mourning gowns.

Norah yanked the lapels of her dressing gown together. She could see the picture of scandal through their eyes: she in her scanty garb and Kit kneeling beside her. Even worse, she had been contemplating the very act that society would condemn them for committing.

But she had done nothing wrong except dream of happiness. She raised her chin. "Good afternoon, Winnifred. And Ivy."

"Oh, my dear." Ivy trotted forward, her face pale beneath the frothy lace cap. She twisted a handkerchief, the lace embroidered with tiny black crosses. "Last night, when we received Lord Blackthorne's message at the museum, Winnie and I came straight here. But he sent us on home. I could scarcely sleep for worrying about you."

Fondness flooded Norah's heart. "I'm much better now."

Winnifred arched an accusing eyebrow. "You don't appear to be suffering from any grave injury. His lordship gave us to believe you couldn't be moved."

Rising with easy grace, Kit went to the tea tray on the bed. "My physician said Norah's ankle is badly sprained."

"Lord Blackthorne told us you tumbled down the stairs at the museum." Ivy bent to Norah and grasped her hand. "Oh dear, you have a nasty bruise on your face. I feel horribly responsible."

Kit spun around, the bone china cup pale against his dark fingers. "Responsible, Miss Ivy? What do you mean?"

His sharp tone speared Norah. Dear God, he considered her sister-in-law a suspect. Ivy's spidery fingers clung to Norah. Despite the parchment quality of her skin, her hand felt wiry and strong, capable of giving a person a violent shove. Norah tried to put Ivy's age-creased face onto the shadowy figure of her nightmares. But the vision eluded her.

Ivy blinked her aquamarine eyes at Kit. "Why, I should have noticed her hem was too long. I would have been happy to shorten it."

Winnifred snorted. "Might we change the topic to one more pertinent than sewing? We've come to escort Norah home, where she belongs."

His jaw set, Kit delivered the cup of tea to Norah, then took a stance by her. "She's staying here. Now, would either of you ladies like a cup of tea?"

His calm voice surprised Norah. She started to protest, then looked at Winnifred's sturdy hands strangling the cord of her reticule. Was she the killer? Could she have lurked in the darkened museum, waiting for the chance to leap out and strike?

The possibility quaked through Norah. Warming her icy palms on her cup, she sipped slowly at the tea and studied Winnifred's face, now mottled with red.

"Do you think I could drink tea when you propose such a scandalous arrangement?" Winnifred sputtered. "Lest you forget, my lord, Norah is a lady in mourning. Even you should see the folly in letting her reputation be blackened."

"The folly would be releasing her from my protection. You see, someone pushed her down that staircase."

His words dropped like dark stones into the sunny silence.

Ivy gasped. "Why, that's a sin. She could have been killed. I can't imagine who would be so wicked."

"I told you something dreadful had happened, Ivy." Winnifred swung to Norah. "Who did you see? Tell me, and I'll give the name to Inspector Wadding.''

"It was too dark. I only remember a black silhouette darting from the shadows.''

"I must have frightened the person off," Kit added.

Winnifred lifted one thick brown eyebrow. "Didn't you bump your head, Norah? Poor dear, you may be confused. When we get home, I'll brew you a hot tisane, rosemary and peppermint.''

"I know what I saw," Norah stated quietly. "No headache remedy will alter that.''

Kit folded his arms over his broad chest. "So you see the necessity of keeping her here, under my guard.''

Winnifred stood as stiff as a bird of prey poised to strike. "Do you dare suggest Ivy or I committed the evil act? I'm staggered by your accusation.''

"I'm not accusing you. I merely won't take any chances. Don't forget, someone murdered Maurice.''

"Yes, in this very house." Winnifred stabbed a finger at him. "So much for Norah's safety.''

"Is this the room where my brother passed on?" Her voice quavering, Ivy glanced furtively around.

"No," Kit said in a softer tone. "That happened in the master bedroom.''

"Humph," Winnifred snorted. "As if a different bedroom will keep Norah safe. Pardon me for saying so, your lordship, but how can *I* trust *you*?''

"You'll have to. I give you no choice.''

"Then I shall move in here. Someone must chaperone Norah.''

"You needn't worry yourself," Kit stated. "I've taken care of the matter.''

Norah tilted a startled glance up at him. The chaperone was news to her.

"How so?" Winnifred demanded. "I should like to know this woman, to make certain her character is above reproach.''

He placed his hand on the back of the chaise

lounge and moved closer to Norah. "Enough questions. As I said, you'll have to trust me." His voice rang with steely command.

The starch left Winnifred's spine. Her shoulders drooped into a curious facsimile of Thaddeus's posture. Gripping the reticule, she looked at Norah. "Have you nothing to say?" she murmured. "Lord or not, he cannot force you to remain here. If you leave now, we may yet salvage your reputation."

Ivy dabbed the corner of her eye with her handkerchief. "Oh, do come with us, Norah. Marmalade and I miss you so dreadfully."

Norah cradled her cup to keep her hands from shaking. She couldn't stop reliving the horror of that shove, the panic of the long, long fall into oblivion. And now she knew the depths of hell—the despair of losing faith in the people closest to her. She was aware of Kit's nearness, the strength of his doeskinclad legs, the toughness of his body. His indomitable aura of security held an enormous appeal.

"I'm staying."

Winnifred's lips pinched. "Will you blacken Maurice's memory and bring ridicule to your family? You think only of yourself."

Norah sadly shook her head. "Maurice managed to shame himself. I won't accept responsibility for his actions."

"Well! Do not expect the rest of us to fall into the den of iniquity with you. Come along, Ivy."

"Oh, dear," said Ivy. "At least you seem happier here, Norah." Sniffling into her handkerchief, Ivy padded to the door like an obedient dog.

Winnifred stopped short, then strode back to Norah. "I nearly forgot. This arrived by the early post."

As if it disgusted her to touch Norah, she dropped a letter on the chaise lounge. Turning on her heel in military precision, she marched out, Ivy bringing up the rear and closing the door.

Tears flooded Norah's eyes. There went her only relations. Exasperating as they might be, she had grown to love both women, to smile at their eccentricities and to cherish their companionship. Guilt mingled with her grief. How could she mistrust them?

Kit bore away her cup, then sank to his heels beside the chaise and gave her a napkin to wipe her eyes. "I'm sorry you've been forced into this predicament, Norah. But you made the best choice, your only choice."

"Did I?" Bitter regret plagued her. "What if we never find the person who pushed me? This estrangement could last forever."

"Try not to worry." He took her hand and gently rubbed her wrist. "In the meantime, I'll find out the truth somehow. I promise you that."

His steady gaze seemed too wise, too cognizant of her private thoughts. She felt uneasy and strange sitting here in the bedroom with him, as if they were husband and wife discussing how to discipline a laggardly parlor maid. Pulling her hands free, she picked up the letter. Surprise joined the upheaval in her emotions. "It's posted from India. It must be from my agent, Mr. Upchurch."

She tore open the envelope. A single sheet of paper fell into her trembling fingers. Quickly she scanned the thick black script. The bottom dropped out of her stomach. "Oh, no."

"What does Upchurch say?" Kit asked.

"It isn't from Upchurch—it's from a man named Thomas Leach, the district head for the principality of Rampur. The local telegraph office told him about my wires, because no one there has heard of Upchurch. And Leach says the maharaja is gone."

Kit frowned. "Gone where?"

"Here. He's sailing to England on his yacht. To attend the Queen's Jubilee celebration."

"Hell, that's good news."

"No, it isn't. Not if he left Fire at Midnight back in India." The enormity of the dilemma set her head to pounding again. She rubbed her brow. "Oh Blessed Virgin. Whatever happened to Upchurch?"

"Maybe he's on his way back to England. He might even be traveling with the maharaja."

"And if he's not? Kit, the competition is only two months away. And last night we bragged to the Prince of Wales about using the stone."

"We'll purchase another gem."

"There isn't another stone like Fire at Midnight." She lifted her despairing gaze. "It's matchless, the only known lavender diamond."

He rose and took the letter. "Norah, don't fret over this, too. Your health and safety are foremost. I'll look into the matter of the diamond."

His casual attitude lit the fuse of her anger. Didn't he understand what the commission meant to her? The pinnacle of her career, the chance to accomplish something in her own right? "I'm not *fretting*. This commission is vital to my future."

"It's only one sale. If you lose it, there'll be others. I'll see to that."

The gap between them loomed like an abyss. For all her years of training to be a lady, she would never attain his nonchalance about wealth and position, the attitude inherited from centuries of nobility. She had worked hard to carve her own niche in the competitive world of jewelers. And she had survived the painful task of laying her dreams of love and family to rest. She wouldn't—she couldn't—let her hope for success die, too.

She levered up from the chaise and snatched the letter back. "For once, you're not taking care of matters for me," she snapped. "This is *my* problem, and I'll solve it."

His face darkened. "It's our problem. We're partners, remember?"

"Then if you wish to be of assistance, kindly fetch my gown. I must try to find out when the maharaja is arriving." Ignoring the pain in her ankle, she swung her legs to the floor.

He pressed her shoulders back against the cushions. "The side seam of your gown was ripped, and the housekeeper is repairing it. Even so, you're in no condition to go anywhere.''

He was right, but she would never admit it. His handsome face loomed close, his gold-flecked dark eyes shining like fire at midnight. She blazed with the desire to kiss his beautiful mouth. Her appalling lust ignited the explosive mix of her emotions.

She crushed the letter into a ball. ''So you finally have me trapped. The instant you saw me helpless, you carried me off to your house.''

He jerked back. ''What else was I to do? Leave you to be murdered?''

She ignored his sarcasm. ''You saw an advantage and you took it. Just as you did when you kissed me last night.''

''You wanted that kiss as much as I did.'' She lowered her gaze, but he caught her chin and held it, so she couldn't help but see the angry hurt reflected in his eyes. ''Admit the truth, Norah. I won't let you shovel all the blame onto me.''

''I indulged a passing fancy. That doesn't mean I want to have an affair with you, Kit Coleridge.''

''Fine. I haven't asked you.''

Releasing her, he stood up and stalked to the window. His grim posture somehow dismayed her. She groped for the shield of resentment. ''Oh? You said last night that you wanted to make love to me.''

''Contrary to what you believe, I only make love when the woman is willing.''

Something in the chilly set of his mouth suggested pain, yet she couldn't stem the acrid flow of words, not even when she knew she was being unfair to him. ''*You* made me believe otherwise. You brought me here and stripped off my clothes—''

''Betsy did the honors. I wasn't even in the room.''

''—and you gave me no choice but to wear a gown left by one of your hussies.''

Unexpectedly he laughed, a bittersweet sound, his teeth gleaming white in the sunlight. ''That's my stepmother's gown. She forgot it the last time she and my father came to visit.''

Looking down at the flimsy concoction of lace and silk, Norah blurted, ''She would wear something so . . . so . . . ?''

''So sensual?'' His lashes lowered slightly as he walked to the bed and leaned against the post. ''Despite what many dried-up matrons would have you believe, Norah, there are married couples who take great pleasure in the sexual act. It's a way to express love.''

Her cheeks burned. Unable to look at him, she smoothed the crumpled letter against her thigh. Other ladies blissfully welcomed that repulsive joining? For the first time she wondered if Kit could be right. Then she wondered what was wrong with her, that she hadn't found joy in her own marriage bed.

Her throat thick with pain, she murmured, ''Love has nothing to do with what you want—or wanted—from me, Kit.''

Chest aching, she waited for him to answer. The truth crept forth and stripped away the protection of anger. Dear God, she wanted him to deny her statement. She wanted him to clasp her close and declare his eternal love.

Because the same fierce emotion dwelt in her own heart.

The faint ticking of the mantel clock underscored the silence. She watched the letter slip from her numb fingers and flutter to the carpet. How had this warm soft affection for him grown, this hot wild yearning for a man who was destined to marry a debutante? The man with a wicked reputation for using women?

''Norah.''

Her name sounded like a caress. Slowly she lifted her head to find him gazing at her. The floral bed-hangings formed a backdrop for the hard contours of his face, for the whipcord strength of his body. The shadow of displeasure had fled his expression. In its place, a tender fire illuminated his exotic eyes.

"Norah, if I thought you truly wanted—" A sharp rap on the door ended his utterance. "Dammit."

Kit shot her a look of frustration, then strode to the door. *Wanted what?* Dear God, what had he been about to say?

A man brushed past him and hurried toward Norah. He wore a tailored camel topcoat with gold buttons that glinted in the sunlight. His neat silver hair and gentlemanly features brought a rush of happy surprise to her.

"Jerome! You're back from Switzerland."

"Norah, my dear." Dropping to the edge of the chaise, he caught her in a hug. The familiar smells of peppermint and cigars enveloped her in nostalgia, and his mustache tickled her cheek. "Are you all right? My God, what happened to your face?"

"It's only a bruise." Frowning, she drew back. "Winnifred and Ivy only just left. How did you know I was here?"

"Culpepper told me what happened—that you fell down the stairs at the museum and had to spend the night here." Jerome kept a gentle grip on her shoulders. His smile thinned into a strict line as he glanced at Kit, then back at her. "Norah, tell me the truth. Has the cad dishonored you?"

His meaning washed her in warmth. "No, of course not." Ashamed of her earlier outburst and determined to make amends, she softly added, "Lord Blackthorne has been nothing short of wonderful."

Kit's eyes held hers for an eternal moment. He stood with his arms crossed, his feet planted like the roots of a solid oak. In contrast, his lips were slightly parted, giving an impression of vulnerability that clasped her heart. She was at a loss to explain the sense of oneness she felt with him; she only knew he would defend her against any foe, real or imagined.

A muscle leaped in Jerome's jaw. He surged to his feet. "By God, you can't remain with this scoundrel. I'm taking you away from here."

Kit stepped forward. "What do you propose, that she stay with you?"

"Yes. At least she can trust me not to compromise her."

"Can she? I wonder." Abruptly Kit asked, "How long have you been back in town?"

"I arrived yesterday evening. And I resent your vulgar implication."

"Someone pushed Norah down those stairs. Did you by chance visit the museum?"

The two men faced each other. Kit radiated a cold suspicion that froze Norah. "Surely you don't believe *Jerome* is the culprit," she said. "Besides, we're looking for a woman."

As if he hadn't heard her, Jerome clenched his fists. "Why, you haughty bastard. I should call you out for that."

"Someone tried to kill her. Someone close to Maurice and to her. Somebody like you, St. Claire."

Horrified, Norah wanted to jump up between them, but her ankle frustrated her. "Stop it," she said. "Both of you. Jerome would never harm me."

"Maybe you're right." Kit slanted a glance first at her, then at the older man. "After all, you still owe him six thousand pounds."

Jerome paled. "So, you've been examining the shop's ledgers."

"Yes," Norah said. "And I—we—intend to settle with you as soon as possible."

"Consider the debt canceled. You don't owe me a copper."

"How noble of you," Kit mocked. "Or shall I say expedient? Perhaps you see more profit in making Norah very grateful to you."

Jerome hissed a breath between his teeth. "Only a wastrel like you would dream up such a vile suggestion—"

"You're doing it again," Norah snapped. "You're behaving like two dogs fighting over a bone."

"You're far more precious than a bone, my dear," Jerome said, still glaring at Kit. "Not that Blackthorne would ever value you. He'll use you and then discard you, as he does all his women.''

He voiced the fear savaging Norah's heart. In that one vital way, she dared not trust Kit.

He took a step forward. ''You're wrong about me. My intentions toward Norah are honorable.''

''You wouldn't know honor if it kicked you off one of your racehorses.''

''Is that so?'' Kit's icy gaze flitted to her, and warmed to a strange, burning intensity. In a hushed tone, he added, ''Regardless of what you think, Norah *will* stay here. As my wife.''

Chapter 13

Kit watched the surprise unfurl on Norah's face. Her lips parted and her emerald eyes rounded. Her skin glowed pearl-pale in the afternoon sunlight, the freckles scattered like gold dust across the bridge of her nose. Her ruby curls tumbled over the gentle mound of her breasts. Despite his desperate yearning, he couldn't interpret her reaction to his abrupt proposal.

Lord, what had he done?

He had intended to romance her with soft compliments and tender kisses, to ease her into accepting his suit. But Jerome threatened to take her away. Kit couldn't relinquish her to the one man who already owned her affections. The one man who clearly wanted to marry her himself.

Lord Blackthorne has been nothing short of wonderful.

The memory of her words heartened Kit. But only for a moment. Norah frowned down at the wedding band she twisted on her finger.

Jesus God. Maybe his true rival was a dead man. She still loved that bastard, Maurice.

Please don't say no, Kit silently beseeched her. *Please.*

"Norah can't marry you."

He focused cool eyes on Jerome. "What gives you the right to speak for her?"

The older man raked his fingers through his hair,

mussing the shiny silver strands. "We're friends. She has no family. Somebody has to protect her from scoundrels like you."

"I'm proposing to marry her, not molest her."

"She's in mourning, barely eight weeks a widow. People will question your haste. Given the circumstances of her night here, they'll say you compromised her."

"So? Once nine months have passed, everyone will know the wedding wasn't forced."

"Regardless, remarrying so swiftly simply isn't done. I won't let you drag Norah's good name through your own mud."

Dread lay like a rock in Kit's stomach. In the past he had thumbed his nose at society; now he agonized at the prospect of even one critical word spoken against Norah. Years of abuse had hardened him, but she was still so fragile.

The picture of vulnerability, she sat with her head bowed, her unbound hair hiding her expression. Why didn't she speak?

"She'll be the marchioness of Blackthorne and someday the duchess of Lamborough," he said. "Any gossip will eventually die down."

"This is madness.' Jerome paced before the bank of windows. "Title or not, you would make an unfit husband."

The insult echoed a lifetime of slurs. Conscious of the Indian blood that coursed through his veins, Kit balled his fists. "I beg your pardon?" he said in his most chilling tone.

Jerome leveled his keen blue gaze. "May I point out, you've proven yourself incapable of fidelity. Love and integrity are so much dirt under your feet. I won't stand by while you dishonor Norah."

"May I point out, you hardly know me. Yet you presume to pass judgment."

"Yes, by God. You're a rakehell. Everyone knows that. A murder took place at one of your decadent parties, for God's sake." He shook his finger at Kit.

''If she ever remarries, I'll approve the man. And you're at the very bottom of the list.''

His scorn enraged Kit. For half a penny, he'd grind his heel into those suave features. ''And I suppose you're at the top.''

Jerome stopped pacing. His silver eyebrows winged upward. ''Where would you conceive such a notion—?''

''Are you both quite finished?'' Norah broke in. ''If I may be permitted to speak, you've both neglected one vital detail. No one has asked *my* opinion on this proposal.''

She sat with her palms braced on the floral cushions. Her angry frown, her tightened lips, shamed Kit. Oh God. He had offended her again; he had disregarded her need for independence. He had acted like the arrogant lord she thought him.

His own hostile words would drive her toward Jerome. Unless Kit opened his heart.

He crossed to her and went down on one knee. Shoving away the awful memory of kneeling before another girl who had spurned him in disgust, he grasped Norah's small hand and strove for eloquence. ''Norah, please forgive me. Had circumstances been different, I would have courted you the proper way, with gifts and flowers and compliments.''

''I won't be bought,'' she murmured stiffly. ''I'm not like your other women.''

''I know—you're special. There won't ever be any other woman for me. I want to be your knight in shining armor. I want to commit my heart and soul to you. I want to be everything you dreamed of in the ideal husband.'' He groped for the courage to utter the words he'd reserved for nearly thirty years. ''I love you, Norah. Will you do me the great honor of becoming my wife?''

Her eyes grew soft and hazy. The tip of her tongue slid over her lips. She started to melt forward, a goddess garbed in red hair and creamy silk. Then she withdrew her hand and pressed it to her stomach. "No."

Stunned, he sat back on his heels. "No?"

She shook her head, slowly but emphatically. "No."

"You heard her, your lordship." Jerome strode forward, triumph blazing in his eyes. "Norah is a lady. She has the good sense to realize your passion for her won't last, that your promises are more lies. She would never marry a blackhearted heathen like you."

Kit surged to his feet. He couldn't abide the racial innuendo, not in front of Norah. Rage blotted his reason. He swung out with his fist and clipped Jerome on the jaw.

Jerome staggered backward. His back struck the bedpost. Blood spotted the corner of his mouth.

Norah gasped. Kit kept his eyes on Jerome. "If you value your life, St. Claire, you'll watch what you say to me."

The older man brandished his fists. "Why, you bloody bugger—"

"Sweet heavens, stop!" Norah struggled to her feet and hastily limped to him. "No more fighting."

"As you say." Jerome reached out to support her, though his cheeks retained an infuriated flush. "*I'm* a gentleman."

"Are you hurt?" Balancing on one foot, she snatched a napkin from the tea tray and dabbed tenderly at the blood trickling down his chin. "Oh, you poor dear. I'm so terribly sorry."

Her solicitude irked Kit. "For God's sake, don't apologize on my behalf."

Eyes flashing, Norah swung on him. "Someone must! Jerome came here as a friend, to protect my honor. If you were as considerate as you claim to be, you would be glad of that." She looked him up and down. "Knight in shining armor, indeed."

Her words lashed like a horsewhip. Kit rubbed his throbbing knuckles. But the raw wound on his heart stung far worse than his hand. Christ, he had lost any hope of winning her. By indulging an adolescent fit of temper, he had pushed her straight into Jerome St. Claire's waiting arms.

Fear for her life pulsated against his rib cage. He mistrusted Jerome. What thoughts lay behind that urbane exterior? God, what if Jerome were the killer? He could have hired the woman who had murdered Maurice. What if now he meant to woo Norah to her death?

"Thank you, my dear." Jerome took the cloth from her. "If you'll get dressed and collect your things, we'll go now."

"No," Kit said. "She's staying here."

"Now who's speaking for her?" Jerome jeered.

"I'll speak for myself." Norah crossed her arms. "Forgive me, Jerome, but I can't go with you."

"But . . . you just said . . ."

"I am perfectly aware of what I said."

She hobbled away and leaned against the bedpost. Half sick with relief, Kit stood perfectly still. He couldn't flatter himself that she cared for him, but he thanked God she had the good sense to accept his protection. The dressing gown embraced her hourglass shape: the swell of her breasts curved into a slender waist, then flared out again to her hips. But Norah was more than a warm feminine body. Her resolute expression reflected her strength of character and her keen mind.

And Kit yearned as desperately for her respect as he did for her passion. How could he bear to live in the same house with her? To see her every day and know she didn't return his love?

He must. Her safety was more vital than his own pain.

"Norah, please reconsider," Jerome said hoarsely. "He'll ruin you. Your very presence here will besmirch your reputation. You've worked for years to win acceptance as a lady."

She held her chin high. "Then I suppose I shall find out who my true friends are."

"And the business? The scandal will drive clients away from the shop."

"I've weathered worse troubles these past few months. One more scandal won't matter."

"You've no cause for worry," Kit said. "My stepmother is due to arrive at any moment."

Norah's eyes widened. She clutched the robe beneath her chin. "The duchess? Kit, you should have warned me—"

"A likely story." Jerome threw down the bloodied napkin. "I don't believe a word the rascal says."

"Believe what you like. I wired her early this morning. She'll be escorting us to my parents' estate in Kent."

"You might have consulted me when you made your plans," Norah said. "If I go off to Kent, who will watch over the shop?"

"Thaddeus can manage things." Kit went to her and grasped her hand. "Please don't be angry. You need a safe haven until your ankle is healed."

"I forbid you to take her out of the city," Jerome said.

Kit almost gagged on a rise of gall. "Who do you think you are—her husband? Or are you suggesting the duchess of Lamborough is an inadequate guardian of Norah's virtue?"

Jerome's gaze wavered, but only for a moment. He crossed to her and snatched up her other hand. "For the sake of our long friendship, I must ask you one last time to come with me—"

"No. His stepmother will be here, for heaven's sake." She waved them both away, the silk and lace of her sleeve fluttering. "It's time you accepted my ability to make my own choices. I will meet the duchess and then decide whether or not I'll travel to Kent. Now I want the both of you to cease badgering me."

"I'll take my leave, then." Jerome walked in jerky steps to the door. He turned to give Norah a piercing look that held the bitterness of regret. "I'll be in town for at least a month, so please feel free to summon me—at any time, day or night." He wheeled around and stalked out.

Victory left a sour taste in Kit's mouth. Christ, he didn't want to sympathize with the loser. Yet he and Jerome shared one common failing: neither had won Norah's heart.

She limped toward the bell cord by the fireplace. "I must get dressed," she murmured in a curious, breathy voice.

"You should return to bed and rest that ankle."

"Oh, bother my ankle. Kit, I can't meet the duchess looking like *this*." She grimaced at her nightdress, then tugged on the rope. "I do hope Betsy hurries. Do you suppose my gown is ready? Black velvet is hardly suitable for afternoon, but it will have to do."

A faint ray of hope pierced the darkness of his despair. If Norah fretted over meeting his mother, maybe she *did* care for him. "I'll check. And I'll see to fetching the rest of your things." He strode to the door.

"Kit?"

He spun on his heel, "Yes?"

Poised by the marble fireplace, she fingered the tasseled end of her sash. Her slim body stiff and proud, she murmured, "I want you to know I'm honored by your proposal. But I can't marry you or anyone else. I've only just learned to rely on myself."

He harnessed the wild beating in his chest. Once today he had humbled himself on his knees before her, and he could not bear the hurt of another refusal. "Do as you like," he said, affecting an indifferent tone. "And rest assured I shan't badger you again."

Norah sat beside Kit in the dining room at Lamborough Hall and sampled her treacle tart. Though she had spent the past fortnight here at his parents' estate, the beautiful room still awed her: the red damask draperies, the black japanned sideboards, the army of doting servants. Little Chinese lanterns shed pools of soft light over the intimate gathering. His parents occupied opposite ends of the long, white-draped table; across from Norah sat Kit's youngest—and only unmarried—sister, Annabelle, and his newly arrived friend, Lord Adrian Marlow.

In place of the traditional paintings of ancestors, fascinating photographs graced the walls. By now Norah knew them all, from the portrait of a gold-toothed mandarin bedecked in embroidered silk, to the picture of a grubby Indian beggar gazing hungrily at a fruit stand piled high with mangoes and bananas.

The pictures were the work of Kit's father, Damien Coleridge, the duke of Lamborough. Broad-shouldered, with a shock of gray-streaked black hair, he bore a striking resemblance to his eldest son. In Kit the rugged handsomeness had a subtly exotic slant, the sensual fullness of his lower lip, the high slash of cheekbones, the polished teak skin. Warmth spread through her. If she had trusted her heart, she could be sitting here as his fiancee and preparing to join a real family. Instead his parents believed she was merely his business partner.

Rest assured I shan't badger you again. True to his word, Kit had acted the perfect gentleman, solicitous but remote. She found herself longing for the charmer who could melt her with a smile, for the rake who would steal a kiss in the British Museum, for the caring man who had rescued her from a murderer.

"Our first peaceful dinner in days," Damien said, motioning to a footman to remove the china plates. "Thank God the regiment of hellions departed this morning."

"Merciful heavens, Damien. Watch how you speak of our grandchildren." Sarah, the duchess of Lamborough, shook her blond head in mock exasperation. The aqua gown enhanced her eyes, the silk as smooth and serene as her ageless features. "What will Norah think, to hear you complaining about your own kin?''

"She's likely as relieved as I am to see them go, but far too polite to say so."

The gleam in his brown eyes told Norah he was teasing. A pang wrenched her heart. He and the duchess treated her as if she were one of the family, instead of a widow fallen on hard times. "On the contrary," Norah murmured, "I loved meeting Kit's nieces and nephews. And his sisters and brother. They told me about quite a few of his boyhood escapades. Such as the time he faked a fall off the Great Wall of China."

Sarah pressed her fist to her bosom. "He nearly scared me to death."

"Yes, and Papa walloped him so he couldn't sit down for a week," Annabelle said, a smirk shading her lily-pure features.

"How would you know?" Kit scoffed. "You were a baby, still in nappies."

She tipped up her impish nose. "I *can* tell you, Norah, that he's never brought a lady home before. His other women are not the sort we ladies would associate with—"

"Stop right there." Kit aimed his silver fork at her, the tines glinting in the lampglow. "Unless *you* want a walloping."

"You wouldn't dare."

"Try me. You just might lose the bet."

She swung to her dinner companion and touched Adrian's maroon coat sleeve. "Lord Adrian will protect me. Won't you?"

His sandy curls framed languidly handsome features. He gaped at her beauty like a man long starved. "I, er, yes." Clearing his throat, he dragged his gaze to Kit. "I say, speaking of things lost, I've found the maharaja of Rampur."

Norah's heart flew into her throat. Dropping her fork with a clatter, she leaned forward. "Have you? I didn't know you were looking for him."

"Kit set me to the task," Adrian grimaced. "A habit with the old boy lately."

Before she could question the cryptic comment, Kit set down his water glass. "Good God, man, why didn't you say something when you came in?"

"I was distracted, I suppose." Adrian slanted another bedazzled glance at Annabelle; she lowered her blond eyelashes in a mock display of modesty.

Kit frowned from his sister to his friend. "Well?" he said curtly. "Don't hold us in suspense."

"His yacht is docked at the Isle of Wight. I read so in the gossip column in this morning's *Times*."

"Who is this maharaja?" the duchess asked.

Norah explained about the Jubilee tiara and her need to buy Fire at Midnight. An ache started inside her. "This means I'll have to leave soon to seek an audience with the maharaja."

"All in good time." Kit shaped his hand over hers, his warmth flowing into her for a scant moment before he drew back. "Your ankle is only just recovered. I won't let you suffer a relapse."

"I'm fine," she murmured. Yet her belly churned with painful regrets and untimely yearnings. Seldom these past two weeks had he touched her. Because she had spurned him, like that stupid girl, Emma Woodferne. Surely he knew her own purpose hadn't involved prejudice. Did he truly understand she'd had no choice?

"The maharaja of Rampur." The duke tapped his fingers on his wineglass, the light catching the webwork of scars he bore from a tragic fire in his youth. "I wonder if he's the same man I photographed before the Great Mutiny. I suppose the present maharaja might be his son."

"Were the photographs destroyed when your caravan burned?" Sarah asked.

A faraway haze glossing his eyes, Damien nodded. "I lost a a lot that night—but gained so much, too."

"We both gained something precious." Sarah smiled down the table at her husband, a sweetly tender curve of her lips that filled Norah with wistful envy. Her stay here had healed more than her ankle; it had mended her long-shattered dreams. Marriage needn't be the cold, formal relationship she had shared with Maurice, for the affection between Sarah and Damien Coleridge had endured for thirty years. The Lamborough clan was the tender, tight-knit family that had formed the fabric of Norah's yearning during her solitary childhood. Seeing their closeness had shaken her mistrust of Kit. If he had grown up in the glow of his parents' love, perhaps he *was* capable of fidelity. Perhaps . . .

To Norah, Sarah said, "You must be wondering what we're talking about. You see, Kit's father and I were caught up in the Sepoy Mutiny in India, back in '57. Kit was a newborn infant at the time. His mother, Shivina, was slain by a fanatic—"

"For God's sake, Mother, don't resurrect that ancient story again," Kit said. "It's not a part of my life."

A flush tinted his brown cheeks.. He avoided Norah's eyes and scowled into his teacup. Her chest tightened. Though she wanted to spare him embarrassment, she also felt the prod of curiosity, the need to unveil every facet of his past. "But this is fascinating," she murmured. "I'd like to hear the story."

"And so you shall." Flashing Kit a glance that was half remonstrative and half concerned, Sarah related how Damien had rescued Shivina from the fiery death of suttee, then married her before the birth of their son. She spoke with quiet sympathy of the prejudice Shivina had suffered from the English, only to die at the hands of a priest of her own race. Disguised as Indians, Damien and Sarah had fled the mutiny with Kit and found sanctuary in the Himalayan foothills.

The bittersweet tale of strife and triumph brought tears to Norah's eyes.

"Shivina was my friend," Sarah finished, "and I vowed I would always keep her memory alive for Kit."

"She's nothing to me," he said flatly. "Nothing at all."

"She suffered giving birth to you," Damien said. "On her dying breath she asked Sarah to protect you. If it hadn't been for Shivina, you wouldn't be here."

Kit met his father's glare. "As far as I'm concerned, my mother is sitting at this table. I see no need to go on about a dead woman."

Damien pushed back his chair. "That is quite enough, son. I will tolerate no more disrespectful comments."

Kit arched an eyebrow. "As you wish, Your Grace."

He turned his fork over and over, his hand swarthy against the white tablecloth. A lock of black hair slipped onto his brow as his brooding gaze focused on the utensil in his fingers. Norah's heart went out to him. Dear God, she had never realized his scars were carved so deeply. He could not abide references to his dark skin, not even from his own family.

Across the table, Annabelle looked demurely angelic with her hands folded in her lap, though her azure eyes gleamed with interest at the quarrel. Lord Adrian stared as if entranced at a dish of carameled oranges.

In an effort to allay the tension, Norah said to the duchess, "In the library I saw the book you and His Grace published about your travels in India. And the other books, too—about China and Japan and South Africa. How exciting to have lived abroad in so many exotic places."

Sarah smiled. "Once Annabelle was born, we were ready to return to England and put down roots. It grew difficult to live on the road with six active children." Her face sobered. "And by then Damien's brother had died, so Damien succeeded to the title. He had lands and other holdings to oversee. Still, we miss the excitement of new places."

Annabelle batted her eyelashes at Adrian.

"Speaking of travel, Lord Adrian, do tell me more about your trip to Belgium."

The news jarred Norah like an off-key note. "Belgium? You've been there recently?"

"Er, yes . . ."

Kit stood. "Would you ladies care to retire to the drawing room? We wouldn't wish to offend you with our cigar smoke."

He and his friend exchanged a cryptic glance. Adrian rose with fluid grace. "Capital idea, old chap. I could do with one of those Indian *bidis* His Grace keeps on hand."

The sharp teeth of suspicion bit Norah. "Where in Belgium did you go, Lord Adrian?"

Adrian ran his finger inside his starched collar. He looked beseechingly at Kit. "Here and there—"

"It was nothing important," Kit cut in.

"Did you by chance pass through Nivelles, near Brussels? I grew up in a convent there."

"Oh?" Adrian said, his reddened cheeks heightening her suspicions. "How fascinating."

Annabelle linked her arm with his. "*I'm* fascinated by having a guest to brighten our dreary country life. Why must the men and women separate because of some silly custom? We can all retire to the drawing room." She leaned closer to him, her young breasts pressing against her demure neckline. "Better yet, my lord, I could show you the garden—"

"It's pitch-dark outside." Kit pulled her from his friend and marched her away. Norah followed brother and sister to the doorway in time to hear him add in a harsh undertone, "If you flirt with fire, Belle, you'll get burned. Adrian Marlow is no callow lad to worship at your dainty feet."

She set her chin. "I'm to be launched into society this year. That means I'm old enough to make my own judgments about men. Besides, how many big brothers have warned their little sisters about *you*?"

He flushed. "I trust you'll see the value in staying

away from him. Or you'll force me to have a talk with Father.''

The instant Kit turned back to the dining room, Annabelle stuck out her tongue.

Over his shoulder, he said, ''And bear in mind, only children make rude gestures.''

''Bully.'' Cheeks afire, she minced down the corridor toward the drawing room, her kid slippers scuffing on the marble floor.

''Kit, wait,'' Norah called softly.

He returned to her side, but gazed after his sister. ''Now there's a girl who's heading for trouble someday,'' he murmured.

''Perhaps she emulates her elder brother.'' Glancing past his broad shoulder, Norah saw the duke and duchess speaking to Adrian. ''Now I should like to know why Lord Adrian went to Belgium.''

''I'll tell you later.''

''Kit, don't put me off—''

''I'm not. But we can't speak privately here.'' His black lashes lowered slightly, giving him a decidedly indecent appeal. ''I'll come to your room later.''

He moved away before she could protest. She couldn't have protested, anyway, for a pulse of excitement throbbed in her throat. She missed him. She missed the thrill of his touch. She missed the high heat of his kisses. Most of all, she missed his closeness, the easy camaraderie that had flourished during their weeks of partnership.

Her gaze remained glued to the dove-gray coat that encompassed his broad back as he went to the sideboard and poured himself a brandy. Regrets drifted like withered petals into the hollow of her heart. Dear God, she had rejected his marriage proposal. With a pang she knew she had *had* to turn him down. He wanted a large family, and that was the one thing she couldn't give him.

The duchess came over to Norah. Her eyes dancing with warmth, she murmured, ''Men! They do enjoy turning the air blue with their smelly cigars and manly curses.''

"Perhaps we women also need time away from the men."

"Perhaps." Sarah joined arms with Norah and drew her down the passage, their footsteps echoing on the marble squares of tile. "I'm so happy we've had this chance to visit. May I speak frankly, without offending you?"

"Of course."

The duchess stopped near an alcove displaying a statue of the naked Mercury, a fig leaf concealing his manliness. "I've been wanting to tell you how glad I am that Kit has finally found you."

Norah's heart rolled over. "Found me? We're only business partners."

"And I'm the queen of Siam," Sarah said dryly.

Her wise expression seemed to reach inside Norah, demanding honesty in return. "Well," she murmured, "I admit that I'm very fond of Kit. But that doesn't mean I'm the right woman for him."

"On the contrary, he's needed you to fill his emptiness." Sarah sighed. "Kit was ever the rebellious child, never satisfied with himself. Yet he was sensitive, too, taking any slight to heart. More than once he came home with a bloodied nose or a blackened eye."

Remembering his hot reaction to Jerome calling him a heathen, Norah said, "I've seen the bitter side of him, too."

"The love his father and I gave him never seemed enough to assure Kit of his own worth." Sarah took Norah's hand. "I pray all he needs is a good woman in his life, a woman who can be his equal mate."

Denying a rise of yearning, Norah lowered her gaze. "He and I aren't always in accord."

"Because you affect each other deeply. I'm reminded of the quarrels Damien and I had when we first met."

Astonished, Norah tilted her head at the duchess's tranquil features. "You couldn't have quarreled. You're both so perfectly suited."

Sarah laughed merrily. "We're both strong-minded people. And back then, I was a prissy spinster who never lost a chance to criticize Damien's less commendable traits.'' Her smile gentled and she patted Norah's hand before releasing it. ''Trust doesn't magically appear, like the cobra that a snake charmer lures from a basket. You must nurture it. I know my son has a deplorable reputation, Norah, but he's a fine man. A man worthy of your trust.''

Norah didn't correct the mistaken notion that his character was the source of the problem. She ached with the need for a confidante. Since Ivy and Winnifred were both spinsters, Norah had never had anyone to answer her questions. Answers she burned to know now, before Kit came to her bedroom.

Tracing her finger over the tiny wing attached to Mercury's foot, she blurted, ''Is it true that women can't . . . find pleasure in a man's embrace?''

Sarah tilted her head thoughtfully. ''I think those men who fear we would stray from our marriage vows would have us believe so. The Church also teaches submission rather than passion. I would never presume to question your own marital experience, but I *can* say that true love is the vital ingredient to my own happiness with Damien.''

True love. The one element Norah had never known until Kit. Could it be the reason Maurice's touch had repelled her? On impulse, she kissed Sarah on the cheek. ''Thank you. For making me feel welcome and for giving me much to think about.''

Needing to be alone, Norah excused herself. As she took the stairway up to her bedroom, she pictured Sarah Coleridge in the diaphanous nightgown, her husband lifting the silk to caress her most private place, and she positioning herself to welcome his lusty invasion.

A tempest of heat descended upon Norah. The nuns had warned her to accept suffering as a woman's lot. The repellent reality of the matrimonial bed had confirmed their teachings. But now she wondered if an entire dimension of marriage had been lost to her.

Would intimacy with Kit hold no disgust and pain, only bliss?

The daring question both lured and frightened her.

Inside her bedroom she roamed aimlessly from a blue and white Chinese teapot filled with dried heather, to an urn made of Siberian jasper. She trailed her fingertips over the smooth satin coverlet on the bed. Layers of silk in colors of citrine and sapphire draped the posts; the gilded headboard was extravagantly ruched with rosettes and tassels and bows. But the wide mattress with its bank of white pillows seemed cold and lonely tonight.

Kit would come to her soon. For the first time in two weeks, they would be alone. The prospect of yet another strained conversation must be why she felt so restless.

To pass the time, she sat in the comfortable wing chair by the fire and began to sketch. The design began as a brooch, but moments later she gazed at a drawing of Kit, his well-shaped head with the stark definition of wickedly curved lips and compassionate smile. Every nuance of his kiss expanded in her memory like the taste of champagne; even her nipples felt taut and tingly.

Rest assured I shan't badger you again.

Perhaps he no longer wanted her. Perhaps she would never know the joy of his embrace again. She would never *know* . . .

A tree branch scraped against the windowpane, the sound heightening her sense of desolation. She flung down the sketch pad and began to pace. Methodically she ran down the list of arguments against Kit, all the reasons she could never marry again. Then she puzzled over why he would send Lord Adrian to Belgium, what he hoped to learn from the nuns, and wondered in annoyance why he hadn't told her.

As she passed the balcony doors for the umpteenth time, Norah caught her reflection in the murky glass. Her face shone pale against the black of her gown. The woman in widow's weeds. The woman who had let happiness pass her by. The woman who would never know for certain if love-making held a bright bliss beyond the darkness and degradation.

Her throat squeezed tight. Banishing judgment and logic, she flew into the dressing room and undid the buttons down her back. She stepped out of her dress and the myriad petticoats, then kicked off her shoes and peeled away the silk stockings. Corset, chemise, and underdrawers landed on the pile of garments. Cool air struck her fevered skin. Her breath emerged in short puffs. Conscious of her naked state, she crossed to the great mahogany wardrobe, found a fresh nightgown, and slid it over her head.

Then she went back into the bedroom and stopped before the cheval dressing-glass. High color graced her cheekbones. A few corkscrew curls had escaped her chignon to dangle around her shoulders. The bruises from her fall down the stairs had faded, thank goodness. Billows of creamy cotton flannel enveloped her from neck to toe. It was hardly an alluring creation, not sheer in the least, yet she felt freer, hedonistic, aching and ready . . .

The muted glow from a single lamp on the night table augmented the firelight. Mysterious shadows lay within the canopied bed. The scene was made for seduction. A place for a woman to meet her lover.

She pressed her hand to her lips. What was she doing?

Even as a sea of misgivings inundated her, a rap broke the stillness. Kit. The surety of his closeness petrified her. She stood before the mirror, her hand clutching the collar of her nightgown, her knuckles white.

The knock came again. Indecision pulled her to and fro. She could send him away. Or invite him inside.

Then she made her choice.

Hardly daring to reconsider, Norah hastened across the soft carpet. Her fingers curled around the cool crystal knob. A single shining thought sustained her.

Tonight she would know.

Chapter 14

"I didn't expect you so soon, Kit."
Her breathy greeting struck Kit speechless.
His thoughts centered on the lovely picture Norah
made, her cheeks blooming pink and her hair
mussed, as if she had just risen from bed. He wondered if she were naked beneath the voluminous
folds of her nightgown.

Jesus God. Why had she undressed when she
knew he was coming to see her? He rejected the
obvious answer. He'd caught her unawares, that
was all.

To disguise the drumbeat of desire in his blood,
he assumed a formal tone. "Excuse me. If you'd
rather we spoke in the morning . . ."

"No. Come in. Please."

She opened the door wider. Feeling as awkward
as a pubescent boy approaching his first sweetheart,
he stepped into the bedroom and shut the door. The
muted lighting and quiet intimacy struck him. Her
sketch pad lay on the floor beside the wing chair. A
collection of her favorite pencils was scattered over
the oak side table. Just inside the dressing room
doorway, he could see the untidy heap of her clothing, the glimpse of white undergarments—'

"Why do you have one of our cases?" Norah
stood watching him, her fingers gripping the high

neck of her gown, the firelight glinting off her gold wedding band.

He glanced down at the mother-of-pearl presentation box balanced on his dampened palm. The box he'd nearly forgotten.

He passed it to her. "This is for you."

His breath stalled in his chest as Norah lifted the hinged lid. She blinked. For a few heartbeats, she didn't move; then slowly she reached into the white velvet-lined interior and withdrew the glittering contents. Firelight flashed on the moonstones and diamond chips scattered over the woven silver necklace.

"This is the parure you commissioned," she said. "Did you bring it here to show it to me?"

"I brought it to give to you. I asked you to design something you would like, didn't I?"

"But I thought it was for . . ."

"Who?"

"I don't know. One of your other women."

Kit shook his head. "It was for you, Norah. It was always for you."

Her wide-eyed gaze fell to the jewelry spilling like a shiny waterfall over her fingers. He took the necklace and moved behind her to fasten the diamond clasp. His fingers brushed the warmth of her skin, the silken softness of her hair. The feathery down at the nape of her neck brought him to a poignant awareness of her femininity.

She remained motionless, as if mesmerized by the brooch and earrings and bracelet still nestled inside the box. Kit stepped in front of her. Any other woman would have kissed him by now, would have prettily expressed gratitude for the generous present.

"Aren't you pleased?" he asked.

"Yes. Thank you."

She snapped the lid shut and turned to put the box on the dressing table. Her wooden response perplexed him. He felt as if he was foundering in too-deep waters. "Norah, what's wrong?"

She swung around, her hands braced on the table

behind her. A troubled expression knit her auburn eyebrows. "You're still trying to buy my affections."

I won't be bought. I'm not like your other women. Too late, he saw his mistake. In his usual arrogant manner he had taken the easy path; he had hoped to bridge the fortnight-long rift between them in one swift move, rather than rebuild her trust stone by slow stone.

And yet . . . he had put a great deal of planning into the parure. She had unknowingly lured him into becoming a better man, the man of her dreams. Now, her instant misjudgment pricked his anger. "Oh, for God's sake. Since when is it wrong for a man to give the woman he loves a gift?"

Her gaze wavered and her lips softened. Then she steadied her eyes on him again. "I'm the prize in your petty battle with Jerome. You're only trying to win me."

"It isn't petty. He wants you all for himself, Norah."

"That's absurd. In all the years I've known him, he's been nothing short of kind and caring and absolutely wonderful."

The fangs of jealousy tore into Kit. "He's a paragon all right. Let me tell you what Adrian found out when he went to the convent—"

"So you did send him." She planted her hands on her hips, cinching her nightgown into her trim waist. "Why didn't you tell me?"

"Because I didn't want to alarm you." Kit raked his hand through his hair. "When you were first attacked, the night of the fire, I began to worry that Maurice's murderess might be stalking you, too. I wondered if she could be someone from your past, so I went back to your beginnings. I sent Adrian to visit the nuns who raised you."

"Lord Adrian Marlow—among nuns? I gather he's as much the rake as you."

Kit suppressed a smile. "I *was* a rake, but not anymore."

She gave him a strange sidelong look as she swept past him and began to pace. "You had no right to pry."

"Yes, I did. I'm concerned for your safety."

"Well, I don't understand what you hoped to find out. What would *my* childhood have to do with Maurice's murder?"

"I don't know. I just took a chance." Savoring triumph, he added, "And luck paid off. I did find out something interesting."

Norah stopped cold. "Did you learn the identity of my parents?"

She clasped her hands so tightly he could see the delicate bones and fine blue veins. He cursed himself for failing to foresee this need in her. "No. I'm sorry, I didn't. But I did discover that it wasn't the Mother Superior who arranged your marriage. It was Jerome St. Claire."

The light from the fire behind Norah set her hair aglow and limned her nightgown in golden radiance. The moonstones and diamonds on her cloth-draped bosom enhanced her natural beauty. "Jerome? That can't be true," she said, frowning. "I didn't meet him until *after* I married Maurice."

"I see no reason why the Mother Superior would lie."

Norah bit her lip. "I don't, either. So maybe Maurice sent Jerome as an emissary—because he travels so much on the continent. There's nothing so strange about that."

"I wonder." Kit racked his mind for a way to convey his uneasy feelings. "There's something peculiar about Jerome. I think he's hiding something."

She snorted. "Oh, please. Jerome has always been scrupulously honest with me."

"Then why didn't he tell you he arranged your marriage?"

"He probably didn't think it was important. Or maybe Maurice asked him not to." She threw up her hands. "For heaven's sake, it's over and done with. The circumstances of a marriage made nine years ago have nothing to do with our investigation.''

''I wish I could share your certainty.'' Fighting the demons of fear, Kit crossed to her. His fingers formed bracelets around her wrists. The daintiness of her bones, the faint throbbing of her twin pulse points, deepened his terrible sense of helplessness. ''I wish you would marry me.''

Norah heard the tremor in his voice and longed to believe he spoke from his heart. Clad in a dove-gray suit, he towered over her like an exotic prince. His midnight eyes mirrored the flames on the grate. Yet more than his physical perfection drew her. Somehow her need for him had grown beyond that of a friend and a business partner. She admired his strength, his intensity, his dedication, even his new-found honor. The fact that he had planned for so many weeks to give her the parure proved his dedication to loving her.

Agony twisted in her chest. If only she weren't the wrong woman for Kit. If only she dared risk more than a fleeting love affair with him, this one night.

She lowered her gaze. ''You needn't go to such lengths to protect me.''

His grip tightened on her wrists. ''Look at me.''

Slowly she complied, though the steady burn of his eyes singed her. ''Of course I want to protect you,'' he murmured. ''I said I wouldn't badger you, but I won't lose you either. I want the sort of happiness my parents share. I want to spend the rest of my life with you. I want our children to play hide and seek in these rooms. I think you want all that, too.''

A knot of agony formed in her chest. The deep feeling in his voice resurrected the girlhood dreams she had entombed long ago. Yet now the harsh colors of reality stained those fairy-tale images. Once, she had disciplined her outspoken nature and submitted to a husband's will; then Maurice had broken her trust. Even though her heart ached to embrace

Kit's love and the future he offered, her head warned her to guard her emotions.

"I can't," she whispered. "I won't marry again."

"Dammit, why not? If it's your independence, I promise not to stifle you. You can design jewelry until we're both old and gray and you're too feeble to pick up pencil and paper."

She pulled free, walked to the chimneypiece, and pressed her brow against the warm delft tiles. Her hand cradled the cool stones of her necklace. "I know you respect my talent, Kit. But there are so many other reasons why we're wrong for each other."

"Oh?" he scoffed. "Tell me some."

Turning to face him, she plucked an argument from the list she had compiled to console herself on lonely nights. "For one, I lack the breeding to make a suitable wife for a marquis. I can't even tell you who my parents are."

"I'd be the last person to criticize your bloodline."

He stood stiff and straight, a statue chiseled from sun-warmed topaz. Remembering his hostility toward his natural mother, Norah said softly, "Oh, Kit. Don't belittle yourself. I thank God that your father once loved a Hindu woman named Shivina."

Their eyes held, his reflecting unguarded need and hers the tenderness and love she dared not voice. His mouth softened and the tension in his physique eased. His lashes lowered slightly, but not before she spied the glitter of pain.

"How can I believe you?" he said bitterly. "You don't care enough to commit yourself to me."

Dear God, he deserved to know the truth. He deserved to recognize the horrid failure she hid inside herself.

"I do care," she murmured. "But I just couldn't ask you to . . ." Tears scalded her eyes and throat. Mortified by the swift collapse of her defenses, she spun around again, burying her face in her palms.

His hands closed on her shoulders and kneaded her rigid muscles. "Ask me to what?"

"To accept a woman who's less than whole." Her voice dropped to an anguished rasp. "Oh, please don't make me say this."

"Norah, you owe me your honesty."

The desperation to convince him burned away her restraint. "There's something wrong with my body."

A log popped; she heard the quiet swish of his breathing. He drew her close, molding her spine to his chest and crossing his arms beneath her breasts. "Bosh." His exhalation tickled her ear. "Your body is perfect."

"But I could never bear your child. Haven't you guessed?" She forced herself to agonizing candor. "I'm barren."

The damning word lashed like a scourge inside her skull. *Barren. Barren. Barren.*

Focusing on the tiny blue windmill etched on one of the tiles, she braced herself for Kit's withdrawal. Instead he snuggled her closer, subtly fitting her thighs to his, gently pressing her bottom against his groin. The intimate position awakened a memory of pain, yet somehow the turmoil inside her seemed enticing, the antithesis of fear. With vivid intensity, she coveted his nearness. It seemed natural and right for her hands to settle atop his folded forearms, where his warmth guarded her empty womb.

"It takes two people to create a baby," he said. "Maybe the flaw was in your husband."

"No." The suggestion startled Norah into tilting her head back to view Kit. "No, it's in me. The doctor told me so."

"And you accepted his diagnosis?"

"Yes, I consulted our family physician two years ago." Looking into the fire, she relived the nagging anxiety that had driven her to make the appointment, the embarrassment of the examination, the furtive groping of his cold hands beneath the concealing cloth. And she remembered Maurice's fury when the doctor came to consult with *him*. She'd asked him what was wrong, but he had subjected her to a moody silence that lasted for weeks afterward. Haltingly she added, "The physician said that failure to conceive is the fault of the wife—unless the husband had contracted certain illnesses, which Maurice had not."

"Mmm. Well, I can't claim to know much about medical matters, but your doctor could be mistaken. Perhaps my mother knows a specialist you can consult—"

"Please don't involve the duchess." Norah kept the door locked on fruitless hopes. "Even if another doctor declared me healthy, I couldn't let you risk your future. You have a duty to produce an heir."

He shrugged, his chest shifting against her back. "There's Thomas, my younger brother. If need be, he can inherit."

Kit's nonchalant attitude shook the foundation of her assurance. She turned in the circle of his embrace and lay her arms over his, her fingers curling around the smooth material of his sleeves and finding the firmness of muscles beneath.

"Kit, you said you want a marriage like the one your father and stepmother share. But children are a big part of their happiness. I can't give you a family. You wouldn't have a brood of children to bring laughter and light into your life. You wouldn't ever know the joy of holding your own baby, or watching him take his first steps."

"But I'd have you."

His smile illuminated a dark place deep inside her. Wary of her budding hope, she said, "A wife alone can't be enough. Someday you'll regret never having children."

He pressed his finger over her lips. "If it matters so much to you, we'll adopt one of the boys. Lark or Screeve, even Billy. Jesus God, if it makes you happy, we can take in the whole bloody school."

The startling suggestion drew her gaze over the brown column of his throat to his face, to the curve of his mouth and the beauty of his cheekbones, the bronzed skin and the jet-black hair. Now she could discern kindness where she had once seen dissipation, gallantry where she had seen hauteur, sincerity where she had seen a charming deceiver. In defiance of sensible judgment, elation bloomed in her unfurling in a smile.

"Oh, Kit, you're so good for me."

He released a pent-up breath. His stubbled cheek rubbed against hers. "You're good for me, too."

His hand moved in hypnotic circles over her back, massaging away the remnants of anxiety. Yet like weeds in a rose garden, troubling questions marred her contentment. *Could* she bind herself again when she had just sampled the fruits of freedom? Dare she trust the depth of Kit's feelings?

"I'm afraid," she admitted. "What if you want me because I'm the only woman you can't seduce?"

Laughter rumbled deep in his chest. "Now there's one argument I know for a pack of nonsense. Believe me, darling, I've never really tried to seduce you."

"Oh? What about in the museum?"

"That wasn't seduction. *This* is seduction."

He nuzzled her ear, then brushed his moist lips along the side of her neck and tracked over to possess her mouth. The slickness of his tongue, the caress of his hands on her derriere, started shivers that rippled like waves over her skin and penetrated the very depths of her. Wanting the kiss to last and last, she lifted herself on bare toes and outlined his jaw in her hands. Her fingertips rejoiced in the strength there, then greedily moved over his head, learning the intricate design of his ears and sifting through the rough silk of his hair.

Abruptly he pulled back, his expression moody. "Twice before when I kissed you, Norah, you pushed me away. If you're going to do so again, I'd as soon leave right now."

The muscles of her stomach tightened. The specter of painful memories shrouded her in shadows.

Only the familiarity of his face, so close and so be-loved, kept her from falling into the abyss of panic. Like fine wine, the taste and texture of his kiss lin-gered on her lips. The trepidation within her trans-formed into an aching awareness of her own body.

She wanted to take the chance. She wanted to *know*.

Reaching for his hand, she skimmed his hard knuckles and marveled at the dainty paleness of her skin against his dusky flesh. "Kit, I'm afraid to promise you my future. But I do want you to make love to me tonight. That's why I undressed."

His eyes remained steady, though a subtle soft-ening eased the strict line of his mouth. "I have one stipulation," he said. "That you take this off, too." He tapped the wedding band on her finger.

Without hesitation, she worked off the gold ring and dropped it on the side table, among the litter of her pencils. Her hand felt as naked as her emotions. She searched her mind for regrets but found only a boundless sense of release. For nine years she had borne the weight of the ring and the duties it rep-resented; now she reveled in freedom, like a dia-mond pried from a too-heavy setting.

She put her hands on his chest, pushed them beneath the lapels of his coat, and let her palms ab-sorb the thudding there. "Your heart is beating as fast as mine."

"Because we're meant for each other, Norah. We're meant to be partners in more than just a jewel shop. And for more than one night. You'll see."

He caught her by her waist. In one elegant mo-tion, he sank into the wing chair and drew her down onto him. Her bottom met the rock-hard muscles of his thighs; her head fit the cradle of his shoulder.

Confused, she glanced beyond him, at the bed. "But . . . don't you want to lie down with me?"

He smiled. "Eventually. I don't need a bed to prove I love you. For right now, I want to hold you . . . kiss you . . . touch you."

In that instant she knew he appreciated her fear,

and his thoughtfulness intensified the bond between them. She wanted to kiss him, too, partly out of ardor and partly out of a cowardly desire to delay the moment of reckoning.

She tilted her head up in the same moment his hand cupped her cheek. Their mouths melded in a sweetly sensual kiss that whirled her into a realm of throbbing darkness; yet this darkness aroused none of the old familiar alarm, only the profound consciousness of Kit protecting her in the tender power of his embrace.

She clung to his neck and inhaled his musky scent, felt his hands slide up and down her back in a rhythmic motion that mimicked the silken sword thrust of his tongue. Her heightened awareness heated into a fever. She squirmed against him, meeting his kiss with her own. His hands came under her arms and shaped around her unbound breasts. Despite the enfolding fabric, his thumbs flicked over her nipples and sent shock waves radiating down to her belly.

His lips brushed back and forth over hers. "You're naked under this nun's robe."

"Yes," she breathed, awed at feelings so new they had no name. "But I don't feel like a nun."

"Nor will you ever with me."

Gold flecks glimmered in the shadowed pools of his eyes. His lashes were thick, half lowered. Her breasts felt warm and weighted within his palms, aching for his unique stimulation. Abruptly he released her, and she made a sound of dismay.

He smiled in the wicked way that suggested untold pleasures to come. "Patience," he murmured. "You're too precious a gift to open quickly."

He unfastened her necklace and set it aside, then worked his way down the myriad buttons securing the front of her gown. Delving inside, he spread his broad palms on her bare shoulders, then pressed outward, pushing the fabric away and half exposing her bosom. On a rush of modesty, she caught his wrists, where his fine white cuffs delineated brown flesh and black hairs.

"Shouldn't we blow out the lamp?" she said huskily.

"How would I see you then?" he countered.

Already he transported her beyond the realm of her experience. She had known physical intimacy only in darkness, so late into the night that the hearth fire had burned to embers. Even then she had never fully unveiled herself, merely lifted the hem of her gown. But the prospect of Kit viewing what no man had ever seen made her hands melt downward, granting him the liberty to do as he willed.

He guided the garment down over her arms and let it pool at her waist. Oddly, she felt pure and new; Eve before the fall from grace. His hands came up to span her rib cage, his thumbs testing the underside of her breasts. Her heart beat so fast she thought he must surely take notice.

His jaw clenched and his gaze flitted to hers. "God, you're lovely," he muttered. "I want to kiss you."

"I want to kiss you, too."

Her lips parted and she swayed closer. But instead of taking her mouth, he bent his dark head to her breast and suckled her peak. The shock of his tongue circling the delicate point uncoiled a ribbon of delight that hastened downward to the private place between her thighs. The ribbon pulled deliciously taut, provoked by the nip of his teeth and the tug of his lips. Never had she felt so aware of her own body. When he blew gently on her moistened flesh, she felt the sensation unroll straight down to her curled toes.

"Kit," she said on an outrush of air. "What are you doing to me?"

"Loving you." He tilted a look up, and his slumberous smile illuminated the tracery of laugh lines around his mouth and eyes. "Do you want me to stop?"

"No. Please, no."

In shameless encouragement, she threaded her

fingers into his thick hair and urged his head down-ward. He complied by drawing her other nipple into his mouth and paying it the same exquisite homage.

The sideways position on his lap suddenly grew awkward. Norah shifted restlessly, and he seemed to know what she wanted even when she herself did not. Grasping her by the waist, he deftly turned her so that she faced him, her thighs straddling his. She sat with the gown hiked to her hips, the center of her riding the sleek fabric of his trousers and the long staff within.

Alarmed into a gasp, she held an indrawn breath. Though an irresistible rush of liquid heat lured her, she tensed with the thought that Kit would take her to bed now; he would end these dreamy tactile sen-sations with the harsh reality of the act.

But he merely brought her hand up and kissed her fingertips, one by one. "I adore every part of your body," he whispered. "Your skin, so soft and fem-inine. Your breasts, so precious and perfect. Even your wrists, so dainty and small-boned." Turning up her hand, he skimmed his lips over the network of blue veins.

He nuzzled a path up her inner arm to her throat, then his hands massaged her bosom. "You have a beautiful form, Norah. The form of a goddess, silk and warmth and purity."

As he continued his eloquent exploration, the ri-gidity of her muscles abated, altering into a throb of yearning centered low in her belly. Like molten gold, she dissolved onto him, gradually discovering plea-sure in the strange position. She relaxed until her aching pressure point lodged firmly against his maleness.

His eyes darkened. The swift rise and fall of his chest gratified her with the knowledge that he was as affected as she. Yet his movements were easy, posing no threat to her vulnerable state. Reaching behind her head, he pulled out the pins and let her hair fall in tickling streams over her sensitized skin.

"I've wanted to do that since the first moment I

saw you." He rubbed a curl between his thumb and forefinger. "You have sunset hair. Soft as swansdown."

"It's too red, and so curly I can scarcely drag a comb through it." Pursing her lips, Norah focused on the blue fabric of the wing chair. "Winnifred once said that only a baseborn woman had hair in so tawdry a shade."

Kit's hands caught her cheeks. "You have lovely hair. And Winnifred is a jealous, dried-up spinster. If you trust her word over mine, Norah, I'll be sorely disappointed."

His stern avowal gladdened her. Purely on impulse, she put her lips to his palm and followed his solid flesh up over his long, square-tipped fingers. "I wouldn't wish to disappoint you, my lord."

He sucked in a breath. "Then for God's sake, kiss me."

They met halfway in a mutual expression of need. Her open lips welcomed the urgency of his mouth, and before he could take the lead, she traced the tip of her tongue along the ridges of his teeth, then trekked into the moist cavern of his mouth. A groan reverberated in his chest. He returned her kiss, blotting out all but the fervid awareness of him, the caress of his fingers over her breasts and waist and legs, until she felt as radiant as a diamond in the hands of a master cutter.

Without knowing where the urge came from, she rocked her hips against him. The brief friction was not enough to satisfy her; the impulse seemed to deepen and darken. With a moan, she found herself squeezing her thighs to encompass his, pressing herself harder against him.

"Let me help," Kit murmured.

He fingered her in the very spot that had become her flashpoint. Sparks burst inside her, singeing her with arousal, shocking her with wanton passion. She jerked and went still, shaken by her lapse of control and frightened by her perception of hurdling headlong toward an unknown place.

"Kit? This isn't like me . . ."

"Sshh." He touched his lips to her nose; his hand lay warm between her legs, lightly cupping the mysterious folds of her flesh. "Don't hold back, Norah. Let your feelings carry you."

"To where?"

"Relax and you'll see." His eyes were soft and liquid-dark, hypnotic eyes. "Trust me to guide you. Remember how very much I love you."

The certainty of his affection, coupled with the slow circling of his thumb, drew her into sweet surrender. She rested her head on his broad chest and lowered her lashes. The world descended into a voluptuous darkness that held only the two of them, man and woman. The drumbeat of his heart filled her ear; his musky aroma expanded her senses. The love burning in her own heart fired the glow in her loins.

She moved, flirting with his hand, and Kit seemed to understand her needs with unerring accuracy. He quickened his strokes until she surged toward the pinnacle of madness.

Trust me . . .

Letting go of restraint, she writhed in his lap, panting, seeking, climbing . . . then bursting over the verge. She clung tight to his shoulders as joy transported her, one blessed spasm after another, into the light of a thousand sun-struck diamonds.

She drifted back to an awareness of herself, sleepy and satisfied. And brazenly perched astride the marquis of Blackthorne, the most notorious rake in England.

He sat fully clothed, cravat and coat and trousers, while she lolled against him in half-naked splendor.

A laugh of pure delight bubbled from her throat.

Not the notorious marquis, after all. Kit. Her darling Kit. The man who would give her that wondrous pleasure before he used her in his own way.

"Here now," he chided, tipping her chin up so she looked fully into his eyes. "What's so amusing?"

She wreathed her arms around his neck and kissed him. "I love you, that's all."

He blew out a ragged breath. His eyes gleamed with tender fire. "That's all?"

"Mmm. Well . . . now I *know*."

His crooked smile held pride and understanding. "Not everything yet, partner."

Despite his indolent expression, she was conscious that his fingers tightly gripped her arms. The pressure beneath her reminded her of his own unslaked passion. She searched her heart for fear, but found only warmth and willingness. Even if their union hurt, she could endure a few moments of pain if the coupling gave him joy.

She wriggled backward on his steely thighs so that she could shape her hand around him. With a flush of feminine awe, she realized that he surpassed the stretch of her fingers. "You've wrought a miracle, my lord, but there's also the matter of you."

The softness of her voice, the boldness of her touch, nearly brought Kit out of his skin. He could scarcely believe this sultry angel was his Norah. Yet when she brushed her lips over his, a sweetly unschooled quality flavored her kiss. Set afire by the paradox of saucy wench and shy maiden, he knew he could wait no longer. Now that she had been initiated, he could dispense with patience. He could end the delicious agony of waiting.

He drew her to her feet and peeled away the nightgown until she stood in naked glory, her breasts coyly peeking from the veil of curly hair. The ache in his groin flared to an unholy fire. He hoisted her into his arms. "Shall we retire to bed?"

Her smile held a wistful quality. She tucked her face into the crook of his neck. "I'm ready, Kit."

She sounded almost resigned. He was possessed by the fierce need to see her face glow with renewed satisfaction. Maurice Rutherford might have taken her maidenhead, but Kit Coleridge had given her the rapture of her first climax. The first of many.

Stopping beside the bed, he said, "Don't judge

me by another man's ineptness, Norah. Our pleasure has barely begun.''

Her teeth worried her lower lip. "Will you be disappointed if I don't like it?''

"I told you before, you could never disappoint me. Never.''

He kissed her, deep and sure. They fell atop the quilt, his trousered leg flung over her bare thighs as he lost himself to the enticement of her moist and reddened lips. The high fever of love robbed him of rationality; only the barrier of his clothing brought him to his senses. He wanted to feel hot flesh against hot flesh.

"Wait here." Pushing to his feet, he yanked at his cravat.

Humor lit her green eyes. "Where else would I go, my lord? To the library? I understand your stepmother once wrote a book of essays under the *nom de plume* of I. M. Vexed—''

"Imp. If I have my way, tomorrow you'll be writing an essay on the joys of love.''

Norah scooted under the covers and drew the quilt to her breasts. Her hair billowed like a red cloud on the white pillow. The guarded look stole back over her face, a look he meant to banish forever. He also meant to undress in record time. But his adroit fingers became clumsy, fumbling with his buttons, awkward at unscrewing his sleeve links.

Jesus God. Norah loved him. He let himself revel for a moment in paradise. Then doubts crept in. Did she only love her first taste of physical gratification? Would she decide tomorrow that she'd made a mistake? Would she choose Jerome St. Claire as her life mate?

Kit shed the loathsome questions along with the last articles of his clothing. He had never been so unsure of himself with a woman. But he had to believe in her. He *must* believe, for the lonely man inside him cried out with need for her.

God help him, if sex was the only way to hold

her, he would show her a night she would never forget.

Her wide-eyed gaze traveled down the length of his naked body and stopped on his jutting maleness. Her lips parted. The tip of her tongue peeked from between her white teeth. He took a step toward her. His heart hammered from an upsurge of lust, from anticipation of the union to come.

Abruptly she rolled away from him, onto her side. Kit found himself staring at the alabaster smoothness of her back. His jaw dropped. Her rejection ripped into him like a pistol shot.

Driven by pain and passion, he flung himself on the mattress and pulled her around to him. The warmth of her skin mocked him. "Don't turn away from me," he rasped. "My God, not now."

The great green jewels of her eyes blinked. "Why are you angry? I only thought you'd want—"

"This is what I want, Norah."

He covered her with his body and rubbed the thicket of his chest hairs against her sensitive nipples. Her intake of breath rewarded him. His knee nudged apart her thighs, and the crown of his hardened length nestled in the moist heat of her entrance. Sighing his name, she looped her arms around him, and with the keen triumph of a conquerer, he felt her muscles go liquid with surrender.

The savage forces within him defeated his plan for a long, leisurely lovemaking. A powerful tide of fear inundated him with the need to stake his claim, once and for all. In one swift plunge he entered her, met a barrier, and breached it.

She gasped. Her fingers closed convulsively over his back. Kit paused, his lungs heaving, his body aflame, his mind puzzling over the brief resistance. Her eyelids were squeezed shut, her breath quick and light.

"Are you all right?" he said hoarsely.

Her lashes fluttered open. "I'm fine."

Her snug velvet encased him; with effort he gripped the thread of his thoughts. "Forgive me, darling." He caressed her lips with a remorseful kiss. "I didn't mean to be so rough. But I couldn't wait any longer to make you mine."

Dreamy-eyed, she regarded him. "You don't feel rough at all, Kit. You feel . . . wonderful."

When she moved her hips, the stimulus spurred him on a dizzying leap toward ecstasy. He caught himself, the effort bathing him in sweat. Her inner muscles worked him like a fist clenching and unclenching, as if she were experimenting with the newness of him. The awe lighting her face made his throat choke with emotion and his passion blaze like wildfire.

The long weeks of celibacy had honed his desire to a sharp edge. His first time without the dulling shield of a condom lifted his enjoyment to exquisite heights. Most of all, his love for Norah thrust him beyond the scope of his experience, beyond the limits of his control.

"Christ, you excite me," he muttered.

He pushed irresistibly deeper into her tight silken sleeve. With a moan, she lifted herself to him like a maiden offering herself to a deity. He kissed her lips and breasts and throat, until she clutched at him with a need that equaled his own.

"Norah. My Norah. Forever and ever." His fierce chant anticipated the explosion of his seed. Their bodies came together in a starburst of rapture, a shining sense of unity that melded them for all eternity.

Gasping from the sweetest repletion he had ever known, Kit rolled to her side, keeping himself sheathed within her. The ultimate languor spread through his limbs. The sweat cooled on his skin and he grew aware of the cozy snapping of the fire and the wind whispering outside.

Norah fit his arms to perfection. The rose scent of her hair mingled with the musk of their lovemaking. Her head lay back on the pillows. Her lashes formed a thick auburn fringe against her flushed cheeks.

She opened her eyes and feathered her fingers over his jaw. "Oh, Kit. That was so beautiful."

The reverence in her voice wrapped him in pleasure. He kissed her nose. "You're beautiful."

She smiled shyly. "I've missed so very much. I never even knew a man and a woman could make love face to face."

Her naivete enchanted him. Then her meaning penetrated his lassitude. *Face to face . . .*

The chill wind of suspicion blew away the fog in his mind. He withdrew and sat up. A few red droplets stained the sheets. Another smear anointed her inner thigh.

Blood. From her monthly cycle? No, he would have noticed it earlier, when he had first stroked her to climax.

A virgin's blood, then. The barrier had been her maidenhead.

Impossible.

I don't need anyone. Not that way. Not ever again.

So many times she had flinched from his touch. She had recoiled in disgust. As if she loathed the sex act.

Tonight she had turned her back. He remembered her surprised reaction: *Why are you angry? I only thought you'd want . . .*

The pieces of the puzzle fell into place. His mind perceived the abhorrent picture. Norah hadn't been rejecting him. She had been assuming the only sexual position her husband had taught her.

"Kit? Did I say something wrong?"

Her voice penetrated the roaring in his ears. He couldn't breathe. He could only stare numbly at Norah. She embodied womanly innocence, the curly hair tumbling over naked breasts and hips, the dark auburn thatch crowning her slender legs.

Even faced with insurmountable proof, he balked at believing.

"What did he do to you?" His voice sounded odd, a stranger's voice rimed by frost.

"Who?"

"Maurice. I want to know exactly how he entered you."

She blinked. Then her chin dropped a fraction and she shook her head, as if to say she didn't understand why he wanted to know, but she would humor him anyway. "From behind me." She hesitated, looking down at the pillow. "I never . . . liked it. It hurt." She showered him with the light of her smile again. "But the way you make love . . . Kit, I never knew such marvelous feelings existed."

Christ. What he feared was true. And Norah had no inkling of the evil deed done to her.

Done again and again, for nine long years.

Done by that sodomite who had stolen her love and loyalty.

Kit levered himself up off the bed. He couldn't stay still; the tumult of sickness and fury demanded an outlet. Pacing the bedroom, he muttered, "God damn him. God damn him to bloody hell!"

She wriggled up into a sitting position. "You're frightening me. Why are you ranting when we just shared something wonderful?"

The cold draft from the windows brushed his naked body. Yet he felt hot and ill. He slammed his fist against the bedpost. The thick silk hangings and his own rage cushioned him from pain. "Your goddamned husband was a homosexual."

"A what?"

"A man who fornicated with other men." Kit heard himself shouting, but couldn't stop himself. "He was a frigging queer!"

Disbelief shone stark on her face. The lampglow picked out the spattering of golden freckles across her nose. Her lips were parted, ruby lips still sweetly swollen from his kisses.

"No." Norah shook her head, stirring the waterfall of curls. "I don't understand. You know he had a mistress. Maurice may not have been a great lover, but he was a gentleman."

Her certainty drove Kit to furor. He snatched up his cravat, wiped it between her thighs, then dropped it beside her. A red stain streaked the white linen.

"There," he said, towering beside the bed. "Look at the proof. A woman bleeds the first time a man penetrates her in the normal manner."

Gazing at the cravat, she sat with her hands braced on the mattress. "Then . . . how did he . . ."

"How did he enter you? You have more than one orifice, Norah."

Horror darkened her face. She lifted her shaking hands to her cheeks. Her breasts heaved as if she found it difficult to breathe. "No, it can't be," she murmured. "It can't be."

In a flash of remorse, Kit deplored his own bluntness. He'd been too embroiled in his own violent wrath to take care for her sensibilities.

But Christ! She deserved to know how that bastard had misused her.

The bed creaked as he lowered himself beside her. Fighting to master himself for her sake, he said, "I'm sorry, Norah. You're so precious to me . . . I shouldn't have been so abrupt. I wish I hadn't been the one to tell you."

He reached out, his fingers encountering the pale purity of her shoulder. She recoiled against the bank of pillows.

"Leave me. I want to be by myself."

He withstood the lash of her rejection. How alone she must have been, with no one to confide in. "You need someone right now. Someone who loves you—"

"Go away." She drew up her legs and bowed her forehead to her knees. "Please just go away, Kit, and leave me be."

She spoke with wrenching finality. Unsure of what else to say, he rose and donned his clothes. Norah remained curled on the bed in the self-protective pose. The unguarded bow of her back deepened his vast regret.

He ached to hold her close and murmur words of comfort. But their magical evening had burned to ashes. He couldn't even console himself with damning Maurice to hell, because undoubtedly the sod was already there.

Kit picked up the soiled cravat and stuffed it into his pocket. She would feel better come morning. Once she had the chance to think and accept, she would be ready to talk again. They could get on with their life together.

And she didn't realize it yet, but this revelation about her husband's sexual deviance shed disturbing new light on the mystery of his murder. Grimly, Kit conceded that he, too, needed time alone to reflect and plan.

"I'll be nearby if you need me. Good night, love."

Norah heard the heavy tread of his footsteps, then the click of the door closing. Only then did she raise her head. The bedroom looked the same. The yellow and blue silk bed hangings. The fire burning low on the grate. The wing chair where Kit had so patiently guided a virgin to her first glimpse of heaven.

Virgin. The notion was incredible. Unbelievable. But undeniable.

Those years of feeling pain and disgust came rushing back in nightmare waves. Dear God, Maurice had lured her into the sin of sodomy. And she had been too unschooled to know better.

Her numb gaze focused on the small table beside the chair. There lay the necklace from her parure. In the midst of the silver and moonstones, a circle of gold glittered.

Her wedding ring. Symbol of everlasting fidelity. Symbol of cruelty. Symbol of lies.

Rage broke her rigid reserve. She flew off the bed, scooped up the ring, and hurled it into the fireplace. The circlet bounced off the back tiles and rolled into the cinders, where it disappeared into blackness.

She sank to her knees and wept. She wept from shock at her own naivete. She wept from grief for the lost years of her youth. She wept from anger at the husband who had defiled her.

And she wept because Kit knew she had been soiled.

At last the well of tears ran dry. She rose on shaky legs, picked up her nightgown, and blotted the moisture from her cheeks. The black eyes of the windows seemed to mock her stupidity.

What she had perceived to be her marital duty had in fact been an unnatural act, a sin. The horror of it still reverberated inside her.

But how could she have guessed that Maurice hid a dark side? She had scarcely known such perversions existed. Ladies spoke little of intimate matters.

A bittersweet ache lodged inside her breast. No wonder she had felt so pure and new when Kit made love to her. But the nasty reality of her marriage tainted even that precious memory.

Tears burned the back of her throat again. Norah swallowed. She felt unclean from the accumulated grime of years. The desperate urge to be alone suddenly consumed her. She needed time to think, to reconcile herself to the ugly shock of her marriage. Even more, she needed to escape the horrid notion that she had been at fault somehow, that her coldness in bed had spurred her husband to seek out other men, that perhaps she might have changed him if only she had been a more loving wife.

Her rational mind rejected the fear, but doubt kept it alive. Regrets clamped around her, like a deadly serpent squeezing the air from her lungs. She couldn't give herself to Kit again until she came to grips with this awful sense of guilt. Yet the longing for him lay warmly inside her, tempting her.

She must leave here. Now. For if she waited until morning, Kit would try to stop her.

In reckless haste she ran into the dressing room and dragged out a small leather case. She packed a few garments, then dressed herself in warm clothing and sturdy shoes. The routine of her toilette felt alien, performed on a body that had become a stranger to her.

In the bedroom she added the parure to her bag,

letting the delicate jewels sift through her fingers. She hadn't adequately thanked him for the gift, the gift that came from his heart. How astounded she had been, how fearful that it was merely a spoiled aristocrat's method of wooing a woman into bed. Now Norah knew her mistake. Kit had grown into an honorable man. Yet tragically, she felt tarnished beside the luster of his love.

Her hollow-eyed reflection stared back at her from the oval dressing-glass. The black gown hugged the familiar contours of her body, yet she felt inexorably changed. She looked like a woman weighted by sadness yet strengthened by resolution.

Tonight while the household slept she would depart. She knew precisely where she would go, a quiet place where she could be alone to heal her soul. And in that same place she might also find the treasure that would establish her as the foremost jeweler in the land.

If she planned well, she would accomplish her task before Kit even guessed her destination.

Chapter 15

❦

"She's about chin high to me, with beautiful red hair and green eyes," Kit said, his white-knuckled grip on the desk belying his calm tone. "She may have registered under another name."

The hotel proprietress folded her sturdy arms and looked him straight in the eye, an easy task since she matched him in height. "Seems peculiar she'd go to such lengths to avoid you."

He reined in his temper. This formidable Valkyrie with her iron-gray hair and excess of chins had to be the fiftieth hotelier he'd questioned today. He had wasted two agonizingly fruitless days tramping all over London before a flash of inspiration had propelled him to the Isle of Wight.

And Norah had to be here somewhere. The maharaja of Rampur's *abdur* had reported seeing an irksome *memsahib*, but claimed no knowledge of her present whereabouts.

Beyond the window, gulls swooped through the sea mist. Kit felt cold and out of sorts. Christ, he would kiss the hairy wart on this hostelkeeper's cheek if it meant finding Norah. "She's my wife," he lied, leaning over the desk as if to share a secret. "We're newly wed, you see, and we quarreled when she found a note from another woman in my coat pocket—"

"Hah! You look like the sort. Indeed you do."
The Valkyrie peered over the desk at his wind-tousled hair down to his sand-encrusted shoes.

Kit set his jaw. "Norah stormed off before I could explain that the note was from my cousin. I must tell her it was all a terrible misunderstanding." When the proprietress merely fingered the bog oak brooch pinned to her shieldlike bosom, he added in desperation, "Please, ma'am, might I look at your registry? Today's the one-month anniversary of our wedding and I couldn't bear to spend it alone, without my beloved Norah."

"You bring me to mind of me late husband. The smooth-talkin' devil could coax me into the sea durin' a January ice storm." She reached beneath the desk, brought out a ledger, and pointed to an entry. "I'll even save you the trouble of lookin'."

Midway down the list of guests, familiar feminine handwriting graced the ruled page: *Mrs. N. St. Claire.*

Elation and fury and pain detonated in his chest. Kit took a moment to master himself. "What room?"

"Number ten, end of the passage." She jerked her thumb toward the corridor beside the cramped staircase. "Been in there all morning, quiet as a church mouse."

He came around the desk and kissed her cheek, the bristly mole brushing his stubbled face. "Thank you. I'm eternally grateful."

Amazingly, a blush stole over the woman's no-nonsense features. "Go on with you. The lady's looked powerful melancholy these past few days. Seein' you would perk any woman up."

"I'll do my best."

His own fervent words dogged Kit down the dim passage. At the door labeled number ten, he checked the urge to burst inside. He combed his fingers through his untidy hair and faced his fears. Jesus God. Norah might hate him for destroying her illusions about her marriage. She might refuse to speak to him. Worst of all, she might regret the expression of their love that gleamed in his memory like a glimpse of paradise.

He knocked. He paced. He knocked again, harder.

The door opened. He stood transfixed by the solemn-faced woman in the entryway. Color kissed her pale cheeks. Loosely styled red hair framed the face of an angel. Norah. His beloved Norah. The violet smudges beneath her eyes gave evidence to sleepless nights. The black mourning gown enhanced the delicacy of her features. One hand was hidden in her pocket; the bracelet from his parure glinted beneath her other lace cuff.

He couldn't stop himself. He swept her against him and buried his face in her hair. Roses and sea salt perfumed her; joy brought tears to his eyes. "Norah. Oh my God, I found you."

For one heavenly moment she melted against him; then she extricated herself from his embrace. "I'm surprised you found me so soon. You're becoming quite the detective."

Her cool wall of reserve shut him out. He followed her inside and closed the door. The bedchamber had plain furnishings in oak and autumn-toned chintz. The brisk March breeze wafted through the opened French door, which led onto a small stone terrace. He could see a tea tray on a table beside the wrought-iron garden chair where she must have sat watching the white-capped waves roll onto the rocky beach.

The image of her calmly ensconced in a seaside room, as if she were on holiday, uncorked the anger bottled inside him. "Why the devil did you run away?" he demanded. "Didn't you consider how frantic I'd be? I scoured the city of London looking for you."

She stood stiffly by the bedpost. "I left a note saying I was somewhere safe."

"Safe? Here, alone? For Christ's sake, Norah. You have more brains than that. St. Claire could have tracked you down, just as I did."

She brushed past him and went to the terrace

door. The muffled crashing of surf covered her footsteps. "I might have known you were still accusing Jerome."

"He's our prime suspect, now more than ever. He said he was abroad the night of the murder, but we only have his word on that. He could have stolen Ivy's brooch. He could have pushed you down the stairs at the museum."

"Don't be ridiculous."

"Don't *you* be ridiculous." Kit stalked after her and seized her shoulders. The delicacy of her bones belied the strength of her character. "Listen to me. What we found out about Maurice must be a vital clue in the murder investigation. His killer could have been a man. A man dressed as a woman."

"I've wondered about that, too." She frowned at the seascape, the wet beach where the mist had turned into a fine rain. Then she aimed an indignant look at Kit. "But if you're suggesting that Jerome is the culprit, you're mad. We've been through this before, and he had no motive to murder my husband. For heaven's sake, Maurice still owed him six thousand pounds."

Her heated defense made Kit's blood boil. "Maybe he and St. Claire were lovers. Lovers who quarreled."

Horror dulled the sparkle in her green eyes. "I can't believe that. I *won't* believe it." She jerked away from him and hugged herself. "Only you would dream up so vile a suggestion, Kit Coleridge."

Her disdain sliced his heart. "Why do you always trust him before me? You're completely taken in by that suave schemer."

"Jerome is not a schemer. He's a loyal friend."

"See what I mean? He could have knocked on your door with murder on his mind, Mrs. St. Claire," Kit mocked. "And you'd have welcomed him with open arms. When it comes to Jerome, you don't have the sense to protect yourself."

"Well! I certainly don't need you to defend me."

She thrust her hand into her pocket and yanked out a small pistol.

She leveled it at Kit.

For one stupefying instant he feared she hated him enough to pull the trigger. He stood as vulnerable as a fly caught in amber. But only determination shone in her eyes, not the glitter of madness.

She waved the weapon. "You see? I'm perfectly capable of taking care of myself."

"For God's sake! Put that thing away before someone gets hurt."

"I'm only showing you I'm safe—"

"Do you know how to use it? Striking a moving target isn't as easy as it might seem."

"I can hardly miss from this range."

"And what if the man wrested the gun away from you?"

"I'd shoot him first."

"Shall we test your skills?" Propelled by his explosive emotions, Kit strode toward her.

She started to lower the pistol. "On you? I wouldn't—"

He caught her forearm and thrust it outward, so the barrel pointed toward the beach outside. His other arm wrapped around her waist and snared her against him, soft breasts to hard chest, womanhood to manhood. Her muscles went rigid, yet she held still, the rise and fall of her bosom keeping rhythm with the song of the sea. A gust of cold moisture blew through the opened doorway. His fury abated, its heat sliding downward to his groin and sparking the memory of their naked bodies fitting together so perfectly. Norah's green gaze held a wary confusion that told him she too remembered their closeness.

She let go of the pistol; it thunked to the floor. Releasing her, he bent to pick up the compact gun. "Some protection. This is a muff pistol. It only fires one shot."

She made a show of rubbing her forearm. "If I missed, I could have kicked you where you're most vulnerable. So you needn't worry."

Her tone held a thread of teasing. The darkness within him lightened a fraction. "You're wearing too many petticoats to do me any harm. But if you'd care to undress and try again . . ."

"No." Tightening the shawl around herself, she retreated a few steps. "You've already proven your superior strength. That should satisfy you."

Hardly, he thought morosely. Her bitterness reminded him of a wounded bird, withdrawn, mistrustful, and afraid of being hurt again. He regretted letting his anger override his patience.

He lay the pistol on the night table. "Where did you get the gun?"

"In Portsmouth, after I sold the brooch from the parure." Norah caught her bottom lip between her teeth. "I'm sorry I had to break up your gift. I only had enough money to pay for the train."

Kit shook his head. "The piece can be replaced. Your life is far more precious." His tone mellowed into quiet intensity. "Norah, tell me why you ran away from me."

She gazed down at her linked fingers. "I wanted to get the diamond, Fire at Midnight. When I left, I went to London to mislead you; then I came south and took the ferry here. But the maharaja has stayed in seclusion. I've gone back every morning, but I haven't been able to gain an audience." Her nose wrinkled. "I've a suspicion the servant hasn't been passing on my messages."

"You should have invited me to come with you. We're partners, remember?"

"I needed to be alone. To do this alone."

"Why?"

"Because . . ." Still she avoided his eyes, gazing anywhere but at him. "Because my career is important to me. I spent a fortnight at your parents' house when I ought to have been working. Ivy and Winnifred depend on me for their livelihood. And the competition is only six weeks away. I thought it was long past time to finish the tiara."

Determined to ferret out the truth, Kit crossed to

her and grasped her hands. The shock of her cold skin distracted him. "God, you're freezing! Come sit over here while I make a fire."

He settled her into a chair by the brown-painted mantelpiece, wrapped a blanket around her, then closed the terrace door. Returning to the fireplace, he crouched before the coals stacked in the grate.

Watching him strike a match, Norah felt a hunger so great it sparked tears in her eyes. The sight of him fed her starved senses. His face was as darkly alluring as that of a foreign prince. His hair looked charmingly tousled, as if he'd raked his fingers through the ebony strands. The dove-gray suit outlined the muscles in his back and arms and thighs. Her body remembered his with stunning accuracy, the taste of his mouth, the breadth of his chest, the tautness of his loins.

A liquid shudder coursed through her. Not even during the agonizing loneliness of the night had she experienced so poignant a yearning. Praise God he had come after her.

He held the flame to the tinder, but it failed to light. As he tried another match, the sharp scent of sulphur drifted to her. Finally the wood shavings caught. He blew gently on the tiny blaze until the coals began to whiten and glow.

Grimacing, he rose and brushed at the black smudges on his hands. "I've watched the maids light fires a thousand times. Now that I know how difficult it really is, I'll have to raise their wages."

His wry humor in the face of her reticence, his willingness to dirty himself for her comfort, brought home to Norah his kindness and consideration. Yet how diverse their backgrounds were . . . He had been born to privilege while she had had a humble upbringing in a convent, where lighting the morning fires had been her duty. Odd, how their differences made him all the more appealing.

He walked to the washstand and poured a basin of water. Removing his coat, he rolled back his sleeves and soaped his hands. The quiet sounds of his splashing held an intimate quality, and for one heartfelt moment she let herself fantasize that Kit was her husband.

Dear God. If only she could so easily cleanse herself, body and soul. She wanted to be new and untainted for him.

As he dried his hands, she said, "I think you deserve to know the true reason I ran away."

Frowning at her, he replaced the towel on the hook. Then he pulled up a stool and sat close to her, his elbows propped on his knees and his fingers loosely linked. "I'm listening."

She hesitated, not because she thought he wouldn't understand, but because she feared her own weakness for him. She feared opening her heart when her emotions were still so fragile. "I left you because I was confused. I felt . . . soiled and unworthy of you."

"Unworthy?" His eyebrows winged upward. "Norah, I'm the one who had all the affairs, who tried to prove to society that no woman could hurt me. I'm the one with the reputation to live down, not you. You're completely innocent."

"No, I'm not. All those years, I should have guessed something was terribly wrong in my marriage. I should have left Maurice."

Darkness descended over Kit's face. He rubbed the blanket covering her knees. "A lady is told nothing but to close her eyes and endure her husband's touch. What Maurice did to you was vile and unnatural. But it certainly wasn't your fault."

"My mind knows that. But inside I feel responsible somehow."

"Responsible for his sodomizing you again and again? You were a convent-bred orphan who couldn't have known better."

His disgust toward Maurice put her on the defensive. "He didn't . . . come to me so very often. Sometimes months went by, as if he were trying not to desire me that way. The next day he always brought me a gift, a pair of earrings or some other trinket from the shop. I thought—"

"You're making excuses for him."

"Don't interrupt me." Her voice snagged on the lump in her throat. She swallowed. "I thought his gifts were a man's way of buying his wife's affections. But now I can see he must have been trying to assuage his own guilt."

"Any shame he might have felt didn't justify his actions."

"I know that now. But if I hadn't been so horribly naive, perhaps . . ."

"Perhaps what? You could have seduced him into making love to you the normal way?"

"Yes," she whispered on an agonized breath.

Closing her eyes, she tried to fathom Maurice's desire to mate with another male. Did he seek a sense of oneness that he had failed to find in his marriage? Who was that faceless other man? Jerome? Her intellect mulled over the possibility; her heart rejected it outright. What of Maurice's other friends? She couldn't recall any other man he had paid particular attention to.

Kit took her hand and rubbed the back. Though his strokes were gentle, she could sense his latent rage. She opened her eyes to his intent frown.

"Norah, don't torture yourself. Men like Maurice can't feel desire for any woman. Not even for a woman as beautiful and loving as you."

She wanted to believe him. She ached to sink into the purity of his affections. Reluctantly drawing her hand free, she traced the cheery plaid of the lap blanket. "If I could hate him, it might be easier. But in some ways he was a kind husband—"

"So kind he subjected you to perversion."

"Please, just listen." She cast about for a way to make Kit see the man she had lived with for nine years, the man she was only now beginning to understand and pity. "Maurice encouraged me to design jewelry when most husbands would have forbidden their wives to engage in commerce."

Kit slapped his thighs. "It's no wonder he gave you so much liberty. He claimed credit for your work."

"But he left the shop to me. He didn't have to do that. I think it was his form of repayment for the pain he'd put me through."

"Oh, spare me the justifications. He left you with a stack of debts." Kit shot to his feet and snatched up the poker. With an irate jab, he stirred the coals. The flames licked high, radiating warmth throughout the room. "Damn! I can't understand how you can still love a man like him."

His anguished assertion surprised her. "I don't love him. I don't think I ever did."

"Then why are you so quick to jump to his defense?"

She shook her head. "Because I was fond of him in a way. Odd as it might seem, we were accustomed to each other . . . outside the bedroom, at least."

"Then it must be St. Claire."

"Pardon?"

"You love St. Claire. He owns so much of your loyalty that you've nothing left for me."

His blind aversion to Jerome exasperated her. "What utter nonsense. How many times must I tell you, he's only a friend?"

"Well. He certainly wants to marry you." Kit let the poker clatter back into its stand. "Maybe so much that he dressed himself like a woman and murdered your husband."

A blaze of emotion chased away the chill Norah had felt earlier. She threw back the blanket and surged to her feet. "Just a few minutes ago, you implied they were lovers. Make up your mind, for pity's sake."

"Maybe you would prefer to marry him, too." Kit spoke as if he hadn't heard her. "After all, you registered here as Mrs. St. Claire."

Suddenly her own pain dissipated like a sea mist clearing to bright sunshine. All at once she understood the hurt behind his resentment, the vulnerability concealed deep inside the strong, outwardly assured man. Crossing to him, she took his arm. "Oh Kit, please don't be jealous. There's no need."

"I wish I shared your confidence."

"You can." Conscious of the hard muscles beneath his sleeve, she lowered her voice to a murmur. "Despite all that's come to light, one fact hasn't changed. I love you."

Intensity lit his handsome face. "Then for God's sake, marry me."

Her pulse pounded with slow thuds of longing. Surely he hadn't pondered all the ramifications of wedding a commoner, the widow of a murdered man. She walked to the window. The waves curled up to shore, then retreated again, reminding her of the push-pull feelings that plagued her.

Turning, Norah held tight to the sill. "I do want to be your wife," she admitted. "But I can't bind you to a prolonged engagement while I complete my two years of mourning—"

"Forget convention. I want to live with you now."

She shook her head. "Consider the scandal we'd cause. Even the Queen would condemn us. She doesn't believe a widow should ever remarry, let alone after only a few months."

"Leave Her Majesty to me."

His confidence beckoned like a safe harbor to her battered spirits. "What about the license, then? No clergyman would agree to marry us so quickly."

"My family has ties to the archbishop of Canterbury. For years, he's been urging my father to settle me down with a wife. So you see, the highest prelate in England might even dance a jig at our wedding."

Keeping a rigid rein on her ardent emotions, she looked out the window again and groped for the courage to voice her greatest fear. "This is happening too fast. What if you change your mind later? What if you decide you've made a terrible mistake?"

"I won't, Norah."

The conviction in his voice gratified her. The rocky beach, the lowering clouds, took on the blurry aspect of a rain-washed window. Norah grasped the fringes of her shawl. She wanted so badly to be a permanent part of his tomorrows that she couldn't stem the flow of tears.

The tread of his footsteps approached. From directly behind her, he murmured, "Have you started your monthly courses yet?"

She numbly shook her head. The chance of bearing his baby made her smile through her tears. It had buoyed her spirits on the train ride to Portsmouth, and in the solitary days since then.

His arms circled her from behind and his palms settled warmly over her abdomen. "You aren't barren, Norah. You might already hold our child in your womb."

Her breath emerged on a wisp of yearning. "A baby would be a gift from heaven."

"It would also be a bastard if you persist in denying me."

"I know. I know."

"Then trust me, for God's sake. I helped your orphan boys. I took tea with Ivy and listened to Winnifred complain. I tidied the muddle in your account books. I protected you after someone pushed you down a flight of stairs. Do you truly think my feelings for you are shallow? My God, I love you more each day."

She tilted her head back against his chest. Her hands covered his, and she felt the crispness of his hairs, the tempered steel of his bones, the hands of an equal and worthy mate. A man capable of fidelity. The one man who loved her with all his heart. The emptiness inside her suddenly overflowed, rinsing away the uncertainties, cleansing her of doubts, until she felt pure and radiant, and strong enough to endure any opposition.

In that moment she let herself hope again. She let herself dream. She let herself believe.

Turning in his arms, she looked into his midnight

eyes, into the rakishly attractive features of the man who had become the center stone of her life. "I'm ready to be your wife, Kit. Whenever, wherever you like."

His chest lifted; then he released a breath. A smile tilted his mouth. His fingertips traced designs over the side of her neck, sparking delicious chills over her skin. "Then may I propose we get straight to the task of ensuring an heir?"

She slipped her fingers between the silver studs on his shirt and found warm flesh and a forest of hair. "So long as you understand that you might ensure yourself an heiress instead."

He kissed away the tears on her cheeks. "I'd be delighted to commission a few of each."

"Just not all at once, please."

Chuckling, he hugged her tight. "God forbid. As master of the family, I demand the right to create each new life, one by one."

"As you wish, my lord."

Happiness bubbled like champagne through her veins. Yielding to Kit meant not the forfeit of her freedom, but the procurement of his devotion. Between leisurely kisses and liberal caresses, they undressed each other with total disregard for modesty. In bed, his lovemaking engaged her in a celebration of sweetness, a sampling of tastes and scents and tactile sensations. By degrees their passion expanded into the cadence of rich emotion, and they came together in a rush of unbounded pleasure.

Their mutual cries of delight blended with the muted crash of surf outside and the crackling of the fire inside. The aftermath left Norah flushed with satisfaction, rejoicing in their joining, body and soul.

Kit lifted himself on his elbows. The glint of gold in his eyes reflected a tortured intensity. He touched her cheek. "You're precious to me, Norah. So very precious. I couldn't bear to lose you."

"You won't," she murmured. "I'm here for you, always."

He slowly shook his head. "There's a murderer on the loose. You're going back to my parents' estate, where you'll be safe. Then I'll return to London and work with the police. With this new lead, I have more avenues to explore—"

"No." Alarm invaded her lassitude. She pushed up against the pillows. "Kit, I won't be put away like . . . like a ruby kept in a vault and brought out to admire every now and then. I have work to do, a shop to watch over, a royal commission to win."

"I'll handle matters. We can't take a chance with your life." His large hand covered her belly. "Or with the life of our unborn child."

For an instant his argument swayed her. Then in a flash of irritation she recognized what he was doing. "We don't know yet that I'm pregnant, so stop playing on my emotions. I'll be perfectly safe in your house. And elsewhere, I'll stay close to you."

"I won't let you put yourself in danger—"

"And what if the killer is never found? Will we live apart forever?" She took his face in her palms and welcomed the scratch of stubble against her skin. "Now that we've found each other, Kit, I want to be with you. I want to see you when we go to sleep at night and awaken with you each morning. I want us to share every priceless minute of every day."

His warm hand drifted over her bare thigh. He compressed his lips; then she saw his capitulation in the gradual easing of his tight expression, in the wry quirk of one black eyebrow. "Now who's playing on emotions?" he asked.

He bent and kissed her knee; the simple gesture increased the wealth of love inside her. She took a tremulous breath. "I can't leave the island until I see the maharaja. Which means we may have to spend a few days alone here."

"A honeymoon before the wedding?" Kit drawled. "Now there's an appealing idea, partner."

They made love again, a slow delicious coupling

that left Norah gasping with joy. And yet as they lay together afterward, she could sense his disquiet in the moody quality of his gaze, in the tautness of his embrace. He was afraid for her. The same fear nipped at the edges of her happiness, too.

Out of the darkness of memory rushed a black figure. She relived the hard push, the long tumble down the stairs . . .

Norah shook off the sticky cobwebs of horror. Danger lurked only as a distant nightmare, she assured herself.

For now she had the security of Kit's love. She would seize the rare fortune that had brought them to a secluded island off the coast of England. Wriggling closer to Kit, she breathed his fragrant musk and settled her hand on his flat stomach. Let the world pass them by. For a time at least, she would devote herself to dispelling his anxiety and arousing his ardor.

Seven days later, in an old aristocratic mansion near Cowes, she and Kit followed a white-robed *ab-dur* up a graceful flight of stairs.

"Ten minutes," she whispered, clinging to Kit's arm. "I came here every day for over a week, and then you give your name and the maharaja agrees to see us within ten minutes. It isn't fair."

Norah spoke teasingly, but he detected an undercurrent of annoyance. He felt defensive and amused all at once. "I tried to warn you," he murmured. "The Indians are even more patriarchal than we English. So please let me do the talking."

Norah snorted, then fell silent. He knew every nuance of her mind, every inch of her creamy flesh, yet he felt powerless to ease her resentment. The past week reminded him of nirvana, the Hindu version of heaven: long walks on the blustery beach, leisurely picnics in sheltered coves, the cherished perfection of their lovemaking.

Stolen moments, Kit thought. He could distract

her no longer from her quest for the fabled diamond that was linked in some inexplicable way to the mystery of Maurice Rutherford's death.

They entered a dimly lit boudoir. Here, the country manor had been transformed into an exotic palace. Silks of scarlet and saffron draped the walls and concealed the windows. Sandalwood incense drifted from smoking brass braziers. Pagan statuary abounded, from globe-breasted goddesses to impish boy-gods.

Kit felt the instinctive tightening of revulsion, but this time he also experienced a stirring of curiosity and interest. He was suddenly attracted to the notion of learning about the exotic land of his birth. The land of his mother's people.

I thank God that your father once loved a Hindu woman named Shivina.

Norah's fervent words shone like bright stars in his mind. All the slurs and whispers that had infuriated him in the past no longer mattered so much. Even the memory of Emma Woodferne's rejection had lost its power to hurt because now he knew her for what she was, a petty bigot too blind to see the goodness within him. Norah's unconditional acceptance of him enveloped his soul in healing splendor.

Today he had his chance to help her.

In the soft light of the torches, her lovely features were drawn with anxiety. She had shed the drab black of full mourning in favor of a pale gray that complemented her fine complexion. She clung tightly to his arm, and he covered her hand with his, but she was looking toward the far end of the chamber, to the diminutive occupant of a gold throne.

They walked forward until they stood before the man who could cause her to win or lose the most important sale of her career.

The maharaja of Rampur had a wizened face resembling that of the pet monkey perched on the arm of the throne and grooming its long tail. Cloth of gold swathed the ruler's spry, aging body. Adorning his great white turban was a *supeche* in the form of a peacock holding a rope of enormous pearls in its beak. An emerald the size of a dove's egg ornamented his wrist.

Reaching deep into his boyhood memory, Kit folded his palms together and bowed. "*Namaste*, Your Highness."

"We may speak your own tongue with thanks to the British nanny of my youth." The maharaja looked Kit up and down. "Indeed you are the son of Coleridge-*sahib*. He took my photograph once, many years ago."

"Yes, he told me so."

"Yet it is rumored that the blood of my people also flows in your veins."

"My mother once graced the court of Bahadur Shah. She was called Shivina." Saying her name aloud felt good and right, like the lifting of a years-old darkness. He brought Norah forward. "I would like you to meet my intended bride, Norah Rutherford."

She sank into a deep curtsy, her gray skirts billowing around her. "I'm pleased to make your acquaintance, Your Highness. I've waited many days for this moment."

A gleam of humor lit his eyes. "Had I known of your great beauty, I would have welcomed you sooner."

He clapped his hands. A regiment of servants glided in, bearing trays of sweetmeats and a huge, ornate silver tea service. Norah and Kit took seats on a bank of colorful pillows.

"The court of Bahadur Shah," said the maharaja, stroking his beringed hand over the back of the monkey. "I visited there once, before the great mutiny. But alas, I cannot remember a woman of your mother's name."

"More than thirty years ago, she was wed to a court scribe." Kit searched his memory for the story his stepmother, Sarah, had told him so many times, the story he had repressed since boyhood. "When

Shivina's husband died, my father saved her from burning herself on the funeral pyre."

"Ah, the ancient custom of suttee." The maharaja shook his head. "Indeed the British raj brought modern progress to India."

"Will you tell me more?" Kit asked. "I would like to hear about life at the court where my mother once lived."

"Gladly." The maharaja spoke eloquently of cock fights and tiger hunts, of nightingales cooing in the palace garden beside the Jumna River, of the stable of elephants which carried Bahadur Shah and his royal entourage on parade through the streets of Delhi. He described the ancient palace with its many crumbling courtyards and high turrets, the kingdom of past glory ruled by an aging monarch who had become a pensioner of the British raj.

For the first time, Kit let himself picture his mother, her slim dark beauty modestly veiled, gliding through the antiquated stone corridors. Imagining her as a flesh-and-blood woman made him feel both proud and ashamed. For so many years he had been a bigot, too. He had refused to see Shivina as a real woman; it had been easier to curse a shadow figure for the legacy of his Hindu blood. But now he had the chance to make up for past mistakes. He vowed to ask his father and stepmother to share more of their memories of Shivina. Perhaps some day he would even travel to India and go to the places described by the maharaja.

A soft touch on his hand drew his gaze to Norah. She was smiling at him, and the love shining on her face brought a cleansing lightness to his spirits. She loved him for the man he was, and her gentle understanding had helped him come to accept himself.

Their eyes held for a timeless moment; then she turned to the maharaja, who looked on in bemused interest.

"That was a wonderful description, Your Highness," she said. "If I might ask a great favor, though?"

"*Koi baat nahin.*" Petting the monkey's back, the maharaja smiled. "Whatever you like."

"Have you a priest here who might marry Kit and me according to Hindu law?"

Her startling suggestion rocked Kit. He opened his mouth to protest, because he wanted a legal and binding ceremony, not a pagan rite. Yet suddenly the prospect held a certain appeal. Norah was offering him the rare chance to experience for himself the religious practices of his maternal ancestry. They could exchange their Christian vows later.

Grasping her hand, he said firmly, "Yes, we would both like that very much."

"But of course. I will make the arrangements. And give you a wedding present, too." The maharaja removed the emerald from his wrist and passed it to Norah. "A token to match your pretty eyes."

She stared down at the jewel glinting in her palm. "Oh, I could never accept so rich a gift," she murmured.

"Nonsense. It is nothing to me. You of all Englishwomen will esteem the stone, since your departed husband appreciated fine jewels."

Keen attention riveted Kit. "Then you knew of Maurice Rutherford? His agent must have reached you, after all."

The maharaja waved his beringed fingers. "Yes, many months ago, before I left on my voyage here, I sold him the diamond, Fire at Midnight. I was told the stone is to decorate the crown of England's Princess of Wales."

Kit and Norah exchanged a glance. The light of relief brightened her gaze. "Thank heavens," she said, clutching the emerald to her bosom. "Mr. Upchurch must be on his way back from India, then."

"Upchurch?" The maharaja frowned. "I know of no Upchurch."

"But you must," she said, her head tipped to the side. "He's the agent my husband hired."

The maharaja gravely regarded her. "This is most odd. There must be a mistake."

"What do you mean?" Kit asked hoarsely.

"The man who came to my palace in Rampur called himself Jerome St. Claire."

Chapter 16

"**Y**ou're married?" Ivy chirped. "You're truly married?"

The old woman's downturned mouth and tearful aquamarine eyes dismayed Norah. She and Kit had pledged their love first in the exotic Hindu rite and then again in Canterbury Cathedral. A haze of happiness had enveloped them on the train ride to London, a bliss so pure and sweet she had been sure the entire world must rejoice, too.

Dear God, she had looked forward to sharing the wonderful news with the only family she had ever known. In spite of the estrangement, she had hoped for their support and acceptance.

Leaving Kit in the doorway, she stepped across the parlor and gathered Ivy's spidery hands. "Yes, Kit and I are married. Aren't you pleased for me?"

"Can you blame the poor creature for being upset?" Winnifred interjected from her seat by the fire. With a self-righteous jerk, she straightened her black shawl and glowered at Norah's fashionable lilac-gray gown, at the matching jacket with its Russian froggings. "People have been gossiping about your unconventional conduct. When they see that you've abandoned your mourning dress and sullied Maurice's memory by remarrying in haste, Ivy and I will bear the brunt of their censure. We'll be ostracized, ruined!"

"You're overlooking one fact, Winnifred." Walking toward the half circle of chairs, Kit slapped his taupe leather gloves against his palm. "Norah is now the marchioness of Blackthorne. Henceforth, you'll address her more respectfully." He placed his hand on Norah's shoulder. His support buoyed her flagging spirits with the knowledge that he would always be there for her.

Winnifred flushed. "I meant no slight, your lordship."

"Better you should make your apologies to my wife."

As stiff as a marionette, she picked at the lace doily draping the arm of the chair. "Forgive me, my lady."

"Of course." Norah turned her gaze back to the woman whose skinny fingers she still held. "Ivy, I'm sorry if my announcement displeases you. As soon as you know Kit better, I'm sure you'll grow to love him nearly as much as I do."

"Oh, but I already have a great regard for his lordship. And I'm not bothered by silly gossip." Ivy blinked behind the spectacles. "But I do confess I'm worried."

"Worried?" Norah asked. She glanced up at Kit's vigilant features. Bleakness battered her heart; he still considered her loved ones capable of murder. "What are you worried about?"

"Now that you have a home with Lord Kit, you don't need this one. Where will Winnie and Marmalade and I live?"

The fog of suspicion cleared. Norah stroked the papery back of Ivy's hand. Poor Ivy had endured such disapproval from Maurice and Winnifred. "Oh, darling. I'm not planning to sell the town house. You'll have a home here for as long as you like."

"Truly?"

"Truly."

Despite her appearance of frailty, Ivy half skipped over to the hearth, where she bent to stroke the sleeping cat. "Did you hear that, Marmalade? We're going to stay here after all."

The cat stretched its orange striped paws toward the fire, then settled back into slumber.

"I should be happy to continue shouldering all the housekeeping duties," Winnifred intoned.

"Thank you," Norah said. "That would be most helpful."

A shrewd intensity glinted in Winnifred's brown eyes. "May I also reassure you that in your absence I've been tending to poor Maurice's grave? I fear I must report an odd happening there."

Kit tensed his hand on Norah's shoulder. "Explain yourself," he said.

"Last Friday when I went to clip the grass near the tomb, there was a red rose lying atop the marble. When I returned this morning, there was another one, fresh as springtime, dew still on the petals. It would seem someone's been bringing a single new rose each day."

The cold fingers of shock iced Norah's spine. Red roses. A red-cloaked woman. A red-lined jewelry case. Did the clues add up to the same person? The person who had killed Maurice?

"Have you informed the police?" she asked.

"No." Winnifred hesitated. "I thought I had better speak to you first . . . my lady."

"Thank you," Kit said. "We'll notify Inspector Wadding at once."

"You missed him yesterday." Ivy sat down with her tatting. "He came round and gave me back my brooch." She lowered her lacy black shawl to display the mourning piece pinned over her heart. "What a kind man he is."

"Was he able to find the jeweler who engraved the inside inscription?" Norah asked.

"Why, mercy," Ivy said, in wide-eyed innocence. "I never even thought to ask."

"Humph," snorted Winnifred. "Forgot is how I would call it."

"I didn't forget. I simply would never presume to meddle in the business of Scotland Yard."

"How you do like to fool yourself—"

"If you ladies will excuse us," Kit broke into their bickering. "Norah and I must be going."

Out in the blustery day, he helped her climb into the elegant brougham waiting at the curb. Norah gazed through the beveled glass window at the overcast sky, at the trees with their green mist of new leaves. In the weeks since she'd been gone, spring had crept over the city. Yet the old fears piled inside her again, as dark and dank as musty humus in a graveyard.

As Kit seated himself beside her and the carriage rattled off, she said, "Do you think the roses were left by the murderer?"

"It's a bloody good possibility." A grim smile quirked the corners of his mouth. He snapped his gloved fingers. "This could be the most important clue yet. Now the police can post a guard to watch the grave."

"But why would someone leave the flowers?" She shivered from an eerie thought. "It's almost as if this person . . . loved Maurice."

Kit settled his hand over hers. "It *is* odd. I suppose the culprit might be Ivy or even Winnifred herself. But it better fits my theory that he was murdered by a man who was his lover."

One unspoken name hovered in the close confines of the carriage. Jerome. He thought Jerome was the murderer.

"Thaddeus wants the royal commission," she said quickly. "He could have pushed me down the stairs. And he worked closely with Maurice, too. They might have been . . ."

"Lovers? It's a possibility, yes."

But his tone was desultory, his expression distracted.

If Thaddeus were the killer, Norah thought feverishly, poor Winnifred would lose her dream. Then again, perhaps Winnifred *knew*. Perhaps she loved

Thaddeus so much she could abet him in murder. But did she know of his sodomy, the cruel way he would use her if they married?"

"Norah," Kit said, tipping her chin up. "I know it hurts you, but we must consider St. Claire."

Bitter denial choked her. She parted her lips to chastise Kit, then paused. Reluctant to spoil the perfection of their brief honeymoon, they had spoken little of the disturbing news delivered by the maharaja. They had avoided the topic of murder altogether and instead made love with quiet intensity, as if their combined devotion could ward off the perils of a world gone mad.

Now, within their first hour back in London, strife threatened to split them asunder.

She pressed her cheek to his coat sleeve and wished she dared kiss him in public, wished the gold velvet curtains were drawn against the city folk and vehicles streaming past the brougham windows. Instead she clasped his hand. "Kit," she murmured over the clopping of hooves. "Oh, Kit, if only we could run away. If only we could return to the island and live in seclusion forever."

His dark lashes lowered slightly. He slid his arm around her shoulders, turned up her chin, and melded their mouths. The bold move made her stiffen for a few heartbeats; then the irresistible craving beckoned, drugging her to all but the taste and texture of her beloved husband. Blessed heat trickled past the chill in her body and formed an ever-increasing pool within her deepest part. He kissed her with slow sensuality, with tempting tenderness, until she arched mindlessly toward him, her hands sliding inside his coat, riding downward to his firm waist, then lowering to the buttons of his trousers.

He caught her wrist. "Have patience," he whispered in her ear. "We'll be home soon."

The affectionate deviltry in his voice reawakened her to their surroundings. The carriage swayed around a corner. Through the front window, she spied the coachman's blue-clad legs, the prancing rumps of the two black horses, the throng of pedestrians on the crowded Mayfair street.

The heat of passion altered into mortified warmth. She jerked her hands into her lap and sat primly upright. Looking immeasurably pleased with himself, Kit lolled like an Indian prince against the leather seat.

"I'm glad," he said, running his gloved finger down her flushed cheek, "that you prefer me to St. Claire."

"There isn't a contest between you two. There never was."

"So you say." Moody darkness swept away his smile. Kit gripped her hand hard. "I shan't let him harm you, you can be certain of that."

His conviction about Jerome's culpability flooded her with the old irritation. "Don't condemn him yet. For heaven's sake, it's ridiculous to think of him and Maurice . . . in bed together."

"Have you ever known St. Claire to court a woman?"

Her heart tumbled. She felt dismayed and foolish to realize she'd never questioned his bachelorhood. "No, but he travels on the continent for weeks, sometimes months at a stretch. He hasn't the need for a wife."

Kit's upraised eyebrows mocked her explanation. "Every person needs sexual release, one way or another. Surely you understand that now."

She did. Dear God, the need burned like an eternal flame in her heart. "He would hardly speak to me of his mistresses," she went on doggedly. "When we confront him, we'll find out the truth."

"No. I'll call on him alone, Norah. I won't take you into a cobra's nest."

His eyes radiated an arrogant strength of purpose. She flung off his hand. "He's my friend. I have every right to be there."

"Not this time. Anything could go wrong. He

could shoot you before I even moved. He could shoot *me* and then have you at his mercy."

The bloody scenario clashed with the fond memories of Jerome escorting her to the theatre, making her laugh with his amusing tales of the European nobility.

She released a disbelieving breath. "I'm going with you, Kit, and that's that. If you try to stop me, I'll simply follow you. Or will you lock me in my room like a naughty child?"

"Christ, you're a stubborn—"

He bit off the invective and glared out the window. She could tell by the pursing of his lips and the crease in his brow that he didn't intend to give an inch in the quarrel.

Neither did she.

Two hours later, Jerome himself resolved the standoff. He barged into the library, barely a step ahead of the footman who hastened to announce the guest to Kit and Norah.

"M'lord," gasped the servant. "He got past me. I'm most awfully sorry—"

"Never mind, Herriot." Kit shot to his feet, his hand in his coat pocket, where Norah knew his gun lay. "I'll deal with our visitor."

"Yes, m'lord." Herriot bowed and went out, closing the doors.

Norah sat rigid, her hands gripping her teacup and her heart pulsating. Other than a swift glance, Jerome paid her no heed. His fists were clenched, his cheeks reddened.

Like a bull intent on vanquishing a rival, he advanced on Kit. "I demand to know why you've been hiding Norah for nigh on three weeks."

"You aren't welcome here, St. Claire. I said in my message that I'd call on you in the morning."

"The devil take your evil plans." Jerome stripped off his overcoat, the buttons gleaming like gold disks in the dull light of late afternoon. He flung the garment on a chair. The russet handkerchief in his breast pocket mismatched his opal-gray suit, as if he'd dressed without his customary care.

"Norah," Kit said. "I want you to leave."

"No."

Their eyes locked, his hotly furious and hers coolly resolute. Then he wheeled away, toward Jerome. "Keep your distance. If you threaten her, I won't hesitate to use this." He drew his pistol from his pocket.

Jerome went rigid. "*Me*, threaten her? You're the villain who lured Norah into your trap. And don't bother spinning any lies about her staying at your parents' estate. I called on them last week and she wasn't there."

His impassioned words confused Norah. Did the taut mouth beneath the silver mustache reveal true concern for her well-being? Or a madman's determination to track down his quarry? Seeking nuances of expression that might indicate his guilt, she saw only the familiar blue eyes and patrician features of the man who had been a loyal friend.

Kit glowered. "Obviously your visit to my parents preceded the telegram I sent them."

"Explain yourself, by God. Or Norah's leaving with me." Jerome stalked toward her.

Kit brandished the gun. With icy menace, he stated, "Don't touch my wife."

Jerome jerked to a halt. "Your *wife?*" he said in a strange, hoarse tone.

"Yes." Kit moved beside her chair and touched the crown of her hair. The smooth gesture matched his deceptively casual face. "Two days ago, she did me the great honor of pledging herself to me before the archbishop of Canterbury. She is now Lady Blackthorne."

Heedless of Kit's gun, Jerome sank to one knee before her chair and snatched up her hand. "Did he compromise you? If the wretch forced you into this marriage, just say the word and I'll do everything I can to untangle you from his web."

His protectiveness reached out to her aching heart;
his familiar scent of peppermint and tobacco reassured her. Dear Blessed Virgin, Jerome couldn't be
a thief and a killer.

Could he?

She shook her head. "Kit didn't coerce me. I married him out of love."

One silver brow winged upward. "How can you
be so certain of your affections? You've known him
only a few brief months. You've been overwrought
since Maurice's death."

"What a hypocrite you are," Kit drawled. "Especially considering your role in her first marriage."

Jerome frowned up at him. "I don't know what
you mean."

"Then let me make myself clear. You found an
innocent sixteen-year-old girl and arranged her wedding to a man old enough to be her father. To a man
she had never even seen."

He paled. Slowly he rose to his feet, a smaller man
compared to Kit's height and breadth. "Who told
you that?"

"I have my sources. Will you deny the truth?"

Jerome lowered his gaze to the hearth, as if the
low-burning blaze held the answer to a great mystery. Tense, Norah waited for him to look at her.

But when he jerked his chin up, he addressed Kit.
"I admit I acted as an emissary when Maurice told
me he wanted to marry."

"And why did you trouble yourself to travel all
the way to Belgium? Why didn't you choose a girl
from London society?" Kit jabbed his finger toward
Jerome's vest. "Or did you deliberately seek out an
orphan without family or friends, a girl who was too
naïve to see what you were up to?"

"Up to? You speak as if it were some devious
plot." Jerome gave a disbelieving laugh. "Maurice
simply . . . knew the Mother Superior at the convent. They were old family acquaintances who made
a decent alliance for Norah. Surely you wouldn't

have wanted a lovely girl to languish away in a nunnery."

"Decent?" His jaw set, his fingers clenched around the gun, Kit took a step closer to Jerome, so they stood nose to nose. "You wed her to a pervert and you dare call it decent?"

The older man's jaw went slack. "You're ranting. Maurice Rutherford was a respected jeweler, a gentleman of refinement and taste—"

"His taste was for other men. He had no qualms about sodomizing his own wife when there wasn't a boy available to satisfy him."

Jerome recoiled. His cheeks flushed; just as swiftly his skin turned the opal-gray hue of his coat. His harsh breaths rasped into the charged silence. "No . . ."

Alarmed by his pallor, Norah leaped up. "Kit, your bluntness is unnecessary. Let me tell—"

"She's right," Jerome broke in. "You're a cad to speak your coarse lies in front of a lady."

"Didn't you ever wonder why she was so unhappy?" Kit's dark eyes held the savagery of a predator. "Didn't you ever wonder why she never bore him a child?"

"He was a friend of mine for nearly twenty years. I would have known. Surely I would have known." Jerome's beseeching gaze focused on Norah. "Tell his lordship the truth. Please."

Tears made his image shimmer. His distress ripped open the newly healed wound within her own heart. "It wasn't your fault," she whispered. "Maurice deceived me, too."

The dullness of horror glazed his eyes. Jerome stood as if petrified in amber. Then he passed his hand over his ashen face and stumbled away, coming to a halt against the book-lined wall beside the mantelpiece. "God forgive me," he mumbled. "I wanted the best for you. I thought I could make up for everything . . ."

Distressed by his rambling words and unable to bear his pain, Norah started toward him.

Kit caught her arm; his other hand gripped the pistol so tightly his knuckles shone white. Fury quivered in him like a tangible force, and she suddenly feared for Jerome's life. "Put your gun away," she murmured.

"No."

"For heaven's sake, does he look capable of harming me?"

Kit studied Jerome's sagging figure, then slowly pocketed the pistol. "Your display of innocence is touching," he told Jerome. "But maybe the truth is that you found Maurice a wife to cover up the fact that you and he were lovers."

Jerome jerked as if struck by a bullet. "Scoundrel! Bloody heathen scoundrel—"

Norah saw only a blur as Kit sprang like a tiger. His forearm pinned Jerome by the throat against the shelves. Books thudded to the floor in an avalanche.

"Frigging bastard!" Kit snarled. "I ought to kill you for letting her suffer for nine years."

Norah launched herself at him. "Stop! Stop it, both of you!"

She thrust hard at Kit's arm. His flesh might have been granite, the statue of a grim-faced god.

Jerome shoved unexpectedly. Kit stumbled backward, his spine meeting the chair. He would have attacked again, but Norah threw herself between the two men. She slapped her palms flat against Kit's chest. The tailored fabric of his gentleman's suit belied the ferocity of his features.

"Enough," she gasped. "He didn't know about Maurice. Surely even you can see that."

"I see a damned convincing actor. Playing to an altogether too-trusting audience."

"*I'm* trying to keep an open mind."

"Indeed? You're forgetting about the stone, Norah."

He scowled a challenge at her. The frenzied thumping of his heart slowed to a rhythm nearer its normal pace. Cautiously she lowered her hands and turned to Jerome.

His cravat askew, he rubbed his reddened throat. He gazed into the distance, his shoulders slumped. His pensiveness pierced her with the sharp impression of private grief.

"Jerome?"

He blinked and focused. "Norah, I truly didn't know."

His quiet statement held a convincing eloquence. Yet she couldn't resume faith in him, not yet. "Kit and I had an audience with the maharaja of Rampur on the Isle of Wight. We found out that Maurice lied to me about sending an agent named Upchurch to India to fetch the diamond, Fire at Midnight. Why didn't you tell me that Maurice sent you there instead?"

His blue eyes lowered, then fixed to her in a steady gaze. "He asked me not to. I saw no reason to go against his wishes and possibly cause trouble in your marriage." His grimace reflected the irony in his words. "Now I wish to God I'd wrung the blighter's neck."

"But why would he keep it a secret?" Kit demanded. "Norah knew he was sending *someone* after the diamond. What did it matter if that person was you?"

Shrugging, Jerome folded his arms. "I thought perhaps . . . he was jealous of my friendship with his wife."

Norah slanted a look over her shoulder at Kit. "My, how unique," she murmured.

He caught his hands around her waist in a warmly tender gesture that surprised her, considering his foul mood. His hard gaze bored into Jerome. "Now that we know his sexual bent, he couldn't have been jealous."

Jerome averted his eyes. "Who knows what went through his mind? Clearly *I* didn't. Perhaps he had some reason for wanting me out of England for six months. Maybe he thought people would talk if I were seen often with his wife."

"That's a lame excuse," Kit said.

"I'm only trying to read the thoughts of a dead man. If you think you can do better, then get on with it."

At the threat of another quarrel, Norah asked quickly, "So what did you do with the gem?"

"I gave it to Maurice shortly before he was murdered."

Kit snorted. "How do we know that? Or are we expected to blindly accept your word again?"

Jerome's brow pleated. "Now I *am* confused. The diamond is in the vault. You yourself told me so, Norah, weeks ago."

Guiltily she recalled his questions about the royal commission the same afternoon she had received Jane Bingham's "gift." "The stone isn't there," Norah said. "To my knowledge, it never was."

"It likely disappeared on the night of Maurice's murder," Kit added. "Norah saw him with a red-lined jewelry case. He said it contained a South African diamond, but it must have been Fire at Midnight instead."

"My God," Jerome breathed. "I had no idea . . ."

"Forgive me for misleading you," she murmured. "I was reluctant to take advantage of our friendship and burden you with my financial troubles."

Jerome took a tentative step toward her. "You've never been a burden, Norah. Never."

Despite his avowal, he looked tired and old, his dignified features etched by lines she had never before noticed. Yet as always, wistful warmth lit his eyes and his smile. Suddenly the radiance of restored trust shone like a beacon in her heart. Jerome had never betrayed her; he could never hurt her.

She surged toward him and tucked her head onto the shoulder of a true friend. "Thank you for caring so much. Your companionship has been a treasure to me."

"I'm glad," he said. "You've brought light into my life."

The surprise of their hug caught Kit off guard. Instinct urged him to snatch her back, to whip out his pistol. Yet he stood frozen by the agonizing tableau of his wife embracing the one man with the power to steal her affections.

Tears moistened Jerome St. Claire's eyes. He nuzzled his aging cheek against her hair. His arms clasped her with the intimacy of a lover.

Jealousy burned in Kit. Yet in that moment he was certain Jerome wouldn't draw a knife or a gun. The man truly loved Norah.

Did he covet her so much that he'd murdered Maurice in order to free her to remarry?

But that would mean someone else must have pushed Norah down the stairs. Could there be a second killer, someone who hoped his actions would be blamed on her husband's murderer?

Jerome held her by the shoulders. "My lady," he murmured. "I shall have to accustom myself to your new status."

"Please don't be formal," she said. "Our friendship can endure the trials of the past."

"I hope you're right. So much has changed."

Jerome glanced over her head at Kit. The shadowed wariness in those blue eyes roused Kit's suspicions. His mind leapfrogged to a chilling notion. If Jerome were the culprit, would he now seek to kill her second husband?

A deeper fear gnawed at Kit. The cherished flower of her love might be rooted in the uncertain ground of physical attraction. He had known the fickleness of passion enough times to convince him that his own love for her would last into eternity. But Norah lacked his experience. Someday she might regret her impetuous remarriage. When the newness of desire began to fade, she might wish she had wed her devoted friend, Jerome St. Claire.

Unless Kit could keep her passion at a fever peak.

The beginnings of a smile crooked his lips. Jesus God, maybe his years of philandering might prove an asset, after all. He could use his expertise to hold Norah in such a high state of excitement that she would scarcely have time to draw a breath.

Let alone yearn for any other man.

Chapter 17

"May I ask why you're looking at him so strangely?"

Norah addressed Lady Carlyle, who stood on the other side of the glass-topped counter in the jewelry shop. All traces of smoke damage from the fire had been cleared from the showroom. The walls were repapered in subtle stripes of blue and silver. The Waterford chandeliers, cleaned of ash, now sparkled against the scalloped ceiling.

A fair number of customers browsed in the shop. Norah felt the sharp glances of curiosity seekers who had heard of the marquis of Blackthorne's unconventional marriage. London society had never seen a marchioness in trade. But at least business had picked up. As long as they bought her jewelry, and left her and Kit in peace, she refused to care.

Lady Carlyle's attention kept straying to the back corner of the room, where Jerome sat at a small mahogany table and studied a tray of emeralds through his loupe.

At Norah's question, pink misted the woman's pale, ageless cheeks. She focused on Norah, who carefully tucked a diamond-studded bar pin into a velvet-lined case. "*Was* I staring?" Lady Carlyle asked. "Pardon my rudeness."

On impulse Norah touched her ladyship's gray-gloved fingers. "I didn't intend to imply you could be anything but the epitome of politeness. I merely wondered if you knew Jerome.''

"Oh, no. He looks like . . . someone I once knew. Perhaps a beau from my days as a debutante.'' Again Lady Carlyle edged a melancholy look at him. "It's only a quirk of the light, I'm sure.''

To Norah's amazement, Jerome also surreptitiously glanced at her ladyship, his eyes penetrating and interested. Did the spring air nurture a budding romance? She hoped so. "Jerome St. Claire is a dear friend of mine. I'd be happy to introduce you.''

"No," Lady Carlyle said hastily. A frown crimped her milky brow. "You're too busy. Perhaps you would show me a bracelet? I've been admiring the one you're wearing. The mix of moonstones and diamonds is clever and unusual.''

Her ladyship was trying to distract her, Norah realized. Lady Carlyle must be more affected by Jerome than she cared to admit. "Thank you. The bracelet was a gift from my husband. Now do let me call Jerome.''

"Please don't bother yourself—''

"It's no bother. Truly.''

Drawing Lady Carlyle behind the counter, Norah motioned to Jerome. He froze, a green stone sparkling in his fingers, surprise stark on his urbane features. Then he bent and carefully locked the tray of emeralds in the top drawer of the table.

He had come by the shop often in the past few weeks, offering to share his expertise in pricing her gems and evaluating the inventory. No matter how she tried to reassure him, she knew he flailed himself for not guessing the truth about Maurice.

Even as Jerome rose, Kit appeared at her side. Awareness quivered through her. He had an uncanny sense for Jerome's proximity and never once left them alone together. Their rivalry exasperated and frustrated her.

Kit slipped his arm around her, his eyes conveying a covertly erotic promise that flooded her loins with an untimely liquid heat. In the month since their wedding, she had ridden the high crest of dreams and desire. He kept her buoyed on a constant cloud of excitement, and consumed by the perpetual hunger for his touch. It disturbed her to feel this wanton desire even in the presence of others.

Kit turned to the dowager viscountess. "How good to see you again, Lady Carlyle."

"My warmest congratulations on your marriage, my lord. And I must say, I've never seen you so happy, Mrs. Rutherf—" With a nervous laugh, she shook her head, setting the white osprey feather on her gray hat to trembling. "Do forgive me. I must accustom myself to addressing you as Lady Blackthorne."

"Please call me Norah. And here's Jerome now."

A jerky slowness marred his steps. The cordial smile beneath the trim silver mustache held a fixed quality. In an uncommonly anxious gesture, he smoothed his hand over his black suit and adjusted the monogrammed handkerchief tucked in his breast pocket.

"Did you need me for something, Norah?"

"I wanted to introduce you to Lady Carlyle. My lady, may I present Mr. Jerome St. Claire?"

They stared at each other. Jerome's cheeks reddened slightly and his mouth went soft. As if by afterthought, her ladyship presented her kid-gloved hand. He bent and brushed a courtly kiss over the backs of her fingers.

"It's an honor to meet you," he murmured. "In all my travels on the continent, I've never met a lady so fair."

Her blush deepened into a charming rose hue. "Thank you." She compressed her lips, then went on, "So you are an avid traveler, Mr. St. Claire. Will you stay in London for long?"

"For another month at least," he said with a sidelong glance at Norah. "Business often takes me abroad, but personal reasons keep me here at the moment."

"Perhaps we shall encounter each other again

sometime. I, alas, must return to the country on the morning train." Her tone cool, Lady Carlyle drew back her hand and reached for her parcel, lying on the countertop. "I fear I must take my leave now. My son will be wondering where I've disappeared to."

"Give Bruce my regards," Kit drawled. "And perhaps you wouldn't mind passing along a bit of good news."

"News?" asked Lady Carlyle, her expression mystified.

"Since Bruce and I are neighbors of sorts, you might warn him to watch out for the nursemaid wheeling her pram along the square next spring."

Silence as thick as fog enveloped the quartet. The indistinct murmuring of customers and salesmen floated in the background, though Norah knew they couldn't have overheard.

As if to recapture the treasured secret, she crossed her arms. The thought of cradling his sweet, dark-haired baby was like an enchantment so precious that speaking it aloud might break the spell. "Kit!" she chided softly. "You weren't supposed to say anything just yet."

He stroked the nape of her neck. "Forgive me, darling, but I couldn't wait." His eyes caressed her with eloquent love; then he addressed the others in an undertone. "My lady and I are expecting an addition to our household. He—or she—should make a debut sometime after Christmas."

Jerome's widened gaze strayed to her midsection. "Is this true?" he said hoarsely. "You're, er, in a delicate situation?"

"Yes. At least the doctor I consulted yesterday thinks it likely."

Lady Carlyle's gray-green eyes held a sheen of tears. "I'm so happy for you both." She gathered Norah in an embrace that wafted the scent of violets. "I do wish my Bruce would marry. Grandchildren would be such a blessing."

"Indeed," Jerome murmured.

Lady Carlyle's gaze flicked to him. She lifted her hand to her throat in an oddly agitated gesture. "If you will excuse me." Skirts swishing, she glided out of the shop, a liveried footman holding open the beveled glass door.

Poor lady, Norah thought. If Bruce's taste in women included Jane Bingham, he might never marry. Then again, Kit had . . .

Jerome stared at the door, as if willing Lady Carlyle's return. The frown grooving his brow intrigued Norah. Moving closer, she whispered, "Well? What do you think?"

"Think?" Refocusing on her, he blinked. "I'm pleased for you and the marquis. If at least nine months pass between the wedding date and the blessed event, perhaps people will cease their whispering."

"People who gossip," Kit broke in coldly from beside Norah, "are people I don't care for my wife to associate with, anyway."

Disheartened by the enmity between the two men who meant so much to her, she said, "Jerome, I was referring to Lady Carlyle. What did you think of *her*?"

"Oh. She's quite lovely. Is she one of your regular patrons?"

His wooden tone contrasted with his earlier aura of absorption. "She shops here every now and then," Norah said. "Apparently she spends a lot of time in the country since her husband's death last year. But I could find out when she next plans to visit London—"

He cut her off with a slash of his hand. "I appreciate your effort to matchmake, Norah. But I'm far too old for romantic games."

"You're not old." Fondly she viewed his tidy silver hair and handsome features. The lines of humor bracketing his mouth now held a disturbing dejection. "Any woman would be proud to receive your court."

"If Lady Carlyle doesn't interest you," Kit put in,

"I would be pleased to introduce you to an array of suitable women."

"I don't doubt you could," Jerome snapped, "considering how many women you know."

"Stop," Norah hissed. "This is no place to argue."

She felt the pressure of Kit's hand on her shoulder. His nostrils flared as he glowered at Jerome. "My wife is right. I highly recommend marriage, St. Claire. Norah and I share a bliss you couldn't even begin to imagine."

His jealous ownership left a sour taste in her mouth. Why did Kit pursue this absurd rivalry? Didn't he trust her love? Didn't he believe her when she proclaimed Jerome a friend?

She was about to confront Kit on the matter when a voice piped in a stage whisper, "Yer lordship. M'lady."

Around the door that led toward the vault and workroom, Lark peeked out, his boyish face topped by spikes of unruly black hair. Excitement made his brown eyes enormous. A broom in one hand, he beckoned with a stubby forefinger.

Kit drew her toward the lad, who leaped back a step to let them enter the gaslit passageway. "What is it, Lark?"

" 'Tis the peeler from Scotland Yard. He came t' the back door and asked fer you. Mr. Teodecki set 'im t' wait in yer office."

"Inspector Wadding?" Norah said, her pulse leaping. "Perhaps he's discovered something."

"Maybe he finally caught 'er," Lark said in a reverent hush. "The madwoman o' Mayfair."

Kit leveled a stern look at the boy. "Thank you for bringing the message so promptly. That will be all now."

"Aw. Mightn't I listen—"

"Absolutely not. Leave the police to me. You've sweeping to do."

His lower lip thrust out. "Aye, sir." His feet dragging and his shoulders slumped, he preceded them down the passageway and into the workroom.

Watery sunlight flowed through the wall of windows. Over the past weeks the cavernous room had been restored to its original order. The scents of new plaster and paint joined the metallic aromas that spoke eloquently to Norah and renewed her fierce pride. This busy workplace truly belonged to her . . . and to Kit. Winning royal patronage would lure more customers to the showroom. Someday her designs would become as renowned as those of Garrard and Cartier.

Thaddeus glanced up from his workbench, his gaze tracking her progress through the busy room. The gold wire he held glittered against the tan leather of his apron. His pointed goatee and sweep of brown hair gave him a faintly sinister aspect. He turned away, stooping over the neat array of tools on his bench.

Foreboding lowered Norah's high spirits. Could he and Maurice have been lovers? Could Thaddeus have stuck the hatpin through Maurice's heart? Could he have hidden himself in the museum and thrust her down the stairs? After all, he coveted the royal commission.

Controlling a shudder, she clung tightly to Kit's arm as they entered her new office. The lavish gilt furnishings had burned, praise heavens. Now, thanks to Kit, she had a cheerfully efficient workplace with lemon-yellow drapes at the windows, comfortable guest chairs, and a spacious mahogany desk with a hanging gas lamp to provide lighting for her to sketch by.

Scratching his elongated ear with the stub of a pencil, Detective-Inspector Harvey Wadding stood staring at one of her father-in-law's photographs, of an Indian fakir lying on a bed of nails.

"Inspector?" Norah said.

The policeman spun around, his equine face ruddy. He executed a clumsy bow. "Your lordship. Mrs. Ru—ahem—m'lady."

Kit strode forward. "Have you new information? Did you arrest the person who left the roses on Rutherford's grave?"

"I fear not. For the past month, a constable has patrolled Highgate Cemetery, but there hasn't been a single rose delivered, and no visitors to the grave except the two Misses Rutherford." Wadding shuffled his big feet. "I'm afraid I can no longer spare a man to keep a fruitless watch."

"You're giving up?" Norah exclaimed in dismay.

"We must. Last evening, the police commissioner's wife was attacked by footpads outside Drury Lane Theatre. We've orders to place extra patrols in the Covent Garden area."

"And what about the safety of *my* wife?" Kit demanded. "Two and a half months ago, someone pushed Lady Blackthorne down the stairs at the museum. You haven't found the culprit yet."

"We questioned the guests, but since she didn't see who—"

"Someone also sent her that blasted mourning brooch. Why the devil couldn't you track down *that* clue?"

As if to escape Kit's wrath, Wadding ducked his head. "I called on every engraver in the city, even went into the rookeries. I'm sorry—"

"Sorry. Jesus God!" His face stiff with rage, Kit slapped the flat of his palm on the desk. "Suppose the villain chooses tonight to resume delivering the roses?"

"Then we'll set up a watch again." Wadding spread out his chapped hands. "I will, of course, continue my investigation regarding"—he glanced at Norah, and his blush deepened to crimson—"your other information."

She kept her gaze steady. "If you're referring to my late husband's deviant practices, then I'd like to know what you've found out. Have you learned of him frequenting any brothels?"

"Not yet. But it takes time to ferret out places that

cater to, er, peculiar tastes. Seeing as how they don't advertise their services in the *London Times*.''

"Then work harder," Kit growled, with a shake of his fist. "Her ladyship's life is in danger. I want the culprit locked behind bars before I end up putting roses on Norah's grave.''

"Aye, m'lord.''

Outside the office, Lark wielded his broom along the wooden baseboard, his ears attuned to the snatches of conversation that drifted through the inch-wide crack of the opened door.

The tramp of footsteps alerted him. He quickly swept his pile of debris toward the rear of the workroom and hummed a tuneless ditty.

The office door opened, then clicked shut.

He edged a glance over his shoulder. The peeler strode past the rows of workbenches and then disappeared out the alley door.

Agitation beat in Lark's chest. He leaned on his broom, clutching the stick for dear life. Some bedlamite had been lurking about the cemetery, sneaking roses onto Mr. R's grave.

The madwoman! It must be her!

And the peelers, God rot them, were swearing off the case.

Except for checking the brothels. Lark curled his lip. Poor ladyship didn't deserve a man who'd cheated on her with red-caped tarts. At least the barstard had met his just reward. At least now she had a hero for a husband.

Peter Bagley came up from behind and grabbed Lark by the collar. "Lolling about, are you? That's what comes of hiring riffraff. Get on with you now. The privy could use scouring.''

Lark glowered as the portly craftsman ambled back to his workbench. The blinkin' old fart. Never missed a chance to make a bloke's life wretched.

He brandished the flat of his broom at that broad arse. He'd cheerfully give his last copper to see Bagley sprawled out like a gin-sotted drunk.

But he had bigger fish to fry, Lark told himself. Slowly he lowered the broom and headed toward the privy in the rear corner of the shop. He had plans to make. He would keep the marquis's lady safe.

He would nab the madwoman o' Mayfair.

"Jesus God. I can't believe the police failed. The roses were our best clue yet." Kit raked his fingers through his hair. "If I didn't need to stay close to you, I'd keep surveillance on the cemetery myself. This mystery is so bloody frustrating."

Like a caged tiger, he prowled back and forth across the office. He'd removed his coat and rolled up his sleeves. His forearms were as brown and hard as burnished teak. The white shirt embraced his broad shoulders and led Norah's attention downward to his trim waist and taut posterior.

She knew the feel of his long, muscular legs entangled with hers. She knew the arms that could wrap around her as if never to let go. She knew the rasp of his unshaven cheek against her belly, the lick of his tongue on a place so intimate she blushed even to think of it . . .

Languid heat sapped her energy. She shifted in the desk chair and forced herself to concentrate on the list before her. The competition deadline of May first loomed only a few days away. Under her close supervision, Peter Bagley had fashioned the royal tiara. Thaddeus was the better craftsman, but to avoid a conflict of interest, he had declined to make her entry.

She picked up the unfinished tiara. It weighed surprisingly little because she had used platinum instead of the traditional, heavier gold. The innovative metal also made the brilliant white diamonds appear to float around the curve of the headpiece. Cut in graduated sizes, the stones formed a delicate cobweb pattern that resembled the texture of fine lace.

Only the center prongs remained empty. She could no longer put off the inevitable task of finding a replacement for Fire at Midnight.

Worried, she set down the tiara. "I could use the emerald the maharaja gave me," she murmured.

"Pardon?"

"I said, the maharaja's emerald might suit the royal tiara."

Kit stopped pacing. "You're not giving away a wedding gift for God's sake." His stern mouth softened; his ruffled hair made him look enticingly attractive, as if he'd just risen from bed. "Especially not a gift that matches your beautiful eyes."

His aura of sensuality threatened to distract her, as it had so often in the past month. She ought to have found another suitable stone weeks ago. "Well. The Bayhurst estate auction is scheduled for tomorrow." Norah pulled a catalogue from the drawer and flipped through the pages. "See this sketch? Family history claims the Viscaino ruby ring dates back to Henry VIII."

"Impressive." Kit flicked a glance at the opened page. "So let's buy it and reset the stone."

Norah sighed. "I don't know. The ruby is too . . . red. It wouldn't suit Princess Alexandra's ethereal beauty."

"So what else is on your list?"

He circled the desk, propped one hand on the back of her chair, and planted the other on the desk. As he bent over her shoulder, his warm breath stirred the fine hairs above her ear. His male scent disturbed her concentration.

She picked up her pencil and stabbed the point at random on the paper. "There's the Playter necklace. The central stone is a forty-one-carat blue diamond once owned by Peter the Great."

"Who owns it now?"

"Sir Ian Playter, of Edinburgh. Rumor has it he's in debt and needs to sell the piece."

Kit lightly massaged the nape of her neck; tiny shivers rippled down her back and around to her breasts and lower. "It's settled, then," he said. "If you'll give me his address, I'll have my solicitor telegraph him."

She resisted the lassitude spreading like warm honey through her veins. "A man trained in law knows little about jewels. Perhaps Jerome should go instead."

The pads of his fingers faltered, then resumed the magical caress. "Capital idea. We can suggest he take a long holiday in the Highlands while he's there."

The hint of dark humor in his voice annoyed her. She swung her head up. "For heaven's sake, Kit, he'd have to hurry straight back with the stone. And I do wish you and he could be friends—"

"Let's not quarrel, love. Not now."

His white teeth gleamed in the instant before his mouth descended to hers. The pencil slipped from her fingers and plopped unheeded onto the desk. Closing her eyes, she wreathed her arms around his neck and strained upward, the better to feel the thrusts of his tongue. The taste of his lips intoxicated her like fine wine. His incessant desire thrilled her, caused her stomach muscles to contract with voluptuous yearning.

He drew her up out of the chair. Her spine met the hardness of the wall, her bustle cushioning her derriere. The gentle warmth of hand covered her abdomen. "Have I told you how happy I am about our baby?" he murmured.

A rush of pleasure filled her. "At least a dozen times in the past twenty-four hours."

"Mmm. Then this time I'd like to tell you in more than mere words." His hand slid lower, where a wealth of petticoats guarded her womanhood. Pressing his palm there, he rubbed in a slow circular motion that penetrated the layers of muslin and liquefied her loins. "Unbutton my trousers," he whispered against her lips.

She tilted her head back against the wall. "Here?"

"Yes, here." His gold-flecked dark eyes glittered with the promise of treasures to come. "It's time we christened your new office, don't you think?"

Arousal quickened her, enticed her to a deliciously wicked longing. She glanced over his shoulder at the closed door. "The craftsmen—"

"Have orders not to enter without knocking."

"But someone still might hear—"

"So don't cry out loudly."

"I never cry out," she protested, then paused. "Do I?"

He cradled her warm cheeks. "There's no need to look so mortified, darling. Whatever we do together is natural and right, an outpouring of the love we feel for each other."

The adoration in his voice dealt a swift blow to her modesty. The surety of his affections ignited the burn of desire in her heart, a desire that seared downward and coiled tight, like a tendril of fire. Unable to resist, she caressed him; a telltale thickness announced his readiness and stifled any last prickings of propriety. The fevered work of her fingers released his buttons. Reaching inside, she took him into her hand.

His breath emerged in a hot gust against her brow. He rubbed his hands up and down her arms. "Norah, you're mine," he said hoarsely. "No other man will ever have you."

"And no other woman will have *you*."

They kissed again, an open kiss that foretold the mating Norah craved. All the while the pads of her fingers tiptoed up and down his hardened member, from the moist crown to the velvety sacs. He groaned into her mouth and with a dizzying sense of authority, she took hold of his shoulders and pushed him down onto the plush carpet, so the desk shielded them from the unshaded window.

Kit rolled up on his elbow. "Let me undress you—"

"No. Lie still." She knelt beside him, her pale lilac gown fluffing out like a summer cloud. "Your thirtieth birthday is only a few days off. Let's consider this my early gift to you."

He melted back onto the carpet, his fingers digging into the fine pile. "I'm yours. Do whatever you like."

The completeness of his surrender empowered her with wanton urges. She let her fingers roam along the firmness of his collarbone, the breadth of his chest, the rock-solid thighs beneath the smooth fabric of his trousers. He was a beautiful model of manhood, from the sculpted planes of his face to the rigid branch springing from the black forest at his groin.

He lay waiting, watching her, his eyelids half lowered. She ached to assure him of the depths of her love, but words never seemed enough to satisfy him. She wanted to show him once and for all that he had no cause for jealousy.

Cupping him like a gold chalice in her palm, she bent closer and drank deeply. The harsh rasp of his response rewarded her; his fingers dipped into her hair and mutely encouraged her. Following instinct, she kissed and tasted and explored until he caught her by the arms and gasped out, "No more. For God's sake, have pity or I'll spend my seed before I satisfy you."

"Your seed has already taken firm root, my lord," she murmured. "And I trust you'll satisfy me, one way or another."

"How about this way?"

Taking hold of her waist, he lifted her over him so that her skirts billowed and her center settled against steely heat. His hands stole beneath her hem, rode up the path of her silk stockings, and spread the opening in her cambric drawers. Needing no further encouragement, she braced her hands on his chest, lifted herself and plunged. The resulting fullness wrestled a low moan from her throat. Gritting her teeth against further outcries, she shifted her hips and savored the luscious slide of velvet against vigor.

Freedom of movement gave wing to her passion and swept her swiftly toward the crest of completion. The love swelling her heart pushed her over the edge. Even as her feelings burst, inundating her in a shower of shudders, she felt Kit arch upward with the explosive force of his own release.

"Norah. Norah, I love you."

Limp and appeased, she melted onto him. Beneath her ear, his chest rose and fell, gradually slowing to its regular rhythm. Too replete to stir, she let herself drift in a mist of contentment.

A knock erupted into the quiet room. "Norah? May I come in?"

Jerome.

Panicked, she sat halfway up. "No!" Coercing steadiness into her voice, she added, "I'll be out in a few moments."

A pause. Then beyond the door, footsteps tapped away.

Awareness of her wanton posture washed over her in a hot wave. Like a hedonist unable to restrain her physical appetites, she sprawled over Kit, his length still embedded deeply within her.

And just outside her office lay the workroom filled with her employees.

"Oh, dear God," she breathed. "Everyone will guess what we've been doing in here."

"Relax, darling." Kit idly stroked her bottom beneath her petticoats. "You've hardly committed a sin. I certainly hope you're not ashamed for Jerome to know that you love your husband."

Anger seared her, anger at him for his lax attitude and at herself for behaving irresponsibly. Scrambling up, she smoothed her trembling hands over the wrinkles in her gown. She hated the ugly suspicion that took root in her mind, yet she couldn't stop the words from tumbling out. "And *I* hope you didn't seduce me simply to parade your power over Jerome."

His brow creased with annoyance, Kit rolled lithely to his feet. "You're my wife, Norah. I love you, I desire you. Jesus God, I could hardly have known he was going to knock on that door."

His logic failed to soothe the sting of her embarrassment. "I've labored long and hard to win the respect of the men out there. If you truly love me, you wouldn't jeopardize my position here."

"Oh, so this is my fault." He jerked together the buttons of his trousers. "I forced you down onto the floor. I made you suck on my—"

"Don't mock me, Kit Coleridge." She pressed her fingers to her temples in an effort to calm the storm of confusion raging inside her. In a hushed tone, she added, "All I'm saying is that we shouldn't have made love just now. I have work to do, a royal commission to win. These past few weeks, I've barely been able to concentrate."

His brooding eyes studied her. "So is marriage tying you down? Are you already growing weary of me?"

"No! That's not what I mean."

"But you're suggesting I keep my distance."

"Yes. No. I mean you should here at the shop."

"Please yourself, then." Kit thrust his arms into his coat sleeves and yanked the lapels straight. He looked stern and remote, yet a weakening desire washed through her. She longed to throw herself into his warm embrace, but she knew where physical contact might lead. "If you'll excuse me," he added coldly, "I'll leave you to tend to your precious business. Enjoy your visit with Jerome." He strode out, shutting the door.

Norah wilted onto the hard edge of the desk. Blessed Virgin forgive her, she had hurt him. Her turmoil dissipated into the torment of loneliness. "Why can't you understand?" she whispered.

Silence answered her, a dreadful emptiness.

But she wasn't empty. Her hand caressed her belly. Kit had brought spirit and sparkle into her life. Their love had wrought the miracle growing within her. In a matter of months she would hold their darling baby . . . Kit's baby.

Yet she also needed the satisfaction of work. She required it, as she required air to breathe and food to eat.

But most of all, she needed her husband's trust.

In heart-wrenching despair, she fingered the moonstones and diamonds at her wrist. Why couldn't all her needs mesh as smoothly as the silver links of her bracelet?

Aching in body and soul, she reluctantly turned her mind to business. She had best find out what Jerome wanted.

As she walked out of her office, she watched for Kit's dark head, his ready smile, his broad-shouldered form. But she saw only the rows of industrious artisans and assistants, heard the clink of their hammers and the rasp of their drills.

Thaddeus left his workbench and approached her. Bowing, he handed her a small envelope. "Mr. St. Claire left on an errand. He said to tell you that a messenger delivered this."

The envelope was addressed in a curiously familiar feminine script that tugged at her memory. She tore open the envelope and drew out a sheet of lilac-scented stationery.

Her gaze flicked to the initials at the bottom. She blinked in surprise. *J.B.* Jane Bingham.

With dawning anger and horror, Norah read the brief letter.

Chapter 18

The following afternoon, beneath a sky of pewter-gray clouds, Jerome helped Norah from the brougham, then escorted her toward the town house. A cold mist pricked her face and dampened her eyelashes. Despite the shelter of her merino cloak, she felt the wet April chill penetrate her bones.

Jerome halted her by the front steps. Fine droplets coated his groomed silver hair; he seemed to have forgotten the top hat in his hand. "I'm still not sure it's wise for us to come here," he said. "This matter of blackmail belongs in the hands of Scotland Yard."

"Shall I let a troublemaker like Jane Bingham drag Kit's good name through the muck?" Norah asked. "I can't stand by and watch him suffer a false charge."

Jerome sighed. "You're right to defend your husband. I admit I've been suspicious of Lord Kit. But the more I've seen of him these past weeks, the more I've grown to respect him. You've changed him for the better, Norah, and he truly does love you. That's all I ever really wanted for you."

His support gladdened her. She kissed his smooth-shaven cheek. "Thank you for saying so. Your good opinion means the world to me. You're the best friend I've ever had."

He smiled wistfully. "But I couldn't help you win

the royal commission. Are you sure there isn't another suitable stone you can use for the tiara?''

Hiding her acute disappointment, she shrugged. "Don't worry, I'll still enter the competition. Once we're through here, I'll return to the shop and have Peter Bagley fashion a cluster of amethysts in lieu of the center gem.''

"That's a mere shadow of the spectacular tiara you designed.'' He squeezed her hands. "My God, I'd do anything to get Fire at Midnight for you. Anything at all!''

"I know,'' she murmured. "But we don't know who stole the diamond. And the deadline is only two days away. I'll just have to make do with what I have.''

Jerome seemed to realize how painful the topic was, for he sighed and looked up at the three-story edifice. "This place isn't what I expected.''

Norah agreed. As they mounted the steps to the town house, she studied the unobtrusive brown stone dwelling with its plain wooden shutters. A flamboyant mansion decorated by naked statuary would have better suited the occupant.

She tamped out a spark of pity. Jane reaped what she sowed. And today, she would reap a bitter harvest.

Grasping the damp brass knocker, Norah rapped firmly. A coarsely handsome footman opened the door. He ushered her and Jerome through a dim foyer and into a drawing room.

The footman's smile verged on a leer; his gaze slid up and down her form. "May I take your wrap, m'lady?''

Norah clutched the edges of the cloak. "No, thank you. We shan't be staying long. Now kindly fetch your mistress.''

"As you like.'' With a glower at Jerome, he strolled out.

Fury and fear tangled her insides. *Had* she made a mistake in coming here? No. Remembering the threat in the letter, she shuddered. Jane could cost Kit his liberty—even his life.

In the meantime, Jerome would keep her safe. Herriot and Wickham, the coachman, waited outside. And against her thigh, Norah felt the comforting weight of the muff pistol in her pocket. She shied from the notion of needing to use the weapon.

She also tried not to think of how furious Kit would be when he returned from the bank and discovered she had ventured here with the man he completely mistrusted.

"Odd place, this," Jerome remarked, wandering around the room.

For the first time, she noticed the curio shop decor of the gaslit room. Shelves held a hodgepodge of Greek pottery, copper vessels, and jade figurines. A dented bronze shield occupied a place of honor over the fireplace. Display cases exhibited a plethora of coins and shards and ornaments. Even the pair of white turtledoves by the hearth lived in an antique brass cage. Their soft cooing served as a counterpoint to the snapping of the coal fire and the jangling of Norah's nerves.

She picked up a battered Egyptian bracelet and rubbed her thumb over the lapis design. Half the blue stone had broken away, leaving forlorn gaps in the gold. The artistic swirls caught at her imagination. The design could be used in a modern piece of jewelry—

"I thought I told you to come here alone," Jane said.

Swathed in pink silk and frilly ecru lace, she scowled in the doorway. Her elaborate tea gown had a low neckline and half-length sleeves, trimmed with jabots of more lace. A rosette of ribbons dangled long streamers from her upswept blond hair.

Squaring her shoulders, Norah girded herself for battle. "Your letter said not to bring the police or Kit. Mr. Jerome St. Claire is a friend of mine. Jerome, the Honorable Jane Bingham."

He bowed mockingly. "Miss Bingham."

Jane's lips eased into a pouty smile. She stroked one fingertip over her cleavage. "A friend of the brand-new Lady Blackthorne's, are you? If you promise not to interrupt, I may permit you to stay."

"I promise to abide by Norah's wishes." Narrowing his eyes, he glanced around at the jumble. "I've just now realized. You must be the daughter of Sir Hubert Bingham. I've heard of his illustrious contributions to historical research."

"Yes, the man who squandered our fortune on his expeditions to dig up these dusty relics." Jane kicked a brass urn and winced. "The brilliant Sir Hubert Bingham, archeologist extraordinaire. Rubbish collector is what *I* call him."

Surprised interest kindled in Norah. "He must be a fascinating man. I'd love to meet him."

"You'd have to travel to Turkey, then. He's off on a quest to find the ark of the covenant or some such nonsense. I'm left here to contemplate my lovely inheritance." Jane waved her hand at the antiquities that overflowed the drawing room.

Norah fingered the damaged Egyptian bracelet. "I wouldn't so quickly discount these artifacts. If they're genuine, a museum or a private collector might pay you well."

"Truly?" Jane's eyebrows perked up, then lowered in a glower again. She minced closer, her hands on her hips. "Oh, you're a sly one, my lady. Slyer than I gave you credit for. Any woman who could trick the marquis of Blackthorne into marriage is sly enough to try to distract me from our business today. And from the money you'll pay me to keep silent."

"Mind how you speak to her ladyship," Jerome snapped.

The reminder of her purpose struck the air from Norah's lungs. With cool deliberation, she set the bracelet on a littered shelf. "Please, Jerome, I'll handle this."

Looking furiously at Jane, he thinned his lips,

folded his arms, and planted himself in the center of the rug like a robust silver birch.

"I'm not trying to distract you," Norah told Jane. "On the contrary, I'm most anxious to discuss our business and return to my husband."

"Come now, there's no rush." With an impatience that belied her words, Jane drummed her fingers together. "I took the liberty of ordering tea. Where is that laggard, Oswald?"

Pacing to the drab brown mantelpiece, she jerked on the bell cord so violently that the frayed strip of maroon velvet nearly gave way from the ceiling. As if on cue, the rough-featured footman strolled through the doorway, hefting a tarnished silver tray, which he set on the table by the fire.

"It took you long enough." Jane dogged his heels. "Stopped to nip at the brandy again, did you?"

"No, Miss Bingham. If you would care to check for proof in our usual manner . . ." In a crudely sensual gesture, he ran his tongue over his thick lips.

"Oaf." She snatched up a napkin and slapped him on his rump. "You'll show me respect or you'll be back begging in Covent Garden before sundown."

Oswald merely smiled. "Of course . . . mistress." Bowing, he swaggered from the room.

With a grimace, Jerome stroked his fingers over his silver mustache. Poor Jane, Norah thought, reduced to bedding her servant.

Cheeks as pink as her dress, Jane dropped the napkin and picked up the pot. As sweetly as if she were a vicar's daughter, she said, "Do sit down, both of you, and join me in a cup of tea."

Cold resolution hardened Norah. "No, thank you. We would like to see your bogus proof that Kit murdered Maurice."

"All in good time. First, how about a damson tartlet?" Jane offered them a china plate of gooey purple pastries and triangular rolls. "They're far superior to those dried-up scones that Cook insists upon serving."

Norah curtly shook her head. Jerome, bless him, followed her lead. "We didn't come here for refreshments," she said. "Your letter stated that on the night of the murder, you never saw a woman in a scarlet cloak leaving Kit's bedroom. You said that Kit paid you to lie."

Clearly annoyed at her inability to manipulate the meeting, Jane sat down, holding the plate in her lap. "That is correct."

"You also told a preposterous tale that Kit had had an affair with Alexandra, the Princess of Wales. When Maurice found out, he tried to blackmail Kit."

"And so Kit silenced him. Forever."

The woman's cunning smile infuriated Norah. "That is the most utterly ridiculous piece of fabricated nonsense I've ever heard. No one will believe a word of it."

"Oh?" A crafty gleam lit Jane's blue eyes. "Here's a fact, then. It seems your dear departed Maurice needed the blackmail money most desperately."

Norah's legs nearly wilted. To steady herself, she grasped at the shelf of antiquated curios. Only a handful of people knew the truth. Inspector Wadding. Jerome. Ivy. Winnifred. Thaddeus. Kit. Bertie Goswell . . .

One by one, Norah rejected each person.

"Who told you he was in debt?" Jerome asked Jane.

"That's my little secret." Affecting a pout of concern, Jane rose from her chair and glided to Norah. "Poor dear, you look entirely too pale. Here. Sweets can keep one from swooning." Jane selected a scone, then pushed the plate of pastries into Norah's hands. "Do take a tartlet."

The fruity aroma of plum preserves ordinarily would have tempted Norah, but lately her stomach churned at the oddest times from her pregnancy. Swallowing, she set the dish on the tea tray. "No, thank you."

Jane's pretty features twisted sourly. "I suppose it's best. Kit prefers his women slim . . . and lusty."

Hips swaying, she stalked to the brass bird cage and began tearing off bits of scone. The pair of plump doves fluttered down and pecked at the crumbs. "So," she said over her shoulder, "how does it feel to be married to the man who made you a widow?"

"Your accusation is absurd," Norah snapped. "Kit had no motive for murder because he never had an affair with the Princess of Wales. It's common knowledge that Princess Alexandra is a faithful and honorable wife."

"Come now. We both know Kit's persuasive talents in the bedroom." Jane artfully ducked her head. "He does wield a mighty sword, doesn't he?"

"Miss Bingham!" Jerome bit out.

Fury scalded Norah. Her gloved hand closed around a palm-sized pottery vase.

Before she could succumb to her violent impulse, Jerome stepped forward, brandishing his top hat. The startled doves flapped their white wings. "That's quite enough, miss. You'll show Norah the respect due her."

"For the love of God, don't frighten my little darlings." Waving him away, Jane broke apart the rest of the scone. The doves fluttered back down to snatch greedily at the pieces. "There, sweetings. Mama will protect you from that nasty man." She slid her finger between the brass bars of the cage and stroked the snowy feathers.

With effort Norah relaxed her fingers on the vase and banished the image of Jane opening her pale thighs to Kit. Their affair was long over. "No one will believe my husband would commit murder in his own bedroom in the midst of a New Year's Eve party."

Jane arched an eyebrow. "A jury of his peers might disagree. Lest you forget, there are many who resent having a dark-skinned Hindu in their exalted midst."

Men like Lord Carlyle.

Chilled by the reminder of his bigotry, Norah saw the unwelcome scenario in her mind. As a titled no-

bleman, Kit would stand trial before the House of
Lords. Certainly he had allies in the venerated
group, Lord Adrian and his own father among them,
yet in the eyes of the intolerant, Kit's notorious reputation and his mixed blood would damn him.

"Regardless of prejudice, the court will demand
irrefutable evidence," Norah said. "Show me the
letter that you claim to hold."

"Gladly."

Dusting the crumbs off her hands, Jane reached
into her bodice and drew forth a sheet of paper,
which she passed to Norah. "There, feast your eyes
on the proof that will settle a noose around your
beloved husband's neck."

At the top of the perfumed stationery reared a lion
with a black thorn in its paw. Kit's heraldic seal.
Dear God, that bold scrawl was unmistakably his.

Gripping the edges of the paper, Norah breathed
deeply to contain her shock. It was a love letter, addressed to Princess Alexandra, and full of bawdy
references to white breasts and long members and
vows of undying passion. The prominent signature
at the bottom belonged to Kit.

Norah felt ill. Over the past weeks, he had penned
a few notes to her, but never so graphic. Crudeness
wasn't his style.

Jerome peered over her shoulder, his scent of peppermint and cigars somehow giving her strength.
"Is it a forgery?" he whispered.

"It must be." Clearing the fog of fear from her
mind, she studied each inked character. In dawning
excitement, she spied the slight curlicue at the end
of an *E* and a feminine slant to a *T*, reminiscent of
Jane's own hand.

"This is not Kit's handwriting," Norah stated.

Jane snatched back the letter. "Prove it. Or pay
me twenty-five thousand pounds, and I'll destroy
the letter. The choice is yours."

The idea of submitting to blackmail rankled Norah. "*You* wrote the letter." Bolstered by conviction,
she stepped forward. "You concocted the story out

of spite. You want revenge on Kit for spurning you and marrying me.''

Her slim nostrils flaring in anger, Jane retreated to the dove cage. ''He'll spurn you, too. A prissy bore can hardly interest him for long. Put him in a room with another woman, and Kit Coleridge won't keep his prodigious cock inside his trousers.''

''Mind your wicked tongue, you Jezebel.'' Jerome shook his hat again. ''If you dare hurt Norah by letting out this trumped-up charge, you'll only bring the wrath of our Queen onto yourself—''

The walls of Norah's own private hell shut out the rest. She despised the doubts that ripped her heart. *Could* she hold Kit? After their quarrel the previous afternoon, he had acted cool and reserved. For the first time, he had turned his back to her in bed that night. At the moment she'd been relieved, for if he had taken her into his arms, she might have spilled out her anxieties about the threat from Jane.

Regrets slammed Norah like a hammer wielded by a heavy-handed apprentice. She hugged her hands to her stomach. Would her devotion to work drive Kit away? Was he already losing interest in the wife who jealously guarded so much of herself? Would she be forced to make the painful choice between her designing and the family she craved? Of course, she would choose Kit—

Suddenly Jane screamed.

''Where the devil is my wife?'' Kit demanded

Wickham, the coachman, hunched lower in the front seat, as if to elude his master's wrath. Herriot, the footman, caught at the back handle of the brougham to keep from tumbling off the narrow pageboard. His young face was blank with surprise, his brown eyes wide with guilt. ''M-m'lord!''

''Answer me, dammit,'' Kit growled. ''Where is she?''

''Inside, m'lord.'' His Adam's apple working, Herriot pointed at the mist-shrouded town house.

"I know you gave orders not to leave the shop without you, but m'lady insisted—"

A muffled female shriek sounded inside.

"Jesus God!"

Kit sprinted up the wet steps. His heart had been pounding with dread since he found the note Norah had left him at the shop. Pray God he'd reach her in time. He whipped out his pistol, wrenched open the doorknob, and plunged into the dimly lit foyer. The musty odor of lilacs slapped him with the abhorrent memories of sex without love.

Into his mind flashed the image of his wife lying somewhere in a bloodied heap. "Norah!"

A keening feminine wail issued from the drawing room. He veered there, his quickened steps thudding on the marble floor.

In the doorway Norah almost collided with him, her mantle swirling around her slender form. Worry etched her fine cheekbones; alarm shadowed her green eyes. She caught at his arms to steady herself. "Kit! Oh thank God, you're here."

He seized her in a fierce embrace, rejoicing in her warmth and life. "What happened? Why did you scream?"

"I didn't. It was Jane."

Below a freestanding bird cage with its door hanging open, Jane knelt in a frothy puddle of pink skirts. Her blond head was bowed, her ivory shoulders slumped. In her lap she cradled a fluffy white lump.

Jerome St. Claire stood over her, his debonair features stark with shock.

Setting Norah behind him, Kit walked forward, gun in hand. He realized Jane held a pair of fat doves, their bodies still. Their beady black eyes stared sightlessly.

She lifted her tear-blotched face. "They're dead. I found my poor little darlings lying at the bottom of their cage."

Herriot and Wickham crowded the doorway. A crudely handsome manservant pushed past them. "What the bloody 'ell was all the screechin' about?"

"They're dead," Jane repeated. "Oh, Oswald, my sweet babies are dead."

Oswald stared stupidly. "What 'appened to the buggers?"

"I don't know," she cried. "They were cooing and eating just a moment ago."

Kit felt the pressure of Norah's fingers on his arm. Straining upward to his ear, she murmured, "Jane fed them a scone from our tea tray."

Foreboding chilled his blood. A few crumbs lay scattered on the bottom of the cage. The tea tray sat on a nearby table, the silver pot still steaming, the plate of pastries full.

He caught her cheeks in his hands. "Did you eat or drink anything?"

"No."

"Thank God." He pocketed his pistol, grabbed a napkin, and crouched before Jane.

"Oh, please." Her lashes clumped and wet, she held the birds to her breasts. "Please don't take them away, Kit."

"I'm sorry, but I must." He gently wrapped the napkin around the plump bodies, still warm and feathery soft. Rising, he handed the package to Herriot. "Put them in the carriage. The police will want to check for poison."

"Aye, m'lord." He turned on his heel, Wickham following.

The dullness of disbelief glazed Jane's teary face. "Poison?" she gasped. She struggled to her feet, assisted by Jerome. "That can't be, not in the scones. The poison was in the—" She pressed her carmine lips shut.

Jerome released her, then scrubbed his hands together as if to cleanse himself. "I knew we were right not to trust you."

Kit jerked his head at Oswald, who stood gaping. "You—get out. And I'll have no listening ears at the keyhole."

Oswald bobbed a clumsy bow as he moved back-

ward. He bumped into a brass urn, then hastily
righted it. The doors clicked shut.

Kit drew Norah close again. Her scent of roses
invigorated him with heartfelt relief. He'd nearly lost
her. God help him if his trifling jealousies ever drove
her away again.

He turned his hard stare at Jane. "Talk, Jane. I
want to hear about this poison."

Sullenness dragged at her fine features. She
crossed her arms, so that her breasts pillowed above
her bodice. "I don't know anything."

"The police can test the tea cakes. You'll be arrested for attempting to murder Norah."

"But I wasn't going to murder her. It was only a
purgative, in the damson tartlets." Jane cast a glance
of unveiled resentment at Norah. "He said it would
keep her perched on her chamber pot for at least
three days."

"Who is *he*?" Norah asked.

Jane shifted her gaze away. "Why, the chemist
who filled the prescription."

Frustrated beyond control, Kit sprang forward and
grasped her arms. He gave her a shake. "Jesus God,
stop lying. Whoever you're protecting isn't worth
your loyalty. He tricked you. He put his lethal poison in the scones, too. He must have meant to kill
both of you."

Her china-blue eyes went watery again. A fresh
flow of tears streaked down her cheeks. "He
wouldn't," she whispered. "I can't believe that."

"This time you've gone too bloody far with your
pranks," Kit snapped. "While your friend goes free,
you'll be trapped behind bars. You'll go to prison
for abetting a murderer."

Unsightly weeping contorted her face. "For the
love of God, it was supposed to be only a little trick.
I swear I never meant her any real harm."

"Harm?" he said harshly. "Damn you, you almost killed Norah. Or at the very least you might
have caused her to miscarry the baby."

"Baby?" Aghast, Jane sagged against him. "I didn't know she was pregnant."

Norah pushed his hands away and gave him a quelling look. She felt sorry for Jane, who had been an unwitting participant in a murder attempt. "Of course you didn't know," she told Jane. "I'll testify that you fed the scone to the doves yourself, so you couldn't possibly have known about the poison."

She passed a handkerchief to Jane, who blew her nose with inelegant force. "I like you," Jane admitted, sniffling. "That's what irked me so much. You and Kit truly belong together."

"Please help me," Norah said. "Tell me who talked you into this scheme."

Jane dabbed at her reddened eyes. "Bruce. It was Lord Bruce Abernathy."

Jerome emitted a harsh, strangled gasp. "No . . ."

Kit barely heard. The name slammed into him like a blow to his solar plexus. For a moment he couldn't draw a breath. Bruce Abernathy, Viscount Carlyle, had tried to kill Norah.

Why? Could he despise Kit so much?

On the heels of the baffling question sprang another. Had Carlyle and Maurice been lovers? Dredging through his schoolboy memories, Kit recalled that Bruce had been a model student, the favorite of the teachers and, in particular, the pet of one effeminate algebra master . . .

Kit drilled Jane with a pointed stare. "Did Bruce ever make love to you?"

Her woebegone eyes peeked over the handkerchief. "Why would you care? You're no longer my protector."

"Answer me, dammit. He escorted you to the museum the night someone pushed Norah down the stairs. Did you and he make love that evening?"

She lowered the handkerchief. Her chin quivered. "Bruce is a true gentleman. He treats me like the lady I am."

Her oblique denial gave Kit his answer. He met

Norah's troubled gaze. Softly she said, "He and Maurice . . . ?"

"Yes." Seeing the reawakened pain of memories in her eyes, he drew her close and breathed the scent of her skin, rubbed his cheek against her smooth temple. "At last we know."

"Oh, Kit. Bruce must have dressed up in the scarlet cloak. He lured Maurice to your bedroom and murdered him. He must have stolen Fire at Midnight, too."

"Murdered?" Jane squeaked. "No, you're wrong. Bruce was ever so gallant. He brought me jewelry and presents . . ."

"He plotted to kill Norah," Kit stated. "And apparently you, too, to remove any witnesses. The police would have called you the spurned mistress, so distraught you'd commit murder, then suicide."

Sick awareness paled her face. "Bruce suggested I trick Norah with the fake love letter. When he saw how . . . how enraged I was about your marriage."

"Here's where that letter belongs." Bending, Norah scooped the piece of stationery from the floor and flung it into the hearth. The paper flamed, the edges curling to black ash.

Jane pressed her forehead against the empty bird cage. "He told me it was safe to eat the scones. He knew they were my favorite."

"Thank heavens neither of us ate anything," Norah said. Her hand stole over her stomach, and Kit knew with poignant warmth that she was thinking about their baby, their hope for a happy future, untainted by murder and ugly secrets.

One piece of the puzzle didn't quite fit. He stroked her hair, curlier than ever from the mist outside. "Why you, Norah? If Bruce wanted to punish me by poisoning my wife, why did he take particular care to stick *your* hatpin into Maurice's heart? I hadn't even met you back then."

"It must be happenstance. Don't you remember Maurice had taken my stickpin into the shop for repair? Bruce must have found it in Maurice's pocket."

"Maybe. But I'm beginning to think Bruce wanted *you* to be hanged for the murder. If you hadn't had an alibi with the Sweenys, you'd have been the prime suspect."

Norah shook her head. "Perhaps he only meant to direct suspicion away from himself."

"But it's too great a coincidence that he's still trying to kill you. There must be a connection we're missing, a clue we've overlooked."

"There is, my lord," Jerome said, his voice a thin rasp behind Kit. "God help me, I can tell you why Bruce wants to kill Norah."

Chapter 19

Surprised, Norah studied Jerome, who leaned heavily against a shelf crammed with antiquities. He still clutched his black top hat against the front of his dark tweed coat. A sweaty grayness tinged his face and an uncharacteristic grimness pulled at the lines of humor around his mouth. He looked alarmingly old and weary, an aging lion on the verge of collapse.

"Jane," she murmured. "Kindly fetch him a glass of water."

For once, Jane obeyed without protest. Her expression subdued, she trudged from the drawing room.

Norah went to Jerome and helped him to a chair. "Come, sit down." As if he were her child, she released the gold buttons of his coat, pried the hat from his stiff fingers, and set it on the side table.

Falling back against the brown-checkered chair, he drew an uneven breath. "God forgive me, I had no inkling that Bruce even knew of Norah's existence, or I would have spoken out instantly."

Kit pressed his hands to Norah's shoulders, his presence warm and supportive. "Spoken out about what?" he asked.

"The connection between Bruce and Norah." Jerome passed his hand over his face. His gaze lifting to the bronze shield above the mantel, he said haltingly, "Twenty-six years ago, Bruce's mother—the Lady Carlyle—engaged in an illicit romance with a scoundrel. It was an impetuous affair that happened while she was traveling in Italy, without her husband. Understandably, Lord Carlyle was outraged when he discovered her pregnancy. He banished her to Belgium, where she gave birth in secret."

Hot and cold flashes paralyzed Norah. She denied the incredible notion that seized her heart. "What are you saying?"

Jerome focused on her, his gaze both sorrowful and oddly proud. "That baby was you, Norah. Bruce's mother is also your mother."

"No . . ."

The news plunged her into a tight cocoon of unreality. She pictured Lady Carlyle, the fine aristocratic features, the gentle nature, the impression of secret sadness. That sweet-tempered lady was her mother. *Her mother.* The faceless woman Norah had spun dreams about in her lonely youth. The woman who had nurtured her for nine months, then blithely left her to a solitary life, the only child in a convent of pious nuns who had little patience for an inquisitive and rambunctious girl.

Tears washed her vision. Norah slipped her hands over her abdomen, where her womb sheltered her own baby. Stormy protectiveness whirled forth to lash at her. "Dear Blessed Virgin," she said. "How could any woman give up her child?"

Jerome slapped his fist on the arm of the chair. "She had to. Her husband gave her no choice in the matter."

"She could have left him."

"And abandoned her four-year-old son? She was a fallen woman, wife to a powerful lord. A divorce court would have remanded Bruce to the custody of his father."

"So she abandoned me instead."

"She didn't *want* to." Jerome leaned forward, gripping his knees, his knuckles white with strain.

"My God, Eleanor was heartbroken. No doubt she still is."

"How do you know all this, St. Claire?" Kit asked in a strange, soft voice.

Lips pressed tight, Jerome lowered his gaze to his hands. The fire hissed into the silence. Then he looked straight at Norah and said, "Because I'm the scoundrel who seduced Lady Carlyle."

Kit's firm arm held her upright. Through a mist of disbelief, she saw Jerome: his steadfast gaze, his silver hair and mustache, the visage of the man she had cherished as a friend.

"You're . . . my father."

"Yes. I don't deserve you, but . . . yes."

His gruff whisper echoed amid the litter of her long-broken dreams. She tried to reconcile his familiar image with the blow of his revelations. A white-hot fist tightened in her chest. He claimed to love her. Yet he had been a co-conspirator in the plot to foresake a helpless baby. "You've lied to me these past nine years. It wasn't Maurice who knew the Mother Superior, it was *you*."

His blue eyes shimmered, though whether from her tears or his own, she didn't know. "I wanted to tell you," he murmured. "So many times. But I was afraid you would despise me for the mistakes I'd made."

"So you and Lady Carlyle rectified your mistake by hiding me away in a convent, by denying me a loving family."

"We found you a safe haven where you could grow up in peace. Please try to understand why." He furrowed his hands through his hair, rumpling the tidy strands. "Twenty-six years ago, I wasn't the respected man I am now. I was a burglar, a common thief. I met Eleanor when I broke into her hotel room one night. I thought no one was there, but she sprang out of bed and almost unmanned me with the fireplace poker. We quarreled, then somehow began to talk . . . for hours. And well, one thing led to another." He spread his hands wide.

Norah's heart pulsated with the grief of ripped-open scars. "Is your story supposed to make me feel better? To know I was conceived in lust, by a would-be robber and a wife who betrayed her marriage vows?"

"Eleanor was a lonely woman trapped in an unhappy marriage. And I was a lonely man, raised on the streets of London. She encouraged me to stop stealing, to make an honest man of myself."

"You weren't honest, not with me."

He bowed his head in acknowledgment. "I couldn't be. When her husband discovered our affair, she begged me to stay away from her. So I never saw her again until yesterday, in the shop. I felt . . ." A faraway look gentled his face. "I felt the same way I had when she swung that poker at me, her eyes so fierce. I wanted to hold her in my arms and show her how much I adored her."

"Love at first sight," Kit murmured. "Now there's a devilish predicament I can understand."

His tone was thoughtful, commiserating. With a shock, Norah saw that he was actually smiling at Jerome. How could her husband be so disloyal? Didn't he recognize the pain Jerome had put her through since birth?

Jane trotted back into the drawing room with the glass of water. His hands shaking, Jerome drank deeply, heedless of the droplets that spotted his pristine coat.

In a move of typical brazenness, Jane settled into a chair and watched him, her kittenish face keen with interest.

"Leave us," Kit told her.

"For the love of God, this is *my* house—"

"Go."

"But you can't order me around anymore—"

"Now."

Mouth pinched, she rose with exaggerated grace and flounced to the door. "Murderer or not, Lord Bruce has better manners than *you*, Kit Coleridge." She slammed the double doors.

Kit drew Norah over to a settee and pulled her down close to him. Still shaken, she let him take her hands. "Darling, we have to forget the past for a moment and think about the danger you're in now," he said. "At last we have a motive. Bruce is your half brother."

The extraordinary thought struck into the agony that embroiled her heart and soul. After all these years, she did have a sibling . . . and the memory of his cruel disdain chilled her to the bone. "He killed Maurice," she whispered. "And he hates me enough to see me dead, too. My own brother."

"I wonder how he found out about you," Kit mused. "Lady Carlyle must have said something."

Jerome set down his glass with a thump. "It wouldn't surprise me if Eleanor had decided to acknowledge you, Norah. She's free to do so now that her husband passed away last year."

Kit snapped his fingers. "Good thinking. If she voiced her intentions to Bruce, he would have threatened her into silence. Jesus God, he's vain about his flawless bloodline. He'd be livid to learn he had a sister born on the wrong side of the blanket."

"One would think he'd be thrilled," Jerome said. "To claim a beautiful and talented woman like Norah as his sister."

The wistful softness of his mouth and eyes burrowed into her heart. She groped for the angry sense of betrayal. "Why should he? *You* didn't claim me. You denied a helpless child the security of a true family."

"Because I had nothing to offer you. Nothing but the money to pay for your care by nuns who knew more about children than I."

With a stab of torment she recalled the dreamy girl she had once been, crossing the bitter North Sea to wed an Englishman she had never met, with hope in her heart and visions of a real home and a family to love. "I never even knew you until I was sixteen.

How could you have discarded me all those years, like unwanted rubbish?''

"It took me those sixteen years to make something of myself, to take a thief's knowledge of jewels and use it in a legitimate form of trade. And I did. I convinced the European aristocracy that I could broker their family gems. I turned my life around and became the sort of father you could honor and respect.''

Tears seeped down his aging cheeks, but he made no move to wipe away the wetness. His unashamed show of emotion rattled her, made her ache to throw her arms around him in comfort.

Had he really changed his life for her? Or was he only trying to excuse his neglect?

Clenching her fists around the folds of her skirt, she said, "Why did you never tell me?''

"Because I feared the very reaction you feel now. I feared you would despise me, that you would shut me out of your heart forever. I did the best I could. Please forgive me, Norah.''

Sincerity throbbed in his voice. Torn between hurt and yearning, she choked back the sobs that burned her throat. In her agonized confusion one thought shone clear and bright. Her father. Jerome was her *father*.

The notion washed her in a thrill so intense she feared its brilliance. She was his bastard daughter. The disclosure tore apart the familiar ties of their friendship. She felt at a loss to reweave the broken strands of trust.

Seeking solace, she pressed her cheek to Kit's shoulder; he hugged her tight. "I don't know what to say,'' she murmured. "I need time to think.''

"I understand completely,'' Jerome said. He stood slowly and looked at her, his eyes moist and mournful. "I only wish there were some way I could make up those lost years to you.'' Picking up his top hat, he went out.

The minute his dignified form disappeared from sight, she ached to call him back. "Oh, Kit,'' she whispered in a tangle of distress. "What shall I do now?"

He kissed her brow. "Sshh. Don't torture yourself. You'll learn to have faith in him again." He held on to her for a long, soothing moment. His expression hardening, he drew her to her feet. "In the meantime, we must tell the police about Bruce."

Half a block down the street, Lord Bruce Abernathy, Viscount Carlyle, sat inside his carriage and peered through the mist. His muscles tensed as he saw a man emerge from the town house. Jerome St. Claire. The worthless blighter who had ruined Bruce's mother.

Hatred swept hotly through his veins, chasing away the chill of an hour spent biding his time, waiting for the moment to savor victory. But the ambulance had never come, its team of horses blowing steam, its wheels clattering over the cobblestones.

And now, seeing Jerome St. Claire walking sedately off, Bruce knew the bitter sting of failure. The taste was even more galling in light of his ecstatic joy as Kit had burst into Jane's house, the footman and coachman following. Then the servants had come back out to man their posts by the brougham. The small white bundle the handsome one had placed inside the carriage still puzzled Bruce.

St. Claire strode past, one hand holding on to the brim of his top hat, his face tucked downward to ward off the light drizzle. Bruce made no attempt to close the curtains; the carriage interior was dim, the afternoon already beginning to darken into evening. The filthy old goat. How dare the common thief walk the streets of London dressed as if he were a gentleman worthy of esteem?

Not for long. With the information Bruce had so carefully gathered, Jerome St. Claire would be exposed for a petty criminal. Once Bruce relished his revenge, St. Claire would die, too.

But not with the dignity afforded Maurice. St. Claire would suffer. He would be stripped of his bogus gentility and tied up. He would be naked and vulnerable.

Anticipation hardened Bruce. Permitting himself the luxury of fantasy, he reached inside his cloak and stroked himself through his trousers. Intense pleasure rippled through him. God. Wouldn't that be rich? To use the man responsible for seducing Bruce's mother. The man responsible for fathering—

Norah.

Blackthorne at her side, she descended the front steps. Alive and unharmed.

The erection wilted beneath Bruce's fingers. He gripped the leather curtain, his eyes fixed on her flame-red hair and the pale oval of her face. She held her dainty chin with the hauteur of the aristocracy, as if she'd been born to privilege instead of sin.

His half sister.

He had always sensed that Mother had a secret. How keenly he recalled the year of her absence, first to Italy on holiday, then home for a mere fortnight before she'd gone off again, for eight long months. He had spent his fifth birthday alone. Upon her return, she'd brought him lavish presents, but even the model of Wellington's battleship couldn't distract him from the truth. Everything had changed. He recalled the chill between his parents, the banked fury in his father, so easily sparked that Bruce had learned to avoid him. There had been many times when Mother had closed herself in her studio and painted dull landscapes for days.

Now he knew why. She had been grieving for her beloved bastard. After his father's death the previous winter, she had told him the truth. With the fervent light of hope in her eyes, she had expressed her intent to acknowledge Norah. In secret, of course. It wouldn't do to let society learn of her indiscretion.

Bruce had put a swift end to his mother's misguided plan to welcome Norah into the family fold. He had threatened to expose the whole sordid story to the public, to make his mother and Jerome St.

Claire objects of scorn, and to hurt Norah in the process. His mother had quickly backed down. Yet she stood firm on one issue: she meant to make Norah an heiress.

Resentment burned him with furor. He would never split the family wealth with a by-blow. That was why she must die.

Suspense held him on the edge of his seat. He watched Blackthorne help Norah into the brougham. Had they discovered the strychnine? Or had the poisoned tartlets simply not worked yet?

He considered grilling Jane. But he hated to let Norah out of his sight. When she fell, he wanted to be close enough to see her writhe in agony.

Putting his mouth to the speaking tube, he snapped to his driver, "Follow them."

The carriage jolted through Mayfair, along Piccadilly, down Whitehall, and made a sharp left turn. A grouping of stone houses loomed through the mist. In the yellow glow of a street lamp, a squat-faced constable stood guard at the door of one building.

Bruce's blood chilled. Scotland Yard. The medieval lodging of the ambassadors of Scotland now housed the Metropolitan Police.

The curtain slipped from his fingers. The interior of the carriage plunged into gloom. Hoarsely he ordered the coachman to drive on.

God! He'd been found out. Jane had turned informant. He'd wring her lily-white neck.

He clamped down on his fear and rage. He hadn't time to waste on that bitch. He must act, and act fast. Only Norah mattered. How the devil could he pry her away from Blackthorne?

Thinking hard, he plucked the red rose from the cushion beside him and breathed deeply of its petals. The lush aroma washed him in single-minded loathing. Norah's scent.

An idea pricked him, sharp as the thorn that scraped his gloved finger. The previous night he'd driven past the cemetery. No constable patrolled there anymore, but a couple of urchins had lurked among the gravestones. He had recognized one of them, the spike-haired lad who worked for Norah and lived at the orphan school where she taught.

Bruce smiled. Excitement grew in him, mounting into visceral pleasure. That fresh-faced boy would bring her running.

No sooner did he close the door to the master bedroom than Kit drew Norah into his arms. Her silky scent, delightfully damp from the outdoors, washed him in a wave of love so powerful he might have fallen had not he needed to hold her. "It's nearly over, darling. Praise God the nightmare is nearly over."

"But Bruce wasn't at his town house across the square." Shivering, she looked toward the window, into the misty dark where the distant pinpricks of lights through the trees marked the Carlyle residence. "If he went back to Jane and found out that his plan hadn't worked . . ."

Wishing he could shed his own fears, Kit rubbed her arms. "The police are waiting at Jane's house, too. He won't get away."

She tilted her head back. "He's my brother. How could he hate me so?"

Moody sadness haunted her lovely features, lent fragility to her fair skin. He kissed her freckled nose, then brushed his lips across the warm satin of her cheek, to the mysterious glow of moonstones at her earlobe. "Maybe he's afraid you'll lay claim to the family fortune. He should realize you're more precious than a vault full of diamonds."

"Oh, Kit. I'm sorry for pushing you away yesterday in my office." She nestled her face in the crook of his neck. "I *don't* want you to keep your distance. I love you so much."

A band of emotion tightened around his heart. Resting his jaw atop her fragrant head, he stroked her back. When he regained his composure, he murmured, "You were right to criticize me. I should have trusted you. Norah, I have a confession to make."

She lifted her head. "You do?"

"I deliberately played on your physical passion as a way to distract you. To keep you all to myself. Because I was jealous of Jerome."

Gazing into his solemnly handsome face, the darkly sensual features she had come to adore, Norah felt the flash of a joy so radiant it banished the darkness of despair. "At least now we know you haven't any cause for jealousy," she murmured. "However, I do hope you won't ever stop seducing me."

She slipped her finger between the silver studs of his shirt. Crisp hairs and warm skin met her touch, then the smooth disk of his male nipple.

He sucked in a breath and caught her wrist. Bringing her palm to his lips, he kissed her gently. "Charming as you are, we need to talk about Jerome and Lady Carlyle first. It's not every day a woman learns the identity of her long-lost parents."

She sighed at the reminder, the memories that crowded her. "I suppose they did what they had to, by giving me away."

"But they never forgot you. Lady Carlyle is your faithful patron. And Jerome has been your devoted friend for the past nine years."

"I know, but the memory of growing up alone still hurts."

"That's only to be expected, love. No matter what wonderful things my parents told me about my own mother, I couldn't accept her for a long time. Because I wasn't ready to see her as a real person, with strengths and flaws." He cupped her cheeks in his big palms. "Your parents aren't perfect, either. What would your childhood have been like if you'd been raised by a fallen woman and a thief? They coped the best they could with an unhappy situation. They settled you in a place where you could thrive and be safe."

She closed her eyes. On a rush of nostalgia she

saw the mossy stone fence enclosing the convent garden, felt the warmth of the sun on her face, smelled the incense drifting from the chapel. She had spent hours among the roses, fashioning neck-laces from the petals, pouring her soul onto drawing paper and sketching dreams of the world beyond the cloistered walls.

Now she could see that she hadn't been aban-doned, but sheltered with the best of intentions. By two people who loved her dearly.

Pauvre petite. She is the product of sin. She can never wash away the taint of her bad blood.

But she had. Through their love, both she and Kit had vanquished the demons of the past. Together, they had created the new dream of a glorious future.

Smiling, she opened her eyes to her husband, solid and warm and all hers. She slipped her arms around his trim waist. "I suppose if I'd been a more devout girl, I'd have been content living among the nuns."

His lips crooked upward. "I worship your irrev-erent streak. As long as you're not throwing a box of condoms at me. Or running off and putting yourself in peril."

"Never again, Kit." She thrust away the abhor-rent premonition of danger lurking beyond the pro-tection of his arms. "I missed making love with you last night."

"I had a devil of a time lying beside you in the dark and not reaching out. I was aching to kiss you here." His palms molded around her breasts. Then one hand slid down between her legs, caressing her through the silk of her skirt and petticoats. "And here."

"Mmm." Her brief satisfaction dissolved into the longing for a more intimate touch. Impatient with talking, she pushed off his coat. He assisted her, shrugging his arms free, then reaching around to unfasten the back of her gown. He slipped his hands inside and found her bottom, rubbing their hips to-gether.

Their mouths melded in a deep kiss of equal need. They undressed each other, dropping their clothes in a heedless heap on the floor, until she could stroke his magnificent arousal. He lengthened and heated under her caresses, allowing her only half a minute before his need grew too great.

He carried her to the bed, came down onto her, and, in one bold drive, penetrated her. Norah moaned at the divine pressure of him inside her. His own harsh growl of urgency stirred her hair.

"God, Norah. I love this. I love *you*."

She smiled, entranced by the ardor in his voice. "Who would have thought three months ago, we would be married? A widow afraid of lovemaking, and a rake who couldn't commit himself to one woman."

He grimaced. "Don't remind me of my checkered past."

"I'm glad for it. Otherwise you might have married someone else, years ago."

"I waited for you. Only you."

He pressed deeper, withdrew almost to her entrance, then slid inside her again. The seductive friction scattered her thoughts like sunlight off the facets of a diamond. Lifting her hips in welcome, she wrapped her legs around his. She smoothed her hands over the ropy muscles of his shoulders and down his back, the slick strength and musky scent of his skin expanding her pleasure.

With earthy reverence, he kissed her breasts, her throat, her mouth until the world held only their hot impassioned bodies, their mingled cries and groans, the eloquent expressions of mutual adoration. The ultimate joy took Norah first, pulsing in sweet-sharp spasms that seemed to go on forever before fading, then peaked again when Kit surged into her one last time on the path to his own release.

She drifted back to the awareness of his harsh breaths, his trembling muscles. He rolled onto his back, draping her atop him. He rested his forearm across his brow and with his other hand worked his fingers through the tangle of her curls. "My sweet wife," he said with husky satisfaction. "Love is quite the aphrodisiac. I never knew that until I met you."

"Kit." Too mellow and replete to do more than sigh his name, she laid her cheek on the springy black hair of his chest. His closeness was pure paradise. Thinking of Kit as her husband still held a faint surprise, a leap of joy at unexpected moments. Once she had resigned herself to a barren future. Never in her wildest imaginings had she thought her life would take this course, that she would marry again and look forward to the birth of their baby, that she would know the bliss of true contentment.

A knock rattled the door. The sound was a brusque intrusion, shattering the spell enveloping Norah.

Kit pushed up on his elbow. "Who is it?"

"Herriot, m'lord," came his muffled voice. "I've a message, delivered for m'lady."

"Put it beneath the door."

With a papery rustle, a white envelope appeared through the crack and slid onto the rug. Kit rose, crossed the room, and fetched the note for her. His naked splendor stole her breath. With effort, she turned her regard to opening the letter.

"It's from Jerome." Mystified, she read the page. Clutching the paper to her bare breasts, she focused puzzled eyes on Kit. "He says not to redesign the royal tiara just yet, that I might still be able to use Fire at Midnight. What can he mean?"

Kit snatched the note from her and read it. "I don't know. The police will seize the stone as evidence. You won't be able to legally reclaim it for months. And the competition is the day after tomorrow."

I'd do anything to get Fire at Midnight for you. Anything at all.

Jerome's impassioned words reverberated in her mind, setting off an explosion of awareness. Her composure crumbled beneath the weight of panic.

"Oh dear God, Kit! He must have gone to Bruce's town house to steal back the diamond."

Surging up from the bed, she grasped Kit's arm. "The police are watching Bruce's house. If they catch Jerome breaking in, he'll be arrested. They could find out about his past reputation as a thief and use it to convict him."

"Not if I intercede."

Grabbing his shirt from the floor, Kit jerked it over his naked torso. Norah padded after him and reached for her chemise. "I'm going, too."

"No. You're to stay put."

"But he's my father—"

"And Bruce is still out there somewhere. He wants to kill you." Kit pulled her tight against him. "You'll be safe here, with Herriot and Wickham and the other servants to protect you."

"But I feel safest with you."

"Sshh. I won't drag you into a volatile situation."

Her panic deepened into fright. "You could be hurt—"

"Don't. Please don't fret." His breath gusted warm against her cheek. "I'll take care. You do the same."

Releasing her, he picked up his trousers. Norah watched, her numb fingers clutching the chemise to her breasts. Dear God, her hunger for the royal commission now endangered the two men she loved most.

Fully dressed, Kit brushed a kiss over her lips. "Be patient, darling, and I'll return shortly. With Jerome."

He strode out the door. Its closing eddied a current of air against her naked skin. Shivering, already missing his closeness, she dressed slowly. Then she leaned on the window seat and peered out. There were no stars, no moon tonight, only the occasional glow of a street lamp. The mist had grown too dense for her to detect more than the hint of lights beyond the blackened tangle of trees in the square. The fog swirled thickest near the ground, denying her any chance of spying Kit's broad-shouldered form.

Too agitated to sit, she paced. Since that long-ago morning when she had come to see where Maurice had died, the master bedroom had been refurbished in sunshine silks. The change reflected the bright path her life had taken.

Her heart pulled taut. Dear God, if anything happened to Kit, she would know true grief, an irreplaceable emptiness. She breathed a prayer for the safety of her husband and her father.

To distract herself, she repaired her disheveled curls and then went down the passage toward the grand staircase. The marble pillars, the lofty ceiling painted in the palazzo style, gave her a thrill of pride. Kit's home was hers now, too. Soon these walls would ring with the laughter of their children.

The sound of argumentative voices made her move to the balcony. Touching the cold marble guardrail, she gazed down into the entrance hall.

To her surprise, the door stood wide open. Herriot waved a pistol and held a black-haired urchin by the scruff of his neck. The lad swung his fist at the footman's stomach. Herriot doubled over and the boy ducked past him, darting into the grand hall.

"Lark!"

Norah hastened down the wide steps, her slippers scuffing against the marble. Lark met her halfway. His brown eyes were white-rimmed against his stricken face. "M'lady. You gotta come. Sumfink turrible's 'appened."

Herriot stumbled up the stairs and snatched at Lark. "When I wouldn't open the door," he gasped out, "the cheeky beggar picked the front lock and tried to walk right in."

"It's all right," Norah said. "Lark is a friend. He works for me."

Taking Lark by the arm, she guided him into the library and shut the doors. He was breathing hard, and she realized with a twist of alarm that the dirty streaks on his face were tear tracks. She rubbed him soothingly on his shoulder.

"Calm down now, and tell me what's wrong."

He scrubbed at his nose with his sleeve. " 'Tis the madwoman o' Mayfair. Only she ain't no woman. She's a *man*."

A chill whispered over Norah's skin. "Who told you that?"

"Nobody. I saw 'im. Me and the boys, we been takin' turns watchin' the grave. T' see 'oo left the roses."

"How did you know about the flowers?"

"Sorry, m'lady, but I listened at yer door. Tonight 'twas me an' Screeve 'oo went t' watch." Lark stopped, gulping, his eyes watery.

"Go on, please."

"Somebody tried t' grab me from behind. I jabbed 'im in the ribs an' got away. But the blighter caught Screeve instead. The red-caped bloke put a knife t' Screeve's throat an' told me t' fetch you, t' bring you back inside an hour."

"We must notify the police at once—"

"No! 'E said 'e'd *kill* Screeve if I told anybody else but you—" Lark's voice choked on a sob.

An ice-cold fist of fear squeezed Norah. Unwillingly her mind saw the gruesome image of the freckle-faced boy sprawled on the ground, blood seeping from his slit throat.

His hands clasped, Lark fell to his knees before her. "Oh, please, m'lady. Please 'elp 'im. Please don't let the bastard murder me best mate."

Chapter 20

Silence cloaked the dark, terraced hills of High-gate Cemetery. The damp night held only the swift tap of Lark's footsteps and the muted rustle of Norah's petticoats. Adjusting the hood of her mantle, she yearned for the heartening glow of a lantern.

But light would announce their approach to the murderer who lay in wait for her.

She edged a glance over her shoulder. Behind her stood the massive archway of lotus-decorated columns that marked the entrance to Egyptian Avenue. On the winding roadway beyond, she could discern the black shape of the hired hansom cab floating like a disembodied entity atop a cloud of fog. The high-perched driver looked none too pleased to be left waiting alone in the spooky chill of the graveyard.

Through the swirling mist ahead lay tombs decorated by granite angels and ivy-shrouded crosses. The shadowed maws of burial vaults were carved into the hillside on either side of the path.

At the juncture where the walk diverged into the two curves of a circle, Lark tugged at her mantle. His eyes were round and scared, and moisture dewed his spiky hair. "Maybe we should wait for 'is lordship," he whispered.

She wanted to. Dear Blessed Virgin, she wanted to feel the security of Kit's presence at her side. If only they had had the time to fetch him. If only Bruce hadn't ordered her to come alone.

She turned a composed face to the boy. "You know I dare not," she murmured. "Herriot ran to alert Kit, to bring him here. But only I can save Screeve."

Norah suppressed a bone-deep shudder. An hour had passed since Lark had hailed a cab and hastened to fetch her. An hour in which an innocent boy had been at the mercy of a deviant. A murderer.

"You'll stay right here," she said in a low voice.

"Nay, m'lady! I can protect you—"

"Beyond the trees, Bruce could spot you. He said I was to come alone. He might panic if he saw you."

"But I want t' 'elp."

"You have. His lordship doesn't know the precise location of the sepulcher. You can listen for his arrival and then guide him to me."

"You might be killed—"

"You'll hear if I scream for help. If you don't obey, Lark, you'll endanger Screeve."

He hunched his shoulders and hung his head. "Aye, m'lady."

Before she could lose her nerve, Norah started down the left curve of the path. The faint aroma of cedar and earth hung in the damp air. The trees that looked so neatly manicured in the daylight now appeared to reach for her with bony limbs. Drawing out her muff pistol, she hurried past the black outlines of crypts, the pale oblongs of tombstones. Her advance stirred thick snakes of vapor that coiled along the ground.

Taking care to be quiet, she mounted the stone steps cut into the terraced hillside. At the top of the short flight, she paused to get her bearings. The heaviest of the fog hung below, though the misty darkness here obscured her vision. Were the evening clear, she would have seen the vast expanse of the cemetery and the glow of London to the south.

Tonight, the gloom pressed as heavily as a funeral shroud.

Relying on memory, she cautiously picked her way along the murky path. A pebble went rolling down the slope, the sound as loud to her heightened senses as the hooves of a runaway horse. She froze. Nothing moved against the charcoal canvas of the night. Hearing only the swish of blood in her ears, she went on.

When she reached the inky facade of the Catacombs, she used the wall to guide her. Cold rough stone met her fingertips. Tendrils of ivy tickled her skin as she groped along the curved length of the structure. Every few feet, there yawned an open door and a tomb hidden within the darkness.

At the end of the row, a faint glimmer beckoned. Maurice's crypt. The place Bruce had designated for their meeting.

Heart hammering, Norah tightened her hand on the diminutive stock of the gun. Her index finger caressed the slim metal crescent of the trigger. She tiptoed forward, hoping to take Bruce by surprise. It was a dismal plan, but her choices had dwindled to none.

She dared a peek around the corner. A candle guttered atop the marble sarcophagus. Its yellow glow bathed the single red rose lying on the tomb. Shadows played over the visage of a life-sized stone archangel. And there, bound and gagged at the feet of the statue, sat Screeve.

A bolt of relief pierced her. Though unhurt, he looked small and forlorn, his freckled face pale against his fair hair. He saw her and his blue eyes widened over the white cloth covering his mouth. He wriggled frantically. Mewling sounds emerged from his throat.

Where was Bruce? Could it be he'd given up on her?

Or was this a trick?

Shaking and anxious, she rushed to untie the boy. She had only started to jerk open the knot at his ankles when she heard a sound from behind. Before she could whirl, an arm clamped around her neck to cut off her breath. Yanked backward, she slammed into solid flesh. The cold steel of a knife met her throat.

"Give me your gun, Norah."

Her brother's voice sluiced over her like ice water. The pressure of the blade at her throat held a deadly threat. Her head spun from lack of air. Glancing down at the tears pooling in Screeve's blue eyes, she relaxed her fingers.

Bruce snatched the weapon away. Awareness of her own vulnerability plunged her into terror; then her emotions ascended into rage.

He abruptly released her and she stumbled away, rubbing her sore throat. "You horrible bastard," she choked out.

A scarlet cape fringed in jet beads hugged his black suit like a splash of blood. His face was as hard as marble beneath his styled blond hair. He might have been a study in perfection but for the scar that made his eyebrow slant in diabolical query.

He pocketed the knife and aimed her own pistol at her. "Tut, tut, my lady. Haven't you guessed the truth yet? *You're* the bastard. My own mother's by-blow."

His condescending smile taunted her. Out of the corner of her eye she saw Screeve wriggling his ankles. The rope appeared less than taut. Pray God she had loosened his bonds enough that he might work himself free. She stepped in front of him, so that her gown shielded him from view. "If you think to shock me," Norah said, forcing steadiness into her voice, "I already know about the love affair Lady Carlyle had with Jerome."

"Love had nothing to do with it," Bruce growled. "St. Claire violated her, then abandoned her."

"Did he? I'll be happy to tell you his side of the story if you'll let the boy go."

Bruce stood still. Only his eyes moved, assessing her up and down. "And allow him to sound an alarm before I'm through with you? I think not."

Through with you. The words shivered like a nightmare inside her. Dear God, the baby. She would never see her own sweet baby. She would never again feel the tenderness of Kit's embrace.

Norah fought a sickening wave of panic. She must stall Bruce, divert his attention from Screeve until Kit arrived.

Suddenly behind her, the boy scrambled to his feet. Bruce lunged out, but Screeve ducked under his arm and sprinted off into the darkness.

"Come back, you little scum!" Bruce started out of the crypt. Then he wheeled around again, his red cape swirling. "The brat had better not run for help, or I'll make *you* sorry."

Screeve's departure gave her a brief twist of triumph before the horrid despair returned. Striving to blank her expression, she said, "Whatever you have planned won't work. The police know everything. There isn't a corner in England where you'll be safe. So you may as well let me go, too."

As she spoke, Norah inched toward the doorway. He stepped over to block the opening. He cocked the pistol with a sharp click. "No. When I go down, dear sister, you'll go with me."

Determination glittered in his frosty blue eyes. She stood petrified. The eerie hoot of an owl drifted from outside the crypt.

Distract him, she thought. Distract him.

But her mind emptied of all save the black eye of the gun, glaring at her heart. She wrenched her gaze away. And saw the red rose.

"Why have you been leaving flowers on Maurice's grave?"

His face changed, bitterness drawing down his fine mouth. "Because you never did. You're his widow, but you never honored him the way he deserved."

Carefully she said, "I gave Maurice nine years of my life. I made a comfortable home for him, obeyed his every wish. I even cared for his relations, and let him take credit for my designs. Given his predilections, I think that was enough."

"Obviously it wasn't. He strayed from you. He needed a lover who could satisfy his desires the way I did."

His contemptuous scorn sickened her, but she dared not anger him. Pressing her damp palms together, she said, "Please, I must know. How did it start? How did you meet him?"

"It started when Mother confessed the truth last spring and told me she was changing her will. I investigated you and found out that your husband sometimes frequented establishments that catered to . . . sophisticated tastes. I thought it might prove amusing to dally with my own brother-in-law." His head cocked in contemplation, Bruce lowered the gun a fraction. "Maurice was like a ripe plum, waiting to be plucked. We met several times a week, sometimes every evening. Your husband was quite the passionate lover. He showered me with expensive gifts, especially with jewels."

Norah swallowed a glut of infuriated disgust. Now she knew why Maurice had left her so deeply in debt. "So why did you murder him?"

"Later, he tried to end our liaison. He said it wasn't fair of him to deceive his wife. Imagine . . . he wanted to discard me in favor of you."

Ugliness twisted all humanity from his features. He stood like a demonic apparition in the doorway of the crypt, the weak candlelight wavering over his bestial yet beautiful face.

She wished she had the courage to run. Run from those feral eyes, run into the sheltering darkness of the cemetery. But he had the pistol. She'd never get past him. "Of course Maurice felt guilty. He was betraying his marriage vows."

"What about betraying me? My God, he didn't even love you. He loved me."

The painfully raw edge to his voice roused a dawning awareness in her. "And you fell in love with him, too." On impulse she added, "Oh Bruce, I am sorry."

His harsh breaths rasped into the quiet crypt.

Stepping closer, he leveled the gun at her. "Don't you dare pity me."

Her brief softening dissolved into terror. She backed up against the stone archangel, into the outstretched granite arms. "I'm only saying I understand," she said hastily. "I know what it's like to love someone."

"Blackie?" Bruce stopped and gave an unpleasant laugh. "God, you two deserve each other. A heathen and a bastard."

Norah stiffened. "My husband is a fine man. He has a rich and wonderful heritage. You're too blind to see his goodness."

"He's a black devil. It's a shame I went through all the trouble of dressing like a woman and tempting Maurice to Blackthorne's bedroom. I was hoping the scandal would taint him."

Tamping down her anger, she asked, "How did you convince Maurice to sneak into Kit's house in the middle of a New Year's Eve party?"

A sly smile curled Bruce's lips. "Much as he tried to resist his base urges, Maurice still lusted after me. But I played the spurned lover, too hurt to give in to his advances. I told him he could have me again only if he proved his love by the ultimate test: risking discovery by a houseful of people." He swept his hand dismissingly. "And so he did. The rest was simple."

Repugnance twisted deep in her belly. "If you truly loved Maurice, how could you look him in the eyes and kill him?"

"I didn't." For a brief moment, Bruce had a faraway luster to his gaze, as if he peered into the past. "He was unconscious by then from the morphine I put in his sherry. He never even felt the pin pierce his heart."

Norah kept her gaze on the gun. Dear God, he was close. Too close. If she kept him talking, he might lower his guard. It was her only hope. "You tried to put the blame on me."

"The emerald hatpin was a nice touch, was it not?"

"But your ploy didn't work." Surreptitiously she felt behind her; only cold smooth stone met her fingers. She had no weapon but her tongue. "I'm curious, what did you hope to accomplish by sending me that mourning brooch with Maurice's hair inside?"

Bruce scowled. "You were getting too close to Blackie. I wanted to remind you of your duty to mourn your own husband."

"None of your schemes has hurt me. Not your pushing me down the stairs at the museum. Not your attempt to break into my shop and hit me."

"That wasn't me," he spat. "It was a felon I hired. Needless to say, the bungler didn't live long enough to collect his fee. Just as you won't live long enough to bring Blackie's heir into the world."

Her legs shook. Somehow she managed to keep standing, her eyes fixed to his aristocratic features. His scent drifted to her, an elegant hint of spice that mixed with the musty smell of decay in the air and the acrid taste of fear in her mouth. "I'm your sister. My baby will be your niece or nephew, your own flesh and blood."

"You're a by-blow," he snapped. "Yet you had the temerity to outrank me by marrying Blackthorne. Both of you are a blemish on English society."

Norah saw the tension in his slim body, the faint tightening of his hand on the gun. "If you murder me," she said in desperation, "the whole story will come out. You'll bring shame onto the Carlyle name."

His face darkened with diabolic hatred. "*You* brought shame onto my family's honor. You, by the filthy fact of your existence—"

A sudden movement erupted behind him. Lark and Screeve came barreling inside the crypt, each boy brandishing a tree branch like a sword. "*En garde*, you bloody bugger," Lark shouted.

Bruce started to wheel around.

Norah acted without thinking. She lunged at him, bringing both her fists down on his forearm. The gun flew from his hand. It landed with a thump and skidded into the shadows beside the sarcophagus.

She dove for the weapon. Her cold fingers closed around the warm metal stock. In a crouch, her skirts pooled around her, she lifted the pistol.

But the boys were too close for her to risk a shot.

Their sticks jammed into Bruce's stomach, Lark and Screeve forced their opponent against the side wall near where Norah knelt. Their young faces, one rough-featured and the other scrawny, reflected a kindred sense of bloodthirsty purpose.

"Give up or die," Lark snarled.

Bruce stood with his cloak thrown back, his arms raised in surrender. The cunning in his blue eyes alarmed Norah. "Careful," she murmured. "Don't trust him—"

Even as she hastened to her feet, he lashed downward with his arms. Both sticks broke under the swift blow. Rather than attack the boys, Bruce thrust himself sideways, straight at Norah.

She leaped in swift retreat to the back corner of the crypt. She aimed the barrel at his chest. But her finger hesitated on the trigger. Bruce was her brother. Her brother.

The second of opportunity vanished. He caught her wrist and twisted hard. Pain streaked up her arm. The pistol dropped from her bloodless fingers and into his hand.

He yanked her around and imprisoned her arms. The gun barrel was a tiny cold circle against her temple. "Bitch! This time you'll die—"

"And you'll answer to me, Carlyle," Kit said.

He loomed in the doorway of the crypt. Norah's heart took a giddy surge. Grim-featured, his black hair tousled, he leveled his own gun at Bruce while Lark and Screeve watched, big-eyed, near the wall.

Bruce's arm tightened reflexively. The pistol remained a deadly pressure against the side of her face. "Throw down your gun," he said. "Or I'll shoot your beloved wife."

Kit hesitated. Then his mouth tightened to a strict line. Never taking his eyes from Bruce, he carefully dropped his pistol. It thunked to the ground.

"Now kick it away."

Kit obeyed, his shoe scuffing on the damp earth as he knocked the weapon into the pitch darkness beyond the door. "I see you have Norah's muff pistol," he said. "It carries only a single shot. So you can be damned sure I'll take you alive. And by God, I'll make you pay for hurting my wife. The sordid story of your trial will be splashed across every newspaper in England."

"No one will believe you, Blackie."

Kit laughed, a harsh sound that echoed off the stone walls. "Your petty bigotry is meaningless now. The entire country will learn the intimate details of your tryst with Maurice. Your precious name will be dragged through the dirt. Even the lowliest barmaid will be laughing at you, the pitiful viscount who fornicated with other men and abducted young boys."

Norah felt the hot gust of Bruce's breath against her ear. His muscles were strained around her. He exuded the sweaty scent of a cornered beast. Bile burned her throat. She was so afraid to die. Kit couldn't help her. She could only help herself.

"You can't possibly get away," Kit said in a low, taunting voice. "The police should arrive at any moment. So what will you do with your one shot, Carlyle? Use it on Norah and get arrested for murder? Or use it on yourself?"

Jerome dashed into the doorway. Panting, he burst out, "My God! Let her go!"

Now or never. She drove her heel down onto Bruce's instep. He yelped in surprise.

Wrenching herself free, she threw herself to the ground. And heard the deafening blast of a single shot.

The sound echoed in her ears. She tasted dust in her mouth.

Behind her, Bruce lay sprawled on his side by the sarcophagus. The scarlet cape pooled around his slim body. The gun barrel was still pressed in his mouth. The back of his head was a bloodied hole. His wide eyes stared at nothing.

Dear God. He had shot himself.

She trembled, too stunned to speak. Then Kit bent over her and drew her up. She clung to him, craving his warm strength, the blessed life of the man she loved.

"Thank God you're safe," Jerome said.

He stood by the wall, heartfelt relief shining in his blue eyes. Smiling tremulously at his familiar debonair features, she threw herself into his arms. "Oh, Father. I was so afraid when I heard you'd gone after the diamond."

He hugged her tight, then held her at arm's length. "Your husband caught up to me and raked me over the coals. But not before I found this in Carlyle's safe."

Reaching into his pocket, he drew forth a purple stone the size of a baby's fist. The pale candlelight sparked a mysterious glow within its dark depths.

Norah caught her breath. "Fire at Midnight."

"My skills were a bit rusty," Jerome said modestly, "but a good thief never forgets how to crack a safe. Now my daughter can earn the first of many royal commissions."

"You're a fine man for wanting to help me," Norah said. "The best father in the world. But you didn't have to steal the stone to win my heart."

"We tried to 'elp, too," Lark piped up. His face mournful, he added, "We used our brains instead o' brawn , m'lord, just like you taught us."

"But our sword ploy didn't work," Screeve added, hanging his towhead in dejection.

Kit put an arm around each boy. "I'd call you both heroes for trying."

They smiled, then glanced back at the corpse in disgusted awe.

"Time to go," Kit said.

He drew Norah out of the tomb, into the misty darkness and the fresh damp air. But a tug of sadness brought her to a halt.

"Wait," she murmured.

She went back inside, lifted the red rose from Maurice's tomb, and bent to lay the flower on her brother's still chest. Tears blurred her eyes, but she blinked them away.

Then she left the crypt and walked into her husband's waiting arms.

Epilogue

London, June 21, 1887

"Do you think the Princess of Wales will come
here tonight?"

Norah heard someone in the crowd whisper the
question that occupied everyone's mind. Resisting
the pull of excitement, she greeted the earl who had
just arrived at her front door.

With the windows thrown open to the balmy evening, the Mayfair mansion blazed with gaslight. The
air reverberated with chatter and laughter from the
glittering array of gentlemen and ladies who
thronged the grand staircase hall.

As she and Kit welcomed their noble guests, Norah felt buoyed on a dreamy cloud of bliss. A few
busybodies murmured behind their fans, no doubt
rehashing the old gossip about the indecent swiftness of her remarriage. Yet in her heart she could
only pity the people who had nothing better than
tale-telling to amuse them.

Her gaze strayed to Kit's princely features, the
bold jaw and handsome cheekbones, the warm dark
eyes that could convey both teasing and tenderness. Six months ago, she had been locked into a
barren, unhappy marriage. Now she was blessed
with a devoted husband, a precious baby due by

year's end, and a future illuminated by the radiance of love.

Near a massive marble column, Thaddeus and Winnifred and Ivy stood conversing with a matronly countess.

Upon seeing Norah and Kit approach, Winnifred smiled, her sturdy features softer since she and Thaddeus had made plans to marry at the end of the summer. Kit had bestowed a generous dowry on her. "A splendid party, my lord and lady," Winnifred said. "A true celebration of the Queen's Jubilee Day."

Kit gallantly kissed her hand. "The true celebration is in honor of my wife's accomplishments as a jeweler."

Ivy nodded vigorously, the lace fringe of her cap bobbing, her blue eyes merry above her black gown. "Oh Norah, how thrilling that Princess Alexandra wore your tiara today, when Victoria was honored at Westminster Abbey."

"Perhaps so." The countess of Romney sniffed loudly, looking like an overstuffed pillow swathed in layers of ruffled tangerine silk. With her sausage fingers, she adjusted the heavy gold tiara circling her iron-gray hair. "But *I* was just telling Mr. Teodecki that a crown worn by a royal personage should be grand and regal, like this one he designed for the competition."

Thaddeus clicked his heels and bowed. "I thank you, my lady. Yet perhaps the unique simplicity of Lady Blackthorne's design better suited the princess's rank. I predict that Norah's novel use of platinum as a setting for diamonds will launch a new fashion."

His loyalty and praise warmed Norah's heart. She lightly touched his arm in appreciation. "I'm hardly one to launch a craze, but you're kind to say so."

"Alas," he added, "no one got a close look at the tiara because the princess was sitting with the royal family."

"Isn't she coming here tonight?" asked Winnifred.

"I hear they're engaged at a dinner at Buckingham Palace." Her cheeks puffed like a fat squirrel's, the countess peered through her lorgnette at Norah. "Even so, I rather doubt the princess would deign to visit a household so . . . beset by tragic happenings."

Norah felt Kit's fingers tighten on her arm. With one glance at his thunderous expression, she said swiftly, "Then may I say his lordship and I are pleased you were open-minded enough to attend our humble gathering."

The countess preened. "I am not one to be put off by idle gossip, of course."

Oh no, Norah thought in wry amusement. You're only a prig who's afraid of missing the latest scandal.

From beside her, a boyish voice piped, "Champagne?"

Lark held up a silver tray in his white-gloved hands. Resplendent in blue livery with shiny gold buttons, he had slicked down his hair, with only a single errant spike springing free at the crown of his head. He and Screeve and Billy were serving tonight to hone their skills at gainful employment.

She accepted a thin-stemmed glass. "Thank you, Lark."

"Ye're welcome, m'lady." He gave Norah a secret, impish wink that belied his servile appearance. Affection overflowed her heart and emerged in a smile. Yes, she pitied the nobles who set themselves above the poor masses, for they lost the treasure of many friendships.

Lady Romney tilted her glass and drank, and Norah took the chance to guide Kit away into the throng of guests. He growled in her ear, "I'd like to stick that glass down her ladyship's stuffy throat. How dare she imply the princess is avoiding our house."

Norah tamped out a spark of yearning. "Shush.

We don't require Lady Romney's approval to make us happy."

Displeasure lowered his brow for only an instant longer. Then he grinned, his teeth a white flash against his teak-hued features. "You're right, as always," he murmured. "And later I intend to show you just how happy you make me."

His fingers made a small, erotic circle against her back, his warmth penetrating the silk of her gown and corset. A delicious heat showered through her and roused memories of their joy in each other. To distract herself, Norah sipped her champagne and looked toward the crush of people, where she spied a blond woman talking animatedly with a sedate, balding gentleman wearing a monocle. The jeweled doves in her hair bounced as she gestured at a Roman statue perched on a pedestal in an alcove.

"There's Jane and her fiancé," Norah said. "Fancy her taking up with Lord Melbrooke—a collector of classical antiquities."

Kit chuckled. "He's also the richest lord in Northumberland. At last Jane will have the security she always wanted."

"And perhaps," Norah added dryly, "marriage will keep her from playing any more pranks."

"Speaking of pranks," Kit said, frowning, "I see Annabelle and Adrian coming through the garden doors. She looks suspiciously smug. I wonder what mischief my baby sister is up to now."

Norah strained to follow his gaze, but unlike him, she couldn't see over the heads and shoulders of the guests. Clinging to his arm, she let him lead her through the assemblage. In the drawing room she caught sight of a delegation of Indian princes, including the maharaja of Rampur, who wore a dazzling array of rubies and emeralds that winked against his white turban. Sarah and Damien Coleridge stood talking to the monarch.

Their familiar smiling faces were now as dear to Norah as those of her own parents. At last she had a family, a close-knit clan who had welcomed her as one of their own. She slipped her hand over her stomach, slightly rounded and firm with her pregnancy. Soon she would add a grandchild to their dynasty.

She and Kit came upon the garden doors, open to the lantern-lit night. Oblivious to the guests going in and out, Annabelle stood whispering into Adrian's ear. His cheeks were flushed, his expression enraptured.

Kit took hold of his sister's arm and marched her just outside, into the dimness of the veranda. "What the devil's going on here?" he asked in a harsh whisper.

Trotting after them, Lord Adrian jumped guiltily. Annabelle primped her golden curls and fluttered her lashes at him. "Shall we tell them our news?"

He gulped. "Er, you may do the honors."

"Adrian and I are to be married," she announced. "*After* I have my London season, of course. I wouldn't miss the chance to turn aside all the other offers."

Pleasure broke forth in Norah, and she gathered the girl into a hug. "How wonderful!"

Kit stood still, his shocked expression focused first on Annabelle, then on Adrian. "Married?" His dark eyes bored into his friend. "I trust you haven't been to Buckingham Palace to visit Queen Victoria's suite."

Mystified, Norah asked, "Aren't you happy for them?"

"Of course I'm pleased." But he continued to glower at Lord Adrian, who ran his finger under his starched collar. "Well?"

"Well, nothing!" Annabelle said with a disdainful sniff. "Big brother or not, we have a right to our privacy."

"Ahem—yes. A gentleman does not kiss and tell." Turning, Adrian marched Annabelle into the drawing room.

"Jesus God," Kit said softly, staring after them.

"If it hadn't happened to me, I'd never believe love could reform a rake."

Glad for his change from roué to devoted husband, Norah pressed her cheek to his smooth sleeve. "What did you mean about visiting Queen Victoria's suite?"

Kit grimaced. "It was a wager Adrian once made. He said he wouldn't marry until he found a lady bold enough to make love to him in the Queen's own bed."

The report took her aback; then she giggled. "It would seem Lord Adrian has at last met his match."

"As I have."

Kit plucked the champagne glass from her fingers and set it on a stone bench. Taking advantage of the darkness, he bent to capture her lips in a stirring kiss. The taste and feel of her brought him to instant fire; only Norah could scatter his concentration and fill him with this impassioned wonder, this agonizing tenderness. His hand found the shape of her breast, voluptuous with maternal fullness. He thought of his child inside her, the culmination of their love, and he wanted Norah with a sweet, throbbing intensity that would burn into eternity.

She broke the kiss, her soft hand caressing his cheek. Her face was tilted up, her eyes like shadowy green jewels. His parure of moonstones, the diadem and earrings and necklace, glinted through the night. Yet the richness she had given him was infinitely more precious than any gems.

"We should return to our guests," she whispered.

"Mmm." He kissed the fragrant skin of her throat. "I'd rather love you."

"Later, remember?"

A teasing note in her voice, she slipped out of his arms and darted toward the drawing room. He caught up to her at the opened doors. Awash with love and laughter, he took her slender arm and escorted his wife into the densely packed throng. They fielded greetings from peers and peeresses, and slowly wended their way back toward the grand staircase hall.

"Look, darling." Kit bent closer to her. "Jerome and Lady Carlyle have arrived." He indicated the front door, where a footman took their wraps.

Norah's heart leaped in her breast. The moment held a shining newness, the marvelous thrill of having a mother and father at last. Her future lay with Kit, and now she had her past as well.

The perfect mate for Jerome's dapper refinement, Lady Carlyle wore an elegant black silk gown and seed pearl mourning jewelry. In the two months since her son's tragic suicide, she had made no public appearances until today.

Yet she and Norah had met often in private, each hungering to fill the long-lost years when Lady Carlyle's marriage had been an insurmountable barrier separating mother and daughter. Lady Carlyle had learned about Norah's girlhood at the convent, the peaceful hours in the rose garden, the strict nuns who had curbed her wayward impulses and taught her to behave like a lady. In turn, Norah had learned that Lady Carlyle had kept up a faithful correspondence with the Mother Superior, had followed her daughter's progress in schoolwork, and had rejoiced in her budding artistic talent. She had diverted funds from her dressmaking allowance in order to provide Norah with sketch pads and art lessons.

And now, with a lump in her throat, Norah could see beyond her own youthful loneliness. She could comprehend the agony her mother had endured, to entrust her only daughter to the care of strangers. She knew, because she felt the same fierce protectiveness toward the baby inside her.

She threaded her fingers through Kit's, thankful for the strength there. Praise God their children would grow up in the closeness of a family.

His lips crooked into an understanding smile that saw into her very soul, into the hopes and dreams and joys that shaped their future. "Let's go welcome them," he said.

He drew her through the bejeweled multitude until they stood before her parents. With a huge potted aspidistra providing a modicum of privacy, she took Lady Carlyle's hands and kissed her smooth cheek. "I'm so pleased you're here," she murmured. "Your presence means the world to me."

Her ladyship's face bloomed with a gentle smile. "I wouldn't have missed this chance to witness your triumph, Norah, dear."

"This is a day we'll tell our grandchildren about," Jerome declared. "Queen Victoria celebrating half a century as sovereign of the British Empire."

Kit smiled down at Norah. "And the beginning of a half century of happiness for all of us."

"Is Princess Alexandra here?" asked Lady Carlyle, peering around. "One of her ladies-in-waiting told me she might attend."

Norah felt a surge of excitement, which she promptly denied. Today she had gained professional success. She should be content without the ultimate honor of entertaining royalty. "I doubt she'll leave the family celebrations at the palace."

"Perhaps our request will hearten you," Jerome said. A whimsical sparkle lit his eyes, and he kept her ladyship's hand firmly tucked in the crook of his arm. "Eleanor and I would like to give you an important commission, Norah."

"I'm pleased, Father."

Jerome glanced at Lady Carlyle. "We'd like you to design our wedding rings."

Norah went weak with a powerful mix of emotion: surprise and delight and joy, all so encompassing that tears misted her vision. Her parents were getting married! She clung to Kit to keep from melting in pleasure. "Is this true? After all these years?"

They nodded in unison. "I haven't been so happy since a certain holiday a long time ago in Italy," Lady Carlyle murmured.

Their hands were clasped, their gazes joined in heartfelt bliss. Kit moved his thumb over Norah's palm, and he said in a husky tone, "Congratulations. This is indeed an auspicious day for love."

Norah smiled through her tears; then a buzz of conversation swept the crowd, followed by an awed hush. Curious, she turned and saw everyone staring at the front door.

"Their Royal Highnesses, the Prince and Princess of Wales," the footman intoned.

They stood in the doorway, Edward's rotund figure clad in black evening dress and Alexandra slim and regal in a cream silk gown. In her upswept dark hair shone an airy curve of white diamonds that peaked above her high brow. A glowing purple stone winked in the gaslight. Fire at Midnight.

Norah was too stunned to move; then Kit whispered in her ear, "This is your moment to shine, love."

With a slight pressure at the small of her back, he guided her forward. Bowing before their royal guests, he said, "Good evening, Your Highnesses."

Norah sank into a deep curtsy and echoed the greeting. "We're so pleased to welcome you both."

Edward gave her a hand up. His gaze moved over her slender form, the elegant ivory satin gown. "Our pleasure, my lady. To you and to my friend, Blackthorne."

Smiling warmly, the princess presented her white-gloved hand. "I especially wanted to express my appreciation for your talent, Lady Blackthorne. Perhaps you would find the time to design a necklace for me, too? The one you're wearing is so very pretty."

"Thank you." Awash with pleasure, Norah stood back as people lined up to address the royal pair.

Noble guests surrounded her and vied for commissions. Lady Romney elbowed her plump form through the crush and planted herself before Norah. "I inherited a fine topaz necklace from my great-grandmother, the duchess of Kent," she said. "I should like you to reset the stones into earbobs."

The imperious request made Norah's lips quirk

upward. So the countess, too, intended to ride the crest of popularity. "As soon as I can fit your order into my schedule, my lady."

"But I warn you," Kit added, "my wife's talent will cost you dearly."

"Whatever you say," the countess proclaimed. "I want only the best."

Kit drew Norah back, away from the multitude and into the warm bower of his embrace. He murmured in her ear, "She can't have the best. Because I already do."

Now that you've enjoyed
Barbara Dawson Smith's
FIRE AT MIDNIGHT,
sample another of Avon Books'
Romantic Treasures—
ONLY WITH YOUR LOVE
by Lisa Kleypas

Newly married Celia Vallerand is torn from her husband's arms when their ship is attacked by ruthless pirates, only to be rescued by the notorious Griffin, a dangerous, darkly handsome pirate who stirs Celia's desire . . . and who is her husband's brother . . .

Celia woke up fighting against the arms that confined her. ''No! No—''

''Quiet,'' a low voice said above her head. ''It's over now.''

She shuddered convulsively, burying her wet face in her hands. ''Philippe? Philippe—''

''No. You know who I am.'' Large hands smoothed over her head and back, and she lay folded up and gasping against a hard chest.

''Justin,'' she said weakly, not certain why his real name sprang to her lips when she was more familiar with him as Griffin.

''You were having a bad dream, *petite*. Just a dream.''

''I saw . . . Philippe . . . H-he was alive.''

Griffin continued to stroke her back. ''If he were,

I would go back and find him. But Legare leaves no survivors.''

She swallowed hard, beginning to regain her wits. ''Why?''

''It was a practice he began years ago, when—''

''No,'' she interrupted. ''Why would you care if Philippe were alive?''

There was a long, taut silence. ''I'll tell you when we reach New Orleans.''

''Why not now? Why does it have to be a mystery? What does it matter if I reach safety or not?'' She began to cry brokenly. ''You're no less guilty th-than the men who killed him,'' she said through her raw, angry sobbing. ''You're no better than they! You've killed before, many times. His blood is on your hands as much as theirs!''

Even in her torment, she sensed she had somehow hurt Griffin. The arms around her withdrew, and he stood up from the bed, walking away. The shock of aloneness and encroaching darkness caused something inside her to shatter. She had to escape from the demons howling around her, run, find a place to hide. Wildly she sprang from the bed and stumbled to the door, tearing at it until it was open. But Griffin's arm came around her waist before she could slip outside. A panicked scream burst from her lips, and she clawed at him ferociously.

''Stop it, damn you!'' He shook her slight frame. ''Stop it!''

''No . . . let me go . . . *Philippe!*''

Griffin raised his hand to slap her, unable to think of any other way to stem her rising hysteria.

''No,'' she sobbed, collapsing against him.

Griffin's hand lowered. He stood there, breathing hard, looking down at her small, cowering figure. Her face was hot against his chest, her closed fists pressing hard on his shoulders. Bleakly he realized he would rather confront a shipboard battle than this frail slip of a woman—he could face danger, death, far more easily than he could deal with her tears.

She needed comfort, kindness, things he was incapable of giving anyone.

Fear had made her spine grow rigid and her teeth chatter. The roots of her hair were wet, and her skin was clammy. He held her against his warm body, easily taking her weight. She felt like a child in his arms, small and slight. But she was no child, and he was uncomfortably aware of the texture and scent of her. The sight of her naked on André Legare's bed was still fresh in his memory. His pulse raced at the thought. He had fought for Celia Vallerand, claimed her. It was his right to take her. But some remaining shred of civilized feeling stirred within him, reminding him that she was a defenseless woman.

Celia wiped her nose on her sleeve. "I had a gun wh-when the ship was taken. I was going to kill myself before they . . . but I-I didn't. I was a coward. If I had another chance, it would be different. I wish I had died with Philippe."

"No," Griffin said, brushing at her wet cheeks with his thumbs.

"*I should have died,*" she whispered with scalding intensity, her eyes streaming with tears.

He bent down and picked her up, carrying her to the bed. She clung to him and cried helplessly, giving vent to the sorrow and fear that had gathered inside her since Philippe's death. Silently Griffin set her down and leaned over her, his hand gliding over her hair, her shoulders, the back of her neck. Her body was light and delicate underneath his palm. Celia's crying finally dissolved into soft hiccups, and she wiped her face with a handful of the shirt, feeling drained.

"My head hurts," she said in a thin voice.

"Don't talk."

Surprised by the trace of kindness in his tone, Celia glanced up at him. He was so quiet, so self-controlled, it seemed impossible that he was the same man who had savagely killed André Legare right before her eyes.

"I did not mean what I said to you," she whispered. "About his blood on your hands—"

"You meant it. Don't be a coward."

Celia hesitated and nodded slightly. He was right; it was better to be truthful. She could not deny she was revolted by what he was—a thief, an outlaw, a murderer. "But you helped me," she said in confusion. "I do not understand why. You must want something from the Vallerands, or . . . perhaps you owe something to them. What is it?"

Her hand seemed to burn. Unconsciously she had placed it on his chest. She could feel the frighteningly strong thud of his heart, the heat that radiated from his skin. Pulling her hand away, she closed her fist, but her palm still tingled from his vital pulse.

Griffin flinched as if he had been touched by a branding iron. The feel of her in his arms was too much. He tried to call forth what little compassion and honor he still possessed, but he could not force himself to let her go. Never in his life had he wanted anything as much as he wanted her. "I'm in no one's debt," he said thickly. "But you owe *me* something."

There was no mistaking his meaning. Celia's heart gave a frightened leap. "When we r-reach New Orleans," she stammered, "Monsieur Vallerand will give you a reward for saving my life."

"I want it now." His voice was harsh and strained.

"I have no money—"

"It's not money I want."

She made a sudden bolt out of his lap, trying to crawl off the bed. His arms became bands of steel that locked around her chest and hips.

"*No,*" she gasped.

The bristle of his beard scratched the back of her neck, the velvet heat of his mouth rubbed over the top of her spine. Celia gave a low cry. His hot breath roamed over her neck, and hair, sinking into her shirt.

"Please," she said wildly, "don't do this—"

He turned her to face him and grazed her mouth with a surprisingly soft kiss. She jerked her head back and struggled furiously, a short scream escaping her lips. His hands tangled in her hair, pushing her head down to the bed. A powerful thigh swung over her body, and he straddled her hips, crouching over her intently. She whimpered in fear, clawing at his face, his chest, but nothing would stop the ravenous mouth that wandered over her throat, cheeks, chin, and salty-wet lashes. Her cries were smothered as his lips forced hers open, his tongue plunging into the hollow of her mouth.

At first Griffin intended to take her without delay. It didn't matter if his desire was reciprocated or not—he had to bury himself inside her and satisfy his hunger. Roughly he pulled at the clothes that covered her.

Suddenly Celia went still. She turned her face away from him, closing her eyes, steeling herself to endure what would follow. Griffin stared at her naked body. She was slim and fragile, softness and silk, her skin translucent in the moonlight. He could see the delicate tracing of veins above her breasts, the pale satin points of her nipples, the glint of down that formed a line along her midriff.

Her lips were wet from his kisses. Slowly he bent over her, tasted those soft lips with a gentleness that was foreign to him. She clenched her teeth and held herself immobile while his mouth brushed over hers. He touched the side of her breast, traced the shallow curve underneath. A sweet scent clung to her, the natural fragrance that belonged to her alone. He pressed his mouth to a soft pink nipple until it formed a hard bud, brushed his beard against the aroused peak, then soothed it with his tongue.

Celia quivered in outrage. The way he touched her seemed like a mockery. "Don't," she said hoarsely. "Just have done with it! Don't pretend I'm willing . . . don't pretend . . ."

He seemed not to hear her. His mouth left a trail of fire as it skimmed to her other breast. Strangling a moan, she rolled to her stomach, trying to douse the burning in the pit of her belly and between her thighs. Immediately he found the back of her neck and tormented the vulnerable spot with nibbling kisses. His warm fingers dipped into the hollows of her spine, pressing and kneading, working down to the smooth place where her buttocks began. Celia clenched her fists and turned her perspiring face into the cotton ticking. "I hate you," she gasped, her voice muffled. "*Nothing* could change that. Let me go!"

"I can't."

"I-it doesn't matter what you have done for me, I am not yours and you have no right—"

"You are mine. Until I give you to the Vallerands." He bent over her unwilling mouth once more, thinking that he'd never had to seduce a woman before, not when every corner of the world was filled with willing ones. For him, the act of mating had always been quick and intense. But now he wanted something different, wanted it enough to wait with unnatural patience.

He slid his large hand over her breast, covering it completely. Her heart beat wildly into his palm. "Don't be afraid," he said, stroking her breast in a calming movement. "I won't hurt you."

She gave a choking laugh at the incongruity of such words, when his muscular body was poised over hers so threateningly. She sensed the violence of the passion contained inside him, expected that at any moment he would tear open his breeches and fall on her like an animal. His mouth touched hers, and the unfamiliar laugh died away, melting beneath the scorching heat of his lips. The hammering rhythm of her heart seemed to drive the air from her lungs. Slowly he acquainted himself with the inside of her cheeks, the sensitive places under her tongue.

Celia felt herself slipping into a dreamlike trance. She no longer cared who she was, or what she was doing. All that mattered was that the feeling didn't stop. Her breasts ached, and she moaned as he circled them with gentle fingertips. The muscles of his arms tightened, and he pulled her upright until her nipples were buried in the mat of springy hair on

his chest. His hand moved up the ridge of her spine
clutched the hair at the back of her neck. "Say my
name," she heard him mutter against her throat
The feel of his rough beard against her skin sent a
wave of shocking excitement through her.

"No—"

"Say it."

Celia sobbed in anguish, trying to conjure up Phi
lippe's image, trying to recall herself to sanity. Bu
Philippe's face had vanished, and there was nothing
left but darkness and the tormenting caresses of a
stranger. Tears slid down her face. "Justin," she said
brokenly.

"Yes," he whispered, gripping her small head between his hands, lowering her to the bed.